LOVE, ROSIE

LOVE, ROSIE

Cecelia Ahern

hachette
BOOKS

NEW YORK   BOSTON

Copyright © 2005 Cecelia Ahern

Hachette Books
1290 Avenue of the Americas
New York, NY 10104
www.HachetteBookGroup.com

Hachette Books is a division of Hachette Book Group, Inc.

The Hachette Speakers Bureau provides a wide range of authors for speaking events. To find out more, go to www.hachettespeakersbureau.com or call (866) 376-6591.

The publisher is not responsible for websites (or their content) that are not owned by the publisher.

Printed in the United States of America

First United States mass market edition, December 2006

20 19 18 17 16 15 14

For Mimmie, the dearest of them all . . .

PART I

CHAPTER 1

———※———

To Alex

You are invited to my 7th birthday party on Tuesday the 8th of April in my house. We are having a magician and you can come to my house at 2 o'clock. It is over at 5 o'clock. I hope you will come,

From your best friend Rosie

To Rosie

Yes I will come to your brithday party on Wensday.

Form Alex

To Alex

My birthday party is on Tuesday not Wednesday. You can't bring sandy to the party because mum says so. She is a smelly dog.

From Rosie

To Rosie

I do not care wot your stupid mum says sandy wants to come.

Form Alex

To Alex
   My mum is not stupid you are. You are not aloud to bring the dog. She will brust the baloons.
   From Rosie

To Rosie
   Then I am not going.
       Form Alex

To Alex
   Fine.
       From Rosie

Dear Ms. Stewart
   I just called by to have a word with you about my daughter Rosie's birthday on the 8th of April. Sorry you weren't in when I called, I'll call around again later this afternoon and hopefully we can talk then.
   I think there seems to be some sort of little problem with Alex and Rosie lately, I don't quite think they're on talking terms. Hopefully you can fill me in on the situation when we meet. Rosie would really love if he came to her birthday party.
   I'm looking forward to meeting the mother of this charming young man!
       See you then,
       Alice Dunne

To Rosie
   I would be happy to go to your brithday party next week. Thank you fro inviting me and sandy.
       Form Alex your frend

To Rosie
   Thanks for the great day at the party. I am sorry sandy brust the baloons and ate your cake. She was hungry be-

cause mum says dad eats all our leftovers. See you at skool
tomorrow.

      Alex

To Alex

    Thanks for the present. Its OK about what sandy did.
Mum says she needed a new carpet anyway. Dad is a bit mad
though. He said the old one was fine but mum thinks the
house smells of poo now.

    Look at Ms. Casey's nose. It is the biggest nose I have
ever seen.

      Rosie

To Rosie

    I no and she has a big snot hanging down too. She is the
ugliest alien I have ever seen. I think we should tell the police
we have an alien as a teacher who has a really smelly breath
and—

Dear Mr. and Ms. Stewart,

    I would like to arrange a meeting with you to discuss
how Alex is progressing at school. I would like to talk about
the recent change in his behavior along with the problem of
his note-writing during class. I would appreciate it if you
called the school to arrange a suitable time to meet.

      Yours sincerely,
      Ms. Casey

To Alex

    I hate that we dont sit together anymore in class. I'm stuck
beside stinky Steven who picks his nose and eats it. It is gross.
What did your mum and dad say about Ms. Big nose alien?

      From Rosie

To Rosie

    Mum did not say much because she kept laffing. I dont no

why. I no it is reall boring up the front of the class. Smelly breath Ms. Casey keeps on lucking at me. Have to go. Alex

To Alex
>   You always spell know wrong. It is KNOW not NO.
>   From Rosie

To Rosie
>   Sorry miss prefect. I no how to spell it.
>   From Alex

Hello form Spain! The weather is really nice. It is hot and sunny. There is a swimming pool with a big slide. It is cool. Met a freind called John. He is nice. See you in 2 weeks. Oh I broke my arm coming down the slide. I went to the hopsital. I would like to work in a hopsital like the man that fixed my arm. My freind John signed my cast. You can too when I get home if you like.
>   Alex

To Alex, Hello from Lundin. My hotel is the one in the picture on the front. My room is the one that is 7 up from the ground but you cant see me in the postcard. I would like to work in a hotel when I grow up because you get free chocolates every day and people are so nice that they tidy your room for you. The buses are all red like your toys you got last Christmas. Everyone talks with that funny voice but are nice. Have met a frend called Jane. We go swimming together. Bye. Love from Rosie

To Alex
>   Why amnt I invited to your birthday party this year? I know all the boys from the class are going. Are you fighting with me?
>   Rosie

Dear Alice,

I'm sorry about Alex's behavior this week. I know that Rosie is upset about not going to the party and she doesn't understand why she hasn't been invited. To be honest I can't quite understand it myself; I have tried to talk to Alex but I'm afraid I can't get inside the mind of a 10-year-old boy!

I think it's just a case of his not being able to invite her because the other boys don't want a girl to go. Unfortunately he seems to be at that age . . . Please give my love to Rosie, it seems so unfair and when I spoke to her last week I could see how hurt she was.

Perhaps myself and George can take the two of them out some other evening during the week.

> Best wishes,
> Sandra Stewart

To Rosie

The party was not very good. You did not miss anything. The boys are stupid. Brian threw his pizza in Jameses sleeping bag and when James woke up he had tomato and cheese stuck in his hair and everything and my mum tried to wash it and it would not go away and then Jameses mum gave out to Brians mum and my mum went real red and my dad said something I didn't here and Jameses mum started to cry and then everyone went home. Do you want to go to the cimena on Friday and go to McDonald's after? My mum and dad will bring us.

> Alex

To Alex

Sorry about your party. Brian is a weirdo anyway. I hate him. Brian the whine is his name. I will ask my mum and dad about the cinema. Look at Ms. Casey's skirt it looks like my grannys. Or it looks like sandy puked up all over it and then did a poo and the—

Dear Mr. and Mrs. Dunne,
    I was hoping to arrange a meeting with you to discuss
Rosie's recent behavior in school and her note-writing
during class. How does Thursday at 3 p.m. sound?
            Ms. Casey

    Alex I don't think my mum and dad will let me go to the
cinema tonight. I hate not sitting beside you. It's so boring.
Frizzy lizzys hair is blocking my view of the blackboard.
Why does this happen to us all the time?
            Rosie

TO ALEX
HAPPY VALENTINE'S DAY!
LOVE FROM YOUR SECRET ADMIRER
XXX

To Rosie,
    You wrote that card didn't you?
            From Alex

To Alex
    I really don't know what you're talking about. Why
would I send you a Valentine's card?
            From Rosie

To Rosie
    Ha ha! How did you no it was a Valentine's card! The
only way you could no is if you sent it. You *love* me, you
want to *marry* me.
            From Alex

To Alex
    Oh shut up, I sent it to you for a joke. Now leave me

alone I'm listening to the teacher. If she catches us passing notes again we're dead meat.

> From Rosie

To Rosie,

Oh. What happened to you? You've turned into such a swot.

> Alex

Yes Alex and that's why I'll go places in life, like going to college and being a big successful business person with loads of money . . . unlike you . . .

> From Rosie

—⁓—

CHAPTER 2

Dear Ms. Quinn
Alex will be unable to attend school tomorrow, the 8th of April, as he has a dental appointment.
Sandra Stewart

Dear Ms. Quinn,
Rosie will be unable to attend school tomorrow, the 8th of April, as she has a doctor's appointment.
Alice Dunne

Rosie
I'll meet you around the corner at 8:30 a.m. Remember to bring a change of clothes. We're not wandering around town in our uniforms. This is going to be the best birthday you ever had Rosie Dunne, trust me! I can't believe we're actually getting away with this!
Alex
PS: Sweet 16 my arse!

Mr. and Mrs. Dunne,

Enclosed is the medical bill for Rosie Dunne's stomach pumping on the 8th of April.

Dr. Montgomery

Rosie,

Your mum is guarding the door like a vicious dog so I don't think I'll get to see you for the next 10 years or so. The kind big sis you love so much (not!) has agreed to pass this on to you. You owe her big time . . .

Sorry about the other day. Maybe you were right. Maybe that tequila wasn't such a good idea. It seemed so wise at the time. The poor bar man will probably be closed down for serving us. Told you that fake ID my mate got would work, even though yours did say you were born on the 31st of February!!

Just wondering if you remember anything that happened the other day . . . write to me. You can trust your sister to pass it on. She's mad at your mum for not letting her drop out of college. Phil and Margaret have just announced that they're having another baby so it looks like I'll be an uncle for the second time round. At least that's taking the attention off me for a change. Phil just keeps laughing at what you and me did.

Get well soon you alco! Do you know I didn't think it was possible for a human being to go *so* green in the face. I think you have finally found your talent Rosie, ha ha.

Alex/ Mr. Cocky,

I FEEL AWFUL. My head is pounding, I have never had such a headache, I have never felt so ill before in my life. Mum and Dad are going ape shit, honestly you never get any sympathy in this house. I'm gonna be grounded for about 30 years and I'm being "prevented" from seeing you because you're "such a bad influence." Yeah right whatever.

Anyway it doesn't really matter what they do because I'm gonna see you at school tomorrow, unless they "prevent" me from going there too which is absolutely fine by me.

Can't believe we have double maths on a Monday morning. I would rather get my stomach pumped again. Five times over. See you on Monday then. Can't wait to get out of this hell hole, its doing my head in.

Oh by the way in answer to your question, apart from my face smashing against that filthy pub floor, flashing lights, loud sirens, speeding cars, and puking I can't remember anything else. But I bet that just about covers it. Anything else happen I should know about?

      Rosie

To Rosie

Glad to hear everything is as normal as usual. Mum and dad are driving me crazy too, I can't believe I'm actually looking forward to going to school. At least no one will be able to nag us there.

      From Alex

Dear Mr. and Ms. Dunne,

Following the recent actions of your daughter Rosie we request a meeting with you at the school immediately. We need to discuss her behavior and come to an agreement on a reasonable punishment. I have no doubt you understand the necessity of this. Alex Stewart's parents will also be in attendance.

    The scheduled time is Monday morning at 9 a.m.

      Yours sincerely,

      Mr. Bogarty

      Principal

FROM: Rosie

TO: Alex

SUBJECT: Suspended!

Holy shit! I didn't think that old bogey would go ahead

and suspend us! I'd swear we were axe murderers from the way that they were carrying on! Oh this is the best punishment *ever*, I get to stay in bed for a whole week nursing a hangover instead of going to school!

Thanks for taking me out, you're a real friend!

FROM: Alex
TO: Rosie
SUBJECT: I'm in hell

Glad life is going so wonderfully for you these days. I'm e-mailing you from the worst place in the world. An office. I have to work here with dad for the entire week filing shit and licking stamps. I swear to god I am NEVER EVER going to work in an office in my life.

The bastards aren't even paying me.

A very pissed off Alex

FROM: Rosie
TO: Alex
SUBJECT: To a very pissed off Alex

Ha ha ha ha ha ha ha ha ha em . . . I've forgotten what I was going to write . . . oh yeah . . . ha ha ha ha ha ha ha ha ha ha ha ha ha ha ha ha ha.

Lots of love from an extremely comfy, snuggy, warm, and happy Rosie typing from her bedroom

FROM: Alex
TO: Rosie
SUBJECT: To the lazy bitch

I don't care. There is an absolute babe working in this office. I am going to marry her. Now who's laughing?

FROM: Rosie
TO: Alex
SUBJECT: Don Juan

Who is she?
From a non-lesbian so am therefore NOT jealous.

FROM: Alex
TO: Rosie
SUBJECT: To non-lesbian

I will for the time being humor you by calling you that
although I have yet to see any evidence to suggest otherwise.
When is the last time you had a boyfriend?

Her name is Bethany Williams and she is 17 (older
woman), blonde, has a massive pair of boobs, and the
longest legs I have ever seen.

From the sex god.

FROM: Rosie
TO: Alex
SUBJECT: Mr. Sex god (puke puke gag vomit)

She sounds like a giraffe. I'm sure she is a really nice
person (Not!). Have you even said hello to her or has your
future wife yet to acknowledge your existence? (Apart from
handing you memos to photocopy of course.)

One minute you're a virgin and the next minute you're a
sex god. Are you sure you would even know what to do?

You have an instant message from: ALEX

Alex: Hey there Rosie got some news for you.

Rosie:	Leave me alone please I'm trying to concentrate on what Mr. Simpson is saying.
Alex:	Hmmm wonder why . . . could it be those beautiful big blue eyes all you girls are always going on about?
Rosie:	Nope, I have a great and growing interest in excel. It's so exciting I find. I could just sit in and do it all weekend.
Alex:	Oh you're turning into such a bore
Rosie:	I WAS JOKING YOU IDIOT! I bloody hate this crap my brain is turning to mush from listening to him. But go away anyway.
Alex:	Do you not wanna hear my news?
Rosie:	Nope
Alex:	Well I'm telling you anyway
Rosie:	La la ala la la la la la la la
Alex:	Shut up and read Rosie
Rosie:	OK what's the big exciting news?
Alex:	Well you can eat your words my friend, because virgin boy is no longer
Rosie:	Is no longer than a what? Baby sweetcorn?
Alex:	Ha ha is no longer a virgin boy
Alex:	Hello? You still there?
Alex:	Rosie c'mon stop messing!
Rosie:	Sorry I seem to have fallen off my chair and knocked myself out. I had an awful dream you said you are no longer a virgin boy. I suppose that means you won't be wearing your underwear over those tights anymore.
Alex:	I have no need for underwear at all now.
Rosie:	Uuuugh! So who's the unlucky girl? Please don't say Bethany please don't say Bethany.
Alex:	Tough shit it's Bethany. Well?
Rosie:	Well what?
Alex:	Well say something.

Rosie:	People will stare.
Alex:	Ha ha OK then type something.
Rosie:	Well I really don't know what you want me to say Alex. I think you need to get yourself some male friends because I'm not gonna slap you on the back and look for gory details.
Alex:	Just tell me what you think.
Rosie:	Well to be honest, from what I hear about her, I think she's a slut.
Alex:	Oh come on you don't even no the girl, you've never even met her. You call anyone who sleeps with anyone a slut.
Rosie:	Eh SLIGHT exaggeration there Alex. I call people who sleep with different people every day of the week sluts.
Alex:	You no that's not true.
Rosie:	You keep spelling KNOW wrong. It's KNOW not NO.
Alex:	Shut up with the "know" thing, you've been going on about that since we were about 5!
Rosie:	Yeah exactly so you think you would listen to me by now.
Alex:	Oh forget I said anything.
Rosie:	Oh Alex I'm just worried about you. I know you really like her and all I'm saying is that she's not a one man kind of girl.
Alex:	Well she is now.
Rosie:	Are you two going out with each other?
Alex:	Yes.
Rosie:	YES?????
Alex:	You sound surprised.
Rosie:	I just didn't think Bethany went out with people, I thought she just slept with them.
Rosie:	Alex?
Rosie:	OK OK I'm sorry.
Alex:	Rosie you need to stop doing that.

Rosie:	I no I do.
Alex:	Ha ha
Mr. Simpson:	You two get down to the principal's office now.
Rosie:	WHAT??? OH SIR PLEASE, I WAS LISTENING TO YOU!
Mr. Simpson:	Rosie I haven't spoken for the last 15 minutes. You are supposed to be working on an assignment now.
Rosie:	Oh. Well it's not my fault. Alex is an awful influence on me. He just never lets me concentrate on my school work
Alex:	I just had something really important to tell Rosie and it just couldn't wait.
Mr. Simpson:	So I see Alex, congratulations.
Alex:	Eh . . . how do you know what it was . . .
Mr. Simpson:	I think you two would find it interesting sometimes if you listen to me every now and again. You can really learn some useful tips like how to keep an instant message private so everyone else on the other computers can't see.
Alex:	Are you telling me other people in the class can read this?
Mr. Simpson:	Yes I am.
Alex:	Oh my god
Rosie:	Ha ha ha ha ha ha ha ha ha ha ha ha ha ha ha
Mr. Simpson:	Rosie!
Rosie:	Ha ha ha ha ha ha ha.
Mr. Simpson:	ROSIE!!!
Rosie:	Yes sir.
Mr. Simpson:	Get out of the class now.
Alex:	Ha ha ha ha ha ha ha
Mr. Simpson:	You too Alex.

CHAPTER 3

—⁓—

FROM: Rosie
TO: Alex
SUBJECT: Julie's house party

   Hiya, long time no see . . . I hope they're not working you to death down there in "the office." I've hardly seen you at all this summer. There's a party at Julie's house tonight so was just wondering if you wanted to go. I don't really want to go on my own . . . anyway I'm sure you're busy in that office doing whatever it is you do so just ring me when you get a chance or e-mail me back.

FROM: Alex
TO: Rosie
SUBJECT: Re: Julie's house party

   Rosie, this is just quick e-mail real busy. Can't go out to-night, promised Bethany would go to cinema. Sorry! You go and have fun, Alex

Rosie,

Hello from Portugal! Weather here really hot. Dad got sunstroke and all mum does is lie by the pool which is really boring. Not much people here my age. Hotel quiet (on front of postcard) and it's right on the beach as you can see. You would love to work here! I'm bringing home a collection of those little shampoos and shower caps and stuff that you love. The bathrobe is too big to fit into my bag. See you when I get back, Alex

FROM: Rosie
TO: Alex
SUBJECT: Catching up?

Heard you got back from your holidays last week, haven't heard much from you lately . . . fancy going out tonight to catch up?

FROM: Alex
TO: Rosie
SUBJECT: Re: Catching up?

Sorry have been so busy since I got back. Got you pressie. Can't go out tonight but will drop your pressie by before I head out.

FROM: Rosie
TO: Alex
SUBJECT: Re: Catching up?

Didn't see you last night, I want little shampoos ha ha.

FROM: Alex
TO: Rosie
SUBJECT: Re: Catching up?

Heading to Donegal for the weekend, Beth's parents have a little "hideaway" there. (That's what they call it.) Will drop your pressie by when I get back.

To the most inconsiderate
asshole of a friend,

I'm writing you this letter because I know that if I say what I have to say to your face I will probably punch you.

I don't know you anymore.

I don't see you anymore.

All I get is a quick text or a rushed e-mail from you every few days. I know you are busy and I know you have Bethany, but hello? I'm supposed to be your best friend.

You have no idea what this summer has been like. Ever since we were kids we pushed away every single person that could possibly have been our friend. We blocked people until there was only me and you. You probably haven't noticed, because you have never been in the position I am in now. You have always had someone. You always had me. I always had you. Now you have Bethany and I have no one.

Now I feel like those other people that used to try to become our friend, that tried to push their way into our circle but were met by turned backs. I know you're probably not doing it deliberately just as we never did it deliberately. It's not that we didn't *want* anyone else, it's just that we didn't *need* them. Sadly now it looks like you don't need me anymore.

Anyway I'm not moaning on about how much I hate her, I'm just trying to tell you that I miss you. And that well . . . I'm lonely.

Whenever you cancel nights out I end up staying home with Mum and Dad watching TV. It's so depressing. This was supposed to be our summer of fun. What happened? Can't you be friends with two people at once?

I know you have found someone who is extra special, and I know you both have a special "bond," or whatever, that you and I will never have. But we have another bond, we're best friends. Or does the best friend bond disappear as soon as you meet somebody else? Maybe it does, maybe I just don't understand that because I haven't met that "somebody special." I'm not in any hurry to, either. I liked things the way they were.

So maybe Bethany is now your best friend and I have been relegated to just being your "friend." At least be that to me, Alex. In a few years time if my name ever comes up you will probably say, "Rosie, now there's a name I haven't heard in years. We used to be best friends. I wonder what she's doing now; I haven't seen or thought of her in years!" You will sound like my mum and dad when they have dinner parties with friends and talk about old times. They always mention people I've never even heard of when they're talking about some of the most important days of their lives. Yet where are those people now? How could someone who was your bridesmaid 20 years ago not even be someone who you are on talking terms with now? Or in Dad's case, how could he not know where his own best friend from college lives? He studied with the man for five years!

Anyway, my point is (I know, I know, there is one), I don't want to be one of those easily forgotten people, *so* important at the time, *so* special, *so* influential, and *so* treasured, yet years later just a vague face and a distant memory. I want us to be best friends forever, Alex.

I'm happy you're happy, really I am, but I feel like I've been left behind. Maybe our time has come and gone. Maybe your time is now meant to be spent with Bethany. And if that's the case I won't bother sending you this letter. And if I'm not sending this letter then what am I doing still

writing it? OK I'm going now and I'm ripping these
muddled thoughts up.

   Your friend,
   Rosie

FROM: Alex
TO: Rosie
SUBJECT: Buttercup!!

 Hey Buttercup, you OK? (Haven't called you that for a
long time!) I haven't heard or seen you in a while. I'm
sending you this e-mail because every time I call by your
house, you're either in the bath or not there! Should I begin
to take this personally??! But knowing you, if you had a
problem with me you wouldn't be too shy to let me know
all about it!

 Anyway, once the summer is over we'll see each other
every day, we'll be sick of the sight of each other then! I
can't believe this is our last year in school! It's crazy! This
time next year I'll be studying medicine and you will be
hotel manager woman extraordinaire! Things at work have
been crazy. Dad kind of gave me a promotion so I've more
to do than just filing and labeling! (I answer phones now
too.) But I need the money and at least I get to see Bethany
every day. How's your job as chief dishwasher at The
Dragon? I can't believe you turned down babysitting for
that. You could have stayed in all night and watched TV
instead of watching your hands turn to prunes while you
scrape off egg noodles from a wok.

 I really miss you Rosie, I miss all our chats and jokes,
things aren't the same without you! Mum was asking for
you she said she wants you to call around to her. Oh and
Sandy misses you too!

FROM: Rosie
TO: Alex
SUBJECT: Moonbeam!

It's not because I hate Bethany that I'm not seeing much of you (although I do hate her), it's just that I think Bethany dislikes me just a little. It could have something to do with the fact that a friend of hers told her what I wrote about her in that (not so) private instant messaging thingy in computer class last year . . . I don't think she liked being called a slut, I don't know why . . . some women are just funny like that. But I suppose you already know that she'd heard what I said that day. (Speaking of computer class, Mr. Simpson got married this summer, I'm gutted. I'll never look at excel in the same way again.)

Anyway it's your birthday soon! You have finally reached the grand old age of 18! Want to go out and do some legal celebrating? (Well, legal for you anyway) Let me know.

PS: Please STOP calling me Buttercup!

FROM: Alex
TO: Rosie
SUBJECT: 18th Birthday

Rosie, Good to hear you're alive after all, I was beginning to worry! I would love to celebrate my 18th with you but Bethany's parents are taking me and my parents out for dinner to the Hazel. How posh is that??!

Sorry Rosie, another night definitely.

~~Dearest Alex,~~
~~Well whoopdeedoo for you~~
~~Fuck Bethany~~
~~Fuck her parents~~
~~Fuck the hazel~~

~~And fuck you~~
~~Love your best friend Rosie~~

FROM: Rosie
TO: Alex
SUBJECT: Happy Birthday!

OK then well, enjoy the meal. Happy birthday!

FROM: Rosie
TO: Alex
SUBJECT: DISASTER!

I can't believe this is happening! I was just talking to your mum; called over for a chat and she told me the bad news. I can't believe it, this is the *worst* news *ever*! Please call me when you can, your boss keeps telling me you can't take calls during working hours—QUIT! Mr. I never EVER want to work in an office.

Get in touch with me as soon as you can, this is so terrible, I feel awful!

CHAPTER 4

Dear Mr. Stewart,

We are delighted to inform you that you have been accepted to fill the position of Vice President of Charles and Charles Co. We are delighted that you will be joining the team over here and we look forward to welcoming you and your family to Boston.

I hope the relocation package we offer will be to your satisfaction. If there is anything further that Charles and Charles Co. can do for you, do not hesitate to ask. Maria will call you to discuss a suitable date for you to begin work.

We look forward to seeing you at the office.

Welcome to the team!

Yours sincerely,

Robert Brasco

President of Charles and Charles Co.

FROM: Alex

TO: Rosie

SUBJECT: Re: DISASTER!

I'll call you when I get home. It's true. Dad was offered a

job doing something that sounds incredibly boring . . . I don't really know, I wasn't listening. I don't know why he has to go all the way over to Boston to do a boring job, there's plenty of them right here. He can have mine.

Oh Rosie, I'm so pissed off. I don't want to go. I only have a year left in school; this is such the wrong time to leave. I don't want to go to a stupid American high school or whatever it is they call it. I don't want to leave you.

I'll call you later and we can talk about it. We have to think of a way that I can stay. This is really bad, Rosie.

FROM: Rosie
TO: Alex
SUBJECT: Stay with me!

Don't go! Mum and Dad said that you could stay here for the year! Finish school here and then we can both decide what to do after that! Please stay! It will be so brilliant, us living together. It'll be just like when we were young and we used to keep each other up all night with those walkie talkies! Remember them?!! We used to hear more static than our voices but we thought we were so cool! Remember that time on Christmas Eve absolutely *years* ago we decided to start a "Santa" watch! We planned it for weeks. I can't remember ever being so excited! We drew little diagrams of the road and maps of our houses just so we could cover every angle and not miss him. You were on the 7-10pm watch and I was on the 10pm-1am watch. You were *supposed* to wake up and take over from me, but surprise, surprise you didn't . . . I stayed awake all night screaming down into that walkie talkie trying to wake you up! Ah well, it was your loss, I saw Santa and you didn't . . .

If you stay with us Alex we'll be able to just talk all night! Oh it would be so much fun. When we were kids we always wanted to live together, now's our chance . . .

Talk to your Mum and Dad about it. Convince them to say yes, anyway you're 18 you can do what you like! OK if you can't stay with me then at least stay with Phil. Your parents can't say no to you staying with your brother.

Rosie,
    I didn't want to wake you so your mum said she would pass this on to you. You know I hate goodbyes and it's not goodbye anyway because you're going to come over and visit all the time. Promise me.
    I have to go . . . I'll miss you. Ring you when I get there.
            Love,
            Alex
            PS: I told you, I was awake that Christmas Eve, my battery just went dead on my walkie talkie . . .
            (and I did see Santa, I'll have you know).

Alex,
    Good luck little brother. Don't worry, you'll enjoy yourself once you get there and I can't wait to come and visit. I'll miss you all. It won't be the same without you. Stop worrying about Rosie, her life's not going to fall apart just because you're not in the same country. But if it'll make you feel any better I'll look out for her for you—she almost feels like my little sister in a way. By the way if Sandy doesn't learn how to control her bladder in this house then I'm sending her over to you on a plane.
            We'll miss you,
            Phil. (+ Margaret)

FROM: Rosie
TO: Stephanie
SUBJECT: Urgent sisterly advice needed

    I can't believe he's gone Steph. I can't believe you're gone.

Why is everyone leaving me? Surely you could have "found yourself" a little closer to home? But France? Alex has only been gone a few weeks and I feel like he's dead, which is an absolutely awful thing to think, I know, but it just feels that way . . .

Why did he have to break up with Slutty Bethany just two weeks before he left? Then I wouldn't have gotten used to him being around so much again. Things really got back to normal, Steph. It was brilliant. We spent every second together . . . literally. We had so much fun!

Brian the Whine threw a going-away party for him just last week; I think it was just an excuse for Brian the Whine to get permission from his parents to have a party to be honest because the two of them *never* liked each other. Not since that pizza in James' hair incident. But anyway Whine held the party in his house and invited all of his friends and I don't think me and Alex knew anyone in the entire place! The people we did know we can't stand so we left and headed into town. You know that pub O'Brien's where we held your surprise 21st? Well, we went there and Alex had the bright idea of standing outside the door and pretending to be the bouncer of the pub! (There was none on the door that night because it was only a Monday night.) Well he pulled it off anyway because he's really tall and muscley, you know Alex! Anyway we stood there for ages turning people away; I don't think he let one person in. Eventually we got bored and headed inside to the empty pub. Of course me and Alex ended up getting all weepy about him moving away . . . Apart from that the night was brilliant. I miss the times we had, just us together like that.

You wouldn't believe how lonely it is at school these days. I'm just short of getting down on my hands and knees and begging for someone to be my friend. How pathetic. No one really cares. I spent the last few years ignoring them so they don't feel like they really have to talk to me. I think some of them are even enjoying it. The teachers are loving it. Mr. Simpson called me back after class to congratulate me on how well I'm doing lately. It's shameful; Alex would be appalled if he found out I was actually working at school. I'm horrified that things have gotten so bad that I actually pay attention to the teachers. They're the only people who actually talk to me from one day to the next. How depressing.

I wake up in the morning and I feel like I'm missing something. I know that there's something not right, and it takes me a while to remember what it is . . . then I remember. My best friend is gone. My only friend. It was silly of me to rely so much on one person. It's all coming back on me now.

Anyway, sorry for whingeing on and on all the time, I'm sure you have enough problems of your own to worry about. Tell me how my sophisticated big sis is doing over in France. I can't believe you're over there, you always hated French class. At least it's only for a few months right? And then you're coming back? Dad's still not happy about you dropping out of college. Why you had to go away to find yourself is beyond me. Just look in the mirror. What's the restaurant like? Have you dropped any plates yet? Are you going to work there for long? Any nice men? There must be, French men are yummy. If there are any spare men that you don't want, send them my way.

> Love,
> Rosie
> PS: Dad wants to know if you have enough money and if you've found yourself yet. Mum wants to know if you are eating properly. Little Kevin (he is so tall now you wouldn't believe!) wants to know if you'll send him some video game over. I don't know what he's talking about so just ignore him.

FROM: Stephanie
TO: Rosie
SUBJECT: Re: Urgent sisterly advice needed

Hello my darling little sister,

Don't worry about Alex, I thought long and hard about it and I've come to the conclusion that it's a good idea he's not there for your final year of school because you know how bad you two are when you get together! At least for the first year EVER you may not get suspended from school. Think of how proud you would make Mum and Dad. (Oh by the way tell them I'm broke and starving and currently looking for myself in an Internet café in Paris.)

I definitely know how you feel right now. I'm alone here too, but just stick the year out and when you're finished maybe Alex will move back to Ireland, or maybe you can go to college in Boston!

Aim for something Rosie, I know you don't want to hear it, but it will help. Aim for what you want and the year will all make sense. Go to Boston if that will make you happy. Study hotel management like you've always wanted.

You're only young Rosie, and I know that you absolutely hate to hear that but it's true. What seems tragic now won't even be an issue in a few years time. You're only 17. You and Alex have the rest of your lives to catch up together . . . After all, soul mates always end up together. Silly Bethany won't even be remembered in a few years time. Ex-girlfriends are easily forgotten. **Best friends stay with you forever.**

Take care. Tell Mum and Dad I said hi and that I'm still looking for myself but may have found someone else in the process. Tall, dark and handsome . . .

—⁓—

CHAPTER 5

Dear Ms. Rosie Dunne,

Boston College thanks you for your application to study Hotel Management with us and we are delighted to inform you that you were successful in your application . . .

FROM: Rosie
TO: Alex
SUBJECT: Boston here I come!

I GOT IN!! Boston College, here I come!!! WAHOOO! The letter just arrived for me this morning and I am soooo excited! You better not move a muscle, Mr. Stewart, because I am finally coming to see you. It'll be great, even though you and I won't be studying in the same college (Harvard is far too distinguished for the likes of me!) But I think it's just as well because I don't think we can really afford to get suspended again.

I'm so excited. Are you???! E-mail or call me as soon as possible, I'd call you but Dad put a block on long-distance calls as you know. Mum and Dad are so proud, they're calling all the family to tell them. I think they're hoping I'll be the first Dunne child to go to college and actually finish the course. Dad keeps warning me not to go trying to "find myself" anywhere like Stephanie did. By the way it doesn't look like Steph is coming home anytime soon, she met some chef that works at the restaurant she's waiting at and she's "in love."

The phone hasn't stopped ringing all day with congratulations! Paul and Eileen from across the road sent over a bunch of flowers for me which was really nice. Mum's getting the house ready for a get-together tonight, just a few sandwiches and cocktail sausages, that kind of thing. Honestly Alex, the house is buzzing! Kevin is happy I'm leaving so he can be even more spoiled than usual. I'll miss the brat even though he never talks to me. I'll miss Mum and Dad even more but right now everyone is just so excited I've been accepted to think about the fact that I won't be living here anymore. I'll deal with it the day I wave good-bye but in the meantime we'll continue to celebrate!

> Love, Rosie
> PS: One of these days I can run a hotel and you can be the doctor-in-the-house who saves the lives of the guests I poison in the restaurant . . . Oh this will all work out wonderfully . . .

FROM: Alex
TO: Rosie
SUBJECT: Re: Boston here I come!

This is *brilliant* news! I can't wait to see you too! Harvard isn't too far away from BC (well in comparison to being a whole ocean apart—can you believe Harvard accepted me? It must be the intellects' idea of a hilarious joke). I'm too excited to type, just get over here! When are you coming?

FROM: Rosie
TO: Alex
SUBJECT: September

I won't be over till September, just a few days before the
semester starts because I have got so many things to sort out
you wouldn't believe! The debs are at the end of August, will
you come over for them? Everyone would love to see you
and I need someone to go with! We will have so much fun
and we can annoy all our teachers. Just like old times . . . let
me know.

FROM: Alex
TO: Rosie
SUBJECT: Debs

Of course I'll come home for our debs, I wouldn't miss it
for the world!

Where r u??? I'm waiting at airport. Me and dad have been
here for hours. I tried ur house phone & mobile. Don't
know where else 2 call. Hope everything's ok.

Hi Rosie. Just got ur text. Sent u an e-mail explaining. Can
u check e-mail at airport? Alex

FROM: Alex
TO: Rosie
SUBJECT: Sorry!

Rosie I am so sorry. This whole day has been an absolute
nightmare. There was a foul-up with the flight. I don't know
what happened, but my name wasn't in the system when I
went to collect my ticket. I've been here all day trying to get
another flight. They're all booked because of people flying

home from holidays and students returning home etc. . . .
I'm on standby, but so far there's been nothing. I'm just
hanging around the airport waiting for a flight. This is a
nightmare.

FROM: Rosie
TO: Alex
SUBJECT: Flight tomorrow

Dad's talking to the lady at Aer Lingus ticket desk. She
says there's a flight that leaves Boston tomorrow at
10:10am. It takes five hours to get here so that you will
make it 3pm, then we're five hours ahead which will make it
8pm. We could collect you from airport and go straight to
ball? Or maybe you'd prefer to go to my house first? You
can't wear your tux on the plane because you'll get all
crumpled. What do you think?

FROM: Alex
TO: Rosie
SUBJECT: Flight

Sounds good to me. Doesn't matter if we're late just as
long as I get there. I'll go see if they can get me on that
flight.

FROM: Alex
TO: Rosie
SUBJECT: Flight

Rosie, bad news. That flight is fully booked.

FROM: Rosie
TO: Alex
SUBJECT: Flight

Shit. Think, think, think. What can I do? It seems
that we can get you here every other bloody day except
tomorrow. Somebody up there really doesn't want you to
get on that plane. Maybe it's a sign?

FROM: Alex
TO: Rosie
SUBJECT: My fault

It's my fault, I should have double checked with the
airline yesterday. Please go to the debs anyway. I no I've
messed up your night. You still have the whole day to find
someone else to go with you. Take loads of photos, tell
everyone I was asking for them and enjoy yourself. Sorry,
Rosie.

FROM: Rosie
TO: Alex
SUBJECT: Re: My fault

It's not your fault. I'm disappointed but let's be
realistic, it's not the end of the world. Make sure you
get your money back for that flight, the eejits. And
anyway I'm gonna see you in a little over a month and
we'll be seeing each other EVERY DAY! We'll have
a brilliant time. I better go searching for a man
now . . .

FROM: Alex
TO: Rosie
SUBJECT: Manhunt

Any luck finding a man?

FROM: Rosie
TO: Alex
SUBJECT: Man found

What a stupid question!! Of course I found a man. I'm insulted you even needed to ask . . .

FROM: Alex
TO: Rosie
SUBJECT: Mystery man

Then who is it?

FROM: Rosie
TO: Alex
SUBJECT: Secret man

That would be absolutely none of your business . . .

FROM: Alex
TO: Rosie
SUBJECT: Invisible man

HA! You didn't find a date!! I knew it!

FROM: Rosie
TO: Alex
SUBJECT: Big strong man

   Yes I did.

FROM: Alex
TO: Rosie
SUBJECT: No man

   No you didn't.

FROM: Rosie
TO: Alex
SUBJECT: Yes, man!

   Yes I did.

FROM: Alex
TO: Rosie
SUBJECT: What man?

   THEN WHO IS IT????

FROM: Rosie
TO: Alex
SUBJECT: Almost a man

   Brian

FROM: Alex
TO: Rosie
SUBJECT: Brian?

BRIAN????
BRIAN THE WHINE????

FROM: Rosie
TO: Alex
SUBJECT: Re: Brian?

Maybe . . .

FROM: Alex
TO: Rosie
SUBJECT: HA HA!

Ha ha ha ha ha ha you're going to the debs with Brian
the Whine?!!! I can't believe it! Talk about scraping the
barrel! Brian, who spilled pizza down James's sleeping bag
at my 10th birthday party? Brian who caused mass hysteria
in my house and ruined my birthday? Brian who lifted your
skirt when you were six, in front of everyone in the school
yard to reveal your knickers? The Brian you were stuck
sitting beside for all of second class, who ate fish sandwiches
every day for lunch and picked his nose while you ate yours?
The Brian who followed us home from school every day
singing, "Rosie and Alex up a tree, K-I-S-S-I-N-G?" and
made you cry and ignore me for a week? The Brian who
spilled his beer all down your new top at my going-away
party? The Brian you absolutely can't stand and was the one
person you hated all throughout school? And now you're
going to the last school dance ever, *with Brian*?

FROM: Rosie
TO: Alex
SUBJECT: No the other Brian

Yes Alex, *that* Brian. Now may I ask that you please stop e-mailing me as my darling mother is currently tying knots in my head trying to make me look half decent? She has also been reading your e-mails and wants you to know that Brian the Whine won't be lifting up my skirt tonight.

FROM: Alex
TO: Rosie
SUBJECT: Brian

Well it won't be for lack of trying. Have fun! May I suggest that you wear your beer goggles tonight. Brian, you see, is a bit of a whine. And I don't think you'll find his conversation very interesting . . . hee hee

FROM: Rosie
TO: Alex
SUBJECT: Beer goggles

The beer goggles will be well and truly on! You know as well as I do that I can't go to the debs alone. Brian was the only person I could get last minute thanks to you. All I have to do is stand in with him for the photos so that Mum and Dad can have lovely memories of their daughter going to the debs all dressed up with a man in a tuxedo. The tables seat ten so I won't even have to talk to him at dinner so there's really no problem. Anyway he may have traumatized me as a child but he's not that bad!

You're enjoying this aren't you Alex?

FROM: Alex
TO: Rosie
SUBJECT: Re: Beer goggles

Not really. I'd love to be there instead. Don't do anything with Brian that I wouldn't do . . .

FROM: Rosie
TO: Alex
SUBJECT: Re: Beer goggles

Well that doesn't rule out much. Hair's done now, have to get the rest of me ready. I'll let you know how it went tomorrow.

FROM: Alex
TO: Rosie
SUBJECT: Debs

How were the debs last night? No doubt you're nursing a hangover. I'll wait to hear from you tomorrow but I'll wait no longer! I want to know *everything!*

FROM: Alex
TO: Rosie
SUBJECT: Debs

Did you get my last e-mail? I keep calling and there's no answer, what's up? I hope you're busy preparing for the big move over to me!
          E-mail me soon please.

Steph: Rosie, stop avoiding Alex and tell him how the debs
        went. Alex is even e-mailing me wondering what
        happened and I'm certainly not going to tell him!
        The poor guy missed out and all he wants to know
        is who did what, where and when.
Rosie: Well I certainly won't be telling him who did who.

Steph: Ha ha.
Rosie: It's not funny.
Steph: I think it's hilarious. Come on it's been three
         weeks now!
Rosie: Are you sure it's been three weeks?
Steph: Oh don't try to play that one Rosie!
Rosie: No I'm serious Steph. Has it been *three* weeks?
Steph: Yeah, why?
Rosie: Holy shit.

Rosie has logged off

FROM: Alex
TO: Rosie
SUBJECT: Hello??

Rosie are you there? Are you having problems with your
e-mail? Please reply. You should be getting on a plane soon
to come over here.

FROM: Alex
TO: Rosie
SUBJECT: Please Rosie?

Are you mad at me? I'm sorry I couldn't go to the debs
ball, things with whiney Briany can't have gone that badly,
can they?! What have you been doing all month? This is
ridiculous. Why doesn't anyone answer the phone when I call?
    Answer me,
    Alex

Mrs. Dunne,
    Hi Alice, it's Alex here. I'm just writing to see if Rosie's
OK. I haven't heard from her and I was getting a bit worried
to tell you the truth. It's unusual for me to not hear from

her in so long. Every time I call the house it just goes onto answering machine, are you all getting my messages? Maybe you've all gone away? Please let me know if everything is OK and tell Rosie to call.

> Best wishes,
> Alex.

Dear Sandra,

Alex has been leaving messages with us all week and he's terribly worried about Rosie. I know you're worried about him worrying about Rosie so I'm just writing to let you know the situation . . .

FROM: Alex
TO: Rosie
SUBJECT: You're not coming to Boston??

My mum told me today that you're not coming to Boston. Please tell me what's happening. I'm so worried. Did I do something wrong? Was it because I missed the debs? Because you know I am so so sorry about that but they just couldn't get me on another flight. You know that. I am always here for you when you need me.

Whatever it is Rosie please no that I will understand and will always be here to help you. Please let me no what is happening, I'm going out of my mind here. If you don't get in touch with me, I'm booking a flight back to Ireland and I'm going to see you myself.

> Love,
> Alex

FROM: Stephanie
TO: Rosie
SUBJECT: I'm coming over

My little sis,

Rosie my sweetie, don't worry. Everything happens for a reason. Just take deep breaths and try to relax. Maybe this is the correct path for you, perhaps Boston wasn't. I'm booking a flight and I'll be home as soon as I can. Hang in there little sis,

   Love,
   Stephanie

To Miss Rosie Dunne,

Boston College acknowledges that you will not be accepting your position this year.

   Yours sincerely,
   Robert Whitworth

Rosie, can't believe this is the decision u have made. You *know* I am not in support of it. I'm moving away as I had already planned. Hope everything works out well 4 u.

FROM: Rosie
TO: Alex
SUBJECT: Help

Oh god Alex, what have I done?

CHAPTER 6

—m—

Alex,

It was good to see you again. Please don't be a stranger. I'm really going to need all the friends I can get right now. Thank you for being so supportive last week, I honestly think I will go mad without you sometimes.

Life is funny isn't it? Just when you think you've got it all figured out, just when you finally begin to plan something, get excited about something, and feel like you know what direction you're heading in, the paths change, the signs change, the wind blows the other way, north is suddenly south, and east is west, and you're lost. It is so easy to lose your way, to lose direction. And that's *with* following all the signposts.

There aren't many sure things in life, but one thing I know for sure is that you have to deal with the consequences of your actions. You have to follow through on some things.

I always give up, Alex. What have I ever had to do in my life that really *needed* to be done? I always had a choice, and I always took the easy way out—*we* always took the easy way out. At our age the burden of double maths on a

Monday morning and finding a spot the size of Pluto on my nose was as complicated as it ever got for me.

This time round I'm having a baby. A baby. And that baby will be around on the Monday, on the Tuesday, on the Wednesday, Thursday, Friday, Saturday, *and* Sunday. I have no weekends off. No three-month holidays. I can't take a day off, call in sick, or get Mum to write a note. I am going to be the mum now. I wish I could write myself a note.

I'm scared, Alex.

Rosie

FROM: Alex
TO: Rosie
SUBJECT: Baby talk

No, it's no double maths on a Monday morning. It will be *far* more exciting than that. Double maths on a Monday morning is boring; it makes you sleep and gives you a headache.

A baby will fill you with love and pride, make you laugh, make you cry, make you strong, and help you to be more independent. You will learn far more from this experience than a maths class.

I am here for you for whenever you need me. Boston College can wait for you, Rosie, because you have far more important work to do now.

I no you will be just fine

FROM: Rosie
TO: Alex
SUBJECT: Re: Baby talk

You KNOW I will be fine. Watch the spelling, Mr. Stewart.

FROM: Alex
TO: Rosie
SUBJECT: Re: Baby talk

Rosie, already acting like a mother. Take care, Alex.

You have an instant message from: ALEX

Alex: I thought you said you'd keep an eye on her for me
         Phil.
Phil: I told you, if she didn't learn to control her bladder
         she'd be out of here. She's fine in the garden.
Alex: Not the *dog* Phil, I'm talking about *Rosie*.
Phil: What about Rosie?
Alex: Stop pretending you don't no. I heard mum and dad
         tell you over the phone.
Phil: How do you feel about it?
Alex: Everyone keeps asking me that and I have no idea.
         It's weird. Rosie is pregnant. She's just turned eigh-
         teen. She can barely take care of herself let alone a
         baby. She smokes like a chimney and refuses to eat
         greens. She stays awake till 4 am and sleeps till one
         o'clock in the day. She chose to take a job washing
         pots and pans at the Chinese take-away for less
         money than what her neighbors were offering for
         babysitting. She always said she didn't want to have
         kids till she was forty. I don't think she's changed a
         nappy in her life. Apart from Kevin, I don't think
         she's ever held a baby for more than five minutes.
         What about college? What about working? How the
         hell is she going to manage? How will she meet
         someone? How will she make friends? She's just
         trapped herself into a life that's her worst nightmare.
Phil: Believe me Alex, she'll learn. Her parents are sup-
         porting her aren't they? She won't be alone.

Alex: Her mum and dad will be at work all day Phil. She's
        an intelligent person, I no that. But as much as she
        tries to convince me, I'm not quite sure she's con-
        vinced herself that when the crying starts, she can't
        hand this one back. If only I'd gotten on that flight
        and made it to the debs.

Dear Stephanie,

Let me help you find yourself. Allow my words of
wisdom to rain down on you and shower you with
knowledge. From one sister who greatly loves and respects
you and wishes for nothing but happiness and great
fortune in your life, please take my advice. Never get
pregnant. Or "enceinte" as you would say over there.
Look at the word, say it out loud, familiarize yourself with
it, repeat it in your head, and learn to *never ever* want to
be it.

In fact, never have sex. Might as well try to completely
eradicate the odds. Trust me Steph, it is not pleasant. I'm
not feeling at all at one with nature, I'm not radiating any
sort of magical motherly signals, I'm just fat. And bloated.
And tired. And sick. And wondering what on earth I am
going to do when this little one is born and looks at me and
I shrug back.

Glowing, my bum. Smoldering is more like it. Alex has
started his wonderful life in college, people who were at
school with me are out tasting what the world has to offer. I
know it's my own fault but I feel like I'm missing out on so
much. I've been going to these prenatal classes with Mum
where they teach me how to breathe. All around me I'm
surrounded by couples. They're all at least ten years older
than me as well. Mum tried to start me chatting with them
but I don't think any of them are too interested in becoming
friends with an eighteen-year-old just out of school.
Honestly it's like some sort of play group and Mum keeps
trying to teach me how to make friends. Mum told me not

to worry because they were just jealous of me. I don't think the two of us have laughed so much for months.

I'm not allowed to smoke and the doctor says I have to start eating my greens. I'm going to be a mother and I'm still being spoken to like a child.

> Lots of love,
> Rosie

Mr. Alex Stewart,

You are invited to the christening of my beautiful baby daughter Katie, as you are the godfather. It's this day month. Buy a suit and try and look presentable for a change.

> Lots of love,
> Rosie

FROM: Alex
TO: Rosie
SUBJECT: Christening

It was great to see you, you look amazing! And you are NOT fat! Little Katie was a girl of few words but I am besotted with her. I almost felt like stealing her and bringing her back over to Boston.

In fact that's a lie, I really felt like staying in Dublin. I almost didn't get back on that flight. I love it here in Boston and I love studying medicine. But it's not home. Dublin is home. Being back with you felt like home. I miss my best friend.

I've met some great guys here, but I didn't grow up with any of them playing cops and robbers in my back garden. I don't feel like they are *real* friends. I haven't kicked them in the shins, stayed up all night on Santa watch with them, hung from trees pretending to be monkeys, played hotel, or laughed my heart out as their stomachs were pumped. It's kind of hard to beat that.

However I can see that I have already been replaced. That little Katie is your whole world now. And it's easy to see why. I even loved her when she threw up on my (new and very expensive) suit. That must mean something. It's weird to see how much she looks like you. What's that like? She has your twinkling blue eyes (I sense trouble ahead!) and jet black hair and a little button nose.

I no that you are incredibly busy at the moment but if you ever need a break from it all, you're welcome to come over here and relax. I know things are tricky for you financially so we could help out with the cost of the flights. Let me no when you want to come, the invitation is always open. Mum and Dad would love you to come over too, they've got photos of the christening all around the house.

There's also somebody I would like you to meet. She's in my class in college, her name is Sally Gruber. You would both get along. She's from Boston. When you come over you have to meet her.

College is a lot tougher than I thought it would be. There's just so much studying to do; so much reading. I barely have a social life. I've got four years here in Harvard then I've to do about five to seven years in a general surgical residency so I'm estimating that I'll be fully qualified in my specialized field (whatever that will be) by the time I'm one hundred years old.

So that's all I do here. I wake up at five a.m. and study. Go to college, come home and study. Every day. Not much more to report really. It's really tough. But then I don't need to tell you that. I bet it's a hell of a lot easier than what you're doing right now. Anyway, I'm going to sleep now, I'm shattered. Sweet dreams to you and baby Katie.

Note to self:

Do not bounce Katie on knee after feeding.

Do not breast feed beside football pitch.

Do not inhale when changing nappy. In fact allow Mum and Dad or even random strangers to change nappy as often as possible if they so wish.

Do not push buggy by old school for Ms. Big Nose Smelly Breath Casey to see.

Do not laugh when Katie falls on her bum after attempting to walk.

Do not try to have conversation with old friends from school with whole lives ahead of them, as this will result in huge frustration.

Stop crying when Katie cries.

Bonjour Stephanie!

How's my beautiful sister doing? Sitting in a café drinking a café au lait wearing a beret and a stripy top while stinking of garlic, no doubt! Oh, who says stereotypes are dead and gone!

Thanks for the present you sent Katie. Your goddaughter says she misses you very much, and she sends lots of drool and sloppy kisses your way. I think I could make those words out of the screaming and wailing bellowing out of her tiny little mouth. Honestly I don't know where all the noise comes from. She is the tiniest and most fragile little thing I have ever seen, sometimes I'm afraid to hold her *but then* she opens her mouth and all hell breaks loose. The doctor says she's colicky. All I know is that so she doesn't stop screaming.

It's amazing how something so small can be *so* smelly and *so* noisy. I think she should go into the Guinness book of records for being the smelliest noisiest smallest thing ever. What a proud mother I would be.

I'm so knackered, Stephanie. I feel like a complete zombie. I can barely read the words I'm writing (apologies for mashed banana on bottom of page). Katie just cries and cries and cries through the night. I have a constant headache. All I do is wander around the house like a robot picking up teddy bears and toys that I trip over. It's hard to bring Katie anywhere because she just screams wherever we are; I'm afraid people think I'm kidnapping her or being a terrible mother. I look like a balloon. All I wear are the most unflattering tracksuits. My bum is huge. My stomach is covered in stretch marks, I've flab that won't seem to go away no matter how much I shout at it and I've thrown all my belly tops out. My hair is dry and feels like straw. My tits are HUGE. I don't look like me. I don't feel like me. I feel like I'm about 20 years older. I haven't been out since the christening. I can't remember the last time I had a drink. I can't remember the last time a member of the opposite sex even looked my way. (Except the people who glare at me angrily in cafés when Katie starts to scream.) I can't remember the last time I even cared about a member of the opposite sex not staring at me. I think I am the world's worst mother. I think that when Katie looks at me she knows that I haven't a clue what I'm doing.

She's almost walking now, which means I'm running around saying "NO! KATIE NO! Katie do not touch that! NO! Katie, Mummy says NO!" I don't think Katie cares about what Mummy thinks. I think Katie is a girl who sees something she wants and she goes for it. I dread the teenage years! I can't believe she's one already. Time moves so fast! She'll be grown up and moving out before I know it. Maybe then I'll have some silence. But then again that's what Mum and Dad thought. Poor Mum and Dad. Steph, I feel so bad. They have been so fantastic. I owe them so much and I don't just mean money. Although, there's another depressing situation. I get benefits and all and I'm paying them as much as I possibly can each week. It never feels like enough and you know the situation, Steph, things were always tight for us as it was. I don't know how I'm ever going to move out *and* work *and* look after Katie. Dad and me are going to some clinic during the week to talk to some welfare guy about me getting a place. Mum keeps saying that I can stay with her and Dad but I know Dad's just trying to help me. Anyway that's for another day.

Mum has been fabulous. Katie loves her. Katie listens to her. When Mum says "NO KATIE!" Katie knows to stop. When I say it, Katie laughs and keeps going. I think I am the world's worst mother.

Alex has met someone over in Boston, she's the same age as me and studying at Harvard. But is she *really* happy? Probably is. Anyway I have to go, Katie is wailing for me.

Write soon.
Love,
Rosie

To Rosie,

I'm glad all is well with Katie; the photos you sent of her on her third birthday are beautiful. I framed them and they take pride of place in the house. Mum and Dad were delighted to see you when they visited Dublin, they can't stop talking about you and Katie, we're all so proud of you.

Happy 21st! Sorry I couldn't make it home to celebrate with you, but things have been crazy at college. Because it's my final year here there's just been so much work to do. I'm dreading the final exams. If I fail I don't no what I'll do. Sally was asking after you, I no you've never met but she feels like she nos you from me talking about our old times so much.

From Alex

To Alex
~~Katie's teething is really bad lately~~
~~Katie is starting playschool soon~~
~~Katie said grandma today~~

It was dad's 50th last weekend so we splashed out and went out for dinner to the Hazel restaurant where I believe you went with slutty Bethany and her rich parents all those years ago for your 17th. It was good to be able to let my hair down and relax without Katie. I hired a babysitter, so that was my treat for the weekend.

Rosie

FROM: Alex
TO: Rosie
SUBJECT: (none)

Ah come on Rosie! You're letting the side down! You better have something to tell me about next time!

FROM: Rosie
TO: Alex
SUBJECT: 3-year-old child

In case you didn't know, I have a 3-year-old child which makes it rather difficult for me to go out and drink myself silly, otherwise I wake up with an awful headache and a screaming child who needs me to look after her and NOT to be sticking my head down the toilet.

FROM: Alex
TO: Rosie
SUBJECT: Sorry

Rosie, I'm sorry I didn't mean to come across as being insensitive. I just meant that you should remember that you need to enjoy life too. Look after yourself and not just Katie. Sorry if I hurt you.

FROM: Rosie
TO: Stephanie
SUBJECT: A moment to whinge

Oh Stephanie, sometimes I just feel like the walls are closing in on me. I'm only 23 and I feel like I'm 43. I love Katie. I'm glad I made the decision I made, but I'm tired.

So bloody tired. All of the time.

And that's how I feel with Mum and Dad helping me. I don't know how I'm going to cope on my own. And I'm going to have to do that—I can't live with Mum and Dad forever. Although I really want to.

I wouldn't want Katie depending on me so much when she's older. Of course I want her to know that I'm here for her always and that my love is absolutely unconditional, but she needs to be independent.

I need to be independent. I think it's time for me to grow up now Steph. I've been putting it off, running away from it for so long. Katie will be starting school soon. Imagine! My baby starting school. It's all happening so quickly. Katie will be meeting new people and beginning her life and I have left mine behind. I need to pick myself up and stop feeling so sorry for myself. Life is hard, so what?

It's hard for everyone isn't it? Anyone who says it's easy is a liar. There's this huge divide between me and Alex right now because I feel like we're living in such different worlds, I don't know what to talk about with him anymore. And we used to be able to talk all night. He phones once a week and I listen to what he's been up to during the week and try to bite my tongue every time I go into another Katie story. Truth is I have nothing other to talk about but her and I know it bores people. I think I used to be interesting once upon a time.

Anyway I've decided I'm going to visit Boston finally. I'm going to finally face up to what my life could have been like had Alex gotten on that plane and made it to the debs with me instead of . . . well you know who. I could have a degree now. I could have been a career woman. I know it seems silly to put all that's happened down to the fact that Alex couldn't make it to the debs but if he had come then I wouldn't have gone with Brian. I wouldn't have slept with Brian and there would be no baby. I think I need to face what I could have been in order to understand and accept what I am.

　　　　All my love,
　　　　Rosie

—⁓—

CHAPTER 7

Stephanie,

Honey it's Mum here. I was wondering if you would be able to get in touch with Rosie and maybe have a word with her. She just returned from Boston a week earlier than expected and she seems a bit upset about something, though she won't say what it is. I was afraid this would happen. I know she feels like she has missed out on huge opportunities, I just wish she could see the positive side to what she has now. Will you get in touch with her? She always loves hearing from you.

Love you sweetheart,
Mum

You have an instant message from: STEPH

Steph: Hey you, you're not answering your phone.
Steph: I know you're there Rosie, I can see that you've logged on-line!
Steph: OK I'm going to stalk you until you reply
Steph: Hellooooo!

Rosie: Hi

Steph: Well hello there! Why do I get the feeling I was be-
         ing ignored?

Rosie: Sorry I was too tired to speak to anyone.

Steph: I suppose I can forgive you. Everything OK? How
         was the trip to Boston? Was it as beautiful as it
         looks in the photos?

Rosie: Yeah the place is really gorgeous. Alex showed me
         around everywhere, I hadn't a minute to spare while
         I was over there; he really took care of me.

Steph: As he should. So where did you go?

Rosie: He showed me around Boston College so I could see
         what it would have been like for me to study there
         and it is so fabulous. Oh Steph, it was so romantic
         and magical and beautiful and the weather was just
         fabulous . . .

Steph: Wow it sounds great. I take it you liked it then.

Rosie: Yeah I liked it. It was even better than the pho-
         tographs I saw of it when I was applying. It would
         have been a nice place to study . . .

Steph: I'm sure it would have been. Where did you stay?

Rosie: I stayed in Alex's parents' house. The house is really
         lovely, it looks like Alex's dad is making loads of
         money in that new job. Well it's not so new any-
         more really is it?

Steph: I suppose it's not, time flies by, but the place sounds
         wonderful. What else did you two get up to? I
         know there has to be some exciting story here!
         There's never a dull moment when you two are in-
         volved!

Rosie: Eh well we went looking around the shops, he
         brought me to a Red Sox game in Fenway Park and
         I hadn't a clue what was going on but I had a nice
         hot dog, we went out to a few clubs . . . sorry I've
         nothing interesting to tell you Steph . . .

Steph: Hey that's a hell of a lot more interesting than what
         I did all week believe me! So how is Alex? How
         does he look? I haven't seen him for ages. I suppose
         he's all grown up now too!

Rosie: Yeah he is actually. He looked really well. He's got a
         slight American accent although he denies it. But he's
         still the same old Alex. As lovable as usual. He really
         spoiled me for the entire week, he didn't let me pay
         for a thing, he brought me out somewhere new every
         night, and it was good to feel free for a while.

Steph: You are free, Rosie.

Rosie: I know that. I just don't feel it sometimes. Over
         there I felt like I hadn't a care in the world. Things
         felt so good and it was almost as if every muscle in
         my body relaxed the moment I landed there. I
         haven't laughed so much in years. I felt like a 23-
         year-old, Steph. I haven't felt like that much lately. I
         know this probably sounds weird but I felt like the
         me that I could have been.

         I liked that I didn't have to look out for somebody
         else while I walked down the street. I didn't have
         the fifty near heart attacks per day that I usually get
         when Katie goes missing or puts something in her
         mouth that she shouldn't. I didn't have to dive onto
         the road and hold her back just in time from being
         hit by a car. I liked that I didn't have to give out,
         correct people on their pronunciation or make
         threats. I liked laughing at a joke without my sleeve
         being tugged at and being asked to explain. I liked
         having adult conversations without being inter-
         rupted to cheer and applaud a silly dance or the
         learning of a new word. I liked that I was just me,
         Rosie, not mummy, thinking just about me, talking
         about things I liked, going places I liked to go with-

out having to worry about nappy changes, bottle feeding or sleepy-head tantrums. Isn't that awful?

Steph: It's not awful Rosie. It's good to have time to yourself but it's good to be back with Katie, isn't it? And if things were so great then why did you come home so early? You weren't supposed to be home for another week. Did something happen?

Rosie: Uuuugh not really worth mentioning.

Steph: Oh come on, Rosie, I know when something is bothering you, and you can tell me. It's obviously worth mentioning if you had to come home early because of it.

Rosie: It was just time to go, Steph.

Steph: Did you and Alex have a fight or anything?

Rosie: Ha! I wish.

Steph: What?? What happened?

Rosie: No too embarrassing to explain.

Steph: Why what do you mean?

Rosie: Oh I just made a show of myself one night.

Steph: Oh don't be silly I'm sure Alex didn't mind! He's seen you make a show of yourself in your lifetime.

Rosie: No Steph, this was a different kind of making a show of myself. Trust me. Not the usual kind of Alex and Rosie thing to do. I kind of threw myself at him and the next day I was mortified.

Steph: WHAT?? Do you mean that . . . ? *Did you and Alex . . . ???*

—∿—

CHAPTER 8

Rosie: Calm down Stephanie!

Steph: I can't! This is too bizarre! You two are like brother and sister! Alex is like my little brother! You can't have!

Rosie: STEPHANIE! WE DIDN'T!

Steph: Oh. Then what happened?

Rosie: OK I realize that this was a very silly thing for me to do and I am extremely embarrassed so don't go mental at me . . .

Steph: OK go on . . .

Rosie: Well it's really far more innocent than you think but equally embarrassing. I kissed Alex.

Steph: *I knew it!!!* And what happened???

Rosie: He didn't kiss me back.

Steph: Oh and do you mind that?

Rosie: The unsettling thing is that yes I do.

Steph: Oh Rosie I'm so sorry . . . but I'm sure Alex will come around, he was probably just shocked, oh I'm sure he feels the same!! This is so exciting! I always knew something would happen between you two someday.

Rosie: I honestly don't know what happened to me. I've been lying on my bed, staring at the ceiling ever since I got home trying to figure out what came over me. Was it something I ate that made me feel light-headed? Was it something he said that I could have misunderstood? I'm trying to convince myself that it was more than just the silence of the moment that changed my heart.

At first we had so much to catch up on we were talking a hundred words a second, barely even listening to the ends of each other's sentences before moving on to the next. And there was laughing. Lots of laughing. Then the laughing stopped and there was this silence. This weird comfortable silence. What the hell was it?

It was like the world stopped turning in that instant. Like everyone around us was wiped out. Like everything at home was forgotten about. It was like those few minutes on this world were created just for us and all we could do was look at each other. It was like he was seeing my face for the very first time. He looked confused but kind of amused. Exactly how I felt. Because I was sitting on the grass with my best friend Alex, and that was my best friend Alex's face and nose and eyes and lips but they seemed different. So who was this man that was sending my heart into a frenzy? So I kissed him. I seized the moment and I kissed him.

Steph: Wow. And what did he say?

Rosie: Nothing.

Steph: Nothing?

Rosie: Nope. Absolutely nothing. He just stared at me.

Steph: So how do you know he didn't feel the same?

Rosie: Sally came bounding over. We had been waiting for

her. She was all excited. Wanted to know whether
Alex had told me the good news or not. He didn't
seem to quite hear her the first time. So she
snapped her fingers in front of our faces. Then she
repeated herself. "Alex, honey, did you tell Rosie
the good news?"

He just blinked so she wrapped her arms around
him and she told me herself. They're getting married. So I came home.

Steph: Oh Rosie.
Rosie: What the hell was that silence?
Steph: It sounds like something I'd like. It sounded nice.
Rosie: It was.

Phil: What kind of a silence?
Alex: Just a weird silence.
Phil: Yeah but what do you mean by weird?
Alex: Unusual, not normal.
Phil: Yeah but was it good or bad?
Alex: Good.
Phil: And that's bad?
Alex: Yes.
Phil: Because?
Alex: I'm engaged to Sally.
Phil: Did you ever have "the silence" with her?
Alex: We have *silences* . . .
Phil: So do Margaret and I, you don't always have to talk
        you know.
Alex: No this was *different* Phil. It wasn't just a silence, it
        was a . . . oh I don't no.
Phil: Bloody hell Alex.
Alex: I no. I'm all over the place.
Phil: OK so don't marry Sally.
Alex: But I love her.
Phil: And what about Rosie?

Alex: I'm not sure.

Phil: Well then, I don't see a problem here. If you were in
         love with Rosie and not sure about Sally *then* you'd
         be in trouble. Marry Sally and forget about the god-
         damn silence.

Alex: Once again, you've put my life into perspective Phil.

Dear Rosie,

   I am so sorry about what happened. You didn't have to
leave Boston so soon, we could have worked this out . . . I'm
sorry I didn't tell you about Sally before you got here but I
was waiting until you met her and I didn't want to tell you
over the phone. Maybe I should have . . .

   Please don't distance yourself from me, I haven't heard
from you in weeks. It was wonderful seeing you . . . please
write soon.

                  Keep in touch,
                  Love,
                  Alex

TO ALEX OR SHOULD WE SAY DR. ALEX!
CONGRATULATIONS!
GIVE YOURSELF A BIG PAT ON THE BACK . . .
YOU MADE IT!!
WE KNEW YOU COULD DO IT!
Congratulations on graduating from Harvard, you genius!!
Sorry we couldn't be there,
Love Rosie and Katie
Xxx

You have an instant message from: ALEX

Alex: Rosie, I wanted you to be the first person to no that
         I've decided to become a heart surgeon!

Rosie: Cool, does it pay well?

Alex: Rosie, it's not about the money.

Rosie: Where I come from, it's *all* about the money. Proba-
         bly because I don't have any. Working part-time at
         Randy Andy Paperclip Co. isn't really as financially
         rewarding as it sounds.

Alex: Well in my world it's all about the lives you save. So
         what do you really think? Do you approve of my
         choice of employment?

Rosie: Hmmm . . . my best friend, the heart doctor. I like
         the sound of that.

Alex: Thanks Rosie.

FROM: Alex
TO: Rosie
SUBJECT: Thank you!

I forgot to thank you for the congrats card you and
Katie sent me, the last time we spoke. It has taken pride of
place on the mantel in my new apartment, in fact it's
about the only thing I actually have here. Sally and I just
moved in a few weeks ago, you and Katie are very
welcome to come over and see it whenever you like . . . it
can be Katie's first time on a plane to visit her godfather in
Boston!

The apartment is small but because I've such long
shifts at the hospital, I hardly get to stay here anyway.
I've got another life-long sentence here at the hospital
before I can actually call myself a heart surgeon. In the
meantime I'm being paid a pittance at work and slaving
away till all hours. There's a nice park directly across
the road and it's got a playground for kids, Katie would
love it.

Anyway that's enough about me. I seem to be just talking
about myself these days. Please write to me and let me know

how things are going for you. I don't want there to be any
awkwardness between us, Rosie.

    Keep in touch,
          Alex

TO ALEX,
MERRY CHRISTMAS!
MAY THE FESTIVE SEASON BE FILLED WITH LOVE AND
JOY FOR YOU AND YOUR LOVED ONES.
Love Rosie & kAtIe

ROSIE AND KATIE,
HAPPY NEW YEAR!
May this year bring you lots of fun, love, and happiness!
Love,
Alex and Sally

Dear Stephanie
    You will not believe the card that just arrived through my
door this morning. I was almost sick. I was just cleaning up
the mess Mum and Dad made after their annual new year's
party when it made its grand entrance on the doormat. I was
almost expecting the sound of trumpets to go with it! "Da
da da announcing the arrival of the extremely sad coupley
card!" There was about ten million bottles of wine rolling
around the floor when I came downstairs and I nearly
tripped over a game of Trivial Pursuit (yes it was one of
those nights). There were those stupid paper hats strewn
around the living room, hanging from the lightbulbs, or
dangling in the gravy dish looking extremely unappealing.
There were Christmas crackers pulled apart with their
crappy little miniature toys falling out that no one could
possibly ever use like little torches the size of your
thumbnail and jigsaws with about two pieces, lying in the
leftover food, *the place was a mess!*

Honestly, Steph, when Mum and Dad went away we held the craziest parties *ever* but at least we still managed not to behave like farmyard animals. Plus they were screaming and singing (well *trying* to sing) and dancing (or stamping their feet in some sort of crazy people ritual) *all night*. Poor Katie was terrified of all the noise (she just can't be my daughter), and she spent the night screaming her head off. So I had to sit up with her all night. Eventually everyone started to leave the house at about 6 or 7 A.M., and I was starting to fall asleep when I was jerked awake by a little monster jumping on me and demanding food.

So anyway I think what I'm *trying* to say is that I wasn't in the greatest mood for what arrived on my doorstep. I had a pounding headache, I was so tired and after cleaning the mess downstairs (which is fine because it is Mum and Dad's house after all and they are kindly letting me stay rent-free so I'm not complaining about them) I just wanted peace and quiet and a bit of sleep.

But the card came.

The happy-new-year-make-me-gag card.

On the front was a lovely little picture of Alex and Sally all dressed up warmly in their winter coats and hats and gloves etc. . . . they were standing outside in a park that was covered in snow with their arms wrapped around . . . a snowman. A bloody snowman.

They looked so sickeningly happy. Two little happy Harvard-heads. Uugh.

How sad is it to send a photo of yourself and your boyfriend building a snowman??? Very very very sad. That's how sad. And to send it to me, especially!! The cheek!

I should have sent them a photo of me and . . . me and . . . George (the lollipop man and the only man I seem to speak to these days) standing outside in the freezing cold jumping in puddles. That's how pointless that would have been to them!

Oh god, I'm rambling on and on. Sorry. I have to go before Katie finishes the last of that red wine in the bottle on the floor.

Oh, by the way. It was great to meet your boyfriend after all this time, he's a really nice guy. You two should come home more often, it was fun speaking to people closer to my age for a change.

Happy new year. Whoever thought of that expression?

Love, your festive and extremely joyous younger sister, Rosie.

TO ROSIE,
HAPPY BIRTHDAY, MY FRIEND!
WELCOME TO THE WORLD OF 25 YEAR OLDS! WE ARE GETTING OLD, ROSIE!
WRITE TO ME MORE OFTEN!
LOVE ALEX

TO ALEX
YOU ARE IVNITED TO MY 7TH BRITHDAY PARTY ON THE 4TH OF MAY IN MY HOWSE. WE ARE HAVING A MAJICIN. I CANT WAIT. IT IS ON AT 2 O'CLOCK AND YOU CAN LEAVE AT 5 O'CLOCK.
LOVE KATIE

Dear Katie,

I'm sorry I can't come to your birthday party. The magician sounds like he will be lots of fun. You will have so many friends you won't even no I'm not there! I have to work at the hospital, so they won't let me take a holiday. I told them it was your birthday but they still wouldn't listen!

However I have sent you a little something so I hope you

like it. Happy birthday, Katie, and take care of your
mummy for me. She is very special.

Lots of love to you and Mum,
Alex

TO ALEX,

THANK YOU FOR MY BRITHDAY PRESENT. MY
MUMMY CRIED WHEN I OPENED IT. I NEVER HAD A
LOCKET BEFORE. THE PHOTOGRAPHS OF YOU AND
MUMMY ARE VERY SMALL.

THE MAJICIN WAS GOOD BUT MY BEST FREIND TOBY
SAID HE NEW HE WAS CHEATING AND SHOWED
EVERYONE WHERE THE MAN HID THE CARDS. THE MAN
WAS NOT VERY HAPPY AND HE GOT MAD AT TOBY.
MUMMY LAFFED SO LOUD I DO NOT THINK THE MAJIC
MAN LIKED HER EETHER. TOBY LIKES MUM.

I GOT LOTS OF NICE PRESENTS BUT AVRIL AND
SINEAD GOT ME THE SAME THING. MUMMY AND
ME ARE MOVING HOWSE SOON. I WILL MISS
GRANDMA AND GRANDAD SO MUCH AND I NO
MUMMY IS SAD BECAUSE I HEARD HER CRYING LAST
NIGHT IN BED.

BUT WE ARE NOT MOVING TOO FAR AWAY. YOU
CAN GET THE BUS FORM GRANDMA AND GRANDAD TO
OUR NEW HOWSE. IT DOES NOT TAKE TOO LONG AND
WE ARE NEARER TO ALL THE SHOPS IN TOWN SO WE
CAN WALK.

IT IS MUCH SMALLER THAN THE HOWSE WE ARE IN
NOW. MUMMY IS FUNNY SHE CALLS IT A SHOE BOX!
THERE ARE ONLY 2 BEDROOMS AND THE KITCHEN IS
TINY AND THERE IS NO DINING ROOM OR PLAYROOM.
JUST A PLACE TO EAT AND WATCH TELLY. WE HAVE A
BALCONY AND IT'S NICE BUT MUM WONT LET ME STAND
ON IT ON MY OWN.

I CAN SEE THE PARK. MUMMY SAYS THE PARK IS OUR

GARDEN AND THAT WE HAVE THE BIGGEST GARDEN IN
THE WORLD.

MUMMY SAID THAT I CAN PAINT MY ROOM
WHATEVER COLOR I WANT. I THINK I'LL PAINT IT PINK
OR PURPLE. TOBY SAYS WE SHOULD PAINT IT BLACK. HE
IS FUNNY.

MUMMY HAS A NEW JOB. SHE WORKS ONLY A FEW
DAYS IN A WEEK SO SOMETIMES SHE CAN COLLECT
ME FROM SKOOL AND OTHER TIMES SHE CANT. I
PLAY WITH TOBY UNTIL SHE COMES HOME. HIS MUM
ALWAYS BRINGS HIM AND COLLECTS HIM BECAUSE
THEY SAY WE ARE TOO YOUNG TO GET THE BUS. I
DON'T THINK MUM LIKES HER JOB. SHE IS ALWAYS
TIRED AND CRYING. SHE SAID SHE WOULD PERFER
TO BE BACK IN SKOOL DOING DUBBLE MATTS. I DON'T
NO WHAT SHE MEANS. ME AND TOBY HATE SKOOL BUT
HE ALWAYS MAKES ME LAFF. MUMMY SAYS SHE IS TIRED
OF HAVING TO KEEP GOING BACK TO MY TEACHER MS.
CASEY. GRANDMA AND GRANDAD THINK IT IS FUNNY.
MS. CASEY HAS THE BIGGEST NOSE EVER. SHE HATES ME
AND TOBY. I DO NOT THINK SHE LIKES MUM EETHER
BECAUSE THEY ALWAYS FIGHT WHEN THEY SEE EACH
OTHER.

MUM HAS A NEW FREIND. THEY WORK IN THE SAME
BUILDING BUT NOT IN THE SAME OFFICE. THEY MET
OUTSIDE IN THE COLD BECAUSE THEY HAVE TO SMOKE
OUTSIDE. MUM SAYS SHE IS THE BEST FREIND SHE HAS
HAD FOR AGES. HER NAME IS RUBY AND SHE IS REAL
FUNNY. I LIKE WHEN SHE COMES OVER. SHE AND MUM
ARE ALWAYS LAFFING. I LIKE IT WHEN RUBY IS HERE
BECAUSE MUM DOESN'T CRY.

IT IS REAL SUNNY NOW IN DUBLIN. ME AND MUM
HAVE BEEN TO THE BEACH A FEW TIMES. I AM LEARNING
TO SWIM. BUT I HAVE TO KEEP MY ARMBANDS ON IN
THE SEA. MUM SAYS SHE WANTS TO LIVE ON THE BEACH.

SHE SAYS SHE WOULD LIKE TO LIVE IN THE SEA SHELLS!
OUR NEW FLAT IS IN THE CITY AND I LIKE IT.

    WHEN ARE YOU COMING TO SEE US? MUMMY SAYS
YOU ARE GETTING MARRIED TO A GIRL NAMED BIMBO.
THAT'S A FUNNY NAME.

        LOVE,
        KATIE

You have an instant message from: RUBY

Ruby: Hey you, happy Monday.
Rosie: Oh great, hold on while I get the champagne.
Ruby: What did you do over the weekend?
Rosie: Oh *wait* till you hear this! I was just *dying* to tell
        you all morning, it's *so* exciting! You'll *never* believe
        it, I—
Ruby: I sense sarcasm here. Let me guess: you watched TV.
Rosie: Introducing Ruby . . . and her psychic powers!! I
        had to listen to it with the volume blaring just to
        drown out the loving couple next door screaming
        their ears off each other. Someday they're going to
        kill each other. I can't wait. Poor Katie didn't know
        what was going on so I sent her down to stay at
        Toby's house.
Ruby: Honestly don't some people understand the meaning
        of the word DIVORCE?
Rosie: Ha ha, well, it's a magic word for you.
Ruby: I would appreciate it if you wouldn't make fun of a
        devastatingly difficult time in my life that left me
        feeling shattered and emotionally distraught.

Rosie: Oh please! Getting that divorce was the happiest
         day of your life! You bought the most expensive
         bottle of champagne, went out clubbing, and you
         snogged the ugliest man in the world . . .

Ruby: Ah well people have their different ways of
         grieving . . . OK well it was a happier feeling than
         the one I had on my wedding day . . . The wedding
         day feeling was kind of "Uh oh . . ."

Rosie: Have you finished typing up all that crap Randy
         Andy gave us?

Ruby: No I haven't. Have you?

Rosie: No.

Ruby: Good let's take a coffee break as a reward.
         We really shouldn't overwork ourselves. I hear
         it's quite dangerous. Will you bring your fags,
         I forgot mine.

Rosie: Yep meet you downstairs in five minutes.

Ruby: It's a date. Gosh how exciting. Neither of us has
         been on one of them for a while . . .

You have an instant message from: RUBY

Ruby: Where the hell were you? I waited for you in the
         café for a half an hour!

Rosie: Oh what hell for you Ruby!

Ruby: Yes I had to force myself to eat *two* chocolate
         muffins *and* a slice of apple pie. Oh it was *awful*
         Rosie . . . if only you had been there . . .

Rosie: Sorry about that, Randy Andy here wouldn't let me
         leave the office.

Ruby: Oh he is such a slave driver! You should complain
         to head office, get the asshole fired.

Rosie: He is head office.

Ruby: Oh yeah.

Rosie has logged off

ഌ

Dear Rosie and Katie Dunne,
Shelly and Bernard Gruber proudly invite you to the marriage
ceremony of their loving daughter Sally to Alex Stewart.

ഌ

FROM: Stephanie
TO: Rosie
SUBJECT: No way in the world I'm going to that wedding!

I am so angered by your last letter! You cannot miss
Alex's wedding! That would be completely unthinkable!

This is *Alex* we're talking about, not some archenemy of
yours! Alex, the boy who used to sleep on a sleeping bag on
your floor, the boy who used to sneak into my room and
read my diary and look through my underwear drawer!
Little Alex, who you used to chase down the road and shoot
at with a banana for a gun! Alex, who used to sit beside you
in class for twelve years, giggle with you all the time and
nobody else would ever know why!

He was there for you when you had Katie. He was so
supportive throughout the entire thing when I'm sure it was
difficult for him to adjust to the fact that little Rosie who
slept in a sleeping bag on *his* floor was having a *baby*.

Go over to him Rosie. Celebrate this with him. Share in
his happiness and excitement. Share it all with Katie. Be
happy! Please! I'm sure he needs you right now, this is a
huge step for him and he needs his best friend by his side.
Learn to get to know Sally too as she is an important person
in his life now. Just as he has learned to get to know Katie—

the most important person in your life. I know you don't
want to hear it, but if you don't go you will be ending what
was once and what still is one of the strongest bonds of
friendship that I have ever seen.

I know you are embarrassed by what happened a few
years ago when you visited, but swallow your pride, hold
your chin up. You are going to be at that wedding because
Alex *wants* you to be there for *him*; you are going to be
there because you *need* to be there for *yourself*. Make the
right decision, Rosie.

Dear Rosie,

Hey there! I have no doubt you have received our
wonderful wedding invitation that took Sally about three
months to choose. Why, I don't know, but it seems that a
cream-colored invite with a gold border was so much more
different than a white invite with a gold border . . . you
women . . .

I don't know if I should be worried or not, but Sally's
mom hasn't seemed to have received an RSVP from you yet!
Now I no I don't need one from you because I'm just
presuming you will be there!

The reason why I am writing and not ringing is because I
want to give you time to think about what I'm asking you.
Myself and Sally would be honored if you would allow
Katie to be our flower girl at the wedding. We would need to
no quite soon so that Sally and Katie can pick out a dress.

Whoever thought this would be happening, Rosie?! If
someone had told us ten years ago that *your daughter*
would be a flower girl at *my wedding* we would have just
laughed and laughed at the ridiculousness of it all. But it is
happening. And I can't quite believe it.

The second question I have to ask you is the one I'm sure
you will need to think about. You are my best friend Rosie;
that goes without saying. I have no best friend over here. No
one that measures up to what you mean to me; therefore I

have no best man. Will you be my best woman? Will you
stand beside me at the altar? I no I will definitely need you
there! And I trust you will organize a better stag night than
any of my male friends over here!

Think about it and let me no. And say yes!

Love to you and Katie,

Alex

You have an instant message from: ROSIE

Rosie: You won't fucking believe it.

Ruby: You got a date.

Rosie: No, worse than that, Alex has asked me to be his
         "Best Woman."

Ruby: I don't suppose that means you'll be standing to the
         left of him in the church??

Rosie: Eh no . . . to the right.

Ruby: What about his brother?

Rosie: He's an usher or something.

Ruby: Wow so he really is going ahead with it?

Rosie: Yep. Looks like it.

Ruby: I think you should stop waiting for him now, honey.

Rosie: I know. I probably should.

—⌇—

CHAPTER 10

My "Best Woman" speech

Good evening everyone, my name is Rosie and as you can see Alex has decided to go down the non-traditional route of asking me to be his best woman for the day. Except we all know that today that title does not belong to me. It belongs to Sally, for she is clearly his best woman.

I could call myself the "best friend" but I think we all know that today that title no longer refers to me either. That title too belongs to Sally.

But what *doesn't* belong to Sally is a lifetime of memories of Alex the child, Alex the teenager, and Alex the almost-a-man that I'm sure he would rather forget but that I will now fill you all in on. (Hopefully they all will laugh.)

I have known Alex since he was five years old. I arrived on my first day of school teary-eyed and red-nosed and a half an hour late. (I am almost sure Alex will shout out "What's new?") I was ordered to sit down at the back of the class beside a smelly, snotty-nosed, messy-haired little boy who had the biggest sulk on his face and who refused to look at me or talk to me. I hated this little boy.

I know that he hated me too, him kicking me in the shins under the table and telling the teacher that I was copying his schoolwork was a telltale sign. We sat beside each other every day for twelve years moaning about school, moaning about girlfriends and boyfriends, wishing we were older and wiser and out of school, dreaming for a life where we wouldn't have double maths on a Monday morning.

Now Alex has that life and I'm so proud of him. I'm so happy that he's found his best woman and his best friend in ~~perfect little brainy and annoying~~ Sally.

I ask you all to raise your glasses and toast *my* best friend Alex and his new best friend, best woman, and wife, Sally, and to wish them luck and happiness ~~and divorce~~ in the future.

> To Alex and Sally!

OR SOMETHING TO THAT EFFECT. WHAT DO YOU THINK, RUBY?

You have an instant message from: RUBY

Ruby: Gag gag puke puke puke. They'll all love it. Good luck Rosie. No tears and DO NOT drink.

To Rosie,

Greetings from Seychelles! Rosie, thank you so much for last week! I had such a good time. I never really thought I could actually enjoy my wedding day but you made it so much fun. Don't worry, I don't think anyone noticed you were drunk for the entire ceremony (maybe they did for the speech—but it was funny), but I don't think the priest was too impressed when you hiccupped just as I was about to say "I do!"

I can't quite remember the stag night but I hear it was a great success, the boys just keep going on and on about it. I think Sally is a little angry that she had to marry a man with one eyebrow and I don't care what anybody says, I no it was you who did it! All the wedding photos are of the left side of my face but it doesn't matter because Sally says it's my best side. Unlike you, who says my best side is the back of my head.

The wedding went really well, didn't it? I thought I was going to be a bundle of nerves all day but you just made me laugh so much I think it helped to get rid of the nervous energy. Although we shouldn't really have laughed when the wedding photos were being taken, I doubt we'll find any decent shots where my face and yours aren't distorted from laughter. Sally's family thought you were really terrific. They weren't really keen on the idea of me having a best woman, to be honest, but Sally's dad thought you were great. Is it true you made him knock back a shot of tequila?!

My mum and dad were *so* glad to see you and Katie. It's funny; they say Katie is exactly how you looked when you were eight. I think Mum kind of kept hoping that it *was* you and that I was that age again too. She was very teary that day! But they just wouldn't stop going on and on about how beautiful you looked in that dress! It's as if you were the bride!

But you did look beautiful, Rosie, I don't think I've ever seen you in a dress before (not since you were Katie's age anyway). Well I suppose I would have seen you in one had I made it to the debs all those years ago. God, listen to me. I sound like an old man reminiscing on years gone by!

Everyone said the best woman speech was brilliant, I think all my friends have a crush on you. And no, you can't have their phone numbers. By the way Rosie, you *were* my best woman that day and you still are my best friend. Always will be. Just to let you no.

Married life is going well so far. We've only been married ten days so we've only had let's see . . . ten fights. I'm sure somebody told me that was healthy in a relationship . . . I'm not worried. The place we're staying in is fabulous, which I'm glad about because it's costing us an absolute fortune. We're staying in this little wooden hut-type place that's built

on stilts high up over the water. It's beautiful. The water is
that turquoise green color that you can see through right
down to the multicolored fish below. It's paradise; you
would love it. Now, this is the hotel you should work at
Rosie. Imagine your office being the beach . . .

I would just love to laze on the beach and drink cocktails
all day, to be honest, but Sally always has to be doing
something so every second I'm being dragged into the sea or
I find myself flying in the sky hanging out of some odd
contraption. I wouldn't be surprised if she decides to eat our
lunch while scuba-diving.

Anyway I bought you and Katie presents so I hope they
arrived to your house safely and that they weren't crushed in
the post. They're supposed to be a kind of a good luck
charm over here but I no you always loved collecting shells
on the beach when we were kids so now you can wear the
prettiest ones around your neck.

Well I better go, apparently people aren't even supposed
to send postcards while they're on their honeymoon, never
mind writing novels for letters (according to Sally—so I
must go). I think she wants to do something crazy like be
dragged around on water skis by a dolphin.

God help me, what have I gotten myself into?!!

> Love,
> Alex
> PS: I miss you!

You have an instant message from: RUBY

Ruby: I spotted you out the window coming into work,
         what the hell are you wearing around your neck? Is
         it shells?
Rosie: It brings luck.
Ruby: Uh-huh. Any luck yet?
Rosie: I didn't miss my bus this morning.

Ruby: Uh-huh.
Rosie: Oh piss off

Rosie has logged off

FROM: Rosie
TO: Ruby
SUBJECT: You'll never believe this

I'm faxing you over a letter Sally sent Katie. Let me know what you think.

To Katie,

Thank you for being my flower girl at my wedding last week. Everybody said that you looked beautiful, just like a real little princess.

Myself and Alex are now on holiday in a place called the Seychelles, just where your mummy wants to live. Tell her it is lovely, very hot and sunny, and you can show her the photograph of me and Alex lying on the beach to show her what it looks like here. We are very happy and very much in love.

I am enclosing a photograph of you, me, and Alex on our wedding day so you can frame it and put it up in your house. I hope you like it.

Ring us soon.
        Love,
        Sally

You have an instant message from: RUBY

Ruby: Sounds like the bitch is just pissing around her man
         to mark her territory.
Rosie: By sending a letter to an 8-year-old little girl!??!!

Ruby: Well she obviously knew that it would get into your hands. That's cruel alright. What did Katie say?

Rosie: Oh nothing much, I don't think she realized what Sally was doing.

Ruby: Don't let Sally worry you. She's just trying to let you know who the woman is in Alex's life now. Anyway why is she doing this, did you do anything to make her feel threatened?

Rosie: No way! As if!

Ruby: Rosie?

Rosie: Oh OK then maybe she felt just a little threatened by the fact that Alex and I had a better time at her wedding than she did.

Ruby: Bingo!

Rosie: Yes but that's the way we always are Ruby, it wasn't flirting, it wasn't anything. It was just happiness. However she did not crack one smile for the whole day, she just kept sucking her cheekbones in and pouting at everyone.

Ruby: OK I believe you, but millions wouldn't. Anyway, don't rise to her, just ignore it.

Rosie: Oh don't worry, I won't respond. I'm just sorry that the stupid woman didn't have the common sense to leave my daughter out of her insecurities.

Ruby: Katie will be fine; she's a smart girl. Just like her mother.

To Sally,

Thank you for your letter. I'm glad you liked my dress, but if I were you I would have worn a pretty dress like my mum's for my wedding day. Everyone said that it matched Alex's tuxedo really well. They made a nice couple, don't you think? I showed Mum and Toby (my best friend) the photograph of you and Alex on the beach and Toby says that he hopes that your sunburn doesn't hurt too much. It looks really sore.

That's all for now. I have to go now because Mum's new boyfriend is coming to the flat soon. Tell Alex that me, mum, and Toby said hi.

     Love from Katie,
     Xxx

—~m—

FROM: Alex
TO: Rosie
SUBJECT: Secret boyfriend

Back from my honeymoon; you sly little lady, you never told me about this new boyfriend of yours! Sally was so excited about the news she couldn't wait to tell me, which I thought was rather sweet. I didn't realize Katie and Sally were writing to each other, did you?

Anyway why didn't you say a word about this guy at the wedding? I never knew you to be so secretive, you usually tell me everything. So what's he like? What's his name? Where did you meet him? What does he look like? What does he do for a living? I hope he earns loads of money and that he's treating you well, or else I'm coming home to throttle him.

I'll have to go back to Dublin to meet this guy; make sure he gets the best friend approval. Anyway, let me no all the details (maybe not *all* of them).

Hi Stephanie,
Just writing to see how you are, love, and to share a bit

of good news with you. I'm sure Rosie hasn't told you this already because she's keeping pretty quiet about it, but I just wanted to tell you that she's met someone! We are all so delighted, she seems so happy, those big blue eyes don't look so sad anymore and there's a spring in her step again. More like the Rosie we used to know.

Anyway, she brought the young man over to the house yesterday for dinner to meet us and I have to say he really is a charming man. His name is Greg Collins and he's a bank manager for AIB in Fairview. So I presume he's being reasonably well paid, which isn't important I know but it's nice to see Rosie being treated for a change.

He's quite a short man, to be honest, a little taller than Rosie with a cute little face. He's thirty-something, I would guess, and he is absolutely wonderful with Katie. They spent the day teasing each other, it was very funny. It's been difficult, as you know, for Rosie to meet someone who she likes herself as well as taking into account that it has to be somebody that Katie feels comfortable with too. But there should be no compromises, I keep telling her. Too often she ended up with those other men just because Katie liked them. Anyway, as I said, Katie adores Greg. I'm so pleased. Rosie seems to have found a nice fellow at last.

Anyway how's work? Busy over there as always? Don't work yourself too hard in that restaurant anyway, love; you need to enjoy life too. Your dad and I were thinking of coming over to you for a little holiday soon, would that be OK? Let us know when you're free and we'll work around it. Say hello to Jean-Pierre for us. Looking forward to seeing you.

      Love,
      Mum

FROM: Rosie
TO: Alex
SUBJECT: Re: Secret boyfriend

Oops my little secret is out now thanks to Katie and her big mouth! Well I didn't say anything about Greg (that's his name) at your wedding, because at that stage we hadn't gone out yet! We met in the Dancing Cow nightclub (it's a very long story!) just before I went over to you in Boston, and he took my number and asked me out but I said no! So I must have gone all gushy after your wedding because when I came back I rang him up and asked him out!

Oh Alex I've been wined and dined like never before! He's taken me to restaurants I only read about in magazines and he's terribly romantic, but you said not to give you *all* the details so I won't tell you about our weekend away down the country . . . OK so you wanted to know all about him, here goes: He is 35, works at the bank in Fairview. He's not exactly tall (my height), which isn't exactly small but . . . OK if he was to stand beside you, you would have a fantastic view of his scalp. But he has sandy-colored hair and wonderful twinkling blue eyes.

He is always bringing Katie little gifts when he comes, which I know he shouldn't do, but I love seeing her being spoiled especially as I haven't exactly been able to do that myself over the years. I can't believe I have finally met a man that doesn't mind that I have a daughter, all the others looked at me like I was diseased when I told them and would suddenly think of a great excuse to have to leave the dinner table. I also can't believe that Katie and I have finally agreed on the same man. She only seemed to like the young pretty ones that she fancied herself probably. We need to be realistic here, though, I can't exactly afford to be picky!! Her idea of a great partner for me was someone who would play games with her all the time, pull silly faces, put on unattractive voices and wear

brightly colored clothes that should only be worn on
Saturday morning TV.

Anyway I seem to have found him. He is a very generous,
caring, and thoughtful man, and I think I am very lucky to
have met him. It may not last forever but I'm enjoying
myself Alex. I know I've been such a misery guts for the
past, oh I don't know . . . 10 years or so (!) but now I have
realized that Katie and I are a team and if they can't love us
both, then they can get lost.

But I *think* I may have met a man who does. Fingers
crossed.

PS: I notice you have stopped referring to Ireland as
home . . . your heart must finally be in Boston now.

FROM: Alex
TO: Rosie
SUBJECT: Oooh Rosie's in love!

Oooooh! Rosie sounds like she's in love!!!

With a bank manager who goes clubbing in a place
called the Dancing Cow?? What kind of bank manager (or
any man for that matter) goes to the Dancing Cow? Fair
enough, you and your friend Ruby seem to have gone off the
rails altogether, so therefore I wouldn't expect anything
more from you. But I don't no, I'm not yet convinced this
man is the right one for you.

And I have to say I was slightly insulted by your last
letter. What do you mean by the statement "I have finally
met a man who doesn't mind that I have a daughter"? I
think that I have always been supportive of you and Katie,
in fact I no I have. Whenever I can, I visit you and bring you
out to all your favorite restaurants and bring my
goddaughter presents.

Anyway I better go, just worked a double shift at the hospital so I'm feeling kind of ratty and tired.

FROM: Rosie
TO: Alex
SUBJECT: Thanks Mr. Supportive

Well thank you, Mr. Supportive, for being so happy for me. In case you haven't noticed, you and I are not involved in a romantic relationship. Yes, you are a wonderful friend (supportive and generous), but you are not here every day with me. I'm sure you will understand when I say that finding a friend and finding a partner are two very different things. You accept me warts and all, some men don't. But you're not here.

OK well that's all. Hope married life is going wonderfully!

You have an instant message from: RUBY

Ruby: Katie told Sally what??
Rosie: I know, it's crazy isn't it? And Katie wrote that let-
         ter after I had only been on *one* date with Greg!
Ruby: Wow, she must really like him to be telling people
         about him so soon. Ah well maybe Sally won't feel
         like you're trying to get your grubby little mitts on
         her husband now.
Rosie: Ah who cares anyway, I have my Greg!
Ruby: Ugh you make me sick, you've turned into one of
         those sickening couples that we hate. You two are
         carrying on like love-struck teenagers; I think I'll
         have to find a new single friend so that I don't feel
         like a *complete* gooseberry the next time we go out.

Rosie: Oh you're such a liar! You were having a great time
         with all those guys every time I looked at you. You
         were the center of attention!

Ruby: Oh a girl does what she has to . . . Anyway you
         must only have spotted me on the rare occasion
         you detached your head from Greg's face. Oh by
         the way that guy called me last night so I'm think-
         ing of—

You have an instant message from: GREG

Greg: Hello gorgeous how's your day going?

Rosie: Oh hello! Oh it's the same as usual . . . better now
         though!

Ruby: Hello? Are you still there or has Randy Andy at-
         tacked you?

Rosie: Sorry Greg just a second, I'm chatting to Ruby on-
         line too!

Greg: Do you two ever do any work?!

Rosie: Enough to keep ourselves from getting fired.

Greg: I'll try you again later.

Ruby: No no! Don't be silly! I'm perfectly capable of
         carrying on two conversations at the same time. Be-
         sides I want to chat to you and if I tell that to Ruby
         she'll be even more angry at me for becoming one of
         them . . .

Greg: Who's "them"?

Rosie: Part of the secret couple elite . . .

Greg: Oh, *them*! Of course, silly me . . .

Rosie: Sorry Ruby, Greg is e-mailing me too so bear with
         me for a few minutes.

Ruby: Can you two not live without each other for a few
         hours?!

Rosie: No!

Ruby: Oh I miss Rosie . . . Who are you and what have
         you done to my man-hating friend?

Rosie: Don't worry she's still here, just taking a well-
         deserved break. So what were you saying about this
         guy you met the other night?

Ruby: Oh yeah his name is Ted (a real teddy bear), he's
         overweight but then again so am I so who cares; we
         can bounce off each other. He's a truck driver and
         he seemed like a nice guy because he kept buying
         me drinks, which puts him up pretty high on my
         Decent Man scale. Plus he was the only person who
         wasn't ignoring me in the pub that night.

Rosie: Oh I'm so sorry but you know what it's like when
         you meet someone new, you want to get to know
         everything about them.

Ruby: No I don't quite want to know everything about
         Ted . . . I don't want to be put off him.

Rosie: So Greg what are you doing tonight?

Greg: Rosie my dear, I am all yours for the night! Why
         don't we get a bottle of wine, some take-away, and
         stay in for the night. We can get Katie a video or
         something.

Rosie: Yep, that sounds like a great idea! My stomach
         is rumbling at the thought of it. I'm starving!
         Randy Andy will only let me take two lunch
         breaks now. Anyway Katie will be really excited to
         see you.

Ruby: So should I call him?

Rosie: Call who?

Ruby: TED!

Rosie: Oh yeah, of course! Ring the teddy bear! Then I
         won't feel like such a bitch for leaving you on your
         own when we go out. Actually ask him out, I can

get Kevin to babysit and then we can all go on a double date, I've always wanted to do that!

Ruby: Oh please, the innocence of the young and inexperienced. Ted and Greg will have absolutely nothing in common, they're like chalk and cheese; a bank manager and a possible bank robber. They will hate each other, the atmosphere will be awkward, no one will talk, all you'll hear is the munching of food in our mouths over the deafening silence like some kind of weird Chinese torture, we'll all refuse dessert, skip the coffee, pick up the check, and leg it out the door and feel relieved and promise ourselves never to meet up again.

Rosie: How does next Friday sound?

Ruby: Friday's fine.

Greg: I hope Ruby is OK with us after the other night; we were kind of in a world of our own.

Rosie: Don't be silly, she didn't mind at all. She met some guy called Teddy Bear, oh and by the way, are you free to go out on a double date thingy on Friday night? That's if I can get a babysitter for Katie.

Greg: A dinner date with Ruby and a man named Teddy Bear. Sounds interesting.

Rosie: Greg said he's free for dinner on Friday.

Ruby: Well that's all very well but I haven't asked Ted yet. What did Alex say about you and Greg being *in love*?

Rosie: Well I didn't say I was *in love* Ruby! Greg and I haven't even said that to *each other* yet! But Alex sent me some weird letter telling me that he thinks that Greg sounds like a freak of nature and that he's insulted that I don't think that he's supportive of me and Katie. He just went on a bit of a rant to be honest but I won't take any notice because he

had worked all night at the hospital and he was
tired—

Ruby: Uh-huh.

Rosie: What's that supposed to mean?

Ruby: This is just as I suspected.

Rosie: Why Jessica Fletcher, what did you suspect?

Ruby: He's jealous.

Rosie: Alex is *not* jealous!

Ruby: Alex is jealous of your relationship with Greg; he
feels threatened.

Greg: So what time should I call over to you tonight? 7 or
8?

Rosie: No, Alex is *not* jealous of my relationship with
Greg! Why should he be? He's married to perfect
pretty little Sally, happily might I add (at least according to Sally) *and* I have a lovely photograph
of the two of them lying on the beach together
looking *very* much in love just to prove it. I gave
him a chance to be part of Katie's life and mine
and he chose to remain my friend, which is what
I have now come to terms with. It's fine. Now I
am in a relationship with Greg, he's wonderful and
I no longer care about Alex in that way *at all
whatsoever*! So that's all I have to say about that
thank you very much! I am over Alex, he is not interested in me and now I am in love with Greg!
So there!

Greg: Well . . . thank you for sharing all that with me
Rosie, I can't tell you enough how thrilled I am to
hear that you are no longer in love with a man
named Alex "*at all whatsoever*" as you so articu-
lately put it . . .

Rosie: Oh my god Ruby!! I just sent Greg the message that

was supposed to be for you!! Fuck fuck *FUCKETY*
FUCK! I TOLD HIM I *LOVED* HIM!!!!

Greg: Em . . . that eh . . . went to me again Rosie . . .
       sorry . . .

Rosie: Oh . . .

Ruby: Oh what??

—m—

Rosie: OK so that has to be the singularly *most embarrassing* thing that has *ever* happened to me, without *any* doubts, NO exceptions!!!

Ruby: What about the time you wore that white dress out to a club with no underwear on and someone spilled water all over you and it was suddenly completely see-through?

Rosie: OK so that was pretty embarrassing.

Ruby: And what about the time you were in the supermarket and you grabbed another little girl's hand by mistake and started dragging her out to the car while Katie waited inside crying her eyes out.

Rosie: That little girl's mother said it was fine and she dropped the charges . . .

Ruby: And what about the time—

Rosie: OK that's enough thank you! I take back what I said, it was not *the* most embarrassing thing that has ever happened, but it's pretty much up there with the all-time classics. The number one embarrassing moment being the time I kissed Alex.

Ruby: Ha ha ha ha ha ha ha.

Rosie: Oh come on you're supposed to make me feel
         better.

Ruby: Ha ha ha ha ha ha ha ha.

Rosie: Oh the joy of having supportive friends. I'm going
         now; Randy Andy is glaring at me like a schoolmas-
         ter over the rim of his incredibly sexy brown-
         rimmed spectacles.

Ruby: Maybe he wants you to be the naughty schoolgirl.

Rosie: Well he's just a few years too late for that. I think
         he wants to kill me, his nostrils are flaring and he's
         breathing quite heavily

Ruby: Are his hands above the desk?

Rosie: Uuugh! Ruby stop!

Ruby: What?! You don't think they call him Randy Andy
         for nothing do you?

Rosie: I hate open plan offices, he can see me from every
         corner of this room, and he can also see my legs
         underneath the desk. Oh my, now he's staring at
         my legs.

Ruby: Rosie you really need to get out of that office. It's
         not healthy.

Rosie: I know, I'm working on it but I can't quit until I
         get another job and that's proving to be rather
         difficult. Apparently no one really cares about
         whether or not you work as a secretary in a
         paper-clip factory.

Ruby: Hmm . . . how odd . . . And it *sounds* so glam-
         orous, you would think . . . Honestly, *some*
         people . . .

Rosie: Oh my god, he has now moved his chair over so he
         can get a better look. Hold on a minute while I send
         him a message, I've had enough!

Ruby: Don't!

Rosie: Why not? I'll just send him a polite message asking
         to stop looking at me because I find it distracting
         while I'm trying to work.

You have an instant message from: ROSIE

Rosie: Stop staring at my tits you pervert.

Rosie: OK Ruby, I sent it.
Ruby: Oh you are so fired; Randy Andy doesn't take too
         kindly to brash young ladies who stick up for
         themselves.
Rosie: Screw him! He can't fire me for that!

Ms. Rosie Dunne,
     Andy Sheedy Paper Clip & Co. will no longer be
requiring your services, which means that your contract will
therefore not be up for renewal next month as was
previously discussed.
     You are, however, entitled to remain as an employee of
Andy Sheedy Paper Clip & Co. until the end of the month,
i.e. June the 30th.
     Andy Sheedy Paper Clip & Co. thanks you for the work
you have put into the company over the past few years and
we wish you luck in the future.
                    Yours sincerely,
                    Andy Sheedy
                    Owner of Andy Sheedy Paper Clip & Co.

You have an instant message from: ROSIE

Rosie: I faxed the letter over, did you see it?
Ruby: Ha ha ha ha ha ha.
Rosie: Do you know what? The more I read it, the more
         I'm glad that I'm leaving. The name Andy Sheedy
         Paper Clip & Co. says it all really, doesn't it? I won-
         der who wrote the letter for him, seeing as I'm his
         secretary and that's my job and all. I probably did it
         myself and didn't even realize it. I never pay atten-

tion to half the stuff he gives me to type up anyway.
Ah well, so what do you think? .

Ruby: Ha ha ha ha ha ha ha ha ha.

Rosie: Well I'm glad you find me losing my job *so* funny.

Ruby: Oh please it's not like you weren't leaving anyway.
This is the best way to go. Rosie Dunne, you will go
down in history in this building as the woman who
told Randy Andy to f off. I will spread the word
Rosie; you being fired will not have been in vain.
I'll miss you! Where will you go?

Rosie: I have absolutely no idea.

Ruby: Why don't you apply for a job in a hotel? Ever
since I've met you you've been going on and on
about hotels.

Rosie: I know. I have a slight obsession with them. Perhaps
it's the huge furniture that makes me feel so safe in
them, like oversized vases the size of people and
couches that wouldn't fit in my living room and
kitchen put together. I feel like Alice in Wonderland
in hotel lobbies. At least I have a month to find
somewhere, it shouldn't be *that* hard. I better start
writing up my CV.

Ruby: That shouldn't take long then.

FROM: Rosie
TO: Alex
SUBJECT: Is my CV OK?
         Attachment—CV.doc

Please, please, please help me with my CV or my poor
daughter and I will starve to death. How do you make all
my crappy jobs look impressive? Help! Help! Help!

FROM: Alex
TO: Rosie
SUBJECT: Re: CV
         Attachment: CV.doc

As you can see (by the attached document) I have rewritten your CV. The one you sent me was practically perfect as it was of course but I just fixed the grammar and a few spelling mistakes . . . you no how great at spelling I am!

By the way Rosie, just to let you no, you haven't been doing a "crappy job" as you so nicely phrased it. I don't think you understand the difficulty of what you are doing. You are a full-time *single* mum who has a job as a personal secretary to a very successful businessman. I only changed the words around; I didn't alter the truth in any way. What you have been doing day after day is incredible. When I come home from work I'm so shattered that I just collapse; I barely take care of myself, never mind another person.

Don't underestimate yourself, Rosie, don't play down what you do. When you go into your interviews keep your head held high and feel confident with the knowledge that you are an incredibly hard worker (when you want to be), you have the wonderful ability to work with other people as you are always well liked (except that time when we had to do a group project in school on the planets and you insisted on drawing little men on Mars and little women on Venus over Helen Corrigan's picture that took her weeks to do in art class which ended up causing every one in the group to walk out in protest leaving just the two of us having to start another one all by ourselves. God what is it about you and me being together that makes everyone hate us?!) You are wonderful, beautiful, smart, and intelligent, and if you knew anything about coronary heart diseases I'd hire you myself.

I mentioned that you were offered a place in Boston College which is impressive so everything will be fine, just be yourself and they'll love you.

Just one more thing, I *strongly* suggest that you apply for a job that you actually *like* this time. You would be surprised at how easy it is to get out of bed in the morning when you're going to do something that doesn't make you want to jump off the top floor of the bus (I was a bit worried when I got that e-mail). How about finally trying to find a place in a hotel? You've wanted to do that since you stayed in the Holiday Inn in London when you were seven, remember?

Go for it and let me no how you get on.

CHAPTER 13

—w—

FROM: Alex
TO: Rosie
SUBJECT: Boston visit?

Just taking a sneaky break from performing "lobotomies" to send a quick e-mail to see how you're getting on with the job search. You have one week left till Randy Andy throws you out of his paper clip empire, so there's still plenty of time, and if by any chance something hasn't caught your eye by then, I can send a check over to help tide you over for a while (but only if you *want* my help.)

I would love to go home right now and go to bed, I am so tired. I've worked a double shift so I don't have to get my hands bloody tomorrow; I have the day off, such bliss . . . The problem is that when I get home Sally will be getting ready to go on her shift. We don't have the most sociable hours in the world; well not unless you count talking to people who are rolling around in agony on hospital beds. Sorry that wasn't funny.

I'm just tired, and Sally and I don't really get to spend a lot of time together, and when we do we're usually so tired we just pass out.

Here's a good idea. If you come over with Katie and whats-his-name then I'll take a few days off and we can see all the sights, eat out, enjoy ourselves, and I can *sleep*. And I'll finally get to meet whats-his-name. I've had a lousy few weeks; I really need your comic relief! Work your magic Rosie Dunne and make me laugh.

FROM: Rosie
TO: Alex
SUBJECT: Rosie is here!

Hello there misery man, have no fear, Rosie is here! Sorry things have been shit for you lately. I think life likes to do that every now and again. Every so often it likes to dip and when you feel like you can't take any more it smoothes out again. But until then my dear friend I will try to humor you by explaining the events of my life.

OK firstly you are a bad, bad influence on me. After I read the masterpiece that was my CV, and after I read your letter I felt so motivated and hyped up that I donned my tracksuit, headband, wrist bands, and jogging shoes (not really) and I raced around Dublin city like a woman on a mission.

You horrible, horrible man. You made me feel like I could do anything, like I could take on the world (never *ever* do that again) so I proceeded to drop my CV into every single hotel I've ever wanted to work in but was always too afraid to try. Shame on you for giving me strength, because it quickly disappeared and I found myself faced with a million billion interviews with a million billion snotty companies that hated me and my cheek for even *thinking* I could work for them.

So let's see, which embarrassing interview should I tell you about first? Hmm . . . there are so many to choose from. Well let's start with the most recent, shall we?

Yesterday I had an interview to work at the reception in the Two Lakes Hotel; you know that really posh one in the city? The front of the building is entirely made of glass so you can see the big bright glistening chandeliers dripping down, from miles away. At nighttime the building looks like it's on fire, it's so bright. The restaurant is on the top floor so that you can look out over the entire city. It really is very beautiful.

But it's also one of those places where there's a guy (actually more of a gentleman) dressed in one of those cloak things and a top hat who stands at the door and refuses to let anyone in. It must have taken me about ten minutes just to get inside the door, he just wouldn't listen, and he kept saying that I needed to be a resident. Honestly, how could anybody ever get to be a resident if they don't let you in the door? Anyway, finally he let me in and I nearly slipped on the marble floor that was *so* shiny.

The place was so quiet you could hear a pin drop. No, I mean it literally; the woman at reception actually *did* drop a pin. I heard it. Well I suppose the hotel wasn't *that* quiet, there was the twinkling sound of a piano filtering out from the lounge, there was a water fountain trickling down through the lobby area, the sounds were just so calming. It even had all those giant pieces of furniture that I always loved as a child, like huge mirrors, gigantic chandeliers, doors the length of my apartment wall. When I stepped onto the carpets I thought I was going to bounce up to the balcony, they were so spongy.

I was seated at "The Longest Table Ever" for the interview. Two men and a woman sat at one end, at least I think that's what they were, I was so far away I could barely see (I almost felt like asking them to pass the salt).

So I thought that I would try and make myself sound interested in the company, just like you told me to, so I asked them how the hotel got its name as I wasn't aware of any lakes in that part of the city. The two men started laughing and introduced themselves as Bill and Bob Lake. They own the place. How embarrassing.

So I basically just kept talking about what you told me to say: how I like working as part of a team, that I'm good with people, how I'm very interested in the running of a hotel and about how I'm such a hard worker and always put my mind to working on tasks and always finishing off what I start. And then I waffled on for what felt like an hour about how I've loved hotels since I was a child and have always wanted to work in one. (Well, the luxury is in *staying* in one but we both know I can't afford *that*.)

And then they go and spoil it all by saying something stupid like: "So Rosie, from the time you spent working at Andy Sheedy Paper Clip & Co. what have you learned that you think you can bring to the table here at the Two Lakes?"

Please, like that's even worth asking.

OK I have to go now, actually, because Katie just got home from school with the look of evil on her face and I haven't made dinner yet.

FROM: Alex
TO: Rosie
SUBJECT: Two Lakes Hotel

It's a shame you had to rush off, I was enjoying that e-mail. Glad to hear your interviews are going so well—it's cheered me right up!

But I'm dying to no, what did you tell them you could bring to the company?

FROM: Rosie
TO: Alex
SUBJECT: Re: Two Lakes Hotel

Alex, isn't it obvious??

Paper clips!

(They just laughed so I got myself out of that one easily.) OK so I'm really going now, Katie is shoving pictures that she drew in school in my face. (Oh by the way, she drew one of you . . . you look like you've lost a bit of weight. I'll scan it to you . . .)

Dear Ms. Rosie Dunne,

It is our pleasure to inform you that we are offering you the position of head receptionist at the Two Lakes Hotel.

On a more personal note, I am proud to say that Bob and I are very excited about having you here following the success of your interview last week. You come across as being a bright, intelligent, and witty young woman; the kind of person we like to have working at the hotel.

We take pride in hiring people we ourselves would like to be greeted by in a hotel and we have great faith that the smiles you brought to our faces when we met will also be brought to the customers of the hotel when they arrive at reception. We are proud to have you as a member of the team and hope our working relationship will continue on successfully for many years into the future.

We ask that you get in touch with Shauna Simpson at reception with regard to your work uniform.

> Yours sincerely,
> *Bill Lake*   *Bob Lake*
> Owner and manager   Owner
> PS: We would also appreciate it if you would bring those paper clips with you—office supplies are rather low!

You have an instant message from: ROSIE

Rosie: My god Ruby could it be possible that I'm actually

going to have a *nice* boss/bosses?! I think everything
is finally falling into place.

Ruby: And then she goes ahead and jinxes herself . . . she
        will never learn . . .

FROM: Rosie
TO: Stephanie
SUBJECT: Congratulations

I'm delighted to hear that you and Pierre got engaged! I
know we spoke on the phone for hours last night but I
wanted to send you this e-mail too. Congratulations!

Something rather bizarre is happening in my life,
Stephanie. I have a boyfriend who loves me, and who I love
back, I'm about to start work in the hotel of my dreams,
Katie is beautiful and healthy and funny and I finally feel
like a good mum. I feel happy. I want to enjoy this feeling
and revel in my good fortune but there's something niggling
at me in the back of my mind. There's a little voice
whispering to me, "Things are too perfect." It almost feels
like the calm before the storm.

Is this how normal life is supposed to be? Because I'm
used to drama, drama, drama. I'm used to things refusing to
go my way, I'm used to having to struggle, moan and
whinge my way into getting something that's not exactly
what I want but that will *just do*.

This is not something that will "just do," this is perfect;
this is exactly what I wanted. I wanted to feel loved by
someone, I wanted Katie to stop wondering if it was all her
fault that she didn't have a daddy like all the other kids, I
wanted to feel that the two of us not only belong together
but that someone else would accept us in their lives too, I
wanted to feel important, I wanted to feel like *somebody*, I
wanted to know that if I called in sick to work that I would

be *missed*. I wanted to stop feeling so sorry for myself, and I have.

Things are going great. I'm feeling really good about myself and I'm not quite used to that. This is the new Rosie Dunne. Young and confused Rosie is gone. Phase two of my life now begins . . .

PART 2

CHAPTER 14

Dear Ms. Dunne,

I was hoping that you could come to the school to discuss Katie's rapidly deteriorating behavior in class. Her attention span is short and she distracts other students by her note-passing.

How does Wednesday after school sound? You can reach me at the school. You know the number.

Ms. Casey

To Katie,

What do you mean your mum just laughed?

From Toby

FROM: Rosie
TO: Alex
SUBJECT: Flight details

Hey there, OK our flight is landing at 1.15 p.m.—flight number is EI-4023. I'll be the woman dragging a terrified-looking man by the hair through arrivals, carrying a hyperventilating child by the other arm, and pulling twenty suitcases along by my toes. (Greg hates flying, Katie is so excited I'm really very concerned that she's going to explode, and I couldn't decide what to bring with me so I packed my entire wardrobe.)

Are you sure Sally knows what she's got herself into, allowing me and my mad family to stay with you?

FROM: Sally
TO: Alex
SUBJECT: Re: Rosie's stay

Of course it's not OK Alex. You couldn't have chosen a worse time to invite her and you know it.

FROM: Alex
TO: Rosie
SUBJECT: Re: Flight details

Of course Sally doesn't mind. I can't wait to see you and Katie and to meet what's-his-name. I'll be waiting at arrivals for you.

Dear Alex,

I just want to thank you so much for the holiday! I had such a fantastic time. Boston seemed even more beautiful than I remembered, and I'm glad I didn't have to run home early in embarrassment this time round (ha ha best way to deal with it is to make fun of oneself). Katie just loved the whole experience, and the child will just not stop talking about you!

Greg really enjoyed it too, I'm glad you finally got to meet him and also learn that his face isn't usually the greenish kind of color that it was when you met him coming off the plane. It was such a treat to finally have my two favorite men in the same country together, never mind in the same room! So what do you think of him? Does he get the best friend seal of approval?

So apart from the fact that your wife absolutely hates me, everything else was very comfortable and enjoyable. But I actually don't mind Alex; I'll just accept it. It just makes it official and confirms what I already thought: for some unknown reason, any girlfriend or wife of yours will forever hate me. And that's fine with me. I'm over it.

I just hope she lets me see your son or daughter when he or she is born. Now there's something else I never imagined would happen! Alex Stewart is going to be a daddy! Every time I think about it I just have to laugh out loud. God love your child to have a father like you! Just joking, you know I'm thrilled! Although I can't believe you kept it a secret from me for three months. Shame on you.

By the way, I'm really sorry Katie spilled her drink over Sally's new dress. I don't know *what* got into her; she's usually not so clumsy! I've told her to write a letter of apology to Sally. Hopefully she won't hate us all so much then.

Anyway, my few weeks of fun are over now; it's back to reality again. I start work at my new job on Monday; I'm just hoping I'll like it. All my life I've wanted to work in a hotel and I've put the thought away, with the rest of my dreams. I just hope it isn't hell, or all my little dream bubbles will burst in an instant.

There's one more thing I forgot to tell you, Greg has asked me and Katie to move in with him. I'm not quite sure how to feel about it. I'm over the moon of course but you know the saying, "If it ain't broke don't fix it." Things are going really well at the moment between us and it's not just me that I have to think about. Katie really likes Greg, and she loves to spend time with him (it may not have been that obvious in Boston because she was so excited to see you), but I don't know if she would be ready for such a huge change in her life. We're only in the flat together two years now and we're learning to live our lives with just the two of us as opposed to having the rest of my family around. I'm not sure if uprooting her *again* would be the right thing. What do you think?

Well, I suppose all I need to do is ask her. But what if she says no? Do I say to Greg, "Eh . . . sorry I love you and all but my eight-year-old daughter doesn't want to live with you?" Do I tell Katie, "Tough luck you're moving house," or do I do what she wants? I clearly can't just do what *I* want because there's two other people involved. I'm going to think about it for the next while anyway.

Thanks again for the break, I really needed it. I'll make sure Katie sends on that letter to Sally.

> Love,
> Rosie

Welcome to your first day at the Two Lakes. I hope everyone has helped you to settle in so far. I'm sorry I'm not there to greet you but I am currently in the States finalizing a few things at our new Two Lakes Hotel in San Francisco.

In the meantime, Amador Ramirez, the hotel manager, is there to show you the ropes. Let me know if you have any problems.

> Once again, welcome!
> Bill Lake

You have an instant message from: RUBY

Ruby: Remember me?

Rosie: I'm sorry Ruby, it's just that I don't get to spend much time on the computer like the last job; it's a bit difficult to pretend I'm doing work here.

Ruby: So you're still there then?

Rosie: Ruby you know I am.

Ruby: I'll give you one month . . .
Rosie: Thank you for your support; it's always very much
        appreciated.
Ruby: No problem. So how's life with Greg?
Rosie: Great thanks.
Ruby: So you don't hate each other yet?
Rosie: No not yet.
Ruby: I'll give you one month . . .
Rosie: And once again, thank you.
Ruby: Just doing my duty as a friend. Gary has a girl-
        friend now.
Rosie: Gary?! Your baby Gary?!
Ruby: Well he's 20 now but I can see how you could be
        confused, he's yet to lose all that baby fat . . . like
        his mother.
Rosie: Oh stop it! Who's the girl?
Ruby: Gemma is her name. To be honest I think there's
        something a bit wrong with her.
Rosie: In what way?
Ruby: In the way that she has deliberately chosen to go out
        with my son.
Rosie: Oh Ruby that's awful! Gary is a nice boy.
Ruby: Nice my bum! I don't know what she sees in him;
        all he does is occasionally make grunting sounds
        and point to things. Usually at food, and then to his
        stomach. Any news with you?
Rosie: Well actually I have a bit, I've only told Alex so far
        but you're not allowed to tell anyone.
Ruby: Ooh lovely, I love it! The most magical words you'll
        ever hear in a sentence. What is it?
Rosie: Well a few weeks ago when I came home from
        work Greg had a beautiful dinner cooked, the table
        was set, candles were lit, and the music was
        playing . . .
Ruby: Go on . . .
Rosie: Well he asked me—

Ruby: To marry you!

Rosie: No actually, he asked me if I was interested in mov-
        ing in with him.

Ruby: Interested?

Rosie: Yeah.

Ruby: Were those his exact words?

Rosie: Eh, yeah, I think so why?

Ruby: You think that's romantic, do you?

Rosie: Well he went to a lot of trouble to cook the meal,
        and set the table and—

Ruby: Jesus you do that every day Rosie. Do you not think
        it sounds a bit like a business proposition?

Rosie: A business proposition? In what way?

Ruby: If I wanted to open a joint bank account with
        Teddy I would say, "Teddy, would you be interested
        in opening a joint bank account?" If I wanted to
        move in with Teddy, I would not say, "Teddy would
        you be interested in moving in together?" Do you
        see what I mean?

Rosie: Well I suppose I—

Ruby: That is not the way to broach the subject. And what
        about marriage? Did he say anything about that? Or
        about Katie? If you and he get married, will he want
        to adopt Katie? Did you discuss any of those things?

Rosie: Well actually . . . no we didn't even discuss mar-
        riage. Moving in together is the same commitment
        as a marriage, Ruby. Anyway I thought you were
        anti-marriage.

Ruby: I am but I'm not the one who does want to get mar-
        ried and who is in a relationship with a man who
        doesn't. There lies a problem.

Rosie: I never said that I wanted to marry him.

Ruby: Well then if neither of you feel comfortable marry-
        ing each other then go ahead and move in together;
        that sounds like a fabulous idea!

Rosie: That's exactly what you and Teddy are doing!

Ruby: I've been married before and so has Teddy, we both
        don't want to go through it again. I've been there,
        done that, while this is just the beginning for you.

Rosie: Anyway it doesn't matter because I told him that I
        wasn't ready to move in with him right now. It's a
        bad time, with me trying to settle down in the job
        and everything and Katie settling down in the flat. I
        need to allow a little more time to pass so that Katie
        can adjust to the whole situation. It's been a huge
        change in her life—

Ruby: So you keep saying.

Rosie: What's that supposed to mean?

Ruby: You've been in the flat for two years now, you've
        been in that job of yours for a few weeks now, I've
        seen Katie and she's fine Rosie, she's very happy.
        She's adjusted to this "huge change," I think that
        maybe it's *you* who needs to adjust.

Rosie: Adjust to *what*?

Ruby: Alex is married now Rosie. Move on and make
        yourself happy!

Rosie has logged off

Steph: Why didn't he ask you to marry him?

Rosie: I wasn't aware that he had to.

Steph: Would you have liked to?

Rosie: You know me Steph, if anyone got down on one knee
        and proposed (on the beach with a four-piece orches-
        tra in the background) I'd like it. I'm an old romantic.

Steph: Are you disappointed he asked you to move in with
        him and not marry you?

Rosie: Well I presume if he had proposed it would mean
        I'd be moving in with him anyway so I'm really not
        that heartbroken. I'm lucky to have met someone
        like Greg.

Steph: Come on Rosie, you're not just "lucky" to have met
         Greg. You *deserve* to be happy. It's OK to want
         more than you're offered.

Rosie: I've decided to move in with him. We'll take it one
         step at a time.

Steph: If that makes you happy.

Rosie: *Then* if things are still as perfect between us as they
         are now, I'll expect the room filled with roses and lit
         with candles.

Dear Sally,

   Sorry I spilt my orange juice on your new dress when
we visited a few weeks ago, it is just that when I heard
you slagging my mum's new dress I got a shock and spilt
my juice all over you. Just like you laughed to your
friend, the next day, about my mum having me, accidents
happen.

   I sure hope your dress doesn't stain seeing as it was so
expensive and all. I hope you will come to visit us sometime
in our new house. We are moving in with Greg. It's bigger
than your apartment.

                   Love,
                   Katie
                   PS: My friend Toby says hi and says that he spilt
                   orange juice on his school shirt and it wouldn't
                   come out when it was washed. His mum had to
                   throw it out. It was white too. But lucky for him,
                   the shirt was not as expensive as your dress.

You have an instant message from: ALEX

Alex: Hi, what you up to?

Phil: I've been surfing the Net for hours looking for the
         original chrome exhaust pipes on a 1968 Ford Mus-
         tang. And do you think I could find the original

badges as well as two-tone leather seats for the 1978 Corvette?

Alex: Eh . . . no?

Phil: Exactly but I don't suppose you want to hear about my problems. How was the Rosie trip? Any more silences?

Alex: Oh drop it Phil.

Phil: Hee hee. What's the boyfriend like?

Alex: He's OK. Nothing special. He's not the kind of man I'd have put Rosie with.

Phil: He's not you, you mean.

Alex: No that's not what I mean. He's not exactly the life and soul of the party.

Phil: Should he be?

Alex: For Rosie, yes.

Phil: Maybe he's a calming influence on her.

Alex: Yeah maybe. He's polite and friendly, but that's all he lets you no about him. He doesn't talk much about himself. I couldn't quite figure him out. He's one of those people that don't seem to have an opinion on anything, he would just agree with absolutely everything everyone is saying. It's hard to get a sense of him. Sally and he got along very well though.

Phil: Maybe he just had a problem with you then.

Alex: Thanks Phil, you always have such a good way of making me feel comfortable.

Phil: And isn't that why you discuss all of life's little problems with me?

Alex: Yeah. How are Margaret and the kids?

Phil: Great. Maggie thinks she's pregnant again.

Alex: Jesus, another one?

Phil: I'm one fully loaded man, Alex.

Alex: Good to no Phil.

Alex has logged off

FROM: Alex
TO: ROSIE
SUBJECT: Moving in with Greg?

So I take it you're moving in with Greg. Sally got a letter ·
from Katie during the week, but she wouldn't let me read it.
She just said that they have an understanding between each
other now. I'm glad. Whatever that means.

In answer to your question about Greg, yes he's a nice
man. Not the kind of person I expected you to settle down
with, he's very quiet and reserved. A lot older than you as
well. He's what . . . 37? And you're 27. That's 10 years,
Rosie. How will you feel when he's old and decrepit and
you're still young and beautiful? How will you ever look
into those faded watery eyes and kiss those wrinkly dry
cracked lips? How can you rub your hands over the varicose
veins in his legs and go running through fields holding hands
while all the time secretly worrying about his weak heart?

These are the things you need to worry about, Rosie.

You have an instant message from: ROSIE

Rosie: Are you on drugs???!
Alex: Only the little pink ones . . . sometimes I hear them
          calling out to me during the night . . .
Rosie: You're a doctor, help yourself. OK, I take it from
          that attempt-at-being-humorous-but-meaning-every-
          word-of-it reply that you don't like Greg. I've had
          enough of your snide comments about Greg. Well to
          let the truth be known, I can't stand Sally. Ta-da!

          I hate Sally and you hate Greg. Now we have
          learned that we all can't love each other. We're mov-
          ing in with him next week. Everything is wonderful.
          We are blissfully happy. I've never been so in love in

my life blah blah blah. Now stop annoying me and get over it. Greg is here to stay. So what have you got to say to that?

Alex has logged off

ROSIE, KATIE, AND GREG,
MERRY CHRISTMAS AND A HAPPY NEW YEAR!
LOVE FROM ALEX, SALLY, AND BABY JOSH

TO ALEX, SALLY, AND BABY JOSH!
WARM WISHES FOR THE NEW YEAR!
WITH LOVE,
KATIE, ROSIE, AND GREG

Hello sis,

Stop worrying! Rosie, for the last time, it is absolutely normal for friends not to get along with each other's spouses/partners. Pierre's sister drives me up the wall but that's neither here nor there. Anyway, it doesn't mean that you and Alex are never going to speak to each other again.

The problem with you two is that you're too honest. I can't think of one friend of mine that I would feel comfortable saying, "I hate your husband/wife" and if I even say one miniscule thing to Pierre about how frustrating his sister is, then he jumps down my throat and defends her. There's never going to be anyone good enough for your best friend, Rosie. So therefore Alex thinks that you could do far better than Greg and you think the same of Sally. Sally and Greg aren't stupid, they probably sense that. When Sally met you I'm sure she felt you checking her out. Of course she's going to be defensive! And likewise with Greg. He knows that Alex was the most important man in your life (he also knows that you once had a crush on him, which doesn't make things any better). And Alex knows that he's been replaced. So both Greg *and* Alex are going to be a bit competitive with each other. This is all quite natural.

But in order to maintain your friendship I do think that you need to care about what Alex cares about and that doesn't necessarily mean caring about *Sally* but it means caring about the fact that *Alex* cares about her. Does that make sense?

Anyway stop giving yourself a headache with all this stuff, just ring the man or e-mail or write or whatever it is that you two do . . . By the way if you don't like Pierre, I don't care. I love him so keep your opinions to yourself!

Send me your measurements over will you? And don't lie Rosie, this is for your bridesmaid dress and if you pretend you're two stone lighter than you actually are and the dress doesn't fit, tough, you have to wear it because I can't afford to get you another one. Do you prefer red or wine? Let me know.

> Love,
> Your agony aunt
> PS: By the way, will you ring Alex and tell him that he and his wife are invited to the wedding. Now there's your excuse to talk to him.

FOR MY GODFATHER,
HAPPY 28TH BIRTHDAY!
I HOPE YOU LIKE YOUR PRESENT; MUM SAID THAT YOU LIKED RED BUSES! AREN'T YOU A BIT OLD FOR TOYS?
LOVE,
KATIE

TO ROSIE,
BIRTHDAY WISHES FROM US TO YOU!
HAPPY 28TH—YOU'RE CATCHING UP ON ME!
LOVE,
ALEX, SALLY, AND JOSH

TO KATIE,
YOU ARE 9 TODAY!

BEST WISHES! I HOPE YOU CAN BUY SOMETHING NICE
WITH THIS!
LOVE,
ALEX, SALLY AND JOSH

FROM: Rosie
TO: Alex
SUBJECT: Great news!

Alex Stewart, why don't you ever answer your phone? I
have become best friends with Josh's nanny now and we
have both come to an agreement over the fact that you and
that wife of yours work far too much. Does poor little Josh
even know who Mummy and Daddy are, or are you both
happy with him thinking you two are just the nice people
who pick him up and cuddle him a few times every day?

Anyway, the reason why I'm e-mailing you is because
you are, as I said, *never* home to answer your phone and I
have something brilliant that I really want to tell you and I
refuse to announce it to you on a computer! So ring me
when you get this message. Your good advice may have been
helpful after all, and I thank you for it!

Ring me, ring me, ring me!

FROM: Alex
TO: Rosie
SUBJECT: Re: Great news!

I am refusing to ring you on the grounds that I am far
too angry over your attacking my parental skills. If one
more person tells me how to be a father to my son I will
explode.

The main problem we're having is that Sally and I just
don't work regular hours. The majority of the time we arrive
home when Josh is asleep and I have to stop myself from

waking him up just to say hello. We never have the same days off together so we can't go out on the weekends to the park and play happy family. We just can't seem to spend any quality time together, it's like we're passing each other in the halls and grabbing quick moments of forced happiness before we run out the door.

It's not the greatest situation for Josh to be in but we just simply can't afford to stop working to be there for him all of the time. Things are tough at the moment. And by the way, *never ever* get married.

FROM: Rosie
TO: Alex
SUBJECT: Surprise!

Oh shucks, you've gone and spoiled my surprise.

FROM: Alex
TO: Rosie
SUBJECT: Re: Surprise!

Rosie Dunne, are you getting married?!

—᙮᙮᙮—

CHAPTER 16

FROM: Rosie
TO: Alex
SUBJECT: Re: Surprise!

Surprise! What a lovely, lovely way to tell you, I can't have imagined a better way of sharing my delightful news with my best friend . . .

FROM: Alex
TO: Rosie
SUBJECT: Marriage!

Oh I'm so sorry, that's great news. Don't mind what I say, I'm just tired and whingeing. So how did it all happen? When's the big day? I thought what's-his-name didn't want to get married.

FROM: Rosie
TO: Alex
SUBJECT: Marriage at last!

Oh, Alex, you don't have to pretend to be interested in all the little details, it's OK. And his name is Greg, by the way. You've plenty on your mind now so I'll bore you another time; I just want to let you know that the "big day" won't be so big. It's only going to be a small gathering with close friends and family. Greg doesn't really want anything too OTT and I'm happy enough to go along with that.

Katie is my flower girl/bridesmaid type person and I want you to be my best man. If Greg is allowed to have one then so should I. Please say yes. Sally and Josh are more than welcome too. Make it a family holiday, I bet you haven't had one of those yet. You can relax and enjoy yourselves because you all deserve it. You can finally spend a few days together as a family.

I won't go into any detail about the proposal: I knew it was going to happen so it wasn't that amazing . . .

FROM: Rosie
TO: Stephanie
SUBJECT: So romantic!

Oh Stephanie it was *so* romantic. I had absolutely *no* idea he was going to propose! He took me away for the weekend to this tiny little village in the west that I've never even heard of so I won't even attempt to spell it. We stayed in this charming little B&B and we ate in a restaurant called "The Fisherman's Catch." The place was empty so we had the entire place to ourselves. The atmosphere was magical and then he proposed over dessert! Then we went for a stroll around the lake and headed back to the B&B, it was low-key and quiet but so romantic!

FROM: Stephanie
TO: Rosie
SUBJECT: Re: So romantic

That's funny, Rosie, because I always thought you said
you wanted fireworks and romance, rose petals and violins
while your man went down on one knee and proposed
in front of a gasping and tearful crowd. Greg's proposal
sounds *nice* and all but whatever happened to that
dream?

FROM: Rosie
TO: Stephanie
SUBJECT: Fireworks and rose petals

Well that kind of thing just isn't Greg's style; you know
the way he is. It would have seemed silly if Greg hung from
a chandelier singing Sinatra while showering red velvety
petals over my head (although what a *nice* thought . . .).
Besides it's not the proposal that counts, it's the
marriage . . .

Ruby: He proposed to you in Bogger-reef??
Rosie: Yes it's a cute little village—
Ruby: You HATE cute little villages! You like *towns, cities,
        noise, air pollution, bright lights, rude people, and
        tall buildings!!*
Rosie: But we stayed in this sweet little B&B owned by the
        nicest—
Ruby: You HATE B&Bs! You are obsessed with hotels.
        You work in one. You want to run one, own one,
        and live in one. The biggest treat for you is staying
        in a hotel and he took you to a crappy B&B in the
        middle of nowhere.
Rosie: Oh but if you had just seen the little restaurant. It

was called "The Fisherman's Catch" and it had
these fishing nets all draped around the ceiling—

Ruby: Oh my god, you HATE fish! You starved Katie's
goldfish until it floated on top of that stinking bowl
and then you flushed him down the toilet. You gag
whenever you see people eating oysters (which, by
the way is very embarrassing in restaurants). You
block your nose whenever I eat tuna, you think
smoked salmon is the work of the devil, and prawns
make you vomit.

Rosie: I had a nice salad thank you very much

Ruby: You always say salad is for rabbits!

Rosie: Anyway, we finished the evening by strolling hand
in hand in the moonlight alongside the lake—

Ruby: You LOVE the SEA. You want to live on a beach.
You secretly want to be a mermaid. You think lakes
are boring, you say they lack the "drama" of the sea.

Rosie: Oh please *stop* it Ruby!

Ruby: No! You please stop *lying* to yourself Rosie Dunne.

Rosie has logged off

FROM: Rosie
TO: Alex
SUBJECT: SOS

Alex, please save me from my family and friends, they
are driving me absolutely demented.

You have an instant message from: ALEX

Alex: Snap. What's the problem?

Rosie: I don't really want to talk about it. I want to take
my mind off them.

Alex: That's fair enough, I can understand that. This is a
        nice distraction for me too. So why don't you tell
        me about this proposal that what's-his-name "per-
        formed" for you.

Rosie: OK . . . here I go again. *Greg* took me to a quiet lit-
        tle village down the country. We stayed in a gor-
        geous little B&B. We ate in a lovely restaurant
        called "The Fisherman's Catch." He proposed
        while I had my mouth full of chocolate profiteroles,
        I said yes, we took a walk along the lake and
        watched the moon shimmering along the water.
        Isn't that romantic?

Alex: Yes, romantic.

Rosie: That's all you have to say?? Two words on one of
        the most important nights of my life?!

Alex: Could have been better.

Rosie: How much better? What would you have done to
        make it so much better? I'm just *dying* to know!
        Everyone seems to think they know me so much
        better than I know myself so go ahead, humor me!

Alex: OK, that sounds like a challenge! Well firstly, I
        would have brought you to a *hotel* along the coast
        so that your *suite* would have the best *sea view* in
        the hotel. You could fall asleep listening to the
        waves crashing against the rocks, I would sprinkle
        the bed with red *rose petals* and have *candles* lit all
        around the room, I would have your favorite CD
        playing quietly in the background.

        But I wouldn't propose to you there. I would bring
        you to where there was a huge crowd of people so
        they could all gasp when I got down on one knee
        and proposed. Or something like that. Note I have
        italicized all important buzz words.

Rosie: Oh.

Alex: Oh? That's all you can say? One word for the most
         important night of our lives? I get down on bended
         knee and ask that you'll spend eternity with me and
         you say, "Oh"? You have to do better than that!

Rosie: OK so that would *also* be a very nice proposal. Did
         I go on about proposals so much Alex?

Alex: All the time, my friend. All the time. Anyone who
         nos you half well would no that is more or less the
         kind of thing you have always dreamed about. But a
         weekend in a B&B sounds fine too.

                              ✍

To Alex, Sally, and baby Josh,
DENNIS & ALICE DUNNE
Proudly invite you to the marriage
of their beloved daughter
ROSIE TO GREG COLLINS
On April 8th of this year.

                              ✍

—⁊⁊—

CHAPTER 17

Dear Rosie,

So you went ahead and did it. You married what's-his-name. You looked beautiful Rosie, I was proud to stand beside you at the altar, and I was proud to be there with you on your special day. I was proud to be your best man, but just as you said at my wedding, I wasn't the best man that day, what's-his-name was. You both looked great together.

I got the oddest feeling when you turned your back to me to walk down the aisle with Greg. It was a pang of jealousy. Is that normal? Did you get that feeling on my wedding day, or am I going completely crazy? I just kept thinking over and over in my head, "Everything is going to change now, everything is going to change." Greg is the man for you, now *he* gets to hear all your secrets, and where does that leave me? It was a weird feeling, Rosie, one that eventually passed but one that was present all the same.

I didn't dare talk about it to anyone, especially Sally, because then she would be only too delighted to think that her little theory of men and women being unable to be "just friends" was correct. It's not like I was jealous because I wanted to be your husband, it was just . . . Oh I don't no how to explain it. I suppose I just felt left out, that's all.

I'm glad Josh finally got to put his feet on Irish soil, well actually mostly his bum but he's almost there. I meant to bring him home a long time ago but work got in the way . . . That's funny, I just referred to Ireland as home, I haven't done that for quite a while. It felt like home last week. Anyway it was good for Josh to be there, I think Katie was happy enough to mind him all week.

She is you, Rosie. The little girl with the raven-colored hair and pale skin is the girl I used to go to school with. It was amazing. Even talking to her I felt like young Alex again. Toby kept a watchful eye over me though; I think he was afraid I would steal his friend away. I felt like I was keeping a watchful eye over him too, because he was stealing my friend away. I had to keep reminding myself that it wasn't you.

I'm not quite sure how your plan to unite me, Sally, and Josh went. As you could probably tell, Sally wasn't in the friendliest of moods during the few days. I thought the break away would help us, but apparently not. It just gave us a chance to talk to each other too much. And that's not the best thing when neither of you have anything nice to say. I think I can safely say that the honeymoon period is over. We're together eight years now.

Anyway I hope you and Greg are enjoying your honeymoon and I'm sure this letter will be lying on the mat at home awaiting your arrival. I always thought you wanted to go to an exotic beach location for your honeymoon, I never new you were interested in seeing all the sights around Rome. Although I'm sure they are beautiful, I just thought you were too shallow to care! Just teasing.

Get in touch with me when you get back, prove to me that at least some things never change.

    Love,
    Alex

Greetings from Rome!
Hi Alex,
Weather warm,
Buildings beautiful. But more importantly: fabulous
hotels!

Love,
Rosie x

FROM: Rosie
TO: Alex
SUBJECT: I'm baa-aack!

Just got home a few minutes ago from our honeymoon
and I read your letter. You sounded down so I called and
guess what? Surprise, surprise, you weren't there. So I'm e-
mailing you once again.

I know I never really liked Sally much, but I want you
two to get over whatever it is that's bothering you. It's a big
change when a baby comes along, I know that only too
well, and I can understand that it's difficult for two people
who work harder than anyone I know to deal with a new
addition in their lives.

You probably just need time to adjust, but maybe you
should go see a counselor or something. God knows it took
me long enough to accept that Katie was here to stay, as
much as I love her, it was and still is hard work. So do what
you do best and get to work on it.

I certainly don't pretend to be a know-it-all but just stop
talking to me about how you feel and start telling Sally. I
am always here for you Alex, married woman or un-
married woman.

Dear Alex,
I hope you are well. It was good to see you at the
wedding, Josh is really cool. Mummy looked lovely and so

did you. Me and Toby are fighting. He is ten next week and
he thinks he is so cool just because he is a little bit older
than me. He didn't invite me to his birthday party and I
didn't even do anything wrong. We had a fight last week
about whos turn it was to go first on the computer and I
went first even though I remembered I went first the last
time but I don't think he remembered so he is not mad at me
about that. I did not do anything else wrong.

Mum called around to Toby's mum to see why but she
does not no either. Toby will not talk to me. I hate him. I
will make a new best friend. Mum told me to write to you
and tell you because you are my godfather and no stuff
about this.

Mum thinks that it is really really mean of Toby and that
I will be motionally scared when I grow up, from the
xperience of not being invited to a birthday party. She says
you no what she means.

     Love,
     Katie

Dearest Katie,

Your wise and extremely intelligent mother is correct, as
always. I agree that Toby is being terribly cold and
calculative. It is an awful thing for anyone to do to a person,
to not invite your best friend to your tenth birthday party. I
do believe it should be a crime. He is selfish and it is an
unforgivable act that will haunt him for years to come no
doubt, maybe even until he is nearly thirty years old in fact.

I think that there is no punishment bad enough to inflict
on him and he should not get away with this. Toby has
shown no mercy, has been immature and very very . . . bold.
So tell your mother and tell Toby that I shall do my very
best to make sure that he and I redeem ourselves so that we
can walk down the road with our heads held high.

     Love,
     Alex

Dear Alex,

That was a weird letter. I don't know what it ment but mum says that Toby is even worse than all the things you said. But she was laughing when she read the letter so I don't no if she means it. I don't think Toby is *that* bad.

You two are weirdoes.

> Love,
> Katie x

Dear Toby,

It's Alex here (Katie's mum's friend from America).

I heard that you're going to be ten next week, happy birthday! I no you probably think that me writing to you is really weird but I heard that you didn't invite Katie to your party and I couldn't believe my ears.

Katie is your best friend! I no for a fact that your party won't be much fun without Katie there. It happened to me before. I no that you will be watching the door like a hawk, just hoping that she will walk into the room so you can enjoy yourself. Who cares if your best friend is a girl? Who cares if the other guys laugh? At least you have a best friend and trust me on this, it's really hard to live your life without a best friend especially if you're in boring school with Ms. Big Nose Casey giving out to you all day. If you don't invite Katie then you will really hurt her feelings and that's not very nice.

It's the best thing in the world to have a best friend—even if she is a girl. Let me no how you get on.

> Alex
> PS: Hope you can buy something nice for yourself with this present . . .

FROM: Toby
TO: Katie
SUBJECT: KNOW not NO

Your mum's friend spells "know" wrong just like you. He says NO instead of KNOW. By the way, do you wanna come to my party next week?

FROM: Rosie
TO: Alex
SUBJECT: Dunne Women

Very clever, Mr. Stewart, but you haven't quite redeemed yourself yet. We Dunne women are pretty hard to please, you know . . .

FROM: Alex
TO: Rosie
SUBJECT: Done Woman

So I see. You're a done woman alright. Well, I have a theory that I wish to share with you. Shall I?

FROM: Rosie
TO: Alex
SUBJECT: Theory Shmeory

If you must. I might read it if I have time.

FROM: Alex
TO: Rosie
SUBJECT: My theory

Yes I must and you *will* read it. OK, if I *had* invited you to my tenth birthday party then Brian the Whine wouldn't have been invited. If Brian hadn't gone then he wouldn't have thrown pizza all over James's sleeping bag and if he hadn't done that and completely ruined my party then you and I wouldn't have hated him so much. If you and I hadn't hated him so much then you wouldn't have had to drink so much in order to be able to accompany him to the debs. If you hadn't have done that . . . well . . . perhaps you wouldn't have been quite so drunk and your darling little Katie wouldn't have been born. Therefore I did you a favor!

And that, Rosie Dunne, is my theory.

FROM: Rosie
TO: Alex
SUBJECT: *My* Theory

Very clever, Alex, very, very, clever. But you needn't have gone that far back to accept responsibility for Katie. Here's my theory.

Had I not been stood up by you at the debs, I wouldn't have had to go with Brian the Whine at all. Had you showed up at the airport that day our lives could have turned out very differently.

FROM: Alex
TO: Rosie
SUBJECT: Life

Yeah, that's something I'm beginning to wonder about.

Ruby: They WHAT??? They *split up??*
Rosie: Yeah, they're finished. Sad isn't it?
Ruby: Well not really actually. Why did they split up?
Rosie: Irreconcilable differences. Isn't that what people always say?
Ruby: Not in my case, mine was a lazy cheating bastard. So who has Josh?
Rosie: Sally took him and went to stay with her parents.
Ruby: Oh poor Alex. So come on spill the beans.

Rosie: Well I don't know everything—

Ruby: Liar. Alex tells you everything which is probably the
         reason in itself.

Rosie: Excuse me; please do nòt accuse me of being the
         reason for his marriage breakup. That is very insult-
         ing. It was a million little things that all finally blew
         up in their faces.

Ruby: So when are you going over to him?

Rosie: Next week.

Ruby: Are you planning on coming back?

Rosie: RUBY! QUIT IT!

Ruby: Oh OK, OK. It's sad though isn't it?

Rosie: Yes it is. Alex is devastated.

Ruby: No I didn't mean that. The irony of it all makes *me*
         sad, I can't even imagine how *you* must feel.

Rosie: What irony?

Ruby: Oh you know . . . you wait and wait for years for
         him until you finally give up and move on with your
         life. You eventually decide to marry Greg and weeks
         later, Alex splits up with Sally. You know, you two
         have the worst timing ever . . . When will you ever
         learn to catch up with each other?

CHAPTER 18

YOU ARE 1 TODAY!
MAY YOUR SPECIAL DAY BE LOTS OF FUN,
IT'S NOT EVERY DAY A BOY IS ONE!
WE LOVE OUR LITTLE SPECIAL BOY,
BECAUSE YOU BRING US SO MUCH JOY!
TO JOSH (AND YOUR DADDY),
WE LOVE YOU BOTH AND HOPE YOU HAVE A VERY
HAPPY BIRTHDAY AND THANKSGIVING TOGETHER.
LOTS OF LOVE,
ROSIE AND KATIE

Dear Rosie and Katie,

Thank you for the teddy you sent me for my birthday, I call him "Bear." Daddy made the name up all by himself, he is very clever. I love to chew on his ear and drool all over him so that when Daddy hugs him, it leaves my slobber all over his face. I also like to throw Bear out of my cot in the middle of the night and then scream at Daddy until he picks it up for me. I just do it for the laugh, Daddy doesn't need to sleep. He's only here to feed me and clean my diapers.

Anyway I better go now, I have a very busy schedule, I'm being fed at nine o'clock, followed by a burping, and then

I'm going to try to take a few steps across the living room. I no I can do it . . . one of these days I won't land on my bum . . .

   Thanks for Bear,
   Love you and miss you both,
          Josh (and Daddy)

FROM: Rosie
TO: Alex
SUBJECT: Happy 30th!

I can't believe you're not having a thirtieth birthday party! Or are you having one and you're just not inviting me? I know you've been inclined to do things like that in the past. Jesus, imagine that was a whole twenty years ago. I never thought we would reach the time when we could remember anything happening that long ago. Anyway happy birthday, have a slice of cake on me.

FROM: Alex
TO: Rosie
SUBJECT: Thanks

Sorry I haven't been in touch, I'm almost ready to finish up my residency here so I can move on to do two more years of cardiothoracic residency program. I just have to figure out where exactly. My one hundred years of study are almost up! No celebrations for me this year, too busy trying to pay back my million-dollar student loan.

You have an instant message from: GREG

Greg: Hi honey, how's your day going?
Rosie: Oh it seems to be one of those never-ending days.

The hotel is completely booked out this weekend because of the St. Patrick's Day parade, the place is jammed. There's been a steady flow of big groups of people arriving all day so I've been constantly checking them in. It has quieted down now for a little while so I'm pretending to be really busy on the computer with reservations right now so don't make me laugh whatever you do or my cover will be blown.

Well, when I say *quiet* I mean no one is bothering us at reception, the noise level of the hotel is a completely different story altogether. There's a huge group of Americans in the bar singing along to old Irish songs, would you believe they got the *Paddy Band* in to the hotel as a special treat? I've never seen so many green faces and dyed red hair in my life.

Unfortunately some of Bill Lake's family have flown in from Chicago. There are thirty of them so I'm on my best behavior. Apparently his nephew is a trombone player in the Chicago high school marching band that's marching in the parade on Sunday.

I'm just dying for the day to end, my face is sore from smiling and my eyes are stinging from staring at this bloody computer screen. I can't believe Bill gave me the weekend off! I am so thrilled! He's such a sweetie; I can't remember the last time I had a Saturday off or two days in a row for that matter. Well it means that for once we can go out tonight and I won't have to worry about getting up in the morning. Have you been talking to Ted? What time do he and Ruby want to meet up at? I was thinking of bringing Katie and Toby to the parade on Sunday, what do you think?

Sorry for rambling on, I feel like I'm back at
school on a Friday afternoon waiting for the final
bell to ring for the weekend. For my freedom.
Whatever use double maths has in life is beyond
me, but it sure prepares you for the boredom of
work.

Greg: Oh Rosie I'm sorry to dampen your good spirits but
I have to head up north to Belfast tonight. I only
found out this morning so it's completely last
minute. I'm sorry.

Rosie: Oh no! Why do you have to go to Belfast?

Greg: Oh there's this seminar that's on that I have to go to.

Rosie: What kind of a seminar?

Greg: A financial one.

Rosie: Well of course it's a financial one. I hardly expect it
to be on French cuisine. Do you *have* to go? Will
they even notice if you're there?

Greg: Well, no they wouldn't notice to be honest, but I
want to go. They're quite interesting you know, and
I have to stay ahead of my game.

Rosie: Oh how much more could you possibly learn about
bloody banks? They give you money and ask for ten
times more back. That's about it.

Greg: I'm sorry Rosie.

Rosie: Oh this is so annoying. Of all the bloody weekends
Bill gives me off, it's the one you have to go away
for. You do know that I will not get a weekend off
for another year don't you?

Greg: I love the way you never exaggerate Rosie. Listen, I
have to go, OK? Talk to you later, love you.

Rosie: Oh hold on, before you go, did you see the phone
bill this morning?

Greg: What was it like, high?

Rosie: Guess.

Greg: Damn. That's you and all that time you spend on
that Internet sending e-mails you know. I don't un-

derstand why you and Ruby can't just arrange to
meet like normal people.

Rosie: Because no establishment allows us to sprawl across
their couches in our pajamas and smoke. It's far
more comfortable at home. Anyway the price of the
bill couldn't have *anything* to do with all those
hours a week you spend on the phone to your
mother, convincing her she's perfectly capable living
on her own, by any chance?

Greg: I somehow think you don't really mind me spending
those hours convincing her, my darling!

Rosie: True! Oh if only we knew a bank manager who
could give us a loan . . . how simple life would
be . . .

Greg: Unfortunately it doesn't work like that Rosie.

Rosie: And imagine my disappointment when I found out
after I married you.

Greg: You stuck with me all the same, thank you for that.
I have to go now and refuse to give a mortgage to
someone, you know how it is. Love you.

Rosie: Love you xx.

FROM: Kevin
TO: Rosie
SUBJECT: My favorite sister

Hello my most favorite big sister in the whole entire
world. It's Kevin here. E-mail me back when you get a
chance, I'm on the college computer so the Internet is free
and I wanna ask you something.

FROM: Rosie
TO: Kevin
SUBJECT: Re: My favorite sister

Why do I only ever hear from you when you want something?

FROM: Kevin
TO: Rosie
SUBJECT: Re: My favorite sister

You sound like my ex-girlfriend. What makes you think I want something? Maybe I just want to catch up with my sister and see what's going on in her life. How's Katie? Tell her I was asking for her. How's Greg? Tell him I was asking for him. How's Alex? Tell him I was asking for him. See how interested I am in your life? If you ever need a babysitter for Katie just let me know, I'd only be too delighted to help out. Anyway that's all from me, take care of yourself and keep in touch.

PS: Any chance you could ask your boss for a job for me?

FROM: Rosie
TO: Kevin
SUBJECT: A-HA!

A-HA! I knew there had to be a catch! You never usually care about what's going on in my life. Katie is fine, thank you, so is Greg, and so is Alex. You could see how they are with your very own eyes if you ever bothered to call around. Yes I would love you to mind Katie thank you very much, but I'm not sure I could trust you after what happened the last time round.

FROM: Kevin
TO: Rosie
SUBJECT: 6 years ago!

Oh come on Rosie! That was at least six years ago, I was only 17! How could you give a 17-year-old male an apartment of his own and not expect him to invite around a few friends. It's only normal.

FROM: Rosie
TO: Kevin
SUBJECT: Normal!

Kevin, you trashed the place. Poor Katie was terrified and I didn't appreciate finding you asleep in my bed with that . . . whatever she was . . .

FROM: Kevin
TO: Rosie
SUBJECT: Water under the bridge

Well you said make yourself at home . . . Anyway that's all water under the bridge, we're both sensible adults now. (You're getting on a bit—thirty next month!) I would really love if you could help me out. Please help me out, I would be forever grateful and I honestly, truthfully mean that.

FROM: Rosie
TO: Kevin
SUBJECT: You owe me!

Oh OK but I'm not promising any miracles. Don't mess this up Kevin or Bill will hold it against me and it'll ruin my grand master plan of taking over this hotel.

FROM: Rosie
TO: Alex
SUBJECT: Life!

Christ Alex, who knew Kevin had learned to walk and talk? I thought he was still at school. He just suddenly grew up. Not that he was ever one for sharing his life stories with me anyway. He's so secretive. It's people like him, the world has to worry about.

Things change so quickly. Just when you get used to something, zap! It changes. Just when you begin to understand someone, zap! They grow up. The same is happening with Katie. She changes every day; her face just becomes so much more grown-up every time I look at her. Sometimes I have to stop *pretending* I'm interested in what she's saying in order to realize that I *actually am* interested. We go shopping for clothes together and I take her advice, we eat out for lunch and giggle over silly things. I just can't cast my mind back to the time when my child stopped being a child and became a person.

And a beautiful person she is becoming too. I don't quite know where I'm going with this letter, Alex, but I've been thinking about a lot of things lately and my head is a bit of a muddle. It's hard to grasp things and keep them firmly in your grip because quicker than you know it they slide right through your fingers and you lose control.

Our life is made up of time; our days are measured in hours, our pay measured by those hours, our knowledge is measured by years. We grab a quick few minutes in our busy day to have a coffee break. We rush back to our desks, we watch the clock, we live by appointments. And yet your time eventually runs out and you wonder in your heart of hearts if those seconds, minutes, hours, days, weeks, months, years, and decades were being spent the best way they possibly could. In other words, if you could change anything, would you?

Everything is spinning around us, jobs, family, friends, lovers . . . you just feel like screaming "STOP!" looking around, rearranging the order of a few things, and then continuing on . . . It was just a thought. I know you're having a really difficult time right now. Please know that I'm always here for you.

Love, Rosie

CHAPTER 19

Dear Alex,

.OK, so as you probably no, it's mum's 30th next month and me and Toby are arranging a surprise birthday party for her. So will you come?

So far we have invited Grandma, Granddad, Aunt Stephanie, Uncle Kevin (even though we didn't want to because he scares us), Ruby, Teddy, Toby's mum and dad, Toby, and me. That's all so far. Oh yeah and Greg too if he's here. He's always working and Mum is always giving out to him about it. The other weekend Mum was off work and she was real excited about it all week because she had stuff planned with Ruby and Greg. I no how she feels because I hate school and I love when the weekend comes. Anyway Greg had to go away again last minute. Then Ruby called her and said she was sick so Mum stayed in and watched TV with me and Toby and she let him stay over.

Toby got this cool new flashlight. It's like the best one you can get. When Mum went to bed we were shining it out our window and it reached all the way up to the clouds and everything it was so strong. Well we were shining it across the road and we could see Mr. and Mrs. Gallagher across the road. Toby thinks they were playing leap frog. It was real funny except Mrs. Gallagher came across the road in her dressing gown real mad at us and she was banging on the door shouting at Mum. Mum was so mad she said she wouldn't take us to the parade. But she did.

Me and Toby got our faces painted in town and it looked really cool. We even got Mum to get a little shamrock on her face as well and she did but then she wished she didn't because it started raining and the green, white, and gold face paints were running all over our faces. They looked like rainbow tears. Loads of Toby's got in his hair and I rubbed my eyes by mistake and all the green got in. They were stinging so much I couldn't keep my eyes open and I couldn't see so Mum and Toby held my hands and brought me home. We had to leave before the parade even started.

We were soaking when we got home and Mum's new outfit was covered by the green stuff. The lady that put it on our faces said that it washes off clothes. It doesn't. Toby has had green hair for the whole week in school and Ms. Big Nose Smelly Breath Casey isn't happy. Can you believe she is the principal now? Mum says the school must really be desperate. Anyway, when we got back from town we just watched the parade on telly but we only got to see the end because it took us so long to get home because of all the bloody tourists. That's what Mum said.

So will you come to the party? You can bring Josh too, we need more people anyway. Aunt Stephanie can't come because she is due next month and I don't think the pilot will let her fly because she's too heavy or something. Grandma and Granddad are going over to visit her, Pierre, and the new baby if it comes, Uncle Kevin can't come because he's starting his new job as a chef in a new hotel down the country. So it's just Ruby and Teddy and Ruby says that she can't promise Teddy will be there, because she doesn't like to plan dates with him that far in advance. It's only two weeks though.

I wanted it to be kinda special for Mum, because she's been really sad again this week. Things have been kinda weird these days. I think it's because the telephone is broken. Every time the phone rings and Mum answers it, no one is there. It happens when I answer it too. It doesn't happen when Greg answers it.

Greg said he would get someone to fix the phone and Mum just spilled her drink on him. I don't really think it's broken. I think that whoever is ringing just wants to speak to Greg and not me and Mum.

It would be good if you came over, you're loads of fun. You can even sleep here but you can't sleep in the spare room because that's Greg's room now I think. You can sleep on the couch or I have a pull-out bed in my room. Remember, don't ring because it's a secret and Mum just keeps hanging the phone up without saying hello anyway. E-mail me if you want.

> Love,
> Katie

FROM: Alex
TO: Katie
SUBJECT: Re: Rosie's 30th

Thanks for the letter. That's a good idea of yours and Toby's but I won't wait until your Mum's birthday if you don't mind. I'll be over as soon as I can.

HAPPY 30TH SISTER!
SORRY WE CAN'T BE THERE,
LOVE STEPHANIE, PIERRE, AND JEAN-LOUIS!

FOR OUR DAUGHTER,
HAPPY 30TH.
SORRY WE CAN'T BE THERE, ENJOY YOUR DAY LOVE
AND WE'LL SEE YOU WHEN WE GET BACK.
LOVE MUM AND DAD

HAPPY 30TH SIS,
SORRY I CAN'T BE THERE BUT THANKS FOR GETTING
ME THE JOB, I OWE YOU ONE.
ENJOY THE NIGHT.
KEVIN

HAPPY BIRTHDAY, ROSIE,
SORRY WE CAN'T BE THERE BUT WE'RE STUCK
COVERING YOUR SHIFT!
LOVE FROM EVERYONE AT WORK XXX

To Rosie,

I'm so sorry, please forgive me; I have been a complete
fool. Please let's put this behind us and enjoy your birthday
weekend.

>   Love,
>   Greg

HAPPY BIRTHDAY,
LET'S GET PISSED.
LOVE RUBY

Rosie,

I'm returning to Boston tomorrow but before I go I
wanted to write this letter to you. All the thoughts and
feelings that have been bubbling up inside me are finally
overflowing into this pen and I'm leaving this letter for you
so that you don't feel that I'm putting you under any great
pressure. I understand that you will need to take your time
trying to decide on what I am about to say.

I no what's going on, Rosie; you're my best friend and I can see the sadness in your eyes. I no that Greg isn't away working for the weekend. You never could lie to me; you were always terrible at it. Don't pretend that everything is perfect because I *see* what's going on. I see that Greg is a selfish man who has absolutely no idea just how lucky he is and it makes me sick.

He is the luckiest man in the world to have you, Rosie, but he doesn't deserve you and *you* deserve far better. You deserve someone who loves you with every single beat of his heart, someone who thinks about you constantly, someone who spends every minute of every day just wondering what you're doing, where you are, who you're with, and if you're OK. You need someone who can help you reach your dreams and who can protect you from your fears. You need someone who will treat you with respect, love every part of you, *especially* your flaws. You should be with someone who can make you happy, really happy, *dancing on air happy*. Someone who should have taken the chance to be with you years ago instead of getting scared and being too afraid to try.

I am not scared anymore Rosie. I am not afraid to try.

I no what that feeling was at your wedding—it was jealousy. My heart broke when I saw the woman I love turning away from me to walk down the aisle with another man, another man she planned to spend the rest of her life with. It was like a prison sentence for me. Years ahead without me being able to tell you how I feel or hold you how I wanted to.

Twice we stood beside each other at the altar, Rosie. *Twice*. And twice we got it wrong. I needed you to be there for my wedding day but I was too stupid to see that I needed you to be the *reason* for my wedding day. But we got it all wrong.

I should never have let your lips leave mine all those years ago in Boston. I should never have pulled away. I should never have panicked. I should never have wasted all those years without you. Give me a chance to make them up to you. I love you, Rosie, and I want to be with you and Katie and Josh. Always.

Please think about it. Don't waste your time on Greg, this is *our* opportunity. Let's stop being afraid and take the chance. I promise I'll make you happy.

All my love,
Alex

CHAPTER 20

Ruby: I've decided. I'm putting my Gary on a diet.

Rosie: *You're* putting *him* on a diet? How on earth can you control what your twenty-one-year-old son eats?

Ruby: Oh it's easy; I'll just nail down everything to the floor.

Rosie: So what kind of diet is it?

Ruby: I don't know. I bought a magazine, but there are so many stupid diets out there I don't know which one to pick. Remember that ridiculous one that you and I did last year? The alphabet one where we had to eat foods beginning with a certain letter every day?

Rosie: Oh yeah! How long did we do that for?!

Ruby: Em . . . that would be 26 days of course Rosie

Rosie: Oh . . . right . . . of course. You *put on* weight on the third day.

Ruby: That's because the third day was the lucky letter "C" . . . Cakes . . . mmmm

Rosie: Well we made up for it on the last day. I was bloody starving on "Z" day; I was practically chasing zebras with a kitchen knife around the zoo. Could have eaten the zoo I suppose . . .

Ruby: You should have done what I did, I ate like a queen. I became German for the day and ate "ze cakes" and "ze buns." Oh I don't know Rosie. I think I'll just invent a diet of my own and give those stupid magazines a run for their money

Rosie: So what's your idea then?

Ruby: Hmmm . . . OK you should only eat . . . whatever food you look like.

Rosie: I bet those magazines are quaking in their boots . . .

Ruby: No really! I think I'm on to something here! Teddy always reminds me of a tomato with his big ripe fat juicy red face. The two hairs on his head that stick up remind me of the stalk . . . I always feel the urge to stick his head in a blender and mix with vodka and Tabasco. A bloody Teddy. Simon from the office reminds me of a Brussels sprout. He's smelly and . . .

Rosie: Green?

Ruby: No, just smelly.

Rosie: What do I look like?

Ruby: Good question . . . Hmmm, I think you're a bit of an onion.

Rosie: An onion?! Why, do I stink and make people cry? An onion?! Why, do I stink and make people cry?

Ruby: Why did you just repeat yourself?

Rosie: Onions do that don't they, they repeat on you?

Ruby: A funny onion too. No I think it's because there are many layers to you, Rosie Dunne, and as the years go by, another one is peeled away. I think there's a lot more under there than people think. So what am I?

Rosie: Hmmm . . . a cake.

Ruby: A *cake*??

Rosie: Sweet as sugar with a cherry on top. Sweet as pie!

Ruby: And fat and unhealthy.

Rosie: Look Ruby you invented this diet. If you look like a cake then all you can eat are cakes . . . Think about it . . .

Ruby: Yes I take your point . . . I always thought secretly
        that I had a touch of the banoffi pie to me alright.
        Well this is a stupid idea, it's not a proper diet at all
        unless you look like a vegetable or a fruit and my
        Gary (although he may have the *qualities* of a veg-
        etable) ain't no fruit or vegetable.

Rosie: What do you think Greg looks like?

Ruby: Ah that's easy. A cow's testicle.

Rosie: HA! Since when did people ever eat cow's testicles?

Ruby: It's a tribal thing . . . OK then a slug. A slimy, dis-
        gusting, slow slug.

Rosie: I don't think Greg would eat a slug.

Ruby: Who cares what the cheating bastard eats. What do
        you think Alex looks like?

Rosie: A Skye.

Ruby: You think your six-foot-tall, brown-haired, brown-
        eyed, white-skinned friend looks like a chocolate
        bar with nougat inside?

Rosie: Yes

Ruby: Now *that's* stupid . . .

Rosie: Well excuse me Ms. I think Teddy has a tomato
        head . . .

Ruby: Look, all this talk of dieting is making me hungry,
        I'm taking an early lunch OK?

Rosie: OK! You cheered me up Ruby.

Ruby: Ooops sorry, I wasn't supposed to do that was I?

Rosie: No, but you're forgiven.

Ruby: Oh good. Bye honey.

Rosie: Bye . . .

Ruby has logged off

FROM: Alex
TO: Rosie
SUBJECT: More time?

Alex here, it's been a while since I've heard from you . . . I was hoping you would have been in touch by now. If you need more time, I understand. Please let me no what's going on.

FROM: Rosie
TO: Alex
SUBJECT: Re: More time?

Hey there Skye! Sorry I haven't written in a while, I've been up to my eyes at work. It's been really busy around here for some reason. Probably because the sun is beginning to peek its big head up again; the country is so much nicer when the sun shines. What do you mean do I need more time? It doesn't take very long to accept I'm thirty!

Thanks for coming over for my birthday, by the way. It was really sweet of Katie and Toby to organize it even if you and Ruby were the *only* people there. Sorry I was a bit of a sour puss, I suppose I was just down because I turned thirty and most people were away. It just would have been nice if more people had come but never mind, it's not the end of the world. You were there and that was good enough for me. I was so happy to see you. You are always there for me, Alex, and I appreciate that. You keep me strong when I don't feel like it.

Anyway how are things with you? How's Josh? Give him a big huge sloppy kiss and a hug from me.

FROM: Alex
TO: Rosie
SUBJECT: My letter

Didn't you get my letter?

FROM: Rosie
TO: Alex
SUBJECT: Letter?

What's this about a letter? Maybe it's just delayed in the post; I'll probably get it soon. When did you send it?

Dear Alex,
    Thank you for coming over for Mum's birthday party and thanks for my present too.
    She was real sad before you came over but I think you made her a bit happier. I have to go because teacher is looking at me.
              From,
              Katie

Dear Katie,
    Thanks for the letter. I hope you didn't get into any trouble at school for writing to me. I'm glad you liked your presents. Tell Toby I said hi and that I'll send over that baseball gear for him soon.
    How is your mum? How is everything at home? Do you no what a Skye is by any chance?!
              Love,
              Alex

FROM: Alex
TO: Rosie
SUBJECT: My letter

    I didn't post the letter; I left it on the kitchen table in your house just before I left to go to the airport. Didn't you get it?

Dear Alex,

Toby is real excited about the baseball stuff. Things are kinda getting back to normal again. Greg only sleeps in the spare room some nights now. Mum said he's there because of his snoring. I don't believe her because Toby and I put a tape recorder in the room and he doesn't snore. He sleep talks though! He said, "Don't send the horses to the rainbow!" It's true, we have it on tape.

Things are kinda OK but not like before. It was nice when you were here. I prefer to stay in Toby's house now. By the way, a Skye is a chocolate bar. It's Mum's favorite. She loves them. She says she would love a diet of Skyes all day. The other day she said she was in love with a Skye then she started kissing it and laughing.

Why do you want to no? Do you want one too? I can post one over if you want if they don't sell them in Merica. I did that before when I was in England on my holidays and I sent a chocolate bar in the post to Toby because they didn't sell them here and when he got it, it was all melted and stuck to the paper. He couldn't read my letter but I was glad because I missed him when I was away and I wrote some silly things and it was imbarrassing. He is my best friend and I shouldn't write letters like that.

So should I get you the chocolate bar? Mum says she can't live without her Skye. She's a weirdo.

          Love, Katie

FROM: Alex
TO: Rosie
SUBJECT: My letter

Hi Rosie. It's really important that I talk to you right now. It's about the letter. I wrote some really important things in there and I would really love you to read it if you can. Please try and find it?

FROM: Rosie
TO: Alex
SUBJECT: Your letter

Hi Alex, I searched the house from top to bottom
yesterday when I got home from work. No sign of it. Is
everything OK? Can you just e-mail me what it said?

FROM: Alex
TO: Rosie
SUBJECT: My letter

Jesus Christ. Rosie, I'll call you in five minutes.

FROM: Rosie
TO: Alex
SUBJECT: Your letter

Alex! You can't call me at work, you'll get me fired!
What is this about?

FROM: Alex
TO: Rosie
SUBJECT: My letter

So pretend to be talking to a customer, Rosie! I'm
serious, answer the phone.

FROM: Rosie
TO: Alex
SUBJECT: Your letter

Oh hold on, Greg is online. Before you have a heart
attack, I'll see if he's seen the letter.

FROM: Alex
TO: Rosie
SUBJECT: My letter

Don't bloody well ask *him!*

You have an instant message from: ROSIE

Rosie: Greg did you see a letter on the kitchen table for me?
Greg: A letter? No I think there was just your mobile
        phone bill and the electricity bill.
Rosie: No I'm not talking about this morning; I'm talking
        about two weeks ago on the weekend of my birthday.
Greg: But Rosie you didn't want me around that weekend.
        I stayed on the couch in Teddy's flat, remember?
Rosie: Oh you poor soul. Of course I fucking remember I
        thought you might like it seeing as you were sleep-
        ing in everybody else's houses for the past while. I'm
        not stupid Greg, oh but sorry, I forgot that you
        thought that I was.
Greg: Honey I—
Rosie: Don't honey me. Did you see the bloody letter or not?
        You were home on the Monday just after Alex left.
Greg: No I honestly didn't see it.
Rosie: Well there's a reason not to believe you, Mr. Honesty.
Greg: Look Rosie we can't move on if you don't forgive
        and learn to trust me again—
Rosie: Oh go shove your forgiveness up your ass. I don't
        have time for another one of these conversations
        with you. This is very simple. I've got Alex online
        waiting for me. He left a letter for me. He wants
        to know if any of us found it. So I'm asking
        you one more time Greg, did you see the letter
        or not?
Greg: No I promise you that I didn't.

FROM: Bill Lake
TO: Rosie
SUBJECT: Personal e-mails

I hope they're business e-mails you've been sending for the last half hour Rosie. We've got a group of eighty arriving in the next few minutes for the weekend business conference in the De Valera Suite. Lots to do, Rosie.

FROM: Rosie
TO: Alex
SUBJECT: Your letter

Alex, Greg didn't see the letter. Maybe you can just write me another one or ring me later when I'm at home and not when Big Brother is watching me on this stupid bloody security camera pointed right at me. Now both of you men leave me alone before I get fired.

FROM: Greg
TO: Alex
SUBJECT: Your letter?

I was told you were online so I hope I caught you on time. I happened to have stumbled across something I believe you're looking for. I would appreciate it if you would stop sending my wife love letters. Something tells me you seem to have forgotten that she's a married woman. Married to *me*, Alex.

Rosie and I have had our troubles like all marriages do but we are willing to put all that behind us now and give it another chance. You need to understand that none of your letters are going to change that. You said it yourself; you had your chance and you blew it. The moment has passed you by, Alex.

Let's be realistic here for a minute, Alex. You and Rosie are both thirty. You've known each other since you were five. Don't you think that in all that time, that if something was supposed to happen with you two, if it was so *meant to be*, that it would have happened by now? Think about it. She is not interested.

I want no further contact with you again; if you set foot in my house I will be only too glad to show how unwelcome you are. To save you the embarrassment, I won't speak of the contents of your letter again and you're wrong by the way, I do fully appreciate the fact that Rosie is my wife. She is a wonderful woman, loving, warm, and caring and I am so glad she is the woman that chose to spend the rest of her life with *me*. So you can keep on watching her back walk from you at the altar because she won't be turning around.

FROM: Alex
TO: Greg
SUBJECT: Rosie

Do you think your ridiculous attempt to scare me off is going to work? You are a pathetic sad little man. Rosie has a mind of her own and she doesn't need you making those decisions for her.

FROM: Greg
TO: Alex
SUBJECT: Re: Rosie

So what are you going to do if she says yes, Alex? What are you going to do? Move to Dublin? Leave Josh behind? Expect Rosie to uproot Katie, leave the job she loves and move to Boston? *Think*, Alex.

You have an instant message from: ALEX

Alex: She didn't get the letter Phil.

Phil: Oh bloody hell, Alex. I told you not to put it in one
       of those damn letters. You should have just told her.
       I don't know why you can't just use your mouth like
       the rest of us.

Alex: Greg found the letter.

Phil: The idiot husband? I thought they were finished.

Alex: Evidently not. But it doesn't change anything, Phil, I
       still love her.

Phil: Yeah but she's *still* married isn't she? You're not go-
       ing to like what I say, and this is just my opinion
       Alex, and hell knows you never take any advice any-
       way but I wouldn't touch another man's wife. That's
       just me.

Alex: But he's an asshole Phil!

Phil: And so are you but you're my brother and I love you.

Alex: I'm serious, the guy cheated on her. He's all wrong
       for her.

Phil: Yeah but the difference between now and before is
       that *now* Rosie knows he cheated on her. She *knows*
       he's an asshole. But she's still with him. She must re-
       ally love him Alex. I'd say back off. Just my opinion
       but I'd say back off.

Alex: I don't agree with that Phil.

Phil: Fine! You're your own man, do as you wish. I know
       you want the best for Rosie but you're being a bit
       selfish here. Look at it from Rosie's perspective. She's
       just found out that her asshole husband cheated on
       her, it must have been hard, and for whatever reason
       she has decided to work it out and stay with him.
       Then just as she's getting used to that idea, in
       waltzes you, the best friend in shining armor, pro-
       claiming your love for her. Do you want to confuse
       the poor woman even more? Look, if the marriage is

a disaster, then it's a disaster and in a few months
it'll end and Rosie will come to you. Just don't be the
prick that tries to break up her marriage. She'll never
forgive you for that.

Alex: So you think I should let it happen naturally. Let her
        come to me when she's ready?

Phil: Something like that. I'm thinking of starting one of
        those shows that they have on telly. You know one of
        those advice ones?

Alex: You'd have me on it every week Phil. Thanks.

Phil: No probs, now while you go give someone a new
        heart, I'll go give a car a new engine. Off with you.
        Do what you have to do.

Alex has logged off

CHAPTER 21

—∽—

FROM: Rosie
TO: Alex
SUBJECT: Letter?

Alex I searched high and low in the kitchen for your letter, I left no stone unturned and Greg and Katie swear they didn't lay a finger on it so I don't know where else it could be. Are you sure you left it there? We were in such a rush to get you to the airport that morning, maybe you forgot. I checked the spare room you were sleeping in. All I found was a T-shirt you left behind, but it's mine now so you're not getting it back!

So what was in the letter? You didn't call me when I got home from work yesterday. You're really keeping me in suspense, Alex!

FROM: Alex
TO: Rosie
SUBJECT: Letter

How are things with you and Greg? Are you happy?

FROM: Rosie
TO: Alex
SUBJECT: Greg

Wow, talk about a change of subject. That's a very direct question.

OK, I know you can sense that he and I are going through a bad phase and I know you're worried. And I also know that you absolutely can't stand him, which is really difficult for me because I would really *love* you to see him how I see him.

Deep down, underneath *all* his layers of stupidity, he's a really good man. He may act out far too many selfish thoughts, says all the wrong things at all the wrong times, but behind closed doors he's a best friend. I *understand* that he has idiotic tendencies and I can still love him for it. He may not be someone that you feel comfortable sitting next to at a dinner party but for me, he's someone that I feel comfortable sharing my life with.

I know it's hard for other people to understand what he's like. All you see is an overprotective paranoid mess, but god does that make me feel safe and wanted. And his stupidity makes me laugh! We have a long way to go to being the perfect couple, we certainly don't live the fairy tale marriage, he doesn't shower me with rose petals and fly me to Paris on weekends but when I get my hair cut, he notices. When I dress up to go out at night, he compliments me. When I cry, he wipes my tears. When I feel lonely, he makes me feel loved. And who needs Paris, when you can get a hug?

Somewhere along the way, without me even noticing, I grew up Alex. For once, I couldn't take advice from anyone around me about what I should or shouldn't do. I couldn't go running to mum and dad and I can't compare my marriage to anybody else's, we all follow our own rules. Taking Greg back was my decision to make and I wouldn't have if I hadn't felt that Greg, and most importantly that I,

had learned something. I *know* that what has happened will
never happen again and I really, really believe it. Because if I
didn't feel so sure about our future, there's no way that I
could go through with this.

I have a feeling that's what was in your letter Alex but
don't worry about me. I'm fine. Thank you, thank you,
thank you, for caring about me so much. There aren't
enough friends like you in the world.

FROM: Alex
TO: Rosie
SUBJECT: Re: Greg

And that's all I wanted. For you to be happy.

Dear Stephanie,

So how's the new mummy? I hope you're coping well
with everything. I know it's a big change—but a wonderful
one. Are you getting any sleep? I hope you are. I always
knew you would be a fabulous mother, you always knew
just how to take care of your baby sister.

Thanks for all the gory details about his birth by the way.
You're even more wonderful than I thought you were! And
no, I don't want Pierre to send over his video tape of the
"magical" experience. Remember they used to show us
those videos at school when we were kids to scare us all out
of having sex? Well neither of us were obviously *that*
scared. If they really wanted to deter us they should have
just shown us the nappy-changing procedure. That would
have sent us running off in our thousands to the convent.

You all looked so happy together in the photograph. You
looked like the perfect family. Is there such a thing anymore
because if there is, my happy little unit was definitely not in
the queue when they were handing out the titles.

I'm really not sure if I have done the right thing by

taking Greg back. It's so difficult to know what decision to make. Christ, Stephanie, I was always the first person to shout out that if my husband was unfaithful there would be no way I would ever take him back in a million years. I always said that was the one thing I could never forgive (well, that *and* abandoning your unborn child), so what am I doing, taking him back?

What am I doing, allowing him to sleep beside me in bed? Why am I cooking him dinner and calling him when it's on the table? This is not what I said I would do. I need all my strength to stop myself from reaching out and slapping him across the face every time he smiles at me.

I thought that sending him packing would be the easiest thing in the world to do, but part of the reason for taking him back was because I couldn't face doing it all by myself again. I just kept imagining me and Katie alone again and I couldn't take it. Now I'm beginning to question my decision. Should I stay with him and learn to love him again, or should I leave and learn to survive on my own, to be independent? I just don't think I can face another tiny flat and one crappy wage for myself and Katie to survive on.

But if I could just *forgive* him. If I could just erase the image of his lips kissing someone else's every time he talks to me. Every time he touches me my skin crawls and I feel so much hate for him it's unnerving. It's hard for my wounds to be healed by the very same man who put them there.

And he's so bloody gung-ho about everything. He's Mr. Enthusiastic about going to see a counselor together and he takes a few hours out of his day to talk to me, *really* talk to me. It's all just such a textbook solution of "How to please your wife after shagging another woman." First you make an appointment to see the counselor, making sure to make a song and a dance about the fact you're canceling important meetings to go, then cook the dinner every day and fill the dishwasher, ask your wife a million times a day if she is OK and if there's anything you can do for her, do the weekly shopping remembering to include thoughtful little gifts like her favorite chocolate cake or a book that you think she might like, spend a few hours during the day to sit in silence with your wife doing a summary of your day and then discussing in detail how you feel your relationship is going. Do this five hundred times a day, add water, and then stir.

And the thing is, the Greg I married would never do all of those things. He would never bother replacing the empty toilet roll with the new one; he would never wash all the food off his plate before putting it in the dishwasher. Everything has changed. Even the small daily routines that make life so comfortable have changed.

If I could find the strength in me to leave him I would, but I'm stuck in this noncommittal limbo. I just want to make the right decision right now. I don't want to be a bitter old woman in forty years time, still making snide comments to Greg about what he's done. In order to make this marriage work I need to know in advance that I can if not forget, then at least forgive. I need to know that the little bit of love I feel for him right now will grow again, back to the way it was. The one thing that's making me so much stronger is the fact that I know that he won't do this to me again. We've had too many long nights of tears and fights for either of us to want to go through it again.

If Alex lived in this country I would know what to do. All I need is backup. He's the little angel that sits on my shoulder whispering in my ear, "You can do it!" It's funny. I'm thirty years old now and I still feel like a little girl. I'm still looking around to check and see what other people are doing to make sure I'm not completely different; I'm still looking around for help, hoping for a quick nudge and a whisper of advice. But I can't seem to be able to catch anybody's eye. Nobody else around me seems to be looking around and wondering what to do. Why is it that I feel like I'm the only person who is confused and concerned about the choices I've made and where I'm headed? Everywhere I look, I see people just getting on with it. Maybe I should just follow suit and get on with it.

Love,
Rosie

Dear Rosie,

Please do not torture yourself with questions that you don't know the answers to. You are going through a really difficult time right now but you *are* getting on with it, and you do it time and time again. Every knock back makes you stronger.

I can't tell you whether to stay with Greg or not, only you can make that decision, but all I can say is that if there's any love there at all then you should work at it. Every small thing grows when you nurture it, Rosie. Love is just the same. But if that is making you miserable then leave and find something else that brings you the happiness you *deserve* to feel.

Just listen to what your heart is saying and go with your gut instinct and it will lead you the right way. I'm sorry I have no great words of wisdom for you, Rosie, but at least you know that you're *not* alone; other people don't have all the answers to the questions. Sometimes we're all just as confused as you are.

Take care.

Love,
Stephanie

FROM: Rosie
TO: Stephanie
SUBJECT: Silent heart

My heart isn't saying anything and my gut instinct is telling me to go to bed, curl up in a ball and cry.

FROM: Mum
TO: Stephanie
SUBJECT: Is this working?

    I think I've just about figured out this e-mail thingy. Anyway I just wanted to see if our plans are still in place for your father's sixtieth. He thinks it's a few quiet drinks with Jack and Pauline, so don't e-mail me back on this address because he can read it too. Call me on my mobile. I really would love you to come. It would be nice for us all to be together again and I think it would be good for Rosie. I'm worried about her, she's so upset about Greg that she's lost so much weight. Your father is only two steps away from punching Greg in the face which won't do anyone any good. Especially not your father's heart. Kevin isn't talking to Greg either which isn't making life any easier for poor Rosie. However, the more family around her, the better.

—⁓—

CHAPTER 22

Ruby: OK whatever diet you're on, I want my Gary to go on it.

Rosie: I'm not on a diet Ruby.

Ruby: But you look sick and unhealthy; that's exactly the way I want him to look. Unattractive, stick thin, exhausted . . .

Rosie: Thanks.

Ruby: I just want to help Rosie, please tell me what's going on.

Rosie: There's nothing you can do to help; Greg and I just have to work this out on our own. Well, me, Greg, and Ursula, the wonderful marriage counselor. We've all become such a wonderful team it really makes me weep . . .

Ruby: How nice for you all. How is the wonderfully helpful Ursula?

Rosie: Wonderfully helpful. Yesterday she told me I had problems discussing my feelings.

Ruby: And?

Rosie: And I told her that made me feel angry and that she could go fuck herself.

Ruby: Well expressed.

Rosie: Thank you. I don't see where there was a problem, I successfully explained how I felt and she clearly understood what I meant. No problems . . .

Ruby: What did Greg say about that?

Rosie: Oh wait for this; it's wonderful. My amazingly intuitive husband thinks that I "have problems communicating with and understanding Ursula."

Ruby: Oh dear.

Rosie: Oh dear is right so I suggested that myself and Ursula attend relationship counseling in order to have good communication skills during my marriage counseling.

Ruby: Right . . . so what did Greg say to that suggestion?

Rosie: Well I couldn't quite hear what he said over the slamming of the car door. It can't have been very positive though, his nose was flared and I think he was snarling at me. I'm also thinking of purchasing a larger bed so that there's room for Ursula. She may as well know absolutely everything about us. Maybe she could count how many times I fart during the night or something . . .

Ruby: Is it really that bad?

Rosie: I just can't see how this is helping *anything*. She only makes us fight more by forcing us to discuss all the little things that bother us about each other. If we ever start to get along with each other, I can almost *see* Ursula getting worried about her next month's rent. Last week we argued *for an hour* about how much I hate it when Greg leaves a milk mustache on his face purposely just to make me laugh, then when I don't laugh he follows me around the house tapping me on the shoulder with it still on, until I do. It's not funny! It's silly!

Yesterday we fought about how it annoys me when his mouth starts to twitch when I get something wrong. If I said the sky was yellow, his top lip would start to do this odd sort of Elvis twitch. It bugs the hell out of me that he can't just *let it go*. He *needs* to let me know in some form or another that I've gotten a piece of "vital" information wrong. *Oh no*, the grass is green not pink! Oops-a-daisies, what a difference *that* statement makes to our life!

Next week I think I'll bring up the fact that he always wears the silly novelty socks his dear mother buys him. He thinks they're hilarious. Sometimes he just calls her up to tell her he's wearing them. Yellow socks with bloody pink polka dots and blue ones with red stripes. I'm sure his fellow colleagues at the bank think they're absolutely *hilarious*. The wonderfully cool and hip bank manager that wears pink socks, ooh let's all get a mortgage from him! Plus when he sits down, his trousers lift and you can see them from a mile away . . .

Ruby: Wow . . . and they say you have problems expressing yourself . . .

Rosie: My point is that they just love going into such irrelevant detail. It shouldn't matter whether Greg kisses me on the forehead or on the cheek every morning; the fact should be whether he kisses me at all.

Ruby: So is this bizarre counseling having any kind of a positive effect on your marriage?

Rosie: Not really, I think Greg and I would do better without her.

Ruby: Do you think you could both break up with her?

Rosie: Ha ha that's what it would feel like. Well we should, otherwise I can't see us still being together by the time Greg turns 40 . . .

FOR MY HUSBAND
HAPPY 40TH
TO GREG,

HAPPY BIRTHDAY SWEETHEART,
LOTS OF LOVE,
ROSIE

HAPPY 40TH!
YOU ARE NOW UGLIER AND OLDER.
TO GREG,
FROM KATIE AND TOBY

Dear Alex,

I think I'm going to organize a search party. Have you fallen off the edge of the earth? Are you still alive?

I called your mother the other day and they haven't heard from you very much either. Is everything OK? Because if it's not, I have a right to know. You're supposed to confide in me because I'm your best friend and . . . it's law. And if things are OK then contact me anyway, I'm your friend and I need gossip. It's section two of the same law.

Everything here is as crazy and unpredictable as usual. Katie is eleven now as you know (thank you for her present). She is so grown up that she tells me that she doesn't need to inform me where she is going during the day or when she'll be coming home. Unimportant information like that, which a mother apparently doesn't need to know. I thought I had another few years left until she became a monster; saw me as being in the way, interfering, and deliberately setting out to ruin her life. (OK so *occasionally* I do.) The child wears lipstick now, Alex. Pink, glossy, glittery lipstick. She wears glitter on her eyes, glitter on her cheeks, and glitter in her hair; I am raising a disco ball for a daughter. I am now under instructions to knock on her bedroom door three times before I'm allowed to enter, just so she can identify the intruder. (I'm quite jealous because Toby only has to knock once. However Greg on the other hand has to knock thirteen times. Poor Greg. Sometimes, most of the time, he loses count and Katie refuses to let him in for safety reasons.

I mean really, who else could it be at her door knocking thirteen times, or at least *trying* to knock thirteen times?! Although I have become very clever and only knock once sometimes; that way she thinks I'm Toby and lets me in to see the inner sanctum of Katie Dunne. You would expect it to have black walls, no light, scary posters on the wall but it's surprisingly neat and tidy.)

I'm not sure if she is still writing to you, but if she fills you in on any interesting aspects of her terribly busy and secretive life, please let me know. I'm her mother and that is *definitely* law.

Everything at work is going well, I'm still at the hotel and I'm the longest employee they have there now. Funny isn't it? But . . . and there's always a "but" with me. I know I've always been obsessed by the inner workings of hotels but I kind of feel "Is this it? Is this all there is to it?" Doing what I'm doing is fine and all, but I would like to move on a bit. More importantly I'd like to try to move up a bit. I won't rest until I'm managing the Hilton hotels.

Greg says I'm mad. He says I would be crazy to give up a job with good pay, a good boss, good hours. He thinks I have it easy here. I suppose he's right though. I really can't afford to take the risk because you never know; I could end up back working for Randy Andy. Now that would have to be the most depressing thing that could ever happen to me.

How is Josh? I would love to see him again. We must make arrangements to meet up soon. I don't want him not knowing who I am. We always promised our kids would be best friends, remember? I don't want to be one of those strange people to him that visits and once in a blue moon squeezes money into his hands. Although I very much liked those kinds of people myself, I would personally rather mean more to Josh.

OK so I think that's all my very exciting news for you for now. Write to me, ring me, e-mail me, or fly over and visit me. Or you could do all of those things. Just do anything to let me know that you're still walking the earth.

Miss you.

Love,
Rosie

Dear Rosie,

Just to let you know I'm still alive—just about. Sally seems to be sucking all the life out of me these days. We're finalizing the divorce . . . it's a nightmare.

So that's what's going on with me. Must go now; have to stick my hands in someone's chest.

Give my love to Katie,
Alex

FROM: Rosie
TO: Stephanie
SUBJECT: Gossip!

Thanks for your letter, Steph. I am absolutely fine, thank you. Everyone is well and healthy, we have no complaints. I feel I've made the right decision about Greg and from just listening to Alex about the divorce procedure, I'm glad Greg and I didn't take that route. At least Sally and Josh haven't moved far from Alex so he can make arrangements to see Josh quite regularly.

My worst nightmare would be to lose Katie. I don't know what I would do. She may watch MTV all day, blare music from her room, ruin my days off by making me go into school to fight with Ms. Big Nose Smelly Breath Casey, leave glitter all over the couches and carpets, worry me to death when she's one minute late for her nine o'clock curfew, but she's the most important thing to me in my life. She comes first all of the time. I'm so glad Alex missed the debs and I'm so glad that Brian the Whine was such a boring person. The men in my life may have let me down but the little girl in my life makes up for it every single day.

Dear Ms. Rosie Dunne,

I was hoping you would be free on Monday the 16th at 9 a.m. to meet with me at the school. Toby Flynn's parents will also be in attendance. It is regarding the recent results of the summer maths exam. It appears that Katie and Toby have the same answers for all the questions. What jumped out at me was the fact that the majority of these answers are wrong. I have discussed this with Katie and Toby and they insist it was coincidental.

Cheating, as you well know, is considered to be a very serious offense at St. Patrick's primary school. I seem to have a case of déjà vu, Rosie . . . Please ring to confirm your presence.

Ms. Casey

CHAPTER 23

—⁂—

FROM: Rosie
TO: Alex
SUBJECT: Grown-ups

What are the two of us like? I was going to say who knew we'd be going through so much "grown-up stuff" but I don't consider you going through a divorce and me trying to pick up the pieces of my marriage grown-up. I think we both had it pretty much sussed when we were playing cops and robbers in the back garden. It's all been downhill from there!

The weather has been beautiful over here for the past few weeks. I love June in Dublin. The gray buildings seem less gray, the unhappy faces seem brighter. It is so hot here at work though. The entire front of the hotel building is built from glass and it feels like we're working in a greenhouse on days like today. It's such a contrast to our winter months when the sound of the fat raindrops hitting off the glass echoes around the quiet foyer. It's a pretty sound but sometimes the hailstones are so loud and forceful, threatening to smash through the glass. Right now I'm staring up at a rich blue sky dotted with white candy-floss grazing sheep. It is beautiful.

Convertible sports cars have their tops down and music is blaring, businessmen have been casually strolling down the street past the hotel, with their jackets slung over their shoulders and their shirtsleeves rolled up, reluctant to get back to the office. The college students have all seemingly decided to call off their plans to attend lectures to flake out in large circles in the park. The ducks are gathering by the edge of the pond, glad they won't have to search for their own food today. Mounds of soggy uneaten bread float on the surface of the water waiting to be pecked at.

A flirting couple chase each other around the large water fountain catching its cool spray on their bare arms and legs in order to cool their body temperatures. Couples in love stretch out together on the grass and gaze longingly into each other's eyes. Children avail of the playground while their parents relax in the sun keeping one eye shut and one eye lazily focused on their excited offspring who squeal with delight.

Shop owners stand at the entrance doors to their empty shops watching the world go by. Office workers gaze dreamily out of the window from the desks high up in their clammy stuffy offices enviously watching the city throb with excitement.

The sound of laughter is in the air, people are full of smiles, there's a bounce in their step. The veranda of the hotel is busy with people taking drinks out in the sun. Long Island iced teas, gin and tonics, tangy orange with crushed ice, lime green concoctions, fruity cocktails, and bowls of ice cream. Layers of clothes are being discarded and hung on the backs of chairs.

Cleaning ladies hum softly to themselves and smile while polishing the brass, feeling the sun's rays streaming down on their faces. Days like this don't come often and you can tell everyone wishes they did.

And I sit here and think of you. I send you my love.

FROM: Alex
TO: Rosie
SUBJECT: Happy!

You sounded happy! I've just returned from a weekend with Josh. He's a feisty little thing now Rosie, he's running around trying to grab anything and everything from left, right, and center. I was almost afraid to blink in case the room came crashing down around me. But he's in great form and I feel so happy and rejuvenated after the weekend. Seeing him always lights me up, a switch is flicked somewhere in my body. I could watch him forever. Watch how he learns, how he teaches himself, how he eventually finds a way to do things without help from anyone. Josh takes chances; he's braver than I am. He always takes that extra step when he nos he shouldn't. He does it anyway and he learns. I think we adults have a lot to learn from that. Perhaps to not be so afraid and oversensible about reaching for goals.

So I am taking Josh's advice. A surgeon whose work I greatly admire is giving a talk during the week. It's a few days of seminars about a new heart procedure he has developed. I'm going to try and meet him, along with the other thousand or so wannabe heart surgeons who will be there. Rumor has it he's from Ireland and has moved over here to develop his studies further.

Cross your fingers and pray for a miracle.

FROM: Rosie
TO: Alex
SUBJECT: Mysterious meeting

I have a mysterious meeting with Bill, my boss, next week. I have no idea what it's about, but I'm quite nervous about it. He flew over yesterday in a not so good mood and has had a series of secret meetings all day. Lots of suspicious-looking people have been arriving to talk to him on the hour every hour dressed in dark suits. They could, of course, be giving him hourly updates of the news but somehow I doubt that very much. I have an awful feeling in the pit of my stomach.

What makes it even worse is the fact that his brother Bob is flying over tomorrow morning. They only ever get together to do the hiring and firing. I think that's all Bob does, really. His brother does all the work on their hotels around the world and he just spends his share of the money on houses, cars, holidays, and women, so I hear. Why is it that people always put women in the same category as cars and holidays as though we're prizes on a game show?

Jesus I hope they don't fire me. I don't know what I would do. I think I would sleep with him to keep this job. That's how much I love it. Or how scared I am about having to search for another one. Or how desperate I am to sleep with a man other than Greg for a change. I love him but bless him; he's a sucker for routine.

Better go and look like I'm really busy so that they will have absolutely no grounds to fire me. Cross your fingers for me, and I'll cross mine for you.

FROM: Alex
TO: Rosie
SUBJECT: Re: Mysterious meeting

Don't worry, it will all be fine! They have no reason to fire you! (Have they?) You have done nothing wrong since the day you started working there. In fact you've hardly even called in sick! Everything will be fine. Just about to leave the apartment now to go to seminar. Good luck to the both of us!

FROM: Rosie
TO: Alex
SUBJECT: Re: Mysterious meeting

You're right. They can't fire me. I'm just being stupid. I am a great employee. They have no reason to. At least no reasons that they know of. I mean, they could never find out about the time I brought Ruby up to show her the penthouse suite. And even if they do know that, there's no way that they could know that we ordered room service and stayed the night.

Could they?

Maybe it was the missing bathrobes that they noticed. But they were so cozy and I had to take one home . . .

Or maybe it was the empty minibar. But I distinctly remember asking Peter to restock the fridge and he owed me one after I gave his parents a Valentine's Day discount in the middle of May. So it can't be that . . . oh god this is killing me. I really don't want to work for Randy Andy again and I don't think I have energy to go sending CV's out again. And the stress of another job interview.

They only want to meet with me. But Bill didn't smile at me when he said it and his eyes weren't as twinkly as usual. Oh no what does that mean?!

FROM: Rosie
TO: Alex
SUBJECT: Fired!

Oh my god, the new skinny girl has a meeting too next week. She's the worst worker ever. She's called in sick more times than she's been in. Probably because she never eats. Lunch breaks are wasted on her. She just stares across the table at your plate with a horrible face on her as though food is the devil and she sips on a bottle of water. Then halfway through her bottle she gets full, tightens the lid, and leaves it behind.

I better start job-hunting I think.

FROM: Alex
TO: Rosie
SUBJECT: Chill out!

For Christ sake Rosie Dunne, I love you with all my heart but you need to chill out!

You have an instant message from: RUBY

Ruby: Oooh so he loves you with all his heart does he?
Rosie: Oh stop reading my e-mails Ruby.
Ruby: Well, get a less obvious password, "Buttercup." You two are being all flirty with each other lately.
Rosie: No we haven't! How on earth have we been flirty??!
Ruby: You know yourself.
Rosie: Oh please I thought you were going to make a good point for once in your life.
Ruby: I have one and you know it.
Rosie: We're just getting along like we used to do; that's all. Alex has perked himself up, I think he's happy again.
Ruby: Because he's in lurve . . .
Rosie: He is not in love. Well not with me anyway.
Ruby: Oh sorry I was just misguided by the fact that he said in his e-mail that he "loved you with all his heart."
Rosie: As a friend loves a friend Ruby.
Ruby: You're my friend and I do not love you with all my heart. Hell I hardly love Teddy with all my heart.

Rosie: OK then Alex and I are madly in love and we're go-
        ing to run away and have a passionate love affair.

Ruby: You see? It doesn't hurt to admit it does it?

Rosie: Whatever. How's your Gary?

Ruby: Overweight.

Rosie: Jesus do you see anything else other than weight
        when you look at him?

Ruby: Yes, I see memories of hours of agonizing labor. He
        still grunts at me and makes signals. Although I
        heard him on the telephone to his girlfriend
        Gemma. He uses words, you know?

Rosie: That's amazing Ruby.

Ruby: Well a mother is allowed to be proud.

Rosie: Hold on Ruby.

Rosie: Oh my god, celery stick just got back from meeting
        with Bill and Bob and she's crying her eyes out.
        They just fired her. I'm next. Shit. I better go. Shit.
        Shit. Shit.

Rosie has logged off

CHAPTER 24

—⸏⸏—

Kevin,

Hi son. I know I'm not one to write letters, but I'm not sure if you gave your mother and me the correct phone number of the staff barracks. Whenever I call it just keeps on ringing and ringing and that's at all hours of the day and night. You either gave us the wrong number purposely, there's something wrong with your phone, or everybody is working so hard they're not there to answer my calls. I wouldn't like the idea of having to share a phone with thirty staff members. Couldn't you get one of those mobile phones? Then maybe your family could get in touch with you every once in a while.

I hope you're not doing anything daft down there. Rosie really stuck her neck out to get you that job in the kitchen. Don't mess it up like all those other ones you had. This is a good opportunity for you now to get a good start in your life. Your old man is sixty now, I won't be around forever for you to rely on, you know!

It's a shame you couldn't make it home for my retirement party. The company invited the entire family, they really treated us well for the night, treated me well for over thirty-five years in fact. Stephanie, Pierre, and Jean-Louis made it over from France. Rosie, Greg, and young Katie were there too. It was a good night. I'm not picking on you, son, just wished you had been there too that's all. It was an emotional night all the same. If you had been there you would have seen your old man cry.

It's funny how life goes. I spent forty years working for them, remember my first day like it was yesterday. I was just fresh out of school, all eager to please. Wanted to start making money so that I could propose to your mother and buy us a house. In my first week of work we held a party in the office for one of the old guys retiring. I didn't give much notice to him. People were making speeches, giving him gifts, talking about old times. But all I cared about was the fact that they were making me stay late at work, unpaid, when all I wanted to do was get out of there to propose to your mother. The old guy had been there all his working life, he had tears in his eyes, was really upset about leaving, took him a lifetime to make the speech, thought he would never shut up so I could leave. I had the engagement ring in my pocket. Kept sticking my hand in my trousers to make sure the velvet box was still there. I couldn't wait for that guy to finish talking.

Billy Rogers was his name.

He wanted to take me aside and explain a few things to me about the company before he left. Seeing as I was a new boy. I didn't listen to a word he had to say. He talked and talked like he never had any intentions of leaving the damn office. I rushed him. The company wasn't that important to me then.

He kept on coming back to visit us in the office every week. Would hang around our desks annoying all the new guys, some of the old guys too, giving advice and checking up on things that were no longer his business. We just wanted to do our jobs. He lived and breathed for that place. We all told him to find himself a hobby. Keep himself busy. Thought we were helping him. Only suggested it out of the goodness of our hearts, that and the fact he was really starting to get up his pals' noses. He died a few weeks later. Had a heart attack on the golf course. He was taking our advice and having his first lesson.

I hadn't thought about Billy Rogers for almost thirty years. Had completely forgotten about him, to be honest. But that night and since I haven't been able to get the thought of Billy Rogers out of my head. Looking around with tears in my eyes, listening to speeches, accepting gifts, catching the new guys sneakily glimpse at their watches wondering when they could slip away to get home to their girlfriends or new wives or children or whomever . . . I couldn't help but think about all the guys who came through those office doors. Thought about the guys who started off on the same day as me; Colin Quinn and Tom McGuire, guys who never made it to retirement like me. I suppose that's what life's about. People come and go.

So there are no more early mornings for me. I caught up on a whole load of sleep I never even thought I needed. The garden is spotless, everything in the house that was once broken is now fixed. I've played golf three times this week, visited Rosie twice, took Katie and Toby out for the day, and I still feel like hopping into my car, speeding down to the office, and teaching the rookies a thing or two about how to do business. But they won't care; they want and need to learn it for themselves.

So I thought I would join the Dunne women in writing. It seems that's all they do. Keeps the phone bills down, I suppose. Let me know how things are going for you, son.

Did you hear about our Rosie's job?

      Love, Dad

FROM: Kevin

TO: Stephanie

SUBJECT: Dad

How are things? I just got a letter from Dad today. Dad writing a letter is weird in itself but what he was writing was even more bizarre. Is he OK? He was talking about some guy called Billy Rogers who died over thirty years ago. Make sure he's not losing it. Anyway, it was good to hear from him but he sounded like another man altogether. Not necessarily a bad thing. Sorry I wasn't there for his retirement do. Should have made more of an effort to be there.

Tell Pierre and Jean-Louis I was asking for them. Tell Pierre I'll beat his culinary skills hands down next time I see him! Here's a little pair of runners (for Jean-Louis obviously) that I saw in the sports shop. He'll be the trendiest little seven-month-old in France. Dad mentioned something about Rosie's job? What has she done now?

FROM: Stephanie
TO: Mum
SUBJECT: Kevin and Dad

Something must be in the water over there in Ireland because I just received an e-mail from your son, my little brother Kevin—yes Kevin, the guy who never keeps in touch with family unless he needs to borrow money. He was writing to tell me that Dad had written to him and he was worried! Did you even know that dad could lick a stamp?

Anyway, Kevin must be having some sort of quarterly life crisis or he's just going soft because he sent a present for Jean-Louis, the most adorable little booties! But don't tell Kevin that he threw up on them. It was a nice gesture anyway. The buying of the boots, not the vomiting over them.

Kevin also mentioned that Dad was talking about Billy Rogers again. He told me about him too. Is he OK? I'm assuming he is just feeling very contemplative now that he has entered a new era in his life. Now at least he has *time* to think. The both of you have worked so hard all your lives.

Now Kevin your baby is gone, Rosie and Katie are gone, I'm gone, and the house is finally all yours. I suppose I can understand how it's difficult for Dad to get his head around it. You were both used to a house full of screaming kids and bickering teenagers. When we finally grew up, along came a crying baby and you were so good to help Rosie out. I know it was hard for you financially too.

Kevin mentioned something about Rosie's job; I don't want to call her until I've heard from you about it. Let me know.

FROM: Mum
TO: Stephanie
SUBJECT: Re: Kevin and Dad

You're absolutely right. I think your father has a lot of thinking to do and enough time in the day to do it now. I love having him home! He's not rushing off all the time or thinking about a problem at work that needs to be solved while I'm trying to have a conversation with him. It's like he's all here with me now—body and mind. I felt that way too when I left my job but I suppose it was slightly different for me. I already went part-time at work when Katie was born to help Rosie cope. It didn't seem like such a drastic change for me when I eventually left the job completely. But your father is trying to find himself again.

Didn't you hear about Rosie's job?? I thought you would have been one of the first people she'd have told (apart from her darling Alex of course), but perhaps she wasn't ready to discuss it yet. That girl has me so worried at times. Honestly she kept telling me all week that she was going to lose her job, finally she calls me to tell me that she had a meeting with her bosses and she tells me she got a promotion!

Oh Stephanie we were so thrilled for her!! It was only a few days ago! I'm surprised she hasn't told you the good news yet. Anyway I'll let her tell you herself or else I'll be in trouble for spoiling the surprise. I better go now; your father's calling me. We're about to go down to the garden center. If he plants any more flowers or trees in that garden, we'll have to apply for planning permission they're so high!

Take care love, and hugs and kisses to baby Jean-Louis from Grandma and Granddad!

CHAPTER 25

—∿—

FROM: Stephanie
TO: Rosie
SUBJECT: Job promotion!

I know you're at work so I won't ring you. Received a letter from Mum today, what's this I hear about a job promotion??! E-mail me ASAP! So excited to know!

FROM: Rosie
TO: Stephanie
SUBJECT: Re: Job promotion!

Can't believe Mum opened her big mouth!! YES!! The news is true!

FROM: Stephanie
TO: Rosie
SUBJECT: Re: Job promotion!

That's all you're going to tell me??! Aren't you excited?! What's the job? Come on, give me info! I've taken time out

from my busy schedule of breast-feeding, burping and . . .
eh breast-feeding to find out the news!

This is fabulous! Congrats!

FROM: Rosie
TO: Stephanie
SUBJECT: Re: Job promotion!

Thanks Steph, sorry, thought Mum gave you all the info.
Yes I am excited! The job title is "Hotel Host" and before
you get overexcited like our beloved parents did, it's not the
manager's job! I will be the primary source of information
for guests to ensure maximum client satisfaction! (Or so
they tell me . . .)

It was the surprise of *all* surprises! I literally had to
drag my body into the long conference room, where I had
my first interview years ago, with my head hanging and
my body slumped, feeling like jelly. My body language
was all wrong, my palms were sweaty, my knees were
knocking, and I just kept having visions of Randy Andy
and me working together until we became old-age
pensioners. I really had convinced myself that they were
going to ask me to quietly and calmly return to my desk,
gather my belongings, leave the premises, and never
return. I don't know why, but I just had one of those
feelings.

Bill and Bob were so generous to me. They pumped me
full of confidence as they went through what the job would
entail. They said that they were delighted with my *perfor-
mance* within the hotel over the past few years (and I really
hope they weren't referring to the time when I lay across the
piano and sang Barbra Streisand songs after all the residents
had gone to bed. Well you can't blame a girl for trying to
live out a fantasy when she can, but the opportunity just
seemed to present *itself* . . .). There they were telling me I

had an abundance of charm and confidence when deep
down I was just waiting for the moment they would break
into a smile, look at me as though I was a fool for believing
them before telling me the promotion was all a joke. One
big funny ha ha practical joke. I kept looking around for the
hidden camera.

But there wasn't one, unless you count the security
camera in the corner of the room and then the joke really
is on me. So it seems that I will be moving to a new hotel
that's going to be built (hence all the secret meetings with
men and women in dark suits, leather briefcases, gelled
hair, and no smiles masquerading through the hotel lobby,
there was some sort of bizarre Matrix-y thing going on).
But if they *are* serious, then my job is to be solely
responsible for the running of all aspects of the resort and
I'll have to liaise with the head office and provide weekly
reports. I've never had to "liaise" before. It sounds sexy
and dangerous. Any job that tells me that I have to
"liaise" with the big boys in the head office is a winner to
me. I can picture myself all dolled up in a cocktail dress at
a work "do" standing in a circle with the other "suits"
speaking in hushed tones about graphs and pie charts and
financial reports. If people ask us what we're doing, I can
say dismissively, "Oh don't mind us, we're just
liaising . . ."

Apparently I have a flair for organizing and have good
communication skills. Anyone who has seen me rushing
to get all my Christmas shopping done in the last hour
on Christmas Eve knows that I *ain't* a good organizer.
And I hardly count loud cursing, swearing, and lots of
physical abuse while trying to grab the last item of
absolutely everything off the bare shelves of stores
from other panicking Christmas Eve shoppers, good
communication. Although, we all have our different
ways of seeing things.

FROM: Alex
TO: Rosie
SUBJECT: Congratulations!!

I am so proud of you! If I was there, I would twirl you around and give you a great big sloppy kiss! You see Rosie, things *can* happen for you, all you need is a lot more faith and self-belief and to stop being so negative all the time!

So where is the new hotel? Are they opening a second Two Lakes Hotel in Dublin? When they say "resort," what exactly do they mean?

Tell me all.

FROM: Rosie
TO: Alex
SUBJECT: Job promotion

Well I'm not quite sure of the location of the hotel just yet but I have a sneaky suspicion it's along the coast. Can you believe that I will finally get to work in a hotel by the sea? It will take longer to commute to, but it's worth it to be able to leave the city behind for a few hours every day. I should be out there within the next few months. When they say resort they are referring to the new eighteen-hole golf course they are building. There will be a gym and pool and more leisure facilities, unlike here which is in the heart of the city and has nothing but bedrooms, a tiny gym, and restaurants. I'm a bit hazy on all the details because they haven't fully informed me of everything yet, they just asked me if I was interested in this new job and of course I couldn't turn it down!

But this entire experience has taught me something. It's taught me that I'm ready to move on from this job. I'm ready to accept a new challenge and without having any sort of game plan at all, I seem to be moving closer and closer toward my dream. Whoever thought those childhood dreams of running a hotel weren't quite beyond my grasp after all? It's funny because when you're a child, you believe you can be anything you want to be, go wherever you want to go. There's no limit to what you can dream. You *expect* the unexpected, you *believe* in magic, in fairy tales, and in possibilities. Then you grow older and that innocence is shattered and somewhere along the way the reality of *life* gets in the way and you're hit by the realization that you can't be *all* you wanted to be, you just might have to settle for a little bit less.

Or perhaps a variation of what you once wanted.

Why do we stop believing in ourselves? Why do we let facts and figures and anything but dreams rule our lives?

But now my mind is changed again. Nothing is impossible Alex—it was there all the time, I just wasn't reaching out far enough, that's all.

Nothing is impossible.

Not a bad statement to come from the pen of a cynic.

Thank you for your faith in me Alex, I would love to return that hug and kiss to you now! But then again perhaps *some* things just might be beyond our reach after all.

FROM: Alex
TO: Rosie
SUBJECT: Dreams

Again Rosie, you're just not stretching far enough. I'm right here.

You have an instant message from: ROSIE

Ruby: What on earth is Alex's last message to you supposed to mean?

Rosie: For god sake Ruby, *stop* reading my e-mails!

Ruby: Sorry I can't help it but I can assure you that I will
        continue to read them until you decide to change
        your password *and* until I find a job that interests
        me at all.

Rosie: Well it looks like I'll be changing my password
        then . . .

Ruby: Ha ha so come on, I've seen it now, what's he talk-
        ing about? What's this about stretching far
        enough?? Sounds kinda dodgy.

Rosie: What do you think it means?

Ruby: I'm asking you.

Rosie: And I'm asking you.

Ruby: I asked first.

Rosie: Oh Ruby, don't be so childish

Ruby: OK then, he's teaching you some new exercise tech-
        niques—reaching and *stretching* . . . to help the
        abs, the biceps, the triceps, and the whatever-ceps.
        Am I close? No probably not. I give up. What's
        your interpretation?

Rosie: A friend telling me that he will always be there for
        me no matter what and that he's not that far away
        at all from me and all I have to do is call and he'll
        be here.

Ruby: Oh right, OK.

Rosie: Oh there you go again Ruby with the sarcasm!
        What's your theory now then?! I suppose you think
        it's his secret way of telling me that he loves me and
        that he will always be there for me and if I just
        reached out to him then he would drop everything,
        his new life in Boston, his family life, his great big
        amazing job to come rescue me, whisk me away to
        live in a beach house in . . . oh I don't know . . .
        Hawaii where we would live happily ever after away
        from all the stresses and complications of the
        world? I suppose that's what you would interpret it

as. You and your sick mind always twisting things, trying to make out as though the two of us—

Ruby: No Rosie, I really meant "Oh OK." That's fine, I believe you.

Rosie: Oh.

Ruby: Are you OK with that?

Rosie: Yeah sure . . . I just thought you might have read into it a bit more like you usually do that's all . . .

Ruby: No, that's OK. I believe that he meant it in a supportive friend kind of way.

Rosie: Oh . . . OK.

Ruby: Why, did you *want* it to mean something else?

Rosie: Ha ha *god no*, I was just expecting you to go on a rant that's all . . . You know you usually do, don't be silly!

Ruby: Are you sure?

Rosie: Of course!!

Ruby: So you're not disappointed?

Rosie: No why should I be?

Ruby: So you're OK with him being your friend?

Rosie: Of course! That's all he ever was to me! I'm perfectly happy!

Ruby: And you don't want to be rescued and whisked off to Hawaii?

Rosie: NO! Off course not!

Ruby: Good then . . .

Rosie: Yep it's great . . . Everything's great . . .

Ruby: Good.

Rosie: And the new job will make everything better!

Ruby: Good.

Rosie: And my marriage has been saved and I truly believe Greg loves me more than ever . . .

Ruby: Good.

Rosie: And I'm going to be paid a lot more than before which is good. They say money can't buy happiness but I'm a fickle person Ruby . . . I can get that new

coat I saw in the Ilac center yesterday . . . I'm
thrilled!

Ruby: Good.

Rosie: Absolutely! So anyway I'm going to head off now,
got a bit of work to do . . .

Ruby: That's really great Rosie . . .

Rosie has logged off

FROM: Rosie

TO: Stephanie

SUBJECT: It's a wonderful life!

Life is wonderful, life is great! I have a good job, just got
promoted to an even better one. I have a daughter who talks
to me, a husband that doesn't! Only joking, have a husband
who loves me! I have a wonderfully supportive family, mum,
dad, brother, and sister. I've two brilliant friends that would
do anything for me and who I love with all my heart. I
remember telling you years ago just before I started my new
job at reception that phase two of my life was beginning . . .
well this appears to be the beginning of phase three! Things
are looking up for me and I am so happy! I am in a
deliriously giddy mood today, high on the excitement of life
I suppose!

FROM: Ruby

TO: Rosie

SUBJECT: Cork??

What do you mean the bloody hotel is being built down
in Cork?! And they only tell you now? Are you moving
down to *Cork?* I thought you said it was along the *coast of
Dublin?!* Did they think that piece of information was
irrelevant to you? For Christ sake Rosie, how are you

going to drag your family down to the *other side of the country?*

Do you even want to move? Oh my god, I think I'm going to have a heart attack!

E-mail me back ASAP!!!

FROM: Rosie
TO: Ruby
SUBJECT: Re: Cork??

Oh Ruby, right now I have a headache, I don't know what to do. I know that I want this job but there are two other people to think about. I'll have to have a chat with Katie and Greg about it tonight. Pray for me! Please god if you're listening and not busy sprinkling gold dust on all the lucky people of the world, please do me this favor and brainwash my family into thinking of what I want for once. I thank you for your time and patience. You can continue gold-dust sprinkling now.

FROM: Ruby
TO: Rosie
SUBJECT: God

Hello Rosie, this is God. Sorry to bring you bad news but life doesn't work like that. You must be honest with your family and try to convince them yourself. Tell them of your lifelong dream to take the job that you have been offered and if they are unselfish people they will understand your desire to move to Cork. My popcorn's ready so I better leave. I'm already missing the first of this evening's entertainment. I'm watching your friend Ruby's life tonight. Good luck with the family.

Dear Mum & Greg,

Don't worry about us Mum, me and Toby will be OK.
We have run away because we don't want to be away from
each other. He is my best friend and I don't want to move to
Cork. Please don't make us leave Mum.

Love,
Katie and Toby

FROM: Rosie
TO: Ruby
SUBJECT: Re: God

I couldn't help noticing that God logged on under your
name yesterday. If you see him around please tell him that if
he's looking for drama, he should tune into my family today.

PART 3

~~~

CHAPTER 26

Dear Alex,

I was so happy when I finally got around to shutting the door on this horrible day. "It's only a job," Greg said. Well if a job is so unimportant then why is he so adamantly refusing to leave his own? It's not *only* a job though. So they offered me a promotion, but with it they offered me confidence and a little bit of self-belief. To believe that my hard work was being rewarded and I was seen as competent and smart.

But this time I wasn't even given the choice to screw it up myself. That decision was made *for* me. Katie won't leave Toby and I'm not quite hating Greg enough to storm off to Cork in a huff on my own. Although, I'm pretty close to it. God does that man make my blood boil! Everything is always so black and white to him.

In his opinion, he has a great job here that pays well and I have a good job that pays OK. Why on earth would he want to move to a city where his wife will have a brilliant job and earn great money? Oh of course, I forgot they don't have any banks in Cork so there's no way he could ever find a job or be transferred. People just save money under their beds in shoeboxes there.

Plus everything (well a lot of things, like houses for one) is cheaper down there than it is here. Katie would be able to *begin* her first year of secondary school in a perfectly good school so it's not as if she's being taken out of school midway here. It could all be so perfect.

On the other hand, I can honestly say that her friendship with Toby is possibly the most important thing to her. He's a great supportive force in her life; he makes her happy and keeps the innocence in her eyes. Children need close friends to help them grow up, to discover things about themselves and about life. They also need close friends to keep them sane, and due to Katie's little disappearing act I now know that her being without Toby, at this stage of her life anyway, would lead to incredible insanity.

Do you realize that they had actually booked their flights to you over the Internet with Greg's credit card? They were in the queue to check in at the airport when the gardai found them! I can just picture them: a little girl with jet black hair and vanilla skin with no luggage except for a cuddly teddy bear bag on her back. Beside her, a little boy with messy blond curls, in charge of the tickets and passport details. A miniature honeymoon couple. Someday I will look back on this experience and laugh. After I get over the shock, horror, bitterness, and resentment. Probably in my next lifetime.

So I can't accept the job of my dreams because my family won't move with me. Big deal. It's not as though I bend over backwards for them. It's not as though I arrange my life to revolve around them. It's not as though I come home from work tired and still have dinner on the table for them, it's not as though I perform wonderful supportive wifely chores when there's a million other things I could be doing. It's not as though I defend my daughter at school, constantly fighting with the teachers about how she is not Satan's daughter. It's not as though I tolerate Greg's mother for dinner every Sunday and listen to her whinge about how the food isn't cooked right, about my hair, about the way I dress, about the way I have chosen to raise Katie and then have to sit through hours of reruns of her favorite soaps. It's not as though I'm always the one to take a day off work when Katie is sick or drop whatever plans I've made to help people out.

Just as well I don't do any of those things.

But who cares? I get burned toast and milky tea one morning once a year on Mother's Day as thanks. And that should make up for it, shouldn't it? Greg always tells me I'm forever chasing rainbows. Maybe I should stop now.

> Love,
> Rosie

FROM: Alex
TO: Rosie
SUBJECT: Rosie Dunne!

Do not give up! You are Katie's mother and what you say is final. She will learn to adjust and you don't need to worry because kids adjust to things far easier than us adults. As for what's-his-name! Doesn't he have a supportive bone in his body? I suppose he doesn't, not having a spine and all . . .

I just hate to see you miss out on another opportunity, isn't there anything you can do to convince what's-his-name?

FROM: Rosie
TO: Alex
SUBJECT: Family

Thanks, Alex, but no. I can't force my family to leave their home if they don't want to, they're important to me.

I have to respect Greg's wishes; I don't think I would be too happy about moving away from my job and friends if he had to move due to work. I can't live my life pretending it's

just me in the world. But how much easier it would be!
Anyway it's just another missed opportunity.

So enough about me—how are all those lectures going?
Find out who Mr. Fantastic Surgeon is yet?

Thanks for your support, as always.

FROM: Katie
TO: Toby
SUBJECT: Grounded!

I can't believe we are grounded! *And* on our summer
holidays! Our parents didn't have to go all psycho about it!
It's not like we ended up going anywhere—we were less
than an hour away from home. Hardly worth locking us in
our houses for two weeks. I told you we should have taken a
ferry over to France or something. In the films, the first
places the gardai always check are the airports. That was
where we made our mistake. I've been looking into this and
we should have gone to Bus Aras, and got a coach to
Rosslare. Next time that's what we'll do.

What do you think Alex would have done when we
arrived on his doorstep? Mum says he's not even home, that
he's away on some meetings or something but I think she's
just lying to try to prove that our plan wouldn't have
worked. I don't think he would have been mad, Alex is cool.
But he probably would have called Mum and she would
have sent ten million squad cars and rescue helicopters over
to get us.

Poor Mum. I'm glad we're not moving away but I feel
sorry for her. She was so excited about doing that job and
now she's back stuck in that other place she said she was
sick of a while ago. I feel kinda guilty. I no she would have
made me go anyway if Greg had said yeah but I still feel bad
for her. She's just wandering around the house looking real
sad and she keeps on sighing as though she's real bored and

doesn't no what to do next. Just like us on Sundays. She gets up from one couch and moves to another room to sit in another chair. Then she gets up again and moves to another room and stares out the window for *ages*, sighs about three million times, moves to another room, in, out, in, out . . . she makes me dizzy just watching her. Sometimes I just follow her around, seeing as I'm not supposed to be allowed in the outside world and I've nothing better to do.

Yesterday I started following her again and she started to walk faster and faster, by the end of it I was chasing her around the house and it was so funny. She opened the front door and ran outside in her pajamas teasing me because I couldn't go outside (being grounded and all). But I ran out anyway and the two of us sprinted around the block in our pajamas, me in my blue one with the pink hearts and Mum in her yellow dressing gown! Everyone was staring at us but it was fun. We ran to Birdie's shop on the corner and Mum treated me to some strawberry ice cream, the highlight of my day. Birdie didn't look too impressed at the sight of us especially seeing as Mum wasn't wearing anything under her dressing gown but she flashed her legs at old Mr. Fanning who was there to buy his morning paper. He looked like he was gonna have a heart attack. So at least I got to go outside for a little while.

As soon as we got back inside she continued just walking around the house as if she was in a museum or something. Greg says she's got a feather up her arse. Mum said she'd love to shove a pole up his. He didn't say much for the rest of the day.

Toby, if we had made it to the top of that queue in the airport, do you think we would have gotten on the plane? I'm not sure if I could have left Mum, but I don't think she would believe that now if I told her. She would probably just think I was trying to get out of being grounded, *although* that's not a bad idea. OK I gotta go!

E-mail me back before I die of boredom!

FROM: Alex
TO: Rosie
SUBJECT: Family duties!

You and your "duties" to your family. I just don't want
you to be the only person following the rules, that's all.

The lectures are going great. You will never believe who
the surgeon is! Your very favorite man—Reginald Williams.

FROM: Rosie
TO: Alex
SUBJECT: Reginald Williams!

Oh . . . my . . . god. Pass me a bucket while I puke. You
mean slutty Bethany's father? Have they come back from the
evil past to haunt us??!!

A very disgusted and extremely shocked Rosie

FROM: Alex
TO: Rosie
SUBJECT: Re: Reginald Williams!

It's OK Rosie, take deep breaths! He's not so bad. A very
intelligent man.

FROM: Rosie
TO: Alex
SUBJECT: Re: Reginald Williams!

What does he do now, hypnotism? Has he been
tampering with your brain? So that's why he's been all over
the papers over here. I have refused to read them out of
protest for him and his family's existence. Oh my god—
Reginald Williams! So do you think you're in with a chance

to be one of the "chosen few" to work with him, seeing as
you were an almost-son-in-law? There's nothing like a bit of
nepotism to keep the world a just and equal place.

FROM: Alex
TO: Rosie
SUBJECT: Nepotism!

I think the chances of that happening are fairly slim. I
think I sealed my own doom when I dumped his favorite
and only daughter!

FROM: Rosie
TO: Alex
SUBJECT: Slutty Bethany

Oh I don't know about sealing your doom, I think it may
have been the *best* move you have ever made. Come to think
of it, I haven't seen slutty Bethany for about ten years! What
is she up to, I wonder? Probably living in a mansion in the
hills counting diamonds and evilly laughing . . .

FROM: Rosie
TO: Stephanie
SUBJECT: Best friends stay with you forever

Oh wise and wonderful sister Stephanie you were right!
When I was seventeen you told me that girlfriends come and
go but best friends stay with you forever. I found myself
saying today, "I wonder what slutty Bethany is doing these
days . . ." The exact statement I never wanted Alex to have
to say about me. I didn't believe you at the time but I sure
do now!!
Thanks Steph, best friends do stay with you forever!

—〰—

CHAPTER 27

You have an instant message from: RUBY

Ruby: So you're still here then.
Rosie: Oh your words of support are like a breath of fresh
        air my dear Ruby. Yes I am still here. The hands of
        Dublin have got their fists tightly grasped around
        my neck, choking me and refusing to let go. Yes
        Ruby. I am still here.
Ruby: I see; nice little analogy. So you found your daugh-
        ter then.
Rosie: Yes we have her trained to come running back after
        three whistles, a clap of the hands, and a little twirl.
Ruby: Impressive . . .
Rosie: I reminded myself that Alex and I ran off together a
        few times when we were younger. The first time we
        ran away because Alex's parents refused to let him
        go to some theme park to visit Captain Tornado for
        the weekend. I now understand his parents' point of
        view because, well, the theme park was in
        Australia . . . in a cartoon . . . Anyway we must only
        have been about five or six. We packed our school
        bags and ran away. We literally *ran* away, we thought

that was what we were supposed to do, *run* down the road which was extremely inconspicuous of course.

We spent the entire day roaming streets we had never been to before, looking at houses and wondering if the pocket money we had saved up that week was enough to buy a house of our own. We even looked at the houses that weren't for sale . . . we hadn't quite grasped that concept yet. As soon as it got dark the two of us became bored with our freedom and a little scared too. Eventually we decided to head back home to see if our protests had made a difference to the Captain Tornado situation. Our parents hadn't even noticed we'd been gone. Alex's parents thought we were at my house and my parents thought vice versa.

I don't know if Katie would have gotten on that plane had she been given the opportunity. I would like to think that I've done a good enough job as a mother for her to know that running away isn't a way to solve anything. You can run and run as fast and as far as you like but the truth is, wherever you run, there you are. In fact she tried to tell me today that she loved me with all her heart and that she could never leave me. I thought I sensed sincerity in her eyes and voice but as soon as I reached out to cuddle her, her face brightened and asked if that meant she didn't have to be grounded anymore. I'm afraid she's a chancer like her father.

	Ever run away from home when you were a child?
Ruby:	No. But my ex-husband ran away from home with a child half his age if that's any help to you.
Rosie:	Right . . . well no it's not but thanks for sharing it with me all the same.
Ruby:	No problem.

Rosie: So what are you doing for your 40th Ruby? It's
         coming up soon?!

Ruby: I'm going to break up with Teddy.

Rosie: No! You can't! You and Teddy are an institution!

Ruby: Ha! That's my point. OK I mightn't then. I was just
         thinking of new and exciting ways to change my
         life. Funnily enough that was the first one that
         jumped into my head.

Rosie: You don't need to change your life Ruby; it's just
         fine as it is.

Ruby: I'm going to be 40 Rosie. FORTY. I'm younger
         than Madonna would you believe and I look like her
         mother. Every day I wake up in a messy bedroom
         beside a man who smells and snores, I trip over
         mounds of clothes in order to find my way to the
         door, I stagger down to the kitchen and make my-
         self a coffee and eat a slice of leftover cake. On the
         way back to my bedroom I pass my son in the hall-
         way. Sometimes he acknowledges me; most of the
         time he doesn't.

         I fight with him to use the shower and I don't mean
         about who's first to use it, I actually have to *force*
         him to wash himself. I fight with the shower in or-
         der to be neither scalded to a crisp nor frozen to
         death. I get dressed in clothes I have been wearing
         for far too many years in a size that makes me phys-
         ically sick, but that has caused me to lose the will to
         care about doing something about . . . *anything* or
         anything about *something*. Teddy grunts good-bye
         to me, I squeeze myself into my banged-up rusty
         old unfaithful mini that breaks down almost every
         morning on the motorway that bears more of a re-
         semblance to a car-park than a road.

         I park my car, arrive into work late again, and get
         given out to by someone I have been forced to

nickname Randy Andy. I sit at my desk where I
concoct stories which help me escape the office
where I flee to the outside world for a sneaky cigarette. I do this various times a day. I speak to nobody all day, nobody speaks to me and then I
return home at 7 p.m. feeling absolutely exhausted
and starving, to a home that will never be cleaned
and a dinner that will never prepare itself. I do this
every day.

On Saturday nights I meet you, and we go out and I
suffer all day Sunday with a hangover. This means
that I turn into a zombie and lie on the couch like a
piece of broccoli. The house still doesn't get tidied
and despite being screamed at, it refuses to tidy itself. I wake up on Monday morning to that awful
horrible wailing sound of my alarm clock that's beginning to sound like *na na na na na*, just to begin
the week all over again.

Rosie, how could you say I don't need change? I
desperately need change.

Rosie: Ruby, we *both* need change.

FOR A SPECIAL FRIEND,
MAY THIS BE THE BEGINNING OF A TRULY HAPPY
AND SUCCESSFUL YEAR FOR YOU!
SORRY RUBY THIS WAS THE ONLY HALF DECENT CARD
I COULD FIND THAT DIDN'T GO ON ABOUT HOW
YOUR LIFE IS ALMOST ENDING.
THANKS FOR ALWAYS BEING THERE FOR ME, EVEN
THOUGH YOU'D RATHER NOT BE!
YOU'RE A FANTASTIC FRIEND TO HAVE, LET'S ENJOY
THIS BIRTHDAY AND GOOD LUCK IN YOUR NEW YEAR.
LOVE, ROSIE
PS: I HOPE YOU LIKE YOUR PRESSIE, NEVER COMPLAIN
OF *CHANGE* EVER AGAIN!

This voucher entitles the bearer to 10 lessons in salsa dancing.
Ricardo will be your teacher every Wednesday @ 8 p.m. in the school hall of St. Patrick's secondary school.

You have an instant message from: RUBY

Ruby: I'm all salsa'd out! The last time I was in this much pain was when Teddy got that Kama Sutra book for Christmas from the lads at work. I practically had to be fork-lifted to work after the holidays, remember? Well this time I actually had to take the morning *off* work. Can you believe it?!

I woke up suspecting that I had been in a very serious car accident; then I looked across at Teddy and was convinced we had been. But I forgot that the drooling, sweating, and disturbing noises were all part of the Teddy package. You get one, you get them all. It took me twenty minutes to wake him up so that he could help me out of bed. It took me a further twenty minutes to get out of bed. My joints were on strike. They were all just lazily lounging around with their little pickets pitched up screaming, "Joints on strike, joints on strike!" The hips were the leaders of this conspiracy.

So I rang my boss and held the phone to my hips so he could hear them too. He agreed with me and let me have the morning off. (Well he claims *now* that he *didn't* but I'm sticking to my side of the story.)

Childbirth is *nothing* compared to exercise, and Gary was a *big* baby. This is what they should do to prisoners of war when they're trying to interrogate them. Make them take salsa classes. I knew I was

unfit but my god, driving the mini today was hor-
rendous. Every time I changed gears I felt like someone was hammering away at my arm. First
gear—sore, second gear—pain, third gear—torture.
I ended up driving to work in second gear because
it hurt so much. Not safe or healthy for the car at
all but she managed to cough and splutter her way
into work just like her owner.

By the way I was walking you would swear Teddy
and I *had* worked our way through the Kama Sutra
book. Even typing was a traumatic experience as I
suddenly realized that my finger bone is connected
to my arm bone which in some way was pulling on
my hamstring which was giving me a headache. I
should have known I would be this bad. When you
dropped me off last night I was so stiff I practically
had to crawl in the hall door where my ears were
greeted by Teddy and Gary having a mutual grunt-
ing session in the living room. I've learned it's their
odd little method of communication.

I'm thinking of sending Gary to electrocution . . .
sorry, elocution lessons so he can brush up on his
"how now brown cows," instead of his "hugh,
nugh, brugh, cughs." I mentioned it to him last
night and he just grunted, "Why do I want to know
about wiring houses, Ma?"

So I left my wonderfully intelligent family and
soaked myself in the bath and considered drowning
myself. Then I remembered I still had chocolate
cake left over from yesterday so I came back up for
air. Some things are worth living for.

But thank you for the gift, Rosie; we had fun in the
class, didn't we? I can't remember ever laughing so
much in my life, which on second thought is proba-

bly why my stomach is so sore. Thank you for reminding me that I'm a woman, that I have hips, that
I can be sexy, that I can laugh and have fun.

And thank you for bringing the sexy Ricardo into
my life. Can't wait to feel this way again next week.
Now after all my whingeing and moaning, how do
you feel?

Rosie: Oh fine, thanks. No complaints.

Ruby: Ha!

Rosie: OK, OK so I feel a little stiff.

Ruby: Ha!

Rosie: Oh OK so the bus had to lower the wheelchair ramp
for me this morning because I couldn't lift my leg.

Ruby: That's more like it.

Rosie: Oh the beautiful Ricardo, Ruby!! I had a dream
about him last night. I woke up with my top off and
my pillow covered in drool. (OK so, *not really*.) The
sound of that sexy Italian accent shouting, "Ros-ie!!
Pay atten-see-on!" and, "Ros-ie! Stup laff-ing!!"
and "Ros-ie!! Get up ov ze floor!" just sends a
shiver up my spine. But it was the sound of "Vell
done Rosie, *fantabulous* hip action!" that really got
me . . . mmm . . . yummy Ricardo with the hips . . .

Ruby: Yes! The hips! Although as I recall, it was *me* he
was referring to about the "*fantabulous* hip action."

Rosie: Oh Ruby, can't a girl *dream*! I was surprised to see
so many men there, were you?

Ruby: Yes! It reminded me of when I was younger at the
school discos or the ceilis; I was always one of those
girls, stuck dancing with another girl as a partner.
There were more men dancing with men last night
than there were women with women.

Rosie: Yes I know, somehow I get the feeling that was due
to personal choice. Although they took the wearing
high heels a little too seriously don't you think?

Could you imagine Greg and Teddy coming with us to a class?

Ruby: Oh that would be a sight for sore eyes! Teddy can't wrap his arms around himself, never mind hug me. By the time he would get around to doing a twirl, it would be next year.

Rosie: Ha! Yeah and Greg would probably become so obsessed with Ricardo counting the steps aloud that he would begin to calculate them in his mind, add them, multiply them, subtract the first count from the square root of the sixth or something. Greg, the bank manager and his love affair with numbers. It looks like it's just you and me Ruby.

Ruby: Looks like it . . . So what's Alex up to these days?

Rosie: He's still hanging around slutty Bethany's dad trying to get a job chopping people's bodies up.

Ruby: Oh . . . kay . . . who is Bethany, why is she a slut, and what business is her father in?

Rosie: Oh sorry, Bethany is Alex's childhood sweetheart and first love, she's a slut because I say so, and her dad is a surgeon of some sort.

Ruby: Oh how exciting . . . the return of one of Alex's ex-girlfriends . . . this will be a page turner . . .

Rosie: No she's not around anymore; Alex is just attending some lectures being held by her father.

Ruby: Oh Rosie Dunne, expect the unexpected for once. Maybe this time you won't get such a shock when things don't go your way.

—m—

ARIES

The heady combination of Uranus in Aries along with your ruler Jupiter opposing Venus and the sun squaring Pluto means, well, complications.

The new moon brings some light relief—but with a strange twist of fate.

IRISH SURGEON TO JOIN WILLIAMS
by Cliona Taylor

Irish surgeon Reginald Williams, who recently achieved success with his much publicized new cardiac surgery, today announced he would be welcoming fellow Irishman Dr. Alex Stewart to the award-winning team. The 30-year-old Harvard graduate says, "I have always followed Dr. Williams's studies with great interest and admiration." He also says he is "both delighted and honored to become a new member of this ground-breaking and, most important, life-saving new surgery." Dr. Stewart is originally from Dublin, and moved to Boston at age 17 when his father accepted a post with the prominent U.S. law firm Charles & Charles.

Dr. Stewart completed five years residency in Boston Central Hospital for a general surgical residency training program before joining with Dr. Williams for further cardiac surgery studies. Pictured above (from left to right) is Dr. Reginald Williams with his wife Miranda and his daughter Bethany, who accompanied Dr. Stewart to the Reginald Williams Foundation for Heart Disease charity ball last night.

See page 4 of the Health supplement for Wayne Gillespie's report on this new cardiac surgery.

You have an instant message from: ROSIE

Rosie: Hey Ruby, you'll never guess what I just read in the newspaper this morning.

Ruby: Your star sign.

Rosie: Oh please! Give me a bit of credit; do you think I read those things *every day?*

Ruby: I know you read them every day. It helps you decide whether to be in a good mood or bad mood. I can't quite figure mine out today. It says: Take the fullest possible advantage of lively financial conditions to seize the initiative at the end of the month. Mars has moved into your sign and you should be feeling full of energy. New exciting experiences forecast.

I have never been so broke, exhausted, and bored in all of my life. So that's all a load of crap. I'm really looking forward to our next dance lesson though. Can't believe we're going to be finished this week! Soon we'll be moving into intermediate class, can you believe it? The weeks have just flown by, far too fast. I know I'm getting old when I hear myself say that. Anyway what was in the papers if it wasn't your star sign?

Rosie: Read page 3 of The Times.

Ruby: Oh God, do I have to? They always speak
        gobbledy-gook language in that paper.

Rosie: OK then don't read the article just read the headline
        and look at the photo.

Ruby: OK on page three, scanning down through articles
        as I type this . . . oh my lord, look at that. I take it
        that's slutty Bethany?

Rosie: Should you even have to ask?

Ruby: Sorry love but she looks like a normal filthy rich
        well-dressed 30-year-old woman to me . . . but I'll
        call her slutty Bethany if you insist.

Rosie: Humor me.

Ruby: OK . . . oh look Rosie, it's "slutty Bethany" in the
        paper with Alex. On page three. Looking . . .
        em . . . slutty.

Rosie: So I see. Anyway she's 32 . . . My star sign said
        that—

Ruby: A-ha! I told y—

Rosie: Oh shut up with the "I told you so's" and listen.
        My star sign said that I would feel light relief but
        with a strange twist of fate.

Ruby: And . . . ? Mine tells me I'm rich, so what?

Rosie: Well I'm delighted that Alex has finally got the job
        of his dreams that he has wanted for so many years,
        but it's just ironic that it was her he had to meet to
        get it.

Ruby: I told you to expect the unexpected Rosie, *and* to
        stop paying attention to those horoscopes . . .
        they're a load of crap.

FROM: Rosie
TO: Alex
SUBJECT: Congratulations!

Heard about your good news. You've made it into every newspaper over here today (I've kept all the press cuttings for you), and I heard you speaking on the radio this morning. I'm not quite sure exactly what you were talking about, but you sounded like you've got a cold. So you can practically bring people back from the dead but you can't get rid of the sniffles.

How's Josh? I rang your mother the other day and he was over with her for the weekend. She put Josh on the phone and I can't believe I could actually have a conversation with him! He's a very intelligent four-year-old just like his dad was, absolutely nothing like his mum. He was telling me all about the animals he had seen at the zoo and proceeded to make the noise of every single one of them. I suggested to your mother that she work on the gorilla sound with him as he wasn't saying anything, but she informed me that the gorilla is so depressed he just sits in his cage and doesn't make a sound. So Josh is an impressionist too as well as a clever clogs.

I would love to see him again sometime; I would love to see you. We need to catch up on each other's lives. Tell me something about yourself that the papers, television, and radio can't tell me.

Dear Alex,
Rosie here again. I'm not quite sure if you got my e-mail a few weeks ago. I just was congratulating you on your fantastic news. We're all so proud of you over here; Mum, Dad, Steph, Kev, Katie, and Toby are all cheering for you. I think Toby wants to be a doctor when he's older, just like you because he'll get to be on the radio and have his photograph in the newspaper. (Plus he revealed he wanted to rip people's hearts out like they do in some movie, I was deeply disturbed by that thought.) Katie is now insisting she wants to be a dance club DJ. You've had no effect on her in

that department whatsoever; she wants to go into the
business of *giving* people heart attacks.

I'm still at the Two Lakes Hotel. Still at reception; still
providing the big bad public with a glass roof over their
heads. My boss has headed over to the U.S. where he has
opened up yet another new hotel so I don't think either of
the Lake brothers will be here for a very long time. In their
stead they have arranged a series of very sad team-forming
experts to come in and teach us how to be at one with one
another. Next week the team leader, Simon, is taking us out
canoeing so we can communicate outside of a work
environment. We're supposed to learn how to discuss our
problems.

How can I tell Tania from reception that the reason I
don't talk to her is because I can't listen to her unnaturally
high-pitched voice, that I hate the way she says "What do
you think?" at the end of every sentence, the way she wears
perfume that is far too strong for a small office, the way she
wears pink lipstick that sticks to her teeth that does not, will
not, and *never will* look good with her hair color. Steven's
morning breath smells of dirty nappies; I love it when he
goes on his first coffee break because that means he comes
back almost smelling of roses in comparison. Geoffrey has a
serious underarm odor problem; Fiona has a serious
problem with flatulence—I don't know *what* she's eating.
Tabitha nods all throughout my sentences when I'm
speaking to her, says "Right" after practically every single
word, and even more annoyingly tries to finish my sentences
for me, or join in with my last few words. The really
annoying thing is that she always gets it wrong. She never
fully catches the gist of what I'm saying, so I have to keep
repeating the sentence while she keeps trying to guess what
my last words will be. One of these days I'll just say "I'm a
tramp" as my last words and she'll have to say that. Henry
wears white socks and black shoes, Grace hums the same

Spice Girls song every single day which drives me demented
but I always end up singing it to myself when I get home
which causes Katie to despise her old-fashioned "way-
behind" mother who has no idea of the chart positions of
this decade.

They all drive me bloody mad. In fact maybe this
canoeing thing is a good idea after all; I can just drown the
lot of them. Alex, write back and let me know what's going
on in your life.

      Love,
      Rosie

FROM: Alex
TO: Rosie
SUBJECT: New job

Sorry I've been so distant recently, but I've been so busy.
Still, it's no excuse for not being in touch. You pretty much
no all my work news I suppose so there's no need to go into
that. Mum and Dad are both well, they're still framing every
single photo you send them of you and Katie. The place is
beginning to look like some kind of shrine to you two
Dunne girls.

I have good news! I'll be coming back to Ireland to visit
next month, Mum and Dad are coming back too, and Sally
has agreed to let me take Josh for the fortnight seeing as she
had him last Christmas. It's been a long time since the entire
family has been back together and Mum decided she wanted
to be with Phil, his forty kids and the rest of the family and
all her friends, for their fortieth wedding anniversary.

Forty years, imagine. I barely made it to five; I don't no
how they did it. You're doing well though, how long have
you and what's-his-name been together? Long enough I
would imagine.

I can't remember how long it's been since I spent Christmas in Dublin. Long enough, once again. But soon enough Prince Moonbeam and Princess Buttercup shall be reunited.

FROM: Rosie
TO: Alex
SUBJECT: Your visit

That's great news! I'm delighted you're coming home. Would you like to stay over at my house or have you and your parents made other plans?

FROM: Alex
TO: Rosie
SUBJECT: My visit

No, no, I don't want to put what's-his-name out. Actually, there's no need for me to be so polite; I hate your husband. So Josh and I are staying with Phil and Maggie and I've booked Mum and Dad into a hotel. Thanks for the offer, though.

FROM: Rosie
TO: Alex
SUBJECT: G. R. E. G.

Hmm . . . Alex you're going to have to learn my husband's name before you come over. It's Greg. G. R. E. G. Try and remember it please.

Did I tell you that Ruby and I are salsa dancing queens? I got the first batch of classes as a present for Ruby's 40th a few months ago and we enjoyed it so much we kept it up. In fact Ruby has surprised me with her talents but I'm secretly sick and tired of having to be the man all the time.

Greg refuses to come to the classes with me but he doesn't mind being taught in our bedroom when Katie is out, our bedroom door bolted, a chair pushed up against it, the blinds down and the curtains drawn. Even the TV must be off just in case an actor or presenter happens to have the magical powers of seeing into people's houses. Well the whole point is for us to do something fun together but seeing as I'm always the man in class it's hard for me to be the woman at home (and I've *never* been any good at being the woman at home). Then we end up stepping on each other's toes, kicking each other's shins, getting really frustrated with each other, having a screaming match about whose foot was where, whose foot should have been where but wasn't, and then storm out on each other.

I blame Ruby for wanting to be the woman all the time. It's got something to do with her always being the boy at ceilis and school discos. She thinks I should be a man and take it on the chin, I told her I am *always* the man and week after week take it on the shin. She thinks I'm joking. I'm *really* not. She's surprisingly good at it though. She's started taking classes on Mondays too which means that every Wednesday when we both attend our class Ruby knows the dances a little better, knows the other students a little better, and the dance instructor a whole lot better. And nobody likes a teacher's pet. I just can't attend class twice a week because I have to bring Katie to basketball on Monday evenings, there's no way I would let her get that bus alone. And even if she could go alone, I couldn't afford two classes a week. The duties of motherhood call, and all that.

Ruby does insist that it's not as much fun without me, because she has to dance with tutu-wearing Miss Behave, a six-foot-tall drag queen with the longest legs and blond hair who's trying to learn salsa for her show on down at the local gay club.

Anyway, Ruby and I are really enjoying ourselves, and I find myself looking forward to the next class the minute it finishes. Ruby's delighted because she's losing a bit of weight (she's losing pebbles apparently, not stones). It's nice to find a hobby, something that excites you and makes you *look forward* to the week ahead instead of constantly dreading days. I hope you're having some sort of life, Alex, and that you're not overworking yourself. Go on any dates recently?

FROM: Alex
TO: Rosie
SUBJECT: Dating?

I might have . . .

You have an instant message from: ROSIE

Rosie: I'm all ears now. Anyone I know?
Alex: Then again I might not have . . .
Rosie: Stop it! Who's the unlucky girl? Do I know her?
Alex: Maybe . . .
Rosie: Oh please tell me it's anyone but slutty Bethany.
Alex: Well I better rush off because I have to get ready for tonight. Take care, Buttercup.
Rosie: You got a date?
Alex: Maybe . . . then again . . .
Rosie: Yeah, yeah I get it, maybe not . . . Well whatever you're doing enjoy it. But not too much.
Alex: I wouldn't dare dream of it!

You have an instant message from: ROSIE

Rosie: Was just instant messaging Alex a few seconds ago.
Ruby: Yeah? That's very interesting, Rosie.
Rosie: Yep.
Ruby: Well? Did he say anything interesting?
Rosie: No. We were just catching up on old times, you
          know how it is.
Ruby: Good for you both. You and Greg have any plans
          for tonight, then?
Rosie: He's going on a date, Ruby.
Ruby: Who is? Greg is?
Rosie: No! Alex.
Ruby: Oh are we still talking about him? Who's he going
          out with?
Rosie: I don't know. He wouldn't tell me.
Ruby: Well he's allowed to have a private life isn't he?
Rosie: Yeah, I suppose.
Ruby: And it's good that he's able to finally move on after
          having his heart broken and going through a di-
          vorce, isn't it?
Rosie: Yeah, I suppose.
Ruby: Well it's good that you feel that way. You're a
          great friend, Rosie, always wanting the best for
          Alex.
Rosie: Yeah. Yeah, I am.

You have an instant message from: ALEX

Alex: Hi Phil.
Phil: Hi Alex.
Alex: What are you doing?
Phil: Surfing the Internet, searching for a crank hole cover
          for a 1939 Dodge Sedan. It's a rare car. A real
          beauty. Just ordered front bumper bar extensions for
          the 1955 Chevrolet Sedan. It's being shipped in.

Alex: Right.

Phil: Something on your mind, Alex?

Alex: No, no.

Phil: Well then did you message me for any particular reason?

Alex: No, no. Just seeing how you are. Wanted to catch up with my big brother.

Phil: Right. How's the job?

Alex: I'm going on a date tonight.

Phil: Really? That's good.

Alex: Yeah it is.

Phil: Good to see you moving on.

Alex: Yeah.

Phil: Finding happiness again.

Alex: Yeah.

Phil: Meeting someone new will stop you from working so bloody much.

Alex: Yeah.

Phil: Does Rosie know?

Alex: Yeah. Just was chatting to her there by instant message before I messaged you.

Phil: How's that for a coincidence? Well, what was her reaction?

Alex: Not much of one actually.

Phil: She wasn't angry?

Alex: No.

Phil: Or jealous?

Alex: No.

Phil: She didn't beg you not to date other women?

Alex: Nope.

Phil: That's good then isn't it? You've got a good friend there. One that wants you to move on, meet new people, and find happiness.

Alex: Yeah. That's good. Good to have a friend like that.

ARIES

You're still heavily under the influence of Neptune, the planet
that brings you your romantic dreams . . .

You have an instant message from: ROSIE

Rosie: You're right Ruby, star signs are a load of crap.
Ruby: Thattagirl.

CHAPTER 29

To Rosie, Katie, and Greg

You are invited to my 7th birthday praty on November 18th. I am haveing a magicman. He can make aminals out of balloons. He will give you a aminal for keeps.

My party starts at 11 in the morning and there will be lots of candy and then you can go home with your moms and dads.

Thanks.

     Love,

     Josh

You have an instant message from: KATIE

Katie: I look like a goofball.

Toby: You do not look like a goofball.

Katie: Yes I do.

Toby: No you don't.

Katie: You don't even know what a goofball looks like.

Toby: What does it look like then?

Katie: Me.

Toby: It doesn't.

Katie: How would you know? I look like some sort of fu-
turistic human race that got messed up with robots.

Toby: You don't.

Katie: Oh my god why is everyone staring at me?

Toby: Katie, we're sitting in the back row of the class-
room, everybody in the entire room has their backs
to us. They are NOT staring at you.

Katie: Whatever. I can feel their eyes on me.

Toby: Everyone's eyes are on their computers. You're just
being paranoid.

Katie: No I'm not.

Toby: Yes you are. Unless they've got eyes on the back of
their heads.

Katie: My mum does.

Toby: Look, they're only braces Katie. It's not the end of
the world. Anyway, I know how you feel. When I got
my glasses I felt like everyone was staring at me too.

Katie: That's because they were.

Toby: Oh. Could you do me a favor?

Katie: What.

Toby: Just say sizzling sausages one more time.

Katie: TOBY! That is so not funny. You said you wouldn't
laugh. I'm gonna be stuck with these stupid train
tracks for years now, and it's not my fault they're
giving me a lisp. I'll even have them for my birthday
photos next week.

Toby: Big deal.

Katie: It's my 13th birthday. I don't wanna remember myself in photographs when I'm older as being the one
with the gigantic two lumps of metal jammed in
my mouth. Plus *everyone's* coming to the party,
people I haven't seen for absolute yonks and I want
to look nice.

Toby: Let me guess, you'll be trying to look nice in black
again.

Katie: Yep.

Toby: You're so morbid.

Katie: No Toby, I'm sophisticated—the black suits my hair.
        It says so in my magazines. But you can wear your
        ratty tatty shorts and T-shirt if you like. No point in
        changing the habit of a lifetime.

Toby: That's what *my* magazines tell me to do.

Katie: No, I *no* what your filthy magazines tell you to do
        and it's not anything to do with dressing. More like
        undressing.

Toby: So I'm invited anyway.

Katie: Maybe, then again . . . maybe not.

Toby: Katie, I'm going whether you invite me or not. I'm
        not missing your 13th birthday just because you're
        in one of your moods. I just want to see your birth-
        day cake getting all caught up in your braces, ooz-
        ing out through the cracks in your teeth, and then
        hitting people on their faces when you speak.

Katie: Whatever. I'll make sure I speak to you the most then.

Toby: Who's going anyway?

Katie: Alex, Aunt Steph, Pierre and Jean-Louis, Grandma
        and Granddad, Ruby, Teddy and her weirdo son
        that never speaks, Mum of course and a few girls
        from basketball.

Toby: Well yippee. What about your uncle Kevin?

Katie: Does he ever come to anything? He's still working in
        that posh hotel down in Kilkenny. He said he's sorry
        he couldn't come but he sent me a card with a ten-
        ner inside.

Toby: Well that's all you want anyway. What about Greg?

Katie: Nope he's working in the States for a week. He gave
        me 13 euro. A euro for every year.

Toby: Cool you're gonna be rich. Just as well he's work-
        ing, I hate when him and Alex are in the same room.
        It freaks me out.

Katie: I no. It's even worse when Mum's in the room be-

cause she just spends the entire time running from
one to the other like she's a boxing match referee.

Toby: Alex would kick Greg's ass if they were in a boxing
match.

Katie: Definitely. Mum would kick both their asses if they
even dared.

Toby: So is there anyone under the age of 80 coming that's
not on your crappy basketball team.

Katie: Alex is bringing Josh.

Toby: Josh is seven years old Katie.

Katie: Exactly, you'll have lots in common. Same brain
power.

Toby: Oh ha ha metal mouth. Do you think you'll have
any "sizzling cocktail sausages" at your party?

Katie: You're hilarious Toby. Well I suppose my situation
could be a million times worse.

Toby: How?

Katie: I could be stuck wearing glasses for the rest of my
life like you

Toby: Hardy har har. I was just thinking, you might not be
able to leave the country for the next few years.

Katie: Why?

Toby: Because of the metal detectors at the airports. You
could be a real danger to the public. They could be
turned into deadly weapons.

Katie: Whatever.

You have an instant message from: ROSIE

Rosie: My baby is going to be a teenager next week.

Ruby: Thank your lucky stars it's almost over now
sweetie.

Rosie: Almost over? Isn't it just beginning? And if I had
any lucky stars they would be well and truly sacked

by now. What's so great about my beautiful baby growing up and become spotty and bitchy while I decay right in front of my very own eyes? The older my child gets, the older I become.

Ruby: Clever discovery there Rosie.

Rosie: But that's not allowed to happen. Because I haven't even started my own life yet, never mind bringing another one into this world and helping her through her own. I haven't actually done anything of substance yet.

Ruby: Some may argue that creating life is of substance. Anything I should bring to the party?

Rosie: Just yourself.

Ruby: Damn it, anything else instead?

Rosie: You're coming whether you like it or not.

Ruby: Oh alright then. At least Greg won't be there wrapping a leash around your neck to hold you back from Alex.

Rosie: Yeah I just might be able to hump Alex's leg in peace this time.

Ruby: Here's hoping. So what do I get for the teenage girl who wants everything?

Rosie: Straight teeth, magic spot removal cream, Colin Farrell, and an organized mother.

Ruby: Ah, now the organized mother bit I can help out with.

Rosie: Thanks Ruby.

FROM: Alex
TO: Rosie
SUBJECT: Flight Details

My flight is landing at 2:15 p.m. tomorrow. Really looking forward to meeting up with you and Katie again. Will what's-his-name be there to greet me too?

FROM: Rosie
TO: Alex
SUBJECT: my HUSBAND

His name, my *husband's* name, is Greg. GREG. Get it?
And no, he will not be there to collect you because he is
away on business. He's in the States so you two have luckily
swapped countries for the next few days. Let's hope that will
be far apart enough for the both of you.

TO MY WONDERFUL DAUGHTER,
YOU'RE A TEENAGER!
HAPPY BIRTHDAY DARLING,
LOTS OF LOVE,
MUM

TO KATIE,
YOU'RE A TEEN TODAY,
HIP HIP HIP HOORAY!
IT'S A JOYOUS DAY,
YOU'RE A TEEN TODAY!
GREG

YOU'RE A GROOVY CHICK!!
HAPPY BIRTHDAY PET,
LOVE YOU LOTS LIKE JELLY TOTS!
LOVE GRANDMA AND GRANDAD

HAPPY BIRTHDAY GLITTER GIRL,
TAKE THIS MONEY AND BUY YOURSELF AN ITEM OF
CLOTHING THAT'S NOT BLACK. I DARE YOU.
LOVE RUBY, TEDDY, AND GARY (GRUDGINGLY)

FROM: Katie
TO: Rosie
SUBJECT: Re: Grudgingly

In Ruby's birthday card, she has signed it—Love Ruby,
Teddy, and Gary (grudgingly). What does grudgingly mean?

FROM: Rosie
TO: Katie
SUBJECT: Grudgingly

She wrote that? Honestly, I sometimes think she's lost the
plot completely. It means that Gary was only too delighted
to wish you a happy birthday. That's what it means. Now
stop e-mailing me or I'll be fired.

FOR MY NIECE,
HAPPY 13TH BEAUTIFUL!
BON ANNIVERSAIRE!
LOVE STEPHANIE, PIERRE, & JEAN-LOUIS

TO MY GODDAUGHTER,
HAPPY 13TH YOU LITTLE ADULT!
I'M SO HAPPY TO SHARE THE DAY WITH YOU,
ALL MY LOVE,
ALEX

YOU MAY BE A TEENAGER BUT YOU'RE STILL UGLY.
FROM TOBY

FROM: Kevin
TO: Rosie
SUBJECT: Secret visit!

Kevin here. I can't get through to your phone so I

thought I'd send you an e-mail seeing as that seems to be all you do every day.

Sorry I couldn't be home for Katie's birthday, but it's absolutely crazy here at work. The golf open is being held here this week and all the world's greatest golfers and their dogs and goldfish have booked in. I've been rushed off my feet but they'll thankfully be gone by the weekend. I seem to keep missing the family do's. (Or family don'ts)

Anyway the reason I'm e-mailing you is because I can't believe you kept it a secret from me that you were coming down here for the weekend! Don't even ask what I was doing checking the reservations but it seems that you have the honeymoon suite booked out for the weekend!

Good ol' Greg's a bit flash paying for all that isn't he? Anyway I'm glad you're finally coming down to see me. It's about time. Don't think I've seen you since Christmas. I'll make sure all the staff treats you extra-specially and I'll even tell the lads in the kitchen not to spit into your food as an extra treat.

FROM: Rosie
TO: Kevin
SUBJECT: Re: Secret visit!

Sorry my baby brother but it must be another Rosie Dunne. I wish it *was* me!

FROM: Kevin
TO: Rosie
SUBJECT: Re: Secret Visit

There's only one Rosie Dunne! No, the booking is actually under Greg's name. Shit! I hope I haven't spoiled a surprise. FORGET I said anything. Sorry.

FROM: Rosie
TO: Kevin
SUBJECT: Re: Secret visit!

Don't worry Kev—what day is the booking for?

FROM: Kevin
TO: Rosie
SUBJECT: Re: Secret visit!

Friday until Monday. Oh please don't tell him I told you.
It was stupid of me to say anything. I should have used my
head first. I really shouldn't have been looking at the
reservations anyway. What an idiot Greg is, he should have
known I work here.

FROM: Rosie
TO: Kevin
SUBJECT: Re: Secret visit!

And in order for him to know where you work you two
would need to have a conversation with each other once in
a while. Don't worry! Greg's away in the States for the
week so I'll be able to hide my excitement from him! I
better go shopping for a few outfits, that hotel of yours is
very classy!

FROM: Kevin
TO: Rosie
SUBJECT: Re: Secret visit!

Enjoy it and I'll see you at the weekend. I'll have a look
of pretend shock on my face.

Ruby: I have to admit that I'm shocked. That's very ro-
        mantic of him!

Rosie: I know! I'm so excited Ruby. I've dreamed of stay-
        ing in that hotel for years. Oh I bet the little sham-
        poos and shower caps in the bathrooms are just the
        most beautiful things.

Ruby: Christ Rosie, you could open your own shop with
        the amount of hotel products you've stolen.

Rosie: It's not *stealing*. They're not just there to be *looked*
        at. Although, they do seem to be nailing down the
        hair dryers a lot more these days.

Ruby: Just as well you're not strong enough to drag the
        beds out of the rooms.

Rosie: Now that would be too risky. They'd see me at
        reception. Although the bedsheets I got from the
        last hotel I stayed in for my birthday are by far my
        favorite.

Ruby: Rosie, you have a problem. Swiftly moving on,
        when are you being whisked away to the lap of
        luxury?

Rosie: Friday. I can't wait! I completely maxed out my
        credit card buying a few outfits for the weekend.
        I'm so pleased that he's made this effort. Things
        with me and Greg have reached an all-time high
        the last while, it's like we're back at our honey-
        moon stage. I am really, really happy.

from: Rosie
TO: Greg
SUBJECT: Coming home?

It's Friday and I was just wondering what time you'll be
home? You must be on the plane because your phone's going
straight to answer machine. Maybe you can reply via your
laptop from the clouds!

FROM: Greg
TO: Rosie
SUBJECT: Re: Coming home?

Hi love. I told you I'd be here in the States until Monday.
I should be home in the evening sometime. Can I call you
from the airport for a lift? Sorry if there was some
confusion. I'm sure I told you it was Monday and not
Friday. I wish it was today darling, I really do.

How's Katie after her first wild teenage party? I haven't
heard from her. I thought she might have thanked me for the
present by now.

FROM: Rosie
TO: Kevin
SUBJECT: *This* weekend?

Do you think you could be mistaken about that booking
for *this* weekend?

FROM: Kevin
TO: Rosie
SUBJECT: Re: *This* weekend?

It's definitely correct Rosie. Greg checked in this
morning. Aren't you here?

FROM: Katie
TO: Greg
SUBJECT: My present

Hope you are having a good time in America and that
you're not working too hard. I grudgingly thank you for my
birthday present. You will be pleased to know I bought a
black sweater with the money. See you when you get home.

CHAPTER 30

—∞—

FROM: Rosie
TO: Alex
SUBJECT: What's-his-name

What's-his-name is gone. For good.

FROM: Alex
TO: Rosie
SUBJECT: Re: What's-his-name

I'll book flights for you and Katie to come over here immediately. I'll let you know the details within the next hour. Don't worry.

FROM: Rosie
TO: Alex
SUBJECT: Please wait

Just give me a little time before you book those flights. There are a few things I want to tie up here before I leave.

And once I go over to you in Boston I'm *never* coming back here. Just please wait for me.

Hi, it's me, Alex.

Look I'm really sorry but I'm not going to be able to make it out for dinner tonight. I'm sorry to tell you in a letter but it's the best way I no how. You're a wonderful, intelligent woman but my heart lies with someone else. It has done so for many, many years. I hope that when we meet we can remain friends at least.

   Take care,
   Alex

CHAPTER 31

Dear Bill Lake,

It is with great sadness that I submit my resignation. I will remain working in the Two Lakes Hotel for the next two weeks as I'm contracted to do so.

On a more personal level, I would like to thank you for seven great years of allowing me to work in your company. It was an honor.

> Yours sincerely,
> Rosie Dunne

FROM: Toby
TO: Katie
SUBJECT: Disaster!

YOU WHAT?? You CAN'T be moving away, this is awful! Ask your mum if it's OK for you to stay with me for a while. I'll ask my mum and dad too. They'll definitely say yes. You can't leave.

What about school?

What about the basketball team?

What about wanting to DJ for Club Sauce?

What about your grandparents? You can't just leave them. They're old.

What about your mum's job and the house and everything? You can't just leave it all behind.

What about me?

FROM: Katie
TO: Toby
SUBJECT: Re: Disaster!

I can't change her mind. I can't stop crying. This is the worst thing that's ever happened to me in my whole entire life. I don't even want to go to Boston. What's so good about Boston? I don't wanna make new friends. I don't want anything "new."

Oh I hate Greg so much. You no he hasn't even come home because he's so afraid of Mum. She's scary she's so mad. I'm even afraid to talk to her sometimes. She screams down the phone at him like a crazy woman. No wonder he's not coming home. She said that if he did, she'd cut off his • you no what. I'm kinda hoping he'll come home just for that.

It's all his fault. It's all his fault we have to move away. It's all his fault Mum is upset. I hate him, I hate him, I hate him.

At least Alex and Josh are in Boston. That's something. I think we're gonna stay with them for a while. So we're really going Toby. She's not just threatening. She told Greg she couldn't stand to be in the same country as him never mind the same house. I suppose I no how she feels. I feel sorry for her but I really don't want to go. I just cried all night Toby. It's so unfair.

Grandma and Granddad keep trying to talk her out of it. We're staying with them tonight because Mum can't stand to be at home. Every time she touches something of Greg's she shudders and wipes her hands. Ruby keeps telling Mum to go because it's where her heart is or something. It's the first time I've ever seen Ruby cry. I didn't think she knew how to. Mum's cries down the phone to Stephanie for hours every day. Last night I could hear her throwing up in the toilet for ages so I got up and made her a cup of tea. She stopped for a while. She slept in my bed last night. It's only a single bed and we were kind of squashed but it was sort of nice. She squeezed me like I was a teddy.

Mum has started packing her bags now. She's gonna help me do mine in a while. She says she's sorry about moving me to Boston and I believe her. I don't blame her because she's so sad. It's Greg's fault but I haven't really seen him do much to make her feel better.

Mum said you can visit us all the time. Promise me you will. You may annoy the hell out of me Toby, but you're my best friend in the whole entire world and I'll miss you so much. Even if you are a boy.

We can write to each other all the time. That's what Mum and Alex did when they were younger and he had to move away.

> Love,
> Katie

You have an instant message from: RUBY

Ruby: So you're leaving in two weeks.

Rosie: Yep.

Ruby: You're doing the right thing you know.

Rosie: Funny. You're the only one who seems to think that.

Ruby: I'm the only one who knows how you feel about him.

Rosie: Oh no, I'm not in the mood to go jumping into another relationship right now. I don't have the energy. At the moment my heart feels like it's been
ripped out of my chest and tap-danced on. I hate all
men right now.

Ruby: Including Alex?

Rosie: Right now including Alex, my father, George
        the lollipop man, and my brother for telling me.

Ruby: You would have wanted to know though.

Rosie: I know and I'm not blaming him. He hadn't a clue
        Greg was messing around. Again. The lying
        little . . . aaaah! I just feel like punching the shit out
        of him. I don't think I've ever been so angry in my
        life. The first time he did this I was hurt, now I am
        just plain pissed off. I can't wait to get out of this
        country. I'm glad Kevin told me because I will be
        the fool no longer.

Ruby: I heard Kevin's in trouble at work. Is it for checking
        the reservations?

Rosie: No it's for marching through the hotel restaurant
        during dinner and punching Greg in the nose in
        front of his lady friend and the rest of the hotel
        guests.

Ruby: Good for him. I hope he broke his nose.

Rosie: He did. That's what he's in trouble for.

Ruby: So who am I going to go to salsa lessons with
        now?

Rosie: I'm sure Miss Behave will be only too delighted to
        be your partner.

Ruby: I finally get to dance with a man and he wears
        tights. Oh I'll miss you so much Rosie Dunne.
        It's not often in life a woman finds a friend
        like you.

Rosie: And I you, Ruby, but as much as Greg has hurt me,
        he's given me an opportunity to start from fresh. I'll
        be free of him and I'm stronger from it.

I'm leaving next week Greg. Don't try to contact me,
don't try to visit me, I want nothing more to do with you.
You have betrayed me at a time just as I had learned to fall

in love with you all over again. This won't be happening again. You have thrown it all away but I thank you for it. Thank you for letting me see what it is I married and for freeing me from you.

Whether Katie wants to continue seeing you is completely her decision. You can work it out with her yourself. Accept her decision.

So long, shithead.

Alex: You were right Phil. She's coming over to me. I just had to leave it and let her come at her own pace.

Phil: Lucky for me I was right! It was a good guess, wasn't it?! So did she tell you that she loves you, that she never should have married that idiot, and that she only wants to be with you and all that other stuff that they say in the movies?

Alex: No.

Phil: She didn't tell you she loves you?

Alex: No.

Phil: Did you tell her?

Alex: No.

Phil: Then what's she going over for?

Alex: She just said that she wanted to get out of Dublin and that she needed a change of scenery and a friendly face.

Phil: Oh.

Alex: What do you think that means?

Phil: Probably exactly what it says, so you've no idea how she feels about you?

Alex: No. Phil, her marriage has just ended, there's plenty of time when she comes over here to talk about our future.

Phil: Whatever you say bro. Whatever you say.

FROM: Alex
TO: Rosie
SUBJECT: You and Katie

I'm so excited that you'll be here so soon. Josh is
practically running up the walls with excitement. He loves
Katie and is delighted about your decision to come live with
us for a while. I've a friend who has a friend who owns a
hotel and as far as I no, they are looking for a manager. You
are more than qualified for the job.

I can help you through this Rosie, remember I've been in
your shoes. I no how it feels to go through a marriage
breakup. I'm here for you one hundred percent. Moving to
Boston may be thirteen years later than you planned but it's
better late than never. Josh and I will be here waiting. See
you next week.

YOU'RE MOVING AWAY!
GOOD LUCK ROSIE, WE'LL ALL MISS YOU HERE AT THE
TWO LAKES,
FROM BILL, BOB, TANIA, STEVEN, GEOFFREY, FIONA,
TABETHA, HENRY, AND GRACE

SNIFF, SNIFF
I'LL MISS YOU ROSIE DUNNE.
GOOD LUCK WITH YOUR NEW LIFE. SEND US AN E-
MAIL EVERY NOW AND AGAIN.
LOTS OF LOVE,
RUBY

YOU GO GIRL!
LOVE, MISS BEHAVE

Rosie and Katie,
We are so sorry that you feel you have to go. We are so
sorry that you have reason to go. We are so sorry this has

happened. We will miss you both so, so much but we hope
you can both find eternal happiness. No more tears for our
two girls. Let the world be good to you. Phone us when
you land.

>   Love, Mum and Dad

GOOD LUCK WITH THE MOVE. MY FINGERS ARE
CROSSED FOR YOU AND KATIE. WE'RE ALL HERE FOR
YOU IF YOU NEED US.
LOVE,
STEPHANIE, PIERRE, AND JEAN-LOUIS

SORRY YOU HAD TO GO. GOOD LUCK.
KEV

KATIE,
GOOD LUCK IN YOUR NEW HOME. I'LL MISS YOU.
LOVE,
TOBY

Dear Mum and Dad,

It's not like I'm disappearing forever, we're only a few
hours away. You can visit all the time! We love you so much
and thank you for your constant support. This time we need
to find the way by ourselves.

>   Lots of Love,
>   Rosie & Katie

—⁓—

CHAPTER 32

Dear Rosie,

Before you rip this up please just give me a chance to explain.

Firstly, I sincerely apologize from the bottom of my heart for the years gone by. For not being there for you, for not supporting you and giving you the help you deserved. I am filled with regret and disappointment with myself for the way I have behaved and chosen to live my life. I know there is nothing I can do to change or make better the years I acted so foolishly and mistreated the two of you.

But please at least give me a chance to build a better future, to make right what's wrong. I can understand how you must feel so angry, betrayed, and hurt and you must hate me so much but there's not just yourself to think of. I look back on my life and I wonder what have I to show for all these years. I haven't done many things in my life that I'm proud of. I have no stories of success to tell, I haven't made a million. There is only one thing in this life that I'm proud of.

And that's my little girl.

The fact that I have a little girl, who isn't even "little"

anymore. I'm not proud of the way I've treated her. I woke
up one morning a few weeks ago on my thirty-third
birthday and suddenly it was as if all the sense that's been
missing for the past thirty-three years came to me in an
instant. I realized I had a daughter, a teenage daughter who
I know nothing of and who knows nothing of me. I would
love the chance to get to know her. I'm told that her name is
Katie. That's a nice name. I wonder what she looks like.
Does she look like me?

I know I haven't shown any signs of deserving this, but if
you and Katie are willing to let me into your lives I can
prove to you it won't be a waste of time. Katie will meet her
father and I will see my daughter, how could that ever be
considered a waste? Please help me fulfill my dreams.

Please contact me, Rosie. Give me a chance to undo all
the mistakes of my past and to help create a new future for
Katie and me.

      Best wishes,
      Brian

Rosie: No no no no no no no no no
Ruby: I know honey, I understand. But at least just look at
      the other options.
Rosie: Options? BLOODY OPTIONS? I have none.
      NONE! I have to go. Staying here is not an *option*.
Ruby: Rosie, calm down. You're upset.
Rosie: Too right, I'm upset! How on earth am I supposed
      to try and get my life together when everyone
      around me keeps fucking it up? When is it *my turn*
      to live *my* life for *me* instead of for everyone else?
      I'm sick of it Ruby, I'm fed up. I have had enough.
      I'm bloody going. Who is this man? Where the hell
      has he been for the past thirteen years? Where did
      he disappear to for the most important years of
      Katie's life, or *my life* for that matter?

Who stayed up all night breast-feeding, pacing the halls and singing fucking lullabies so the constant screaming would stop? Who changed shitty nappies, wiped snotty noses and cleaned sick from their clothes every day? Who's got stretch marks and scars, saggy tits, and gray hairs at the age of thirty-two? Who went to parent teacher meetings, brought and collected her from school, made dinner, put food on the table, paid the rent, went to work, helped with homework, gave advice, wiped tears, explained the birds and the bees, explained why Daddy wasn't around unlike most of the other kids' daddies? Who stayed up all night and worried when she was sick, taking temperatures and buying medicine, making trips to the doctor or the hospital in the middle of the night? Who missed going to college, took days off work and stayed home at the weekend to care for her? Fucking me, that's who. Where was the bastard then?

And *he* has the cheek to stroll back into our lives after thirteen years when all the hard work has been done, with a little shrug of the shoulders and a pathetic little sorry, just after my husband cheats on me, my marriage is over, I finally decide to move to Boston where I should have been anyway had it not been for that sly little prick ruining my plans, turning my life upside down, and legging it off to another country with his dick between his legs.

Fuck him.

This time it's about me. Rosie Dunne and no one else.

Ruby: But Rosie you're wrong. It's about Katie too. She needs to know he wants to see her. Don't punish her for the mistakes in your own life.

Rosie: But if I tell her, then she's going to want to see him.
         She'll be so excited to meet him and he'll probably
         let her down again and break her heart all over
         again. And who'll be the one who cleans up the
         mess? Me. I'll be the one who tries to mend my
         daughter's broken heart, I'll have to pick up the
         pieces and wipe away the tears. Who's going to have
         to put on the happy face, shrug, and say, "Ah well,
         don't worry my thirteen-year-old daughter, not all
         men are shits—just all the ones you've ever known."

Ruby: But Rosie, it could turn out really well. He may
         have really changed. You never know.

Rosie: You're right, you *never* know. EVER. And another
         thing, how can she get to know her father when
         we're halfway across the other side of the world? I
         don't want to stay here Ruby. I want *out*. I want out
         of this entire mess of a life.

Ruby: It's not a mess Rosie. Life is far from perfect, for
         everyone. You're not the only one, there isn't a great
         big black cloud just hanging over your head and no
         one else's. It just feels that way. But it feels like that
         for a lot of people. You just have to make the most
         of what you've got and you are *lucky* because you
         have a beautiful daughter who is healthy, intelli-
         gent, and funny and who thinks the world of you.
         Don't lose sight of that. If Katie wants to get to
         know Brian then you should support her. You can
         still move away, he can come to see you—or if you
         think it's important enough to stay for, stay.

Rosie: Katie is going to want to stay.

Ruby: Well that part is your choice and your choice alone,
         you're the mother. It's only five hours away any-
         way. Airplanes were invented for fathers like Brian
         the Whine.

Rosie: Last month, I *thought* I was living in paradise. Life
         changed in an instant.

Ruby: Well that's the problem with paradise—nothing at-
        tracts a serpent quite like it.

Dear Stephanie,

Congratulations on the pregnancy! I'm thrilled for you
and Pierre, I'm sure baby number two will be a joy as Jean-
Louis has been. I'm assuming Mum has told you the news.
She's delighted I'm not moving to America anymore. Alex
isn't. He cursed and swore and screamed every bad word
under the sun at me. He thinks I'm giving in again and
letting everyone walk all over me so now he's in a huff and
won't speak to me. I may have let people walk all over me
before but not this time. Katie is number one in my life and
my reason for being is to ensure she gets the best chance at
happiness possible.

She's had to go through a lot lately, with Greg, having to
move back in with Mum and Dad and then preparing to
move again to America. She's been under a lot of stress.
Stress that she shouldn't have had to go through. She's
supposed to be worrying about spots, bras, and boys. Not
adultery, moving continents, and fathers doing magic
reappearing acts. None of this is her fault and seeing as I
brought her into this world the least I could do is continue
on with the good work I've been doing. She isn't a drug
addict, isn't rude, is doing fine in school, has all the right
limbs in all the right places, and hasn't managed to do
anything really stupid with her life. And out of all the awful
stories you hear in life I think I'm doing a great job.

I'm expecting Alex to burst through the door any minute.
I'm sure he has hopped on the first plane to get over here
and beat up Brian. I suppose that's what best friends are for.
I can't even think about what life "could have been" like in
Boston, without crying. It's like deja-vu, I don't think me
and Boston were ever meant to be. I don't quite know where
I should go from here. I have no job, no home, and I'm back
living with Mum and Dad again. As much as I'm grateful,

everything about this house brings back a time when I wasn't happy. I had a wonderful childhood but the years with Katie were so difficult, they're the strongest memories I have of this house—the smells, the noises, the wallpaper, the bedrooms all remind me of late nights, early mornings, and worrying.

Anyway forgive me for not being in contact over the past while, but I've been trying to get my head around all of this. I'm trying to make some sense out of the phrase "Everything happens for a reason," and I think I've figured out what the reason is—to piss me off.

When I started school I thought that people in sixth class were *so* old and knowledgeable even though they were no older than twelve. When I reached twelve I reckoned the people in sixth year, at eighteen years of age, must have known it *all*. When I reached eighteen I thought that once I finished college then I would really be mature. At twenty-five I still hadn't made it to college, was still clueless and had a seven-year-old daughter. I was convinced that when I reached my thirties I was going to have at least *some* clue as to what was going on.

Nope, hasn't happened yet.

So I'm beginning to think that when I'm fifty, sixty, seventy, eighty, ninety years old I still won't be any closer to being wise and knowledgeable. Perhaps people on their deathbed, who have had long, long lives, seen it all, traveled the world, have had kids, been through their own personal traumas, beaten their demons, and learned the harsh lessons of life will be thinking, "God, people in heaven must *really* know it all."

But I bet that when they finally do die they'll join the rest of the crowds up there, sit around, spying on the loved ones they left behind and *still* be thinking that in their next lifetime, they'll have it all sussed.

But I think I have it sussed Steph, I've sat around for years thinking about it and I've discovered that no one, not

even the big man upstairs has the slightest clue as to what's
going on.
        Rosie

FROM: Stephanie
TO: Rosie
SUBJECT: Re: Life

    Well isn't that one thing you're all the more wise for?
Age has taught you something. It seems to me that you
know the big secret. That *nobody* knows what's going on.

Hi,
    My sincerest apologies for that ridiculous note I sent you
last week. Just put it down to a momentary lapse in
concentration, I'm a complete fool (as you're already aware)
and I have absolutely no idea what I was thinking. But you'll
be pleased to no (I hope) that I've landed back on earth with
a thump and I'm willing and able to give us another go. So
let's not waste any more of our valuable time and let's get
down to the important stuff. Are we back on for tonight?
        Alex

CHAPTER 33

You have an instant message from: RUBY

Ruby: So you're still here then.

Rosie: Oh not today Ruby, please. I'm really not in the
mood.

Ruby: I'm getting rather tired of you Rosie Dunne. First
you say you're moving to Cork, then you don't,
then you say you're moving to Boston (again) and
then you don't. Then I expect you to finally profess
your love to Alex and you don't, so he still has absolutely no idea. I can't keep up with you and your
"leaving the country/ changing jobs/ leaving your
husband"-type activities. Sometimes I think you just
need a good kick up the behind for wasting all these
good opportunities. You're an incredibly frustrating
person Rosie.

Rosie: Well I'm an incredibly frustrated woman right now.
And I'm not "wasting" good opportunities; it's
called "presenting my daughter with new ones."

Ruby: You can put whatever name you like on it but at the
end of the day a missed opportunity is a missed

opportunity. But don't worry; I think there's a lesson to be learned in all this.

Rosie: Well please tell me there is *some* sort of reason for all this. What's the lesson?

Ruby: That you needn't bother trying anymore, because you're going nowhere. So really, how are you?

Rosie: OK.

Ruby: Are you sure? Oh come on Rosie, if my heart can't take what's happening to you then I can't imagine how you must be feeling.

Rosie: Oh my heart is broken, stopped beating two weeks ago.

Ruby: Well it's a good thing you know a man who can heal them.

Rosie: No, no, no, it's the unspoken rule. He heals other people's hearts, not mine.

Ruby: Here's an idea, Rosie. Why don't you just *tell* Alex how you feel? Why don't you just finally get all of those feelings out in the open, and clear your messed-up little head? At least then, he'll know that you're not going over *not* because you don't care about him, but that in fact you love him, more than he knows, but that you need to stay here for Katie. Then that will put the ball in his court. He can make the decision whether to come to you or not.

Rosie: But what about his job? And what about Josh?

Ruby: That's *his* decision.

Rosie: Ruby I can't. How do I tell him? Over the phone? In a letter, an e-mail, or an instant message? I can't do that. If we had moved over to Boston I could have sussed things out a little, seen how he felt about me, and then tell him. He was just out on a date last week for Christ sake, how stupid would I look telling him I love him when he's seeing someone? It'll just be the whole Sally situation all over again. It's too complicated and right now the last thing I'm worried about is which man to fall in love with next. Anyway he's not even returning my calls.

Ruby: Just give him time, he's disappointed how things worked out.

Rosie: I'm sorry, he's disappointed? *He's* disappointed? I think me and the rest of the world seem to be having a communication problem here—does everyone think that I'm *ecstatic* by these new revelations? I mean, I'm really not looking for sympathy or anything but—

Ruby: Yes you are.

Rosie: Excuse me?

Ruby: Sympathy. Looking for it. Yes you are.

Rosie: Thank you for decoding that for me. OK so maybe it would be nice if at least some people acknowledged the fact that my husband has had an affair, my marriage has ended, I'm still a million miles away from Alex and will never know how I feel about him, my child's runaway father is back in Ireland, and I HAVE NO JOB! A pat on the back, a sympathetic smile, and a bit of a cuddle would be quite nice actually. A few months spent in my bed curled up into a ball, smothered by blankets, in a room darkened by drawn curtains, dressed in a pair of big unflattering pajamas would be my idea of heaven but unfortunately I can't do that right now because I have a daughter who is hyperventilating over the fact that her father who she hasn't met for thirteen years is back in her life and I need to forget about me and be strong for her. But a bit of sympathy would be nice too.

Ruby: Breathe Rosie.

Rosie: No that's how all my problems happen. If I wasn't breathing then everything would be fine.

Ruby: Don't talk like that.

Rosie: Oh shut up, I haven't got time to kill myself; I'm

too busy having a nervous breakdown. Brian
booked a flight over here as soon as he got off the
phone from me so it seems he is very serious about
his new role of fatherhood. He tells me he's been
living in Spain for the past thirteen years where he
owns a nightclub. Providing the highly sexed under-
age drinkers of Ireland's youth with some binge
drinking memories. Now he's back in Dublin to
work on another project.

Ruby: Is he all tanned and gorgeous?

Rosie: Well never before would I have put the words
         "Brian the Whine" and "tanned and gorgeous" all
         in the same sentence. He's pretty much the same
         with less hair and more belly.

Ruby: How did you feel when you saw him?

Rosie: I had to muster all my strength to stop myself from
         punching him. Katie was so nervous about meeting
         him that she was shaking like a leaf and clinging to
         me. She was expecting me to be the strong one.
         Imagine. Someone was relying on me. We met him
         in the coffee shop in Jervis Street Shopping Center
         and I have to admit, as we were approaching his
         table I felt sick. Sick with anger that the miserable
         little man who I was going to have to force myself
         to be nice to for the next hour and help to become a
         part of my daughter's life, was the very same person
         who caused me so much heartache in the past. *I* had
         to help *him*. It also felt odd that as weak as I felt
         bringing Katie into town on the bus that morning,
         as tired, nervous, angry, and disappointed as I was
         to be doing what I was doing, I realize that these
         two people needed me to bring them together. So
         for the sake of Katie's relationship with Brian,
         whatever feelings of resentment I have for him need
         to be kept to myself.

Ruby: You've done a good thing Rosie. It must have been

difficult, it will probably be difficult for a long time watching them grow closer.

Rosie: I know. I have to bite my tongue to stop myself from telling Katie just how much of a hero her father isn't when she tells me about some of the things he has done in his life.

Ruby: What was he like with her?

Rosie: He was even more nervous than Katie so it was up to me to get the conversation started between them. It was an odd situation but you know, being the strongest out of the three really helped me to see that the decision I made about not moving to Boston was the right one. Katie needed me. They both needed me. He seemed genuinely interested in my life and in Katie's. He wanted to know everything about her and I quite enjoyed sharing our stories from over the years. At first I was telling each story with anger because he wasn't around for any of them and then I realized I was bragging. It perked me up in a strange sort of way and made me realize how lucky I've been, as much as I moan and whinge about the responsibility of motherhood. It also helped me see the "specialness" of Katie and my situation; we're the only two to share all these memories together. And what we choose to let other people know is completely up to us. If Brian messes up absolutely everything else in my life at least he's inadvertently helped me realize that.

However unfortunately, it's not exactly the best time in my life to have an ex back again. In these situations you're supposed to have become so much more since the last time you've seen them, happy and successful in your life so you can say "Na na na na na na, look what I've done since you've been

gone." A failed marriage, no job, and living with
my parents did not have the desired effect.

Ruby: None of that stuff is important Rosie, you should
just be glad he's grown up a bit. How long will he
be around for?

Rosie: He's going back and forth from Ibiza all the time.
He's hiring someone else to keep an eye on it for
him during the winter, but obviously he'll need to
be there during the summer, when he's busiest. He
really seems to be taking this seriously and I'm glad
for Katie's sake. Having him hanging around isn't
exactly wonderful for me, but if it puts a smile on
her face then it's worth it.

Ruby: Any luck finding a job?

Rosie: Well I had just switched on the computer to search
the Internet when you messaged me.

Ruby: Oh OK I'll go now and let you become the responsible parent you should be. By the way I'm making
my Gary come to salsa dancing classes with me.
Miss Behave drank one too many sangrias at the
summer party last week and went over on her ankle
in her 12-inch platforms. All we could hear was a
big CRACK! I turned around and she was on her
back with a run in her tights and her wig beside her
on the floor.

Rosie: Oh god did you have to rush her to hospital?

Ruby: Why on earth would we do that?

Rosie: She cracked her ankle?!

Ruby: Oh no don't be silly, she broke the heel of her shoe
and seeing as they are her "only dancing shoes" she
refuses to come to class until she replaces them. Unfortunately for me they're only available in a store in
New York so she has to wait until they're restocked
and delivered. So I am without a partner and I won't
even ask you because I know you'll say no.

Rosie: You're right. But how on earth did you get Gary to

agree to go to dance classes with you? Did you
threaten his life or something?!

Ruby: Yes.

Rosie: Oh. Well I hope he enjoys it.

Ruby: Don't be silly, he'll hate it and shout at me for
weeks but at least he'll be talking to me again. Alright well I better go; I have to buy him a leotard
and tights on my lunch break. I know we don't actually have to wear them but it will be worth it just
to see the look on his face when I pull them out of
my bag.

Rosie: You evil, evil woman.

Ruby: Thank you, now go find a job. In a hotel. After all
this nonsense in your life, I want you to become the
most successful hotel-worker person in the world.
No. More. Setbacks. You hear me?

Rosie: Loud and Clear.

~~Alex,~~

~~OK, here's the truth. I love you. No, more than that, I am
in love with you. Do you think there's any possibility
whatsoever that you drop your successful career in Boston
and role of fatherhood, to come to Dublin to live with me
and Katie in my parents' house happily ever after?~~

Dear Alex,

When will you stop giving me the silent treatment? You
must understand that I can't make decisions to suit myself.
I've Katie to think about too. It is important for her to get to
know Brian. You of all people should know how it is to
want and need to be there for your child. Brian has finally
realized that he wants to be here for Katie. It's better late
than never as you always say. Some things are.

I think I've stressed my apologies more than enough to
you on your answering machine but now I'm writing to
thank you. To thank you for being there for me as you

always have been over the years. For making all those arrangements for me when I couldn't even think clearly. That week my world was turned upside down and everything that was once secure and solid was uprooted and came toppling down on me. Let's not allow your disapproval of my decision to stay to affect our friendship.

Perhaps sometime, someday we can be reunited in the way we planned when we were seven years old. I'm lucky to have a friend like you Alex Stewart; you really are my moonbeam—guiding the way for me all the time. And even though I can see you and know that you're there, you're just beyond my reach. I don't know how unrealistic the promise we made to each other as children was, to stay together side by side forever, but we sure have remained friends from across the seas for over twenty years, and that I'm sure is some feat.

I've been job hunting all week. My aim was to try and get a job in a hotel surprise, surprise but it seems that as the summer has already begun, students and immigrants only too willing to be underpaid have already taken everything for the next few months. The money they're offering really isn't enough to help me and Katie get back on our feet anyway. I will join in with the insufferable moans of twenty-first-century Ireland in a chorus of "Everything is so expensive these days." I'm waiting to hear from the council about getting a house but I've been here before and the waiting list is so long.

Unfortunately my position at the Two Lakes Hotel has been filled, otherwise I would have left my pride at the entrance lobby and asked for it back. Brian has offered to pay child support but I don't want his money. I managed before without him, I certainly don't need his help now. He can give Katie whatever pocket money his heart desires but his money is neither requested nor required.

There hasn't been a peep out of what's-his-name lately. That man is too afraid of his own shadow, never mind of

me. I filed for a divorce last week; I need him out of my life
for good. I gave him enough love and enough chances but he
threw it all back in my face, I would be a fool to stay
around pinning hopes on him again. It's not healthy for me
or Katie. I'll dance around the streets naked when the
divorce is final.

Did you hear that Stephanie is pregnant? She's due in
November so all the family are naturally thrilled. Mum and
Dad are in great form, always asking for you and Josh and
they're very much enjoying their retirement together.
They're actually talking about selling their house and
moving down to the country where it's cheaper so they can
use the extra money to travel the world together for the rest
of their years. I think it's a great idea, they don't need all
these empty rooms in the house (apart from when I come
home crying to them) and neither of them have any need to
be living in the city. But it also means I have to hurry up and
find a job so I can move out with Katie. They're not rushing
me but they want to put the house on the market so it will
sell quickly during the summer. I'll be the only family
member living in Dublin then which I imagine will be rather
lonely. Kevin is in Kilkenny, Steph's in France, and Mum
and Dad will be off on their travels. It'll just be me and
Katie. And Brian the Whine.

My friend Ruby is starting salsa lessons with her son
Gary this week which should be funny. You've met her son
Gary and I'm sure you'd agree he's not the most expressive
or emotive person in the world. But it's a good idea I
suppose. Katie and I should do something together. She gets
to go out for the day with her father and we never spend any
time like that together. We're always just at home biting
each other's heads off. I'll think of something good she'll
like, maybe bring her to a concert or something. With Greg
in the house I was always the cool mum that came to the
rescue, but now with Brian here, he's the cool new dad who
runs the trendy nightclub and I'm the boring mum who

makes her clean her room. Of course, knowing that Brian
has a nightclub has only strengthened her desire to become a
DJ. I don't know what we've created at all. Her music just
gets louder and louder. Mum and Dad have been so used to
silence in the house for the last few years, I think Dad's
going to blow his top if Katie blasts her music any more.

Anyway that's all my news. I'm getting through each day
slowly, taking each day as it comes and all those clichés.
Please return my calls. The last thing on this earth that I
would want to happen is to lose my best friend. Even if he
is a man.

All my love,
Rosie

Phil: So you're pissed off because she's not moving to
         Boston now, because the father of her child, who she
         hasn't seen for thirteen years, has come back and
         wants to get to know Katie?
Alex: Yes.
Phil: Jesus Christ. Who writes your scripts?

Dear Rosie,

I'm sorry Rosie. I know these have been the worst few
weeks of your life and I should have kept in contact.
Sometimes I just get so frustrated watching your life but I no
I can't control it for you. You have to make the decisions. I
wasn't angry at you at all; I was just disappointed for you. I
want to see you happy all the time and I new that what's-
his-name wasn't making you happy. I could see it for years.
As crap as it feels right now, not being with him is a blessing
in disguise. Anyway I'll speak more about this over the
phone during the week because I could rant about what's-
his-name forever.

If I can help you out financially, just let me no, but I'm
sure you're just skipping past that line and fuming I've even
offered. Still, the offer is there. Business has been going

really well lately. Thanks to the diets and lifestyles of the modern world, heart surgery is really in demand. OK, that's not funny.

Speak soon Buttercup, I no you'll be OK.

Alex

FROM: Rosie
TO: Alex
SUBJECT: Messages

Alex Stewart, you KNOW I'll be OK.

FROM: Alex
TO: Katie
SUBJECT: Catching up

It's your beloved godfather here. I'm just e-mailing you to see how you are and to find out how things are going with your dad.

Keep in touch, haven't heard much from you lately and I no things have been tough. Let me no how your music is going too, still want to be a DJ?

FROM: Katie
TO: Alex
SUBJECT: Re: Catching up

SorE this is just a real quick e-mail 2 say hi & that I'm fine tanx. In a rush cos I'm goin out wit dad in a mo. He takin me to concert in the point theater. He got free tickets cos he nos the band. Felt bad cos mum already got tickets as surprise for me & her. Said me & her should do more 2gether. Whatever. Don't no wot she's talkin bout we c each other every day. NE way dad got better tickets so I'm goin

with him and mum bringin Ruby. They got some crappy
tickets down the bak of theater. Brian is cool. He told me u
& him were friends at school & that u went 2 his 10th bday
party & that he threw goin away party 4 u b4 u moved to
usa. But he said that u & mum disappeared after first 10
mins. That was a bit rude!

Mum laughed when he reminded her. She wouldn't tell
me where u and her went. Where did u go?

Oh here he is now—have 2 go.

Katie: Cool isn't he Toby?
Toby: Yeah
Katie: When I finish school I'll be able to move over to
          Spain and work as a DJ in his club. It's so perfect. It
          all fits in with my master plan.
Toby: Did he say you could work in his club?
Katie: No, but he's hardly gonna say no is he?
Toby: Dunno. What's his club called?
Katie: Dyma Nite Club. Cool isn't it?
Toby: Yeah.
Katie: You can come too if you want.
Toby: Thanks. Would you want to live in Spain?
Katie: To start off with I would yeah. First I'd get the ex-
          perience in his club and then I could travel the world
          and work in loads of different clubs in each country.
          Imagine being able to play and listen to music for a
          living. It sounds like heaven.
Toby: You need to get decks then don't you?
Katie: Yeah. My dad said he'd get them for me. He's got
          loads of friends who are DJs and they can get all the
          best gear for cheaper than the shops. Cool isn't it?
Toby: Yeah. It's weird—you calling him Dad.
Katie: Yeah I no. I don't really say it to him though, just to
          other people. It feels odd. I'll get used to it though.
Toby: Yeah I suppose. Have you heard from Greg?
Katie: No. Why?

Toby: Don't tell your mum but me and my mum and dad
        went out for Chinese last night and he was there
        with some woman. He got all embarrassed when he
        saw me and tried to be all nice and friendly by call-
        ing me over to the table and stuff.

Katie: Oh my god. What did you say to him?

Toby: Nothing. I ignored him. I walked straight past their
        table.

Katie: Good. Serves him right. Did your mum and dad go
        mental?

Toby: No. Mum winked at me and Dad pretended he
        didn't see Greg.

Katie: Who was he with?

Toby: Who, my dad?

Katie: No you stupid. What's-his-name.

Toby: Some blonde.

Katie: Did you no her?

Toby: No

Katie: Oh. Poor Mum.

Toby: Don't tell her. Has she got a job yet?

Katie: No but she's been going to interviews every day.
        She's been in the worst moods EVER lately banging
        around the house like the anti-Christ. Granddad says
        that's the way I'm supposed to be now that I'm thir-
        teen. She's such a grump.

Toby: Are you going to the orthodontist guy soon?

Katie: Yeah Granddad is taking me tomorrow, my brace
        broke again. Why?

Toby: Can I go with you?

Katie: Why do you always want to come? I've got blisters
        all on the inside of my mouth and he hacks away at
        me while you sit there sucking lollipops.

Toby: I like going. I bet you had cornflakes for breakfast
        this morning.

Katie: What are you, psychic?

Toby: No it's all stuck in your braces.

Katie: Oh get a life Toby.

Toby: I have one. So can I go tomorrow?

Katie: What is your obsession with braces you weirdo?

Toby: They're just interesting.

Katie: Yeah about as interesting as this geography test. So
         come on, what's the answer for number 5? Is the
         capital of Australia Sydney?

Toby: Yeah Katie, it is.

Dear Ms. Rosie Dunne,

   We are pleased to offer you the position you recently
applied for. The salary is £25,000 and we would expect you
to start in August. Please reply to us as soon as possible with
your decision and contact Jessica at the phone number below.

—◠◠◠—

CHAPTER 34

You have an instant message from: RUBY

Ruby: Praise the lord for he is a miracle worker! I love my
        son, he is perfect, an absolute genius!

Rosie: There's a turnaround for the books!

Ruby: Well you would agree if, like me, you had just wit-
        nessed the rebirth of Fred Astaire. Not only am I in
        a great deal of pain from dancing like I have never
        danced before but I am shocked to the very core!
        There is no possible way in this world that I could
        coherently communicate to you through the use of
        the English language exactly how good my Gary is.
        Did I mention to you at any stage in our lives that I
        have always loved my son and that he is god's gift
        to salsa dancing and finally *not* to salsa sauce!

        Anyway as soon as the music started, magic hap-
        pened!

        I mean, Ricardo didn't exactly go easy on him even
        though it was his first day. He said, "Rub-ee, zis is
        ze advanceda classa, Gar-ee vill just have to try to
        keep up." And my lord, my Gary kept up so much I

almost passed out. Ricardo even put on 1, 2, 3
Maria by Azuquita and you know Rosie—it's fast.
So fast it had you and me in a slump on the floor
halfway through, watching cartoon stars and birdies
circle our heads. The way Gary moved was incredible, and he's a big lad as you well know. He looked
so graceful, spinning and twirling around the floor
with his sweat glistening like a . . . solar system.

At the end of class Ricardo called me and Gary up
to him and said Gary was a star in the making and
that he and I made a great team. Who would have
thought a lorry driver from inner city Dublin would
be a salsa dancing god! Teddy wasn't too impressed when I shared the good news. Well I was so
excited when I got home that I just blurted it out
but I didn't realize that Teddy's fellow truck driving union friends were in the room having a "beer
and porn night" and they were all equally unim-
pressed. Teddy went even redder in the face than
usual and ranted and raved about all male dancers
being gay and that I shouldn't be influencing Gary
to fancy boys. I told him I was trying to help him
come out of his shell a bit not to literally "come
out." But the lads wouldn't understand, they think
crashing beer cans against their heads, farting (then
sniffing the air and laughing), screaming at the
football players on TV (as if they would do any
better themselves if they got on that pitch), com-
menting on all the overweight women on TV (like
they don't have big beer bellies and haven't let
themselves go ten years ago), calling me every ten
minutes to serve them more cans of beer (of the
fifty cent per dozen variety), and then having the
audacity to *lecture* me on what makes a *real* man.
The lazy selfish bastards—

Rosie: Whoa, whoa, whoa Ruby we seemed to have gotten a bit sidetracked here. How did poor Gary feel when Teddy and co. had a go at him?

Ruby: Well the poor lad was so embarrassed that he stormed out of the room, stomped up the stairs, and slammed his bedroom door shut.

Rosie: Oh dear, poor Gary. I hope Teddy apologized.

Ruby: Are you demented? Of course he didn't. Gary's display only further showed how "gay" he was becoming according to Teddy and co. by pulling a "woman's strop." But who cares what they think? So move over Fred Astaire and Ginger Rogers, Ruby and Gary Minnelli are coming through!

Rosie: Minnelli??

Ruby: It's far more superstar-like. Ricardo said he could train us both for competitions. We could even get to travel the world if we're good enough. For someone that considers walking to the end of her garden an adventure, being able to travel would be a real dream. That's *if* we're good enough of course.

Rosie: Ruby that's terrific news. How does Gary feel about all this?

Ruby: Oh it's not important; he'll soon come around to my way of thinking.

Rosie: What will Miss Behave say when she finds out she has been replaced?

Ruby: I know, I was worried about that; you know how jealous she gets when I even look at other men.

Rosie: I'm glad that you and Gary have found something you can do together. I think it's important, no matter how short-lived it may be.

Ruby: Oh don't be fooled by Gary's lack of enthusiasm, this wonderful moment in my life will not be short-lived. I'm bringing Gary all the way with me to the World Salsa Dancing Championships in Miami. You know you need to look beyond the four walls of St.

Patrick's School Hall. *See* the possibilities, *smell* the
success in the air, *taste* the rewards.

Rosie: Have you been watching Oprah again?

Ruby: Yeah that "Remembering your spirit" part gets to
me every time. Maybe Gary and I can be on it
someday talking about how we came from nothing
to salsa dancing millionaires just by *believing*.

Rosie: Oh don't talk to me about remembering my spirit,
all I can think of is the bottle of wine I knocked
back last night.

Ruby: Not that kind of spirit you fool . . . Any word on
the job front?

Rosie: Well yes actually, I received a job offer in the post
yesterday.

Ruby: Terrific! It's about time. Is it the one you wanted or
the one you didn't want?

Rosie: You've known me all these years and you even had
to *ask* that question?

Ruby: Oh silly me, it's the one you didn't want. *Of course.*

Rosie: Well actually it was neither of the above, it's the one
I really, really, really didn't want and would only
accept it if it was the last job in Dublin, if I was being thrown out of Mum and Dad's house on my
bum, and if Katie and I were so desperate for food
we had to lick stamps.

Dear Mr. and Mrs. Dunne,

Hyland & Moore Auctioneers received your request and
we would be more than pleased to act on your behalf for the
sale of your home. Thank you for choosing Hyland &
Moore to represent you.

Yours sincerely,
Thomas Hyland

You have received an instant message from: ROSIE

Rosie: Hi it's me.

Rosie: Helloooo?

Rosie: I know you're there. I can see that you've logged online.

Alex: Who is this?!

Rosie: Oh ha ha you're so funny, what is this? Let's annoy Rosie day?! Tough luck I am spilling the beans and sharing the sob story of my miserable little life with you whether you like it or not. OK here I go.

I was offered a job. But I turned it down because I didn't think I was desperate enough to have to accept it. It turns out I was wrong. Suddenly Mum and Dad tell me that they're putting the house on the market the *very next day* and before my brain has a chance to register what they're saying, people start trampling in and out of the house, nosying through my bedroom, complaining about the interiors, laughing at the wallpaper, turning their nose up at the carpets, talking about which walls they'd knock down, which wardrobes they'd rip out, and which of my cuddly childhood teddies they would like to burn in a bonfire in the back garden while they danced around it hollering, with strips of animal blood on their faces. (OK so they didn't say *that*.) So then a couple put in an offer of full asking price, can you believe, after only seeing it once! Mum and Dad thought about it for approximately twenty seconds and then said yes!

Alex: No!

Rosie: Yes! Apparently the woman is eight months pregnant and they're living in a really small flat and they need to move house really quickly before the baby is born and has to bathe in the sink and play on the balcony.

Alex: No!

Rosie: Yes! Mum and Dad were really apologetic and
         everything but I don't blame them because it's their
         life after all and frankly they should have had to
         stop worrying about me the minute I moved out. So
         all within a matter of days they've sold the house,
         everything has been boxed up, they bought a house
         for practically next to nothing in Connemara. The
         furniture is being auctioned off tomorrow (apart
         from the pieces I managed to grab), the rest of the
         stuff is being delivered to the house tomorrow
         (which is hours away). Mum and Dad have already
         bought tickets to go on a cruise for two months and
         they're leaving on Monday.

Alex: No!

Rosie: Yes! This means that I had to call back the people
         who offered me the job that I already turned down
         not too politely I might add, I had to apologize pro-
         fusely and try to convince them that I really wanted
         the job after all. They were really pissed off and
         said they didn't need me until August. So today
         Katie spent the day with Brian while I went emer-
         gency house hunting.

Alex: No!

Rosie: Yes! Everywhere that was in any way affordable was
         absolutely disgusting. The apartments were still ei-
         ther too expensive, too small, or too far from my
         job and Katie's school. So Mum and Dad were dis-
         cussing my personal problems (as they generally do)
         with the young sickeningly happy couple who are
         about to embark on blissful family life while
         butchering my childhood home. And because Mum
         and Dad had been so speedy and understanding
         about the whole "moving out in a few days" sce-
         nario they suggested that I move *into* the flat they
         just moved *out* of and had decided to rent out. And
         they also said they would lower the rent for me.

Alex: No!

Rosie: Yes! But the only thing is that they have already
        rented the place out for two weeks to a group of
        male students so I have to wait until they move out.
        By which time it will no doubt be disgustingly
        smelly and dirty.

Alex: No!

Rosie: Yes! So who do I stay with while I wait, I hear you
        ask? Well let's see, Mum and Dad have moved to
        Connemara as you now know. Kev lives in the staff
        quarters of the Two Lakes Hotel in Kilkenny, Steph
        lives in France, Ruby only has two bedrooms and no
        space for me and Katie, and you're in Boston which
        isn't convenient commuting for me. So who is the
        only other human being in Dublin that I know right
        now? (And don't even think of what's-his-name.)

        None other than Brian the Whine.

Alex: No!

Rosie: Yes! I am afraid so. I am e-mailing you from the
        storeroom of Brian the Whine's rented flat where I
        have to stay for two weeks. How much lower can I
        go? And that's not even my worst news. I haven't
        even told you who my new boss is.
        None other than Ms. Big Nose Smelly Breath Casey.

Alex: No!

Rosie: Yes! I am now secretary to the woman we most
        hated while growing up, the woman who made my
        daughter's life hell while in school, and who is now
        principal of St. Patrick's Primary School and my
        boss. I have momentarily rambled off the road of
        reason to find a bush to pee behind but I will soon
        find my way back again. If it's the last thing I do.
        Why on earth Ms. Big Nose Smelly Breath Casey
        even hired me is completely beyond me but she has
        and until I find another job in a hotel I won't com-

plain or ask questions. Perhaps she just wants to make my life a misery well into my adult life and until I'm an elderly woman. And speaking of the elderly, she was old when I was *five years old* for Christ sake, and she's still old. The woman has nine lives.

So what do you think of all that? Any messages you want me to pass on to your favorite teacher?

Rosie: Hello, Alex?

Rosie: Alex?

Alex: Em . . . sorry Alex isn't actually online.

Rosie: Oh ha ha. Well then how is his name on my screen and I am typing to him?

Alex: Oh you're not. I logged on using his home computer. I guess his name automatically comes up on your system. I've never come across this little system, it's fun. Sorry I didn't know you were looking for him.

Rosie: What?? You think I just rant about my private life to all strangers on the computer??? Who is this?

Alex: Bethany.

Rosie: Bethany?

Alex: Bethany Williams? Remember me?

Rosie: What the hell are you doing on Alex's home computer?!

Alex: Oh I'm sorry it all makes sense now. Alex didn't tell you, did he? I thought you two told each other everything. I'll be sure to pass on all your little messages to him though, they were very amusing. Good luck with the new job Rosie; I'll let Alex explain this one to you.

By the way, Alex is working with my father now, he's making good money. Doing very well for himself. Perhaps if you're that stuck for money he could give you a loan.

Rosie has logged off

CHAPTER 35

Welcome to the Relieved Divorced Dubliners internet chat
room
There are currently five people chatting
Buttercup has joined the room

Divorced_1:   Screw him, screw'm, screw'm, screw'm!

Buttercup: Hello everyone.

Wildflower: Wahooooo! You tell her Divorced_1!

UnsureOne: I know Divorced_1 but that's the problem
              now isn't it? I can't "screw him" anymore,
              he's gone. I should never have let him leave;
              oh it's all my fault.

Buttercup: Em . . . hello everyone, is this working, can
              you all read what I'm writing?

Divorced_1:   Oh shut up UnsureOne, I'm sick of listening
              to you moaning night after night. How is it
              your fault? Did you drag him into the car and
              drive him to the hotel room? Did you pull his
              pants down around his ankles and push him
              on top of her on the bed?

UnsureOne: Oh please stop Divorced_1! Stop! Stop! Stop!
              No I didn't!

LonelyLady: Oh leave her alone, there's no need to be so
                graphic.

Divorced_1:   Look I'm only trying to help. If you didn't
                do all those things then how on earth is it
                your fault?

Buttercup: Oh I'm not sure this is working, hello? Hello?
                Hello? Stupid bloody computer. Can anyone
                answer me?

UnsureOne: Well you know, maybe I inadvertently put
                him under pressure to do better at his job.
                You know how things are so expensive these
                days and the kids always want more, more,
                more. Well they were going back to school
                and the uniforms and books are always so ex-
                pensive and I kept telling him we needed
                more money because it was tight and I'm not
                sure but maybe it *was* my fault, you know?

LonelyLady: Oh please Unsure . . .

Wildflower: Oh I have heard quite enough for one
                night . . .

Divorced_1:   Look just forget about him. He's a bastard
                and that's all there is to it. Screw'm.

Buttercup: Well not that anyone cares, but there was
                only one kind of job your husband was think-
                ing of that night and it didn't involve a day at
                the office.

Wildflower: Wahoooo! Welcome Buttercup!

Divorced_1:   You're right Buttercup, screw'm.

UnsureOne: Are you sure Buttercup?

LonelyLady: I tend to agree with the others UnsureOne.
                Welcome Buttercup, you want to chat?

Wildflower: Oh please LonelyLady, every time you ask
                one of our visitors if they want to chat you
                scare them away. You sound like you want to
                talk dirty or something.

LonelyLady: Oh I'm sorry, you know I don't mean to. I

	just have this horrible habit of driving every-one away.
Buttercup:	Why, are you in the taxi business?
Wildflower:	HA. I like you Buttercup, you can stay. What are your stats?
Buttercup:	My what?
Divorced_1:	Oh everyone look, a chat room virgin.
Wildflower:	Your stats Cupcake—age, sex, that sort of thing.
Buttercup:	Oh well I'm 32, I'm female, I have a 13-year-old daughter, and I'm happily divorced.
Wildflower:	Wahoooo!
Divorced_1:	Congratulations Cupcake, screw'm that's what I say.
UnsureOne:	Buttercup, whose fault was the marriage breakup. Yours or his?
Wildflower:	Oh ignore her Buttercup, she's riding the "blame" wave.
Buttercup:	That's OK, I don't mind. It was one hundred per cent *his* fault.
Divorced_1:	Quel Surprise.
LonelyLady:	Well at least you have a daughter, Buttercup, and you weren't left all alone. My husband, well my ex-husband, left me before we even had a chance to start a family. I don't think it would have been so hard if we had children, then at least I wouldn't feel so—
Divorced_1:	Alone yeah, yeah. Well trust me it's harder *with* kids. Unfortunately my rugrats are the spit of my husband and when I look at them I just want to strangle the little bastards.
UnsureOne:	Gosh well I think *that's* a little psychotic.
Divorced_1:	Do your kids look like your ex, UnsureOne?
UnsureOne:	Well yes and no. Some people say they do and others say they don't. I'm not too sure really . . .

Divorced_1: Well unless they look like clones of your husband, save the lecture until you're *sure* of what you're talking about. Does your kid look like your ex, Buttercup?

Buttercup: Well thankfully she's not his so, no, she doesn't.

LonelyLady: My goodness, did he know?

Buttercup: Of course he did, I had my daughter years before I met him.

Wildflower: Oh well that's a shame, thought we were onto something good there. So let's not be rude guys and introduce ourselves to Buttercup. I'm 62 years old, I've 5 kids, and my husband left me last year.

Buttercup: Oh how awful, I'm sorry.

Divorced_1: HA! No need to be sorry Cupcake, the man had good reason to leave her; she was sleeping with their gardener.

Buttercup: Oh!

Wildflower: Oh *please* like you lot never thought of ever doing the same thing.

UnsureOne: Well my gardener was a woman.

Wildflower: I didn't mean *that*.

LonelyLady: I didn't, I really didn't. I never would have done something like that to my Tommy. Never.

Divorced_1: Are you crying again, Lonely?

LonelyLady: Yes.

Buttercup: What's your . . . eh . . . stats, Divorced_1?

Divorced_1: I'm 49 years old, have 4 kids, and my ex-husband was screwing his secretary. Bastard.

Buttercup: LonelyLady what about you?

LonelyLady: I'm 27, I just got married last year but my Tommy left me. He just couldn't take married life he said. We just argued and argued every day and then one day he just left me . . . all alone.

Buttercup: UnsureOne what about you?

UnsureOne: I'm 36, have 3 children, and I'm not techni-
                cally divorced per se. We still live together . . .
                What about you Buttercup, how did you and
                your husband split?

Buttercup: Oh he was seeing a number of different
                women quite regularly and I was oblivious to
                it all.

Divorced_1:   Bastard. Screw him.

Wildflower: Well I believe that we're all put on this earth
                to have as many sexual playmates as we want.

Divorced_1:   Oh shut up you new-age hippy.

Wildflower: There's no harm in expressing my personal
                view. I don't recall ever attacking your opin-
                ions.

Divorced_1:   That's because my opinions are always right.
                So anyway Buttercup, did you get the house?

Buttercup: No actually it was his in the first place, my
                daughter and I just moved in with him.

Divorced_1:   What?! Didn't he put your name down on the
                house after you got married?

Buttercup: Em . . . no, why? Should he have?

LonelyLady: Yes of course Buttercup, equal rights and
                equal ownership. Of course in my case, I got
                to keep the house and it just meant I had to
                stay here all on my own with rooms full of
                memories.

Divorced_1:   Oh drop it Lonely, you sound like a broken
                record today. I was screwed in the divorce set-
                tlement. My ex got the holiday home and I
                got custody of the kids. What I would give to
                swap for a few months of peace and quiet in
                the sun. So if you didn't get the house Cup-
                cake, what did you *get*?

Buttercup: I *got* the hell out of there and away from that
                creep.

Wildflower:	Wahooo!
Divorced_1:	You're right, that's all you need. Screw him.
UnsureOne:	But are you *sure* that's enough for you and your daughter?
LonelyLady:	I would stay with Tommy even if he was a shit. I wouldn't care, I just want him.
Wildflower:	Ignore her. Her balance is all wrong. The best way to get over one man is to get under another. We all know that.
UnsureOne:	I'm not sure that's the correct attitude to have. I certainly have no intentions of sharing a bed with anyone other than my husband.
Buttercup:	I don't understand UnsureOne, you're still married?
UnsureOne:	We're not technically divorced. He sleeps in our bedroom and I sleep in the spare room.
Wildflower:	UnsureOne, you let him kick *you* into the *spare room* when *he* was the one messing around??
UnsureOne:	Oh, is that wrong? I'm not too sure. This is all new to me . . .
LonelyLady:	I wouldn't care if Tommy and I couldn't even stay in the same bed. I just want him home with me.
Divorced_1:	Oh sweet lord have I taught you ladies nothing at all . . . Anyway Buttercup, where are you living now if shit for brains kept the house?
Buttercup:	Oh this may seem a bit bizarre but I'm currently living with my daughter's father.
UnsureOne:	The way it should be I think.
LonelyLady:	Oooh what a wonderful love story!
Buttercup:	Oh no, no, no, don't get me wrong, there's absolutely no love involved in this story. In fact, I hate him.
Wildflower:	Thou doth protest too much.

Buttercup:	Yes I do and if you met him you would too.
Divorced_1:	Well I wouldn't be sure of that, ever since this woman hit 60 she's been eating men for breakfast.
Buttercup:	Well not this one I assure you, unless you mistake his head for a hard-boiled egg.
UnsureOne:	Buttercup, why did you choose that name?
Buttercup:	Oh it's just a nickname my best friend calls me. When we were six we were in a school play and I was Princess Buttercup and he was Prince Moonbeam. He's been calling me that name ever since.
Divorced_1:	You're still in contact after twenty-six years??
Buttercup:	Yep, we're still best friends.
Divorced_1:	You're best friends with a man?! Did you ever sleep with him?
Buttercup:	Only when we had sleepovers in the non-sexual kind of way.
Divorced_1:	Is he gay?
Buttercup:	No he's not. He's divorced, himself.
Divorced_1:	And you weren't married to him?
Buttercup:	No.
UnsureOne:	Well I think that's beautiful. I mean I lost contact with my school friends as soon as I left and got married. Leonard hated me having any male friends.
LonelyLady:	When I moved from Belfast to Dublin with Tommy I left all my family and friends behind and now with Tommy gone, my friends are all up north and I'm—
Divorced_1:	All alone, yeah, yeah, we get the message. Buttercup, is your friend single, what does he do, where does he live and finally is he looking for a hot 49-year-old with 4 kids? He can take or leave the kids, I'm not bothered.
Buttercup:	No unfortunately he's not single.

Wildflower: Why "unfortunately"?

Buttercup: Because she's a real bitch. She's his first love
              from when he was 16—I hated her then and I
              still hate her now. Anyway he ended up work-
              ing with her dad in Boston, of all places, and
              I suppose their love was rekindled.

Divorced_1:   And you're jealous.

Buttercup: I am not.

Divorced_1:   Yes you are. I can hear it in your tone.

Buttercup: You cannot hear me; we're typing to each
              other!

Wildflower: What she means is that she *senses* it and I
              must admit, I agree. What about you ladies?

LonelyLady: I agree. It must be so lonely for you.

UnsureOne: Well far be it from me to be a know it all—

Divorced_1:   Far be it is right.

UnsureOne: But *surely* if you've been friends since you
              were six and you're now thirty-two, you've
              both been married once and are now living
              with other people in different *countries*, then
              if it hasn't happened by now, it won't be hap-
              pening at all.

Wildflower: Oh Unsure, don't be so pessimistic. Soul mates
              have a way of finding their way to each other.

LonelyLady: Does that mean that my Tommy will come
              back to me?

Wildflower: No.

LonelyLady: Oh.

FreeWoman has entered the room

FreeWoman: Yeeeessssss!!

LonelyLady: Welcome FreeWoman, do you want to
                  chat?

FreeWoman has left the room

Wildflower:	Oh Lonely! Stop scaring them off!
LonelyLady:	Story of my life.
Divorced_1:	Are you crying again?
LonelyLady:	Yes.

SingleSam has entered the room

Divorced_1:	Sam!!
Wildflower:	Wahoooo! Sam!
LonelyLady:	Hi Sam, welcome, how are you?
UnsureOne:	Hello Sam.
SingleSam:	Hello ladies, good to see you all here again tonight.
Divorced_1:	Sam meet Buttercup, she's 32, has a 13-year-old daughter, and her husband was cheating on her. Cupcake, meet Sam, he's 54, has 2 daughters, and his ex-wife's a lesbian.
SingleSam:	Nice to meet you Buttercup.
Buttercup:	Nice to meet you too Sam.
UnsureOne:	So what's new Sam? Are you happy or sad today?
SingleSam:	Oh today has been a bad day for me.
Wildflower:	Oh please! This is supposed to be the *Relieved* Divorced Dubliners chat room not the Depressed Divorced Dubliners. I'm heading to bed.
Buttercup:	I better head off to bed too. It was nice to meet you all.
Divorced_1:	See you same time tomorrow night Buttercup.
UnsureOne:	I better put the kids to bed.
LonelyLady:	I think I'll watch the wedding video one more time before I go to bed.

Buttercup has left the room
LonelyLady has left the room
UnsureOne has left the room
Wildflower has left the room

Divorced_1:   Well Sam, it looks like it's just you and me.
               You put the music on and I'll light the candles.

Click on the icon to the left to print this page

FROM: Stephanie
TO: Rosie
SUBJECT: Ms. Casey!

I cannot *believe* you're going to be working with Ms.
Casey! Mum told me over the phone and I could barely
understand her through all her laughing. She's wondering
what her and Dad should do when they receive a letter from
Ms. Casey while they're in Australia, demanding to see them
first thing Monday morning due to your behavior at work!

Whatever persuaded you to take this job? Have you gone
nuts?! I never had a problem with the woman personally but
I sure know that she drove you insane when you were a kid
and then again when Katie had her for a teacher! What does
Alex think about all this? I'm sure he's got some very
interesting views on the subject!

Dear Stephanie,

Well you of course *never* had a problem with Ms. Casey
because you were Ms. Goody Two Shoes! She loved you and
your neat copies and your finished and correct homework
and your tidy uniform and politeness!

I probably am nuts taking this job, but to be honest it's
the best one with the most attractive pay packet by far. It's
Monday to Friday 9 a.m. to 3:30 p.m. which is great

because I had to work all hours and weekends with my last job. It's right beside Katie's secondary school which means we can get the bus together every day. I really don't intend working there for very long, just until a job in the hotel industry opens up.

But the main reason for me taking the job is the fact that I have very little choice. I have a week left here in purgatory (Brian's flat) before I can move into the flat which is a bit of a dump. I'm going to need all the spare cash I can get to fix the place up and make it feel like home. God knows Katie's had so many of them so far.

Before Mum and Dad went away they tried to persuade me to accept the money Brian was offering me. As far as I'm concerned his money is for Katie, not me. I'm a grown woman, I can work and provide a home for Katie all on my own, he can give her all the money he wants, for clothes, CDs and after-school activities. That's all the expensive stuff. I'm not a charity, just a woman on a small budget like millions of other people out there. When the Rosie Dunne Hotel Chain buys over Hilton hotels, that's when I can rip up the budget.

Strange things have happened in my daughter's life but none of them as bizarre as her mother and father living in the same house. What may be a daily occurrence for some children is however something for children like Katie to laugh hysterically at. Actually it's not as if Brian and I dislike each other, it's just that we know absolutely *nothing* about each other. We are two complete strangers who got together once in our lives (and only for a few minutes, trust me) in a moment I can barely even remember, to make the most incredible thing ever. How could two fools like us create something as great as Katie? When Katie comes home from school and starts to go off on one of her stand-up comedy routines about her day I look at her, I look at him, and think how did *him*, mixed with *me*, make *her*. It's scary.

I try to spend as little time as possible here as I can. I

stroll around up and down Henry Street for most of the day
because Brian's flat just doesn't feel like home. I feel like I
shouldn't be here. When I'm at the flat I stay in my room for
most of the time or lock myself into the storeroom and send
e-mails all day. You would think that we would share *some*
sort of bond or friendship or have any kind of relationship.
But we're complete strangers.

Katie thinks it's hilarious. Every evening she calls us
both to sit together at the dinner table to eat. She's not
playing matchmaker by any means, she's just trying to
annoy her parents. I do still feel angry at him now but it's a
different kind of anger. Before I felt angry at him because
he left *me, I* had to do everything. *My* social life was
ruined, all *my* money was being spent, and *I* couldn't get a
job. But now when I look at him joking around with Katie
I just think what a waste. That's all he had to do while she
was growing up—be there for her and she would have
accepted him, as children do, no matter what he was like. I
feel angry at him for not being there for *her.* I've finally lost
that selfish part of me.

Once again, I don't quite know where I'm headed Steph.
It seems that every few years I'm shoveling up the pieces of
my life and starting from scratch all over. No matter what I
do or how hard I try I can't seem to reach the dizzy heights
of happiness, success, and security, like so many people do.
And I'm not talking about becoming a millionaire and living
happily ever after. I just mean reaching a point in my life
that I can stop what I'm doing, take a look around me,
breathe a sigh of relief, and think "I'm where I want to be
now."

I'm missing something, you know? That special
"sparkle" that life is supposed to bring. I have the job, the
child, the family, the apartment, and the friends, but I've lost
the sparkle.

And in answer to your question about Alex, I don't
know what he thinks of my new job because I haven't

heard from him in a long time. He's so busy saving more valuable lives and attending charity functions that I couldn't possibly expect him to get in touch with a friend like me. He's far too busy hooking up with "old" friends. Slutty ones at that.

—◦—

CHAPTER 36

BON VOYAGE!
I'LL MISS YOU BOTH LIKE CRAZY, THINGS WON'T BE
THE SAME WITHOUT YOU BUT I HOPE YOU HAVE A
BRILLIANT TIME!
LOVE,
ROSIE

TO GRANDMA AND GRANDDAD,
HAVE FUN, SEND US LOADS OF POSTCARDS.
LOVE,
KATIE (YOUR *FAVORITE* GRANDDAUGHTER)

ALICE AND DENNIS,
I WISH YOU GOOD HEALTH AND SAFETY ON YOUR
TRIP. AND HAVE FUN TOO!
MY PARENTS WISH YOU THE BEST, THEY SAID THEY
WILL PROBABLY JOIN YOU HALFWAY!
BEST WISHES,
ALEX

TO MUM AND DAD,
BON VOYAGE!

HAVE A WONDERFUL ADVENTURE AND DON'T
FORGET TO LOOK US UP WHEN YOU'RE PASSING BY!
LOTS OF LOVE,
STEPHANIE, PIERRE, AND JEAN-LOUIS

MUM AND DAD,
TRY NOT TO GET SEASICK! SEE YOU WHEN YOU GET
BACK.
LOVE,
KEVIN

You have an instant message from: ALEX

Alex: Hello.
Rosie: Oh so he *is* still alive. Where have you been for the
         past few weeks?
Alex: Hiding.
Rosie: From whom?
Alex: You.
Rosie: Why?
Alex: Because I'm dating Bethany again and I was afraid
         to tell you because you hate her with a passion and
         then you found out from *her* first which made things
         even worse. So I was hiding from you.
Rosie: Why?
Alex: Because I thought you'd come over here and kill me.
Rosie: Why?
Alex: Because you think she's a slut and that she's no
         good for me
Rosie: Why?
Alex: Because you're my overprotective best friend and
         you've always hated my girlfriends (and wife) and
         I've always hated your boyfriends (and husband).
Rosie: Why?
Alex: Well because he had an affair, for one . . .

Rosie: Why?

Alex: Because he was an absolute fool and he didn't no
         how lucky he was. But let's not talk about him any-
         more because he's gone and he's never coming back

Rosie: Why?

Alex: Because I scared him off.

Rosie: Why?

Alex: Because I'm your best friend and I care about you.

Rosie: Why?

Alex: Because I've nothing better to do.

Rosie: Why?

Alex: Because it's the unfortunate way that my life turned
         out, whatever happened made me care about you
         and yours. Anyway it's great that I don't have to
         hide anymore.

Rosie: Why?

Alex: Because I've apologized.

Rosie: Why?

Alex: Because I'm tired of not hearing from you and I
         miss you.

Rosie: Why?

Alex: Because (and I'm now saying this through incredibly
         gritted teeth). You. Are. My. Best. Friend. But I have
         to warn you, I'm not going to listen to any of your
         bitchy remarks about her this time round.

Rosie: Why?

Alex: Because I really like her Rosie and she makes me
         happy. I feel like the little boy working in Dad's of-
         fice again. And just think, if it wasn't for you get-
         ting so drunk on your sixteenth birthday that you
         had to get your stomach pumped, we never would
         have been caught, we wouldn't have been sus-
         pended, and I wouldn't have been punished so se-
         verely by having to file every piece of paper in the
         world in Dad's office where I might add, I would

never have met Bethany. So it's all down to you my
dear friend!

Rosie: OH WHYYYYYY??? Dear god, oh why?

Alex: Ha ha. I better go now because I've got surgery in a
few hours.

Rosie: Why?

Alex: Because I happen to be a cardiac surgeon and
there's a poor man, called Mr. Jackson if you really
must no, who needs aortic valve surgery.

Rosie: Why?

Alex: Because he has aortic stenosis.

Rosie: Why?

Alex: Well the reasons behind aortic incompetence in general are rheumatic.

Rosie: Why?

Alex: It's due to annulo-aorto ectasia, endocarditis, and
aortitis among others. But don't worry (because I
no that you are), Mr. Jackson will be fine.

Rosie: Why?

Alex: Because thankfully due to 75 years of studying I
have learned an operation involving the ball valve
prosthesis which will help him.

Rosie: Why?

Alex: Oh Rosie . . . OK but you asked . . . it will help him
because after induction of circulatory support by
extra corporeal circulation, cooling of the patient
and heart, the aorta is x-clamped and the aorta
valve exposed after the aorta is opened.

Rosie: Why?

Alex: So the aorta valve can be examined and excised for
the aortic valve replacement. So then the sizing of
the aortic annulus is done by a valve sizer.

Rosie: Why?

Alex: To help select the size of the aortic valve prosthesis. Then the valve sutures are placed into the

aortic valve annulus and into the heart valve prosthesis.

Rosie: Why?

Alex: To tie the valve prosthesis secure into the valve annulus *of course*. So then the artificial heart valve is
in place, the aorta is closed by a running suture,
the heart is de-aired and the operation is finished.
And Mr. Jackson will be a healthy man. Any more
questions?

Rosie: The aorta, it's in, like, the heart, right?

Alex: Very funny Rosie. OK I'm really going this time;
I'm really glad we had this discussion and that
we've cleared the whole Bethany thing right up. So
I'm forgiven.

Rosie: No.

Alex: Great stuff, thanks. Speak to you soon.

Alex has logged off

Rosie: Thanks for asking about my job, *Doctor*.

FROM: Rosie
TO: Ruby
SUBJECT: Help!

Help . . . (Meek feeble little voice) Help me . . . Oh dear,
my head. My poor, poor head. My even poorer brain cells,
they never even had a chance, they're gone. Dead. The pain
and suffering my mind and body experience right now is pure
torture. I pray that the end is nigh, let me see the light so that
I may follow thee . . . It's 4 o'clock in the afternoon and I am
bedridden (not exactly half as much fun as it sounds) and bed
is where I shall stay for the remainder of my years. Good-bye
world, farewell all, thanks for the memories.

And of the ones remaining from last night I shall try to explain to you exactly what I got up to, although there seems to be a heavy mist working its way in from the edges of my brain toward the center. I'll try to get it all out before I'm surrounded in fuzziness.

After you threw me out of your house in your mad rush to get to last-minute dance lessons I sat at the bus stop for AN HOUR and waited for the bloody bus to turn up. Honestly Ruby I strongly urge you to think of investing in a fireman's pole for your home so that when Ricardo calls you for one of your emergency dance lessons you can press the panic button of your alarm, slide down the pole, and dive into your mini-mobile, remembering to blare salsa music as a warning for all traffic who dare obstruct the urgent call of hip movement. Next time you invite me out on a "girls' night in" though I'll be careful not to spend my meager amounts of money on booze. So me and my two off-license bags waited at the bus stop and I began to work my way through one of them (out of pure boredom of course). Anyway eventually I arrived at Brian the Whine's house and he informed me as he opened the front door that he had given Katie permission to stay at Toby's house for the night (which by the way really annoyed me because I'm the one who usually tells her what she can and cannot do).

So I started to explain that to him in the hall but I stopped when his face moved uncomfortably close to mine and hovered so near we were practically nose to nose. Well I can tell you now that my heart beat wildly at the thought he was going to kiss me. It beat wildly with fear and disgust by the way, due to the thought that perhaps Brian the Whine would take advantage of a slightly pissed woman, I had visions of a horrifying repeat of when we were eighteen years old at the school dance, then of me being pregnant with Brian the Whine kid number two. But when he started to sniff around my face like he was a dog deciding whether to piss on me or not, I strangely stopped worrying. (Perhaps that's when I should have started?)

Anyway he only ended up asking me if I was drunk and of course I told him that it was absolutely none of his business whether I was or not, I was a grown woman, had raised a daughter all on my own with absolutely no help from him or his family (it always gets back to that fact every time), that it was Saturday night and I could do whatever the hell I wanted, like dance around the street naked without having to answer to him (why I chose that as an example I don't know but I was just pissed off that I had to come back to *his* house and explain to *him* details of *my* own life when *he* shouldn't have to know). As I shouted all this at him I was waving my arms around wildly and the two bags of bottles and cans were clinking together nicely, kind of like background music to my rant.

Of course he looked at me like I was a crazy person that had ten heads (and at this stage from my view he *did* have ten heads) and said he didn't give a damn whether I was drunk or not, he just wanted to let me know that his parents were in the living room and they had come over to discuss getting to know Katie and me. He presumed I wouldn't want to meet them for the first time drunk. That's all.

Well.

While it was thoughtful of him to inform me of their presence (and to send Katie over to Toby's house while we discussed it), I stood in the hall in shock for quite a while. I just thought of the fact that Katie would have another set of grandparents, yet even more people in her life she had never met before. And then I became angry by that fact. And even more angry by the fact that all these years I knew who they were, they knew well who I was, they had passed me in the street on numerous occasions while I was pregnant, then again when Katie had been born, had heard the rumors that she was Brian's child yet never bothered to make any sort of contact or give help of any kind. The last I had heard of them was that they had sold up and had moved to the sun to help heal Mrs. Whine's arthritis.

After the anger had passed I quickly became embarrassed by the fact I had just screamed the house down at their son about my right to drink all I like on a Saturday night and dance the streets naked, while they sat in the very next room in silence listening to my every word. I could imagine them Ruby, sitting there with their noses turned up with disgust at the unemployed young single mother who had their son's baby without anybody's consent and drank to get drunk on the weekends. (Imagine!)

All these emotions and thoughts ran through me in a matter of seconds while Brian watched me digest the information. I slowly put my bags down (making loud clinking noises) and I entered the living room. I introduced myself in my best sober voice and shook their hands politely, thanked them for coming back to meet Katie and me but apologized that I couldn't stay because I had made plans for the evening already and pretended as though they hadn't already overheard what exactly they were. Well I couldn't exactly sit down and have a serious conversation with them could I? My head was spinning and every time I spoke, my voice sounded like it was coming from the other side of the room. So I made my excuses and left. Of course I had absolutely nowhere to go so I just wandered the streets for ages and pondered my life. After a while I decided I hated it and everyone in it (I know, I know—*again*), and seeing as Katie was away safe for the night and Brian the Whine had company I made my way to the nearest pub and drowned my sorrows.

The bar was really awful actually, in retrospect I wouldn't go in there if I was sober, but because I was so upset I didn't really care. All I saw was a friendly barman and two serial killers deep in discussion at the end of the bar. There were only four of us in the entire building. So the barman saw that I was really upset and this is real film stuff, but he actually did ask me what was wrong and seemed genuinely concerned. I told him that Greg had ruined my life. (By process of elimination I reached the conclusion that it was entirely his fault.) It just all came spilling out of my mouth, Ruby, all about Alex missing the debs, Brian the Whine, having Katie, missing college, Alex getting married, meeting Greg, marrying Greg, Greg cheating on me, missing my job promotion, Greg cheating on me again . . . I told him about Greg having all those affairs while he said that he was away on conferences and because he was a bank manager I believed that he genuinely had to go to all that stuff.

So then the other two guys down the end of the bar were suddenly really interested in me, saw how upset I was, and bought me loads of drinks. They were huge guys Ruby, over six feet tall, muscles so big they looked like body builders, bald heads, one guy had a tattoo of a severed head on his forearm but they were so nice! They were really concerned, asked me loads of questions, gave me tissues when I cried, and told me I could do better than Greg. I was just really surprised Ruby, they were kind enough to drive me home and make sure I got back safely because I was in absolutely no state to walk. I pointed out Greg's house as we passed and they seemed really interested and we all gave him the finger. Such nice guys. It just shows, you can never judge a book by its cover.

Anyway I have such a headache so I have to stop typing but last night proved to me that, at least there are *some* caring men in the world and they're not just all out for themselves.

Rosie

BANK MANAGER ATTACKED IN HIS HOME

A bank manager was badly beaten in a vicious attack and £20,000 was stolen in a burglary yesterday morning. The victim was forty-three-year-old Greg Collins of AIB, Wall Road, Dublin.

The savage raid took place when Collins was awaked in the early hours of the morning by intruders in his home on Abigail Road. The two masked men broke into the victim's home and demanded the bank manager open the bank and empty the safe. Terrified Collins put up a struggle but was punched viciously in the face by the thugs. His nose, which was healing from a previous injury, was further damaged.

A shaken Collins described how he was blindfolded and forced into their van in his pajamas.

The thugs are believed to be over six feet tall and according to Collins had the appearance of body builders. Although he didn't see their faces he did notice a tattoo of a severed head on the arm of one thief.

The men stole €20,000 and sped off quickly leaving Collins alone at the bank beaten and dressed only in his nightwear. The gardai arrived on the scene moments after the men had left, after the alarm had been triggered.

Collins is unsure of how they knew his address. "I'm always careful to look out for anyone suspicious following me home each day but I didn't notice anyone that night. It was the worst night of my life—an absolute nightmare," Collins said, visibly shaken. "These thugs invaded my home and attacked me—I'm terrified."

Collins was home alone at the time due to the recent breakup of his marriage. An investigation into the burglary was underway today but the garda in charge says it is unlikely they will catch the culprits due to a lack of leads.

If anyone has any information regarding this crime, the gardai ask that you come forward now.

Photo above: 43-year-old Greg Collins stands outside the bank and shows broken nose.

You have an instant message from: RUBY

Ruby: You see the papers today?

Rosie: Nope. I've given up on my star signs.

Ruby: Well may I suggest you purchase the Daily Star quickly and cast your mind back to Saturday night.

Rosie: Oh no did the paparazzi snap me coming out of the pub? Ha ha.

Ruby: Not funny Rosie, I'm referring to the men. Now quick, look at the paper.

Rosie: What? What men? What are you talking about?!

Ruby: Tabloid newspaper. Now. Quick. Go.

Rosie: OK

Rosie has logged off

FROM: Rosie
TO: Alex
SUBJECT: Today's article

It's me, Rosie. Check your fax machine quick! I've sent you over an article that was in the paper today. While you're reading it bear in mind the story of my Saturday night out that I told you about.

Read the paper and tell me what you think. Quick! I need your advice.

FROM: Alex
TO: Rosie
SUBJECT: Re: Today's article

Ha ha ha ha ha ha ha ha ha ha ha ha ha ha ha ha ha ha ha ha ha ha ha ha ha ha ha ha ha ha ha ha ha ha ha ha ha ha ha ha ha ha ha ha ha ha ha ha

—⁓—

CHAPTER 37

You have an instant message from: ROSIE

Rosie: Oh. My. God. Alex.

Alex: Yes Rosie?

Rosie: Are you free to chat or are you busy?

Alex: I'm just doing a bit of work but go ahead.

Rosie: My goodness, life-saving surgery on the Internet? Is there no end to your talents, Doctor?

Alex: Apparently not. What's the "oh my god Alex" all about?

Rosie: Oh yeah, you will NOT believe what came through Brian the Whine's door this morning!

Alex: A brick.

Rosie: No!

Alex: A warrant for your arrest.

Rosie: No! Don't say that! Why would you say that?

Alex: Oh no reason in particular, I was just wondering what the sentence is for people who hire other people to beat up and terrorize their ex-husbands. Hmm . . .

Rosie: Alex Stewart, stop that talk right now! It's dangerous to say things like that over the computer you know and I did *not* to do that!

Alex: You're right the gardai are probably on a stakeout right now across the road, watching your every move through a pair of binoculars.

Rosie: Stop Alex, you're freaking me out. I did nothing wrong, the only thing I am guilty of is a bit of naivete, that's all.

Alex: A bit? You think those "serial-killer-looking guys" are usually as friendly to lone women in pubs as they were to you?

Rosie: Look, I was drunk, my suspicions were at an all-time low, and my guard was down. In fact, I had no guard. Stupid, I know but I'm still alive so let's not keep telling me how foolish I was. Anyway as it turns out they were caring guys. It just so happens that when I came downstairs this morning there was a brown package on the kitchen table with my name on it. Inside was €5,000, can you believe it?! And you said they weren't caring!

Alex: Well, what happened to the other €15,000? It was hardly split three ways, was it. I think they got a bit of a bargain there Rosie.

Rosie: Oh ha ha.

Alex: Well every crime boss must get *some* sort of percentage.

Rosie: I am not a crime boss! It was an *accident*.

Alex: Was there a note inside, or a little thank-you card maybe?

Rosie: Alex do you not take anything seriously? No there wasn't any note so it may not even be from them.

Alex: Rosie, a brown package appeared on your kitchen table overnight with €5,000 inside. Unless the postman has a key to your front door I think we can presume it was them.

Rosie: So what will I tell the gardai?

Alex: You're not keeping the money?

Rosie: Alex, I have a 13-year-old daughter, I do not think keeping knowledge of a bank robbery (as well as some of the money) is exactly the wisest thing to do. Plus, believe it or not I have a conscience.

Alex: Well usually I would agree with the telling the truth theory and abiding by the rules but this time around I think you should keep your mouth shut.

First those guys no you are the only person who nos anything about this, they no where you live, can enter your home in the middle of the night without disturbing the neighbors or anyone else inside.

I don't think they were giving you this money as a present for a wonderful start to your new life—they don't seem the type. I think they were showing you what they can do and gave you enough to keep your mouth shut. And I would if I was you and yes, I do take this very seriously Rosie.

Rosie: Oh my god, I've shivers up my spine! This is crazy, like a movie or something. But I can't *not* tell the gardai.

Alex: Do you want to die?

Rosie: Yes, eventually.

Alex: Rosie, I'm serious. Keep the money and say nothing. Give it to charity or something if it bothers you that much. You can make a donation to the Reginald Williams Foundation for Heart Disease if you want.

Rosie: Gag, gag, puke, puke. No thanks. But the charity thing isn't a bad idea. I think I'll do that.

Alex: Which one will you donate it to?

Rosie: The Rosie Dunne Foundation for Women Who Haven't Seen Their Best Friends in America for Ages.

Alex: That's a good charity. Very needy too.

Rosie: Indeed it is. I think I'll give it to one woman in particular who is in dire need of a bit of TLC.

Alex: Excellent idea. I'm sure the poor deprived woman
         will be delighted with your donation. When do you
         think she and her daughter will be visiting their
         doctor friend?

Rosie: I already booked them a flight for Friday week.
         They land at nine in the morning and they'll be stay-
         ing a fortnight. You're right; giving makes me feel
         like such a better person.

Alex: Ha ha ha ha ha you had this all planned? I'll be
         there to pick you up so.

Rosie: Good, by the way you *still* haven't said anything
         about my job.

Alex: Job? You got a job? When? Where? What are you
         doing?

Rosie: Alex I've only left approximately 22,496 messages
         on your answering machine explaining this. Don't
         you listen to them?

Alex: I do! But there's never any from you. I think you're
         dialing the wrong number.

Rosie: Bullshit. I think you need to keep an eye on that
         Bethany when she's nosying around your apartment.
         She might accidentally be knocking her fake boobs
         against the "delete" button.

Alex: Don't start this crap again Rosie. Beth has no quar-
         rels with you and her boobs are not fake. You
         haven't seen her for more than ten years so how
         would you no?

Rosie: I've seen the photographs in the paper and they are
         fake.

Alex: Whatever. So what's the job?

Rosie: Promise not to laugh.

Alex: I won't.

Rosie: You have to *promise*.

Alex: I promise.

Rosie: I'm starting in August as a secretary in St. Patrick's
         Secondary School.

Alex: You're going back . . . *there*? But our sentence is up!
          Hold on a minute . . . that means that, oh my god,
          you're going to be working with Ms. Big Nose
          Smelly Breath Casey! Why?

Rosie: Because I need the money.

Alex: Wouldn't you rather starve?! Why on earth did she
          hire you?

Rosie: I'm wondering the same thing.

Alex: Ha ha ha ha ha.

Rosie: You said you wouldn't laugh.

Alex: Ha ha ha ha.

Rosie: You promised!

Alex: Ha ha ha ha.

Rosie: Oh bugger off.

Rosie has logged off

> Dear Rosie and Katie,
> Greetings from Aruba!
> Having a wonderful time here in paradise!
> Hope all is well with you,
> > Lots of love,
> > Mum and Dad

You have received an instant message from: RUBY

Ruby: Watch out Ireland here we come!

Rosie: Here who come?

Ruby: Gary and Ruby Minnelli.

Rosie: You're keeping the name I see?! What are Gary and
          Ruby Minnelli up to now?

Ruby: Yes we're keeping the name and Gary doesn't even
          mind because it means that he's in disguise and
          none of his work colleagues or friends will recog-

nize him. The All Ireland Salsa dancing championships are on in a few months from now. A couple
from each county goes forward and whoever wins
becomes the Ireland champions, then there's the European championship, and the world championship.

Rosie: So you're going for total world domination?

Ruby: Well not quite the *world* but Gary and I are willing
to take on Ireland.

Rosie: Gary has agreed to all this?

Ruby: Absolutely! Now that Gemma and he have broken
up he's got more time to practice.

Rosie: How does Teddy feel?

Ruby: He has no idea and that's the way it's going to
stay. Anyway we haven't even gotten through the
Dublin heats so there's no point in causing may-
hem and bloody murdering sprees until we get further into the competition. It's on in a few weeks,
will you be there?

Rosie: I'm insulted you even had to ask!

Ruby: Thanks.

FROM: Stephanie
TO: Rosie
SUBJECT: Visit

How's my brave little sister? I hope you're keeping well.
You're dealing with everything that has happened so
brilliantly, I'm so proud of you. I know it's been a tough
time and with me being all the way over here I feel like I
haven't been there for you like I should have been. If it's OK
with you I would love to come over and visit you. Maybe
stay for a week or something. With Mum and Dad off
gallivanting around the world it must be very lonely for you
and with them away unfortunately the rest of us don't meet
up like we should. Maybe we should go to Kilkenny and

visit Kevin, the three of us haven't been in the same room together since I don't know how long. (Don't worry, we won't go to the hotel, we can stand outside and throw eggs at the windows if you like!)

I know you're going over to Alex so maybe I could come over the week before? (That's next week!) To be really honest with you I need the rest as well. Jean-Louis is just too much for me right now, he's a bundle of energy and I'm simply not, so Pierre is taking the week off from the restaurant to mind him so that I can see you.

Also I know that you're staying with Brian so I'll stay in a B&B down the road—I certainly wouldn't want to upset the happy family!! Sorry, cruel joke. I haven't seen him since your school dance when he arrived at the house wearing his navy tux (I agree with you it was definitely navy not black). It'll be interesting to see how he turned out and I'll give him a piece of my mind too.

If you have other plans then feel free to let me know. I could wait until you came back from your liaison with Alex!

FROM: Rosie
TO: Stephanie
SUBJECT: Liaison!

Liaison with Alex is definitely the wrong word to use! Didn't I tell you he was a taken man? With all that's been going on in my life recently I can't believe I never told you that Bethany is back on the scene.

FROM: Stephanie
TO: Rosie
SUBJECT: Bethany!

Slutty Bethany? No way! I thought we were well rid of her. I'm sorry Rosie.

FROM: Rosie
TO: Stephanie
SUBJECT: Re: Bethany!

No need to be sorry for me, Alex is just my friend, same
as always. As long as I'm not within a one-mile radius of her
I can still be that friend. But have I a lot to tell you about
Greg that I couldn't tell you over the phone!

Of course I would love you to come over. Next week is
great; in fact it couldn't be more perfect. You see Brian the
Whine's parents have returned from the depths of hell (and
are constantly complaining about the cold here, even though
it's the middle of summer and everyone is wearing shorts.
Every time I open a window they shiver and pull another
blanket around them. Not what they're used to at their
private *villa* at all). Anyway the traumatic thing is that they
are staying in this very flat in a desperate attempt to get to
know me and their "granddaughter." The only thing is it's
the summer holidays and all Katie wants to do is hang
around outside with Toby, not inside with two shivering,
shriveled-up whinge-bags.

The flat feels even more cramped than usual with them
being here and I feel so claustrophobic, imagine I actually
can't wait to start my new job just so I can get out of the
house. Toby is very funny, he keeps telling me and Katie to
be nice to them so we can get to use the villa in the South of
France whenever we want. So Katie and him keep making
them cups of tea and bringing it to them while they're still
in bed. I know the boy is only thirteen but he has a point, so
recently I started putting biscuits on their saucers.

You won't recognize Katie when you see her Steph, she's
so grown up. Toby's voice has broken and he's shot up by
about three feet over the summer. I find myself keeping an
eye on them a bit more just in case, even though I know
they're only friends.

So you coming over my dear sister could not come at a

better time. It is both a genius and life-saving idea. Plus I really miss you too! At least I'm going to have a great summer before I start the job in hell.

FROM: Rosie
TO: Kevin
SUBJECT: Steph's visit

Steph is over from France for the week. What days are you off so that we can come down and visit you? We can all go out for a meal or something. We haven't done that for a while.

FROM: Kevin
TO: Rosie
SUBJECT: Re: Steph's visit

That sounds like a good plan. I don't think the three of us have been in the same room together since Mum and Dad forced us to take baths together! I've good news! I've been promoted to the position of head chef in the hotel! I haven't forgotten it was you that got me the job in the first place so thanks, I owe you one. I've got Tuesday off, so why don't you both come down on Monday and I'll treat you for dinner.

FROM: Rosie
TO: Kevin
SUBJECT: Re: Steph's visit

Congratulations! And don't thank me, you did it all yourself. Going for dinner sounds good as long as we don't go to the hotel to eat. Knowing what's-his-name was there with *her* is enough to put me off it forever.

Stephanie had the wonderfully juvenile idea of me throwing eggs at the hotel to release my anger. Stock up on those eggs dear brother. We'll be down on Monday to celebrate your good news, see you then.

Invoice Number: KIL000321
Our Reference: 6444421

	Fee Invoice
	EUR
Fee for damage to dining room windows of Kilkenny Two Lakes Hotel:	€6,232.00
VAT @ 21%	€1,308.72
Total	€7540.72

FROM: Rosie
TO: Kevin
SUBJECT: Hard-boiled eggs?

I think it's safe to say that I'll never get a job in the hotel business again. You should have told me that those eggs were hard boiled. Thanks for the few days break all the same. I'm still recovering.

FROM: Rosie
TO: Alex
SUBJECT: Flight Details

My flight is landing at 9 a.m. so don't forget!

Hello from Barbados!
We're having such a ball! The weather is fantastic and we've met lots of lovely people,
Love you both,
Mum and Dad

You have an instant message from: ROSIE

Rosie: I'm baaaaack!
Ruby: Oh so you decided to come home! I'm surprised.
Rosie: Well I almost didn't. If it wasn't for Brian the Whine and his parents wanting to be my new best friends and ruining all my plans.
Ruby: Imagine, having to think of other people. So how did it go?
Rosie: It was just so brilliant. That's all I can say. Pure heaven.
Ruby: You two get along well?
Rosie: Even better than usual.
Ruby: Did you—
Rosie: No!
Ruby: Did you tell him how you—
Rosie: No! Why on earth would I do that? There's no point. If I did that then I would lose him as a friend forever and then it would all be a waste of time. He has never suggested to me that he has ever felt that way about me; remember it was me that kissed him the last time. That was embarrassing enough once never mind having to do it a second time.

Anyway he is already with someone and even if it is
slutty Bethany I couldn't bring myself to do that.
I've been on the receiving end of that kind of treatment so I know not to go there. We had a really
long chat about her anyway. He took me out for
dinner one night to a really beautiful Italian restaurant and had wonderful murals of Venetian buildings painted across the walls, the restaurant had
two levels, every table was in its own little alcove
and you could only get to them by walking under
bridges and arches. It was supposed to have the
gondola trip kind of vibe. There was running water
tinkling in the background which was really relaxing although it made me go to the bathroom about
ten times. The restaurant was lit entirely by candles
all held in big gothic-looking black holders, an in-
surance nightmare I would imagine but very romantic. I think he brought me there to talk about slutty
Bethany and to explain the situation.

It doesn't seem to be that serious of a relationship.
He said he's enjoying the company after being alone
for so long and it's good that she understands his
long working hours but they don't see that much of
each other and he thinks she understands that it's a
very casual relationship. It sounds like he's going to
break up with her actually because he got really serious and I thought he was going to cry. It was
weird; he said that she wasn't "the one" for him.

Ruby: Then what?

Rosie: Well then we got interrupted by Josh who rang the
restaurant in a right panic looking for us, he and
Katie had been messing around, Katie had fallen,
and they were convinced she'd broken her wrist. We
had to leave straight away but we had finished
dessert and so everything was finished.

Ruby: Or was just starting by the sounds of things.

Rosie: What do you mean?

Ruby: God, you annoy me so much Rosie. Can a human being really be this stupid?

Rosie: Look Ruby, you weren't there. It's all very well you giving me this advice but I'm the one who physically has to go and do it. I'll tell him how I feel when it's the right moment.

Ruby: When will it *ever* be the right moment for you?

Rosie: When there's the silence again.

Ruby: What silence?

Rosie: It doesn't matter. Anyway Katie's fine, it was only a sprain. She can't play basketball this week though so she's upset about that.

Ruby: Have you penciled the big event into your diary?

Rosie: What big event?

Ruby: Rosie! The Dublin salsa dancing championships!

Rosie: I know, I was just kidding. Of course I'm going. Katie and Toby are coming too. Has Teddy had a change of heart yet?

Ruby: I can't tell him about the competition Rosie. If I did he would probably march with his trucker mates to the Conrad Hotel and protest against men dancing in glittery suits. It's far more enjoyable for myself and Gary if we don't think Teddy is about to barge into the reception hall looking like Homer Simpson on a mission.

           I'm, you know, proud of Gary. I don't want Teddy and his pure ignorance and lack of intelligence to ruin something that has taken years to achieve. Whether we win, lose, or draw.

Rosie: Oh I can't wait to see you two dancing together. I'll bring the camera. So if Teddy ever does have a change of heart he won't have missed the moment completely.

Ruby: Thanks Rosie, that's a great idea. Remind me to be
          nicer to you in the future.

Rosie: Ha, I think I'll take you up on that. So what are you
          going to wear while you're dancing?

Ruby: Well that was proving to be a huge problem. I know
          all the other dancers competing will be baring flesh
          for all to see but the idea of my outfit will be to
          cover up as much as I can.

          Unfortunately "Upsizes" don't make sexy salsa
          dresses even for my size. Unless they expect me to
          wear what looks like a sheet with a hole cut out for
          my head to go through. Gary was having the same
          problem. So after Miss Behave got over being in a
          huff at being replaced, she offered to make us some-
          thing. She said she's used to "making women's
          clothes for people who haven't the natural figure of
          a woman." Worryingly enough, she won't tell us
          what she's making. But I've told her to steer clear of
          pink, fluff, and rubber.

Rosie: Look forward to it!

            Ba'ax ka wa'alik from Mexico!
   What an adventure this is taking us on, met Charlie
and Anne yesterday on the ship. Imagine they've been
here all this time and we didn't even know!
   Hope you're both safe and happy,
        Love Mum and Dad

HAPPY 14TH BIRTHDAY TOBY,
HOPE YOU LIKE THE REMOTE CONTROL CAR I GOT
YOU. THE GUY IN THE SHOP SAID THE RALLY ONES
ARE THE BEST (AND THEY'RE THE MOST EXPENSIVE
TOO). I GOT IT FOR YOU IN THE STATES SO I DON'T
THINK ANYONE ELSE WILL HAVE THEM HERE. JOSH
HAS ONE AS WELL, THAT'S WHAT I TRIPPED OVER AND

SPRAINED MY WRIST ON. THEY'RE REALLY FAST!
ANYWAY HERE'S TO ANOTHER YEAR, MAYBE TEN
YEARS FROM NOW YOU'LL BE POKING AT PEOPLE'S
TEETH. WHY YOU WANT TO BE A DENTIST IS BEYOND
ME, BUT YOU WERE ALWAYS WEIRD.
I HEARD MONICA DOYLE IS GOING OUT WITH SEAN.
TOUGH LUCK MY FRIEND.
LOVE,
KATIE

FROM: Toby
TO: Katie
SUBJECT: Re: Happy birthday

He may have Monica but I have the best Rally remote
control car in the world. Thanks for it. I'm gonna bring it to
the crappy dance thing on Sunday. You girls can paint your
nails and watch them dance while I drive my car.

FROM: Katie
TO: Toby
SUBJECT: Dance Competition

You can't bring the car to the dance competition! How
unfair to Ruby and Gary would that be if they saw you
playing with that on their big day?

FROM: Toby
TO: Katie
SUBJECT: Re: Dance Competition

Fine then, you can just go with your mum then. Have a
good day. Byeeee!

FROM: Katie
TO: Toby
SUBJECT: Remote control car

No no no no! Hang on! OK you can bring it but you'll
have to play with it in the corridor or something. I don't
wanna go to this thing with mum on my own; she'll be
introducing me to the entire world if you're not there.

              Aloha from Hawaii!
      I've sent photos of me, your dad, and some people
that we've met on the cruise. Having a ball. Heading to
Samoa and Fiji next. Can't wait!
      Love to you and Katie,
              Mum and Dad xxx

RUBY AND GARY MINNELLI!
GOOD LUCK!
I WAS GOING TO SAY "BREAK A LEG" BUT I DON'T
THINK IT'S QUITE APPROPRIATE FOR THE OCCASION.
YOU WILL BOTH BE BRILLIANT AND WE'LL ALL BE
CHEERING FOR YOU.
LOVE ROSIE, KATIE, AND TOBY

You have an instant message from: ROSIE

Rosie: Congratulations you Dancing Queen! I'm so proud
         of you! Are you still glowing from your win?
Ruby: I'm not too sure how I'm supposed to be feeling to
         be honest. I really don't think that we should be the
         winners.
Rosie: Oh don't be silly! The two of you danced bril-
         liantly. Miss Behave did such a great job on your
         dress. I'm surprised it was so understated for one of
         her creations. Black with glittery sequins looked

tres chic compared to all the others. They looked like rainbows on E. Look, you won it fair and square—be proud.

Ruby: But we didn't even get through to the final round . . .

Rosie: Well it's not your fault the couple who came first were practicing out in the corridor. Anyone could have slipped on Toby's stupid remote control car. It was their own fault. Anyway her ankle will heal with time. She'll be back next year to reclaim her title.

Ruby: Yes but technically we shouldn't have won at all Rosie, only the two couples who got to the final round were supposed to battle it out. The second couple who were in the final really should have won . . .

Rosie: Yes but once again that wasn't your fault. It was the stupid woman in purple who tripped over Toby's remote control Raleigh car (they're very fast aren't they?), knocking the drink out of Katie's hand causing the second woman in yellow to slip and land on her backside. That automatically put you through. It's not your fault. You should be delighted!!

Ruby: Well I am in an odd kind of way. *Afternoon Ireland* have asked me and Gary on their show during the week to do our winning dance and for a small interview as well and next week me and Gary are performing in Miss Behave's show in The George.

Rosie: That's fantastic! I'm delighted for you Ruby, my friend the superstar!

Ruby: Oh I wouldn't even be doing all this if you hadn't got me the vouchers for my fortieth birthday. Thanks so much Rosie, thanks for cheering for me so loudly, I heard you the whole way through the dance. And I'm really sorry, you, Katie, and Toby were asked to leave the dance hall . . .

—∿—

CHAPTER 38

Rosie and Katie,
Magandang tanghali po from the Philippines!
Left the top end of Australia a few days ago, we were in Brisbane and Sydney—very beautiful. Here for a little while and moving on to China for a few days.
Love you and miss you both,
Mum and Dad

FROM: Rosie
TO: Alex
SUBJECT: Slutty Bethany

So Alex, did you dump her yet?

FROM: Alex
TO: Rosie
SUBJECT: Mind your own business

Rosie, stop! I'll tell you when I do!

Ni hao from China!
Sorry we're not there to help you with the move.
We wish you luck in your new apartment.
We're sure it will bring you lots of happiness,
        Love, Mum and Dad xxx

Rosie: The place is disgusting Ruby. Absolutely disgusting.

Ruby: Oh stop, it can't be any worse than mine.

Rosie: Worse than yours multiplied by one hundred.

Ruby: Such a place exists? God bless you. What's so bad
          about it?

Rosie: Well let's see, where should I start? Hmm . . .
          should I tell you about the fact that it's a second-
          floor apartment over a group of shops, among them
          being a tattoo parlor and an Indian takeaway which
          has managed to leave the stench of Tikka Masala all
          over my clothes already?

          Perhaps I should tell you about the *gorgeous* 1970s
          green and gray floral wallpaper which is just *dan-
          gling* off the walls, and I wouldn't want to forget
          the fact that there's matching curtains too.

          Hmmm . . . actually maybe I should start with the
          brown carpets which have very curious-looking
          stains embedded in the pile, as well as cigarette
          burns and mysterious odors. I think it's been there
          for about thirty years and has never been vacu-
          umed. The kitchen is so small that when two people
          stand in it, one person has to back out to let the
          other leave.

          No wonder the rent is so ridiculously cheap; no one
          in their right mind would want to live here. It's also
          no wonder that they were in such a rush to move
          out, why anyone would want to raise a child in this
          tip is beyond me.

Ruby: You are.

Rosie: Yes well I won't be here for long. I'm going to magi-
        cally save loads of money and get us out of here.

Ruby: And open a hotel.

Rosie: Yes.

Ruby: And live in the penthouse.

Rosie: Yes.

Ruby: And Kevin can be the head chef.

Rosie: Yes.

Ruby: And Alex the in-house doctor so that he can save
        the lives of those you poison.

Rosie: Yes.

Ruby: And you'll be the owner and manager.

Rosie: Yes.

Ruby: So what I can be?

Rosie: The head cleaner.

Ruby: Your downfall.

Rosie: Only joking. You and Gary could be the evening en-
        tertainment. You can salsa till you drop.

Ruby: Sounds like heaven to me. Well Rosie, you better get
        your ass in gear and get this hotel business off the
        ground before we're all old and gray.

Rosie: I'm working on it, but in the meantime I start work
        part-time (with the work experience kids) which
        consists of printing up the school letters explaining
        the return dates for the kids next month, we put
        them in envelopes, stick a stamp on them, lick them
        closed, and post them. I don't know about you but
        I'm enthralled by that idea. But at least it's only for
        a few weeks and when the kids start back at school
        then I work full-time.

        Apart from that I'm trying to make this kip of a
        place look like a home. Brian the Whine has been
        very helpful believe it or not. He's hired out a
        sander for the day and tomorrow we're going to rip

up those smelly carpets and sand and varnish the floors in all the rooms. I'm frightened to think of what we'll find under them. Probably a few dead bodies.

Katie and Toby are having great fun tearing the wallpaper off the walls, what's left of it anyway. We're going to paint the walls white, because even with a million-watt bulb the place still looks like a cave. It needs brightening up and I'm going for the minimalist look, not because I'm trendy and fashionable but because I don't really have that much furniture. I'm going to pull down the old floral curtains and burn them in a ritual.

My darling brother Kevin was only too delighted to come to Dublin and raid what's-his-name's house for all my leftover belongings which he only too gladly gave him probably because he was so terrified of having his nose broken again. I even got the black leather couch which was in the house before I married him but hey, I deserve it.

Ruby: It sounds like it's going to be lovely Rosie. A real home.

Rosie: Now all I need to do is get rid of the smell of curry that's floating around and seeping through the walls of the entire building block. It's turned me off Indian food forever.

Ruby: Now *that's* the best diet I've ever heard of. Live over a restaurant and the smell will make you sick of food.

Rosie: I think you're on to something there.

     Ei Je from Singapore!
   Having such a wonderful time we don't want to come home!
   Good luck with your new job this week love, we're

thinking of you here as we lounge by the pool! (Just joking)

    Love,
        Mum and Dad

You have received an instant message from: ALEX

Alex:	Have you a minute to chat?
Rosie:	No sorry, I'm busy licking stamps.
Alex:	Oh, OK. Can I call you sometime later?
Rosie:	I was only joking Alex. Ms. Big Nose Smelly Breath Casey has asked me to put together the year's first newsletter so I'm on the school website trying to figure out what happened or is happening that's worth writing about.
Alex:	How's the job?
Rosie:	It's OK. I've been here a few weeks now so I've settled in and it's going OK. Nothing to write home about.
Alex:	Sorry I wasn't in touch sooner. I hadn't realized it had been so long. Time has been flying by once again.
Rosie:	It's OK. I assumed you were busy. I've moved into my apartment now and everything.
Alex:	Oh gosh that's right. How is it?
Rosie:	It's OK. It was absolutely dire when we first moved in. The place stunk, there was mold growing on the ceilings, damp rising up the walls but Brian the Whine was a really good help. He fixed all that was broken and cleaned what was dirty. Just like a regular little slave.
Alex:	So are you and he getting along then?
Rosie:	Better. I only have the urge to strangle him ten times a day now.
Alex:	Well it's a start. Any romance?
Rosie:	What? With Brian the Whine?!

Alex: Yes.

Rosie: You need your head examined. The man was created for scraping mold and sanding floors only.

Alex: Oh. Anyone else in your life?

Rosie: Yes actually. A 13-year-old daughter, a new job, and a drawer full of bills. My hands are pretty full at the moment. Although my neighbor did ask me to go out on a date with him this weekend.

Alex: Oh right. So are you going out with him?

Rosie: Let me tell you a little bit about him first and then maybe you can help me with the dilemma I'm faced with.

Alex: That's what best friends are for.

Rosie: His name is Sanjay, he's sixty years old, and he's married, lives with his wife and two sons, and owns and runs the Indian takeaway downstairs. Oh and you'll never guess where he invited me out for dinner.

Alex: Where?

Rosie: His Indian takeaway downstairs. He said he would pay.

Alex: So what's your dilemma?

Rosie: Very funny.

Alex: Well at least you have friendly neighbors.

Rosie: He's not the nicest by far. Beside me there's the owner of the tattoo parlor (which is also below my flat). I can't even tell what color he is underneath the tattoos he has covering his body from head to toe. He's got beautiful long black silky hair that he ties back in a plait and a neatly trimmed goatee framing his mouth. He wears leather trousers, a leather waistcoat, and size a million steel-toed biker boots every day. When he's not drilling away on some-body's skin downstairs he's blaring music from his flat beside me.

Alex: Trust you to move in beside a heavy metal fan.

Rosie: That's where you're wrong. His name is Rupert;
           he's thirty-five years old, a graduate of the presti-
           gious Trinity College Dublin where he got a degree
           in Irish History and a master's in Irish Literature.
           James Joyce is his idol and across his chest is the
           quote: "Mistakes are the portals of discovery."

           He's a huge fan of classical and opera music and at
           5 p.m. every evening when he's closing up and cash-
           ing up the till for the night he blares Brahms Piano
           Concerto Number 2 in B flat major, Op 83. After
           that he heads up to his flat where he proceeds to
           cook the most savory and delicious-smelling meals
           and settles down to read James Joyce's *Ulysses* for
           the billionth time while listening to the sounds of
           The Best of Pavarotti blasting out from his speakers
           (paying particular attention to Nessun Dorma).

           Katie and I practically know all the words to it by
           this stage and Toby stuffs a pillow up his shirt, stands
           up on the couch, and mimes along to the music.

           At least Rupert is educating the children. Katie is
           going crazy about mixing Nessun Dorma into a
           dance song she's created on her new set of decks.
           Brian the Whine bought them for her which made
           me really angry because I was planning on getting
           them for her as a Christmas present. But I've made
           her keep them in his rented house so that she
           doesn't disturb the neighbors. Although to be hon-
           est I really don't know why I bothered caring with
           all the other noises and smells going on around us.

           Oh yes and did I mention that Joan of Arc is living
           across the hall from me.
Alex: Ha ha, no you didn't.
Rosie: Well this woman (her name is either Joan, Mary, or
           Brigid, something meaningful in a religious way)

and she's only in her late twenties. She came over to say hello the first day we moved in and when she realized that it was just Katie and I moving in and that my singledom was not due to the tragic loss of my husband she left rather rudely and hasn't spoken to us since.

Alex: Well at least she's quiet.

Rosie: Just because she ignores me, the sinner of the apartment block, it doesn't mean she's quiet. Every Monday evening I noticed there seem to be a large herd of elephants making their way upstairs to our level and going into Joan of Arc's flat. After further investigation I noticed that it was in fact the same twenty people who visited every week all bearing gifts of Bibles in their hands.

My further powers of investigation led me to believe that she was holding Bible reading groups every week. Now she's put a sign up on the door saying, "Ye shall walk after your LORD, and fear him, and keep his commandments, and obey his voice, and ye shall serve him, and cleave unto him."

I mean, what does "cleave" mean? Whoever has heard of such a word?

Alex: Ha ha Rosie, oh I really don't no!

Rosie: You mean KNOW not NO. You will never learn will you?

Alex: I think not.

Rosie: Then down the hall from me are a family from Nigeria. Zareb and Malika and their 5 kids. And I thought the place was too small for just me and Katie.

Alex: Sounds like Phil and Maggie and their kids. How are your mum and dad?

Rosie: My multilingual mum and dad you mean? Well they're having the time of their lives away from all of us. Mum recently celebrated her sixtieth; she sent me a postcard saying, "Zdravstvuite from Russia!" I can just imagine the two of them enjoying themselves like an old couple from the *Love Boat*. Speaking of the dreaded L word, what was with all the personal questions about my love life?

Alex: Because I want you to find someone that's why. I want you to be happy.

Rosie: Alex, I've never found happiness with another human being and you know it. I'm separated from my husband; I'm not looking for another victim just yet. Possibly never.

Alex: *Never?*

Rosie: Possibly. Well I'll never marry again that's for sure. I'm getting used to my new life again. I have a new apartment, a new job, a teenage daughter, I'm 32 years old and I'm entering a new phase of my life. I think I'm finally growing up. Anyway there's nothing wrong with being single. Being single is the new black. You should know.

Alex: I'm not single.

Rosie: Not *yet*.

Alex: No I'm not. I won't be.

Rosie: Why, have you changed your mind?

Alex: My mind was never made up in the first place to be changed.

Rosie: Oh dear, hello Mr. Chicken Shit, my name is Rosie Dunne. Nice to meet you.

Alex: I'm not chicken shit. I never said I was going to end mine and Beth's relationship.

Rosie: Well it sounded like that to me when we discussed it at dinner last month.

Alex: Yes well never mind that dinner, my head was elsewhere. I didn't quite get to finish that conversation . . . So what I'm saying is that I want me to be happy with Bethany and you to be happy with someone and then we'll both be happy with people. I don't like the idea of you being *without* someone when I'm *with* someone. It's an awful waste of a woman. (Joke.)

Rosie: I know what it is. You just don't want me to be single because I'm a distraction to you. If I'm with a man then you think that *perhaps* you just might be able to keep your hands off me. I know deep down that's what this is all about. I've sussed you out Alex Stewart. You love me. You want me to have your babies. You can't stand another day without me.

Alex: I . . . don't no what to say . . .

Rosie: HA! Bloody hell Alex I was only joking. No need to get all serious on me. So tell me. What happened to make you change your mind about Bethany?

Alex: Oh not back to this again . . .

Rosie: Alex I'm your best friend, I've known you since I was five. No one knows you better than I do. I'm asking this for the very last time and do not lie. What happened to make you change your mind about breaking up with slutty Bethany?

Alex: She's pregnant.

Rosie: Oh dear god. Sometimes because you're my best friend I think that you're normal, like me. Then every now and again you remind me that you're a man.

Phil: Hold on a minute Alex. Last year you were trying to *break up* Rosie's marriage and now you're telling me that you *want* her to meet somebody new?

Alex: Yes.

Phil: Just so that while you're with Bethany, you won't feel *tempted*?

Alex: No! That's not what I said!

Phil: Well that's what it sounds like. At the rate you're going, I don't think the two of you deserve each other at all.

PART 4

—᠁—

CHAPTER 39

Welcome home Mum and
Dad! (Fáilte go h-Eirinn!)
    Glad you arrived home safely and in one piece!
    Can't wait to hear all the stories of your adventures and
see all the photographs.
    See you at the weekend,
        Love,
        Rosie and Katie

DEAR STEPHANIE AND PIERRE!
CONGRATULATIONS ON THE ARRIVAL OF YOUR NEW
BABY GIRL!
WE CAN'T WAIT TO MEET LITTLE SOPHIA, IN THE
MEANTIME HERE ARE A FEW LITTLE OUTFITS TO KEEP
HER AS TRENDY AS HER MOTHER!
LOTS OF LOVE,
ROSIE AND KATIE

HAPPY 8TH BIRTHDAY JOSH,
LOTS OF LOVE,
ROSIE AND KATIE

Hi Katie,

Thanks for your card and present that you gave me fro my brithday. I guess my dad told you guys about Bethinny being pregnint. That means I'm gonna have a brother or sister. I think I'm the only person around here who thinks it's cool.

She is four months gone they say. Gone where, I don't know. I only saw her yesterday. My mom just laughed when my dad told her but then she can't have thought it was too funny cos she was cursing too. She was saying she bets your mom is real happy about it. But she's wrong cos your mom's not happy with Dad is she?

Dad is sad because he said all the grils in his life are mad at him. Your mom is, my mom is, and Bethinny is too. The other night he told me that he should have told your mom sooner and he should have done something about it. I don't know what he was talking about. I hope he starts acting normal again.

Bethinny is mad at him cos he won't marry her. I heard them fighting about it. Bethinny was crying and saying that Dad didn't love her and he was saying that he did but that he needed to take things slower. She said how much slower could they take things seeing as it was fifteen years since they started going out? Dad said that he would mind her and the baby but he said it was too soon to get married. She said she wanted them to buy a house near her parents and Dad said she only wanted to do that so she could lunch with all the other ladies. He said he supposed she wanted a summer house in Nantucket as well and she said of course she didn't. She preferred Martha's Vineyard. I've never met Martha and I don't know how she would feel about us just moving onto her vineyard all of a sudden. And I hate grapes.

Dad said that they needed to get to know more about each other before they got married. Bethinny said he knew everything there was to know about her, that they had known each other since they were sixteen and that she was still the same person and that she was pregnint with his baby and if he didn't marry her, her dad would be really angry and would fire him.

I think dad should marry her. I want a brother, and Dad really, really likes his job. I'll fill you and Toby in on more stuff as soon as I know. Because I'm only here at weekends I miss all the good stuff.

Thank your mom fro my present,
>Form,
>Josh

DR. WILLIAMS REWARDED

Reginald Williams, M.D., was presented with an award last night at the National Health Awards in Boston. He was nominated through a highly selective process that recognizes those who have made major contributions to the advancement of the medical sciences and public health.

This award is considered one of the highest honors in the fields of medicine and health. He was accompanied to the ceremony by his wife, Miranda, his daughter, Bethany, and her newly announced fiancé Dr. Alex Stewart, cardio-surgeon at St. Jude's Hospital in Boston.

See page four of the Health Supplement for Wayne Gillespie's report.

You have received an instant message from: ROSIE

Rosie: You wanted me to learn about this in the newspa-pers first?

Alex: I'm sorry Rosie.

Rosie: You're sorry? You get engaged and you let me read about it in a newspaper? What the hell has hap-pened to you these days?

Alex: Rosie, all I can say is sorry.

Rosie: I don't understand the way your mind works Alex,
         you don't even love her.

Alex: I do.

Rosie: Well that's convincing.

Alex: I shouldn't have to *convince* anyone.

Rosie: Only yourself. Alex, you told me you didn't love her.
         In fact a few months back you were planning on
         breaking up with her. Gee, I wonder what happened
         to make you change your mind all of a sudden.

Alex: You no what happened. There's a baby involved now.

Rosie: That's bullshit. The Alex I know wouldn't marry a
         woman he doesn't know for the sake of the baby.
         That's the worst thing you could do to the poor
         child, raise it in an environment where the parents
         don't even love each other. What's the point of
         that? You're not with Sally and things with Josh
         work out fine. It may not be the most desired posi-
         tion to be in, everyone wants to play happy families
         but it doesn't always work out that way. This is
         ridiculous.

Alex: I'm a weekend dad to Josh; I don't want a repeat of
         that. It's not right.

Rosie: Marrying someone you don't love is not right.

Alex: I'm extremely fond of Bethany; we have a great re-
         lationship and get on well.

Rosie: Well I'm glad you and your future wife "get on
         well." If you don't think this through properly,
         Bethany will be another Sally. Another failed mar-
         riage is not what you want.

Alex: This marriage won't fail.

Rosie: No you'll just be miserable for the rest of your life
         and that's great just as long as the tongues of disap-
         proving people can't gossip about you.

Alex: Why should I take advice from you Rosie? What on
         earth have you done in your life that makes you
         such an expert on telling me how to live mine? You

lived with a man that cheated on you for years and
you kept taking him back time and time again.
What do you no about marriage?

Rosie: I know enough not to go racing up the aisle with
someone else I barely know or love. I know enough
to not allow my life choices to be influenced by my
desire for money and power and prestige. I know
enough not to marry a man so a bunch of rich people will smile at me and tell me how great I am. I
wouldn't marry a man to get my picture in the paper, my name on an award trophy, or for some
dumb promotion at work.

Alex: Oh Rosie, you make me laugh. You have no idea
what you're talking about. You've obviously been
spending too much time in your flat doing nothing
but concocting conspiracy theories.

Rosie: Oh of course, because that's all I do. Sit around my
council flat doing nothing, being the poor uneduc-
ated single mother that I am while you and your
Harvard pals sit in your gentlemen's clubs smoking
cigars and patting each other on the backs. We
may live in very different worlds, Alex Stewart, but
I know you and I'm sick of seeing who you've
turned into.

So what would good old Reginald Williams have
done if he had learned that his daughter was pregnant and that the fool who was responsible
wouldn't marry her? Oh the shame that would
bring on the family, how the people would talk. He
would just have to let you go from the hospital,
have a few words with his fellow colleagues on the
hospital board, and bye, bye Alex.

But at least now, she's got the ring on her finger and
you've got the job promotion and we can all live
happily ever after.

Alex: Not everybody walks away, Rosie. They might in
         your life, but not in mine.

Rosie: Alex, for Christ sake! Not marrying Bethany isn't
         "walking away." As long as you're there for the
         child then you're not walking away. You don't have
         to *marry* her!

Alex: Look I'm fed up with all this Rosie, with you con-
         stantly checking up on me, me having to explain
         everything to you. You're not my wife or my mother
         so give it a rest. Who says I have to run all my life
         decisions by you anyway? I'm tired of you nagging
         at me and moaning at me about people I see and
         places I go. I can make decisions on my own you
         no. I'm a grown man.

Rosie: Then for once in your life ACT LIKE ONE!

Alex: Who are you to insult *me* and lecture *me* when you
         haven't done a thing right in your life yourself? Just
         do me a favor and don't bother getting in touch un-
         til you have something decent to say.

Rosie: Fine! Well then, I think you'll find you'll be waiting
         a long, long time.

Rosie has logged off

Alex: No change there then.

Phil: What are you doing?

Alex: You no what I'm doing.

Phil: Why are you marrying her?

Alex: *Her* name is Bethany.

Phil: Why are you marrying *Bethany*?

Alex: Because I love her.

Phil: Really? Because last time you stepped into the virtual
         confessional box, you told me you were planning on
         ending your relationship. Why do you feel you have
         to do this? Is her dad putting pressure on you?

Alex: No, no, no. There's no pressure. I want to do this.

Phil: Why?

Alex: Why the hell not? Why did you marry Margaret?

Phil: I married Margaret because I love every inch of the woman with all my heart and plan to be with her for the rest of my life, through sickness and in health, till death do us part. She is my best friend, we have five beautiful children and as much as they drive me up the walls, I couldn't live a day without them. I don't sense you have this with Bethany.

Alex: Not all relationships are like yours and Margaret's.

Phil: No they're not but the intention should be there at the beginning. Was there the silence thing with Bethany?

Alex: Oh shut up about the silence Phil.

Phil: You're the one who's obsessed with it. So, come on, was there the silence thing?

Alex: No.

Phil: Then you shouldn't marry her.

Alex: OK I won't just because you say so.

Phil: What does Rosie say about it?

Alex: Nothing. She's not talking to me.

Phil: How do you feel about that?

Alex: At this stage, I'm so mad at her, I don't care what she thinks. I'm moving on from her. Bethany and this new baby are my future. Can I leave the confessional box now?

Phil: Yeah. Say five Hail Marys and an Our Father, and God rest your messed-up little soul.

You have an instant message from: KATIE

Katie: You look very interested in learning about the female reproduction system.

Toby: I'm not. I'd rather figure it out for myself the
        proper way.

Katie: Oh funny but you'll be old and gray before anyone
        lets you get your hands on them. And then it'll prob-
        ably be a man.

Toby: My best friend is a comedienne. You had a salad roll
        for lunch didn't you?

Katie: How do you no?

Toby: KNOW not NO. Because I can see the lettuce hang-
        ing out of your braces. So what do you want?

Katie: Well not that you deserve to be asked, I'm going to
        the orthodontist again later if you wanna come. You
        can ask him a million questions about everything
        he's doing as always and annoy the hell out of him.
        It's so funny the way that vein in his forehead pul-
        sates when he sees you.

Toby: Yeah I know. Sorry I can't go. Monica is coming
        around to my house to watch the football.

Katie: Monica, Monica, Monica. I'm sick of hearing about
        stupid Monica Doyle. She's no more interested in
        football than the man on the moon.

Toby: Neil Armstrong could very well be a fan of football.
        She said she's a fan of Manchester United.

Katie: Yeah right. So why aren't I invited to your house?

Toby: Because you have to go to the dentist.

Katie: Yes, but you didn't no that until a second ago.

Toby: OK then would you like to watch football, the sport
        that you absolutely hate with a passion with the two
        teams you hate even more, in my house today?

Katie: I can't. I'm busy.

Toby: You see? Now don't say I never ask you out anywhere.

Katie: How long have you known that I'm going to the
        dentist?

Toby: All of five minutes.

Katie: How long ago did you invite Monica Doyle to your
        house?

Toby: Last week.
Katie: My point exactly!

You have an instant message from: KATIE

Katie: Mum, I hate men.
Rosie: Congratulations dear welcome to the club. Your
        membership is in the post. I'm so proud of this mo-
        ment I wish I had a camera.
Katie: Please Mum I'm serious.
Rosie: And so am I. So what has Toby done this time?
Katie: He's invited Monica Doyle to his house to watch
        the football match and he didn't invite me. Well he
        did, but only after he new I was busy.
Rosie: Oh dear, he's caught the bug already. Is this moany
        Monica we're talking about? The little girl who
        cried all day at your tenth birthday party until her
        parents came to collect her because her false nail
        fell off?
Katie: Yes.
Rosie: Oh dear. I hate that child.
Katie: She's not a child anymore Mum. She's 14, got the
        biggest chest in the school, dyes her hair blond,
        leaves the top buttons of her polo shirt open in PE
        and leans down so the boys can see down her top.
        She even flirts with Mr. Simpson and pretends not
        to understand what he's talking about in computer
        class so he'll come up behind her and lean over her
        to show her what to do.

        She hates talking about anything other than shop-
        ping so I don't no why she's going to even bother
        watching football. Well actually I do no why.
Rosie: Sounds like she's got a case of the Slutty Bethinitis
        to me.

Katie: What? What do I do about Monica?

Rosie: Oh that's simple. Assassinate her.

Katie: Please Mum for once in your life be serious.

Rosie: I am an incredibly serious woman. The only way to deal with this is to silence her. Because if not, she'll only end up coming back to haunt you when you're 32 years old. Death is the only thing for it.

Katie: Thanks, but I'm open to any other suggestions you may have.

Rosie: You said he invited you?

Katie: Yes but only because he new I couldn't go.

Rosie: My dear sweet innocent daughter, an invitation is an invitation. It would be rude to turn him down. I suggest you turn up on his doorstep this evening, I'll give you the money for the bus to his house.

Katie: But Mum I can't go! I've got an appointment with the orthodontist. My brace broke again. Moany Monica hit me in the face with the basketball.

Rosie: Well the dentist can wait. I'll make another appointment for you. This is a very important football match you know, I wouldn't want you to miss it just because of a silly little thing like getting your teeth fixed.

Katie: Thanks Mum!

Rosie: Now get off the computer before Mr. Simpson catches you and reports me to Ms. Big Nose Smelly Breath Casey and gets me fired.

Katie: You wish Mum. I don't no how you work with her every day.

Rosie: Actually, I'm surprised to admit it myself but she's not so bad. In fact she's not bad at all. As far as bosses go she's been really, really pleasant. Her name is Julie. Can you believe it? She actually has a first name. And all this time I had convinced myself it was Big Nose Smelly Breath. And it's a nice, normal name too; I would have thought it was something more like Vladimir or Adolf.

Katie: Ha, ha me too. But is it not really awkward working with someone who used to give out to you every day?

Rosie: Things are a little awkward between us. It kind of feels like she's an ex-boyfriend of mine and we're meeting after years of separation. Every day conversation becomes a little longer, a little friendlier, a little less about work and a little more about life. We've spent so many years arguing with each other it feels odd to agree on things. It's almost like we're afraid of being tricked if one of us agrees with the other. But each day we talk more and more and earlier today I was surprised to hear her tell me that you are quite the intellect when you're not being distracted by that boyfriend of yours.

Katie: He's so not my boyfriend Mum. Just shows how much she nos.

Rosie: I know, I know. Alex and I had a hard time convincing her of the same thing when we were growing up. Do you know that she thought Alex was your dad?

Katie: Did she?

Rosie: Anyway I told her that Brian was your father and she couldn't stop laughing . . . Actually perhaps this isn't a story to tell you.

Katie: Oh so she's your "friend" now?

Rosie: No, not exactly my bosom buddy friend, you know what I mean. She's a work colleague that I get along with.

Katie: Wait till Alex hears you saying that, he'll drop dead with the shock.

Rosie: I'll let you tell him.

Katie: Oh I forgot you two still aren't talking.

Rosie: Yes well, it's a long story honey.

Katie: People who say it's a long story mean it's a stupid
         short one that they're too embarrassed and couldn't
         be bothered to tell. Why don't you talk to him?

Rosie: Because I don't care about what he does anymore.
         What he does with his life is his own mistake and I
         have nothing to do with it now. Anyway he doesn't
         want to hear about what I have to say.

Katie: Our neighbor Rupert says, "Mistakes are the por-
         tals of discovery."

Rosie: Rupert doesn't say that. James Joyce did.

Katie: James who? Do I no him?

Rosie: He's dead.

Katie: Oh sorry, did you no him well?

Rosie: What on earth are they teaching you at school?

Katie: At the moment it's sex education. It's boring as hell.

Rosie: I would have to agree with you on that one. Anyway
         back to Alex, he has just changed as a person, love.
         He's not the man I used to know. He's different.

Katie: He'd bloody want to be, he was 5 years old and
         drooling when you first met him. If Toby is still
         acting like a 14-year-old when we're your age then
         I'll worry.

Rosie: Oh don't worry Katie, I'm sure Toby will grow up
         to be a mature friend and family oriented dentist.
         But just as a warning, be prepared to meet many
         30-year-old men who still think they're 14 years
         old. Your father being a prime example . . .

Katie: Yeah, yeah, yeah. I've heard all this before. Dad's
         coming home for Christmas you no. He asked me
         to ask you if you we would eat Christmas dinner
         with him and his parents. Seeing as it's only you
         and me this year anyway I thought it would be a
         great idea.

Rosie: Well whoopdeedoo. Bring on Christmas day.

Katie: I new you would be ecstatic at the idea Mum!

Hi love,

Hope all is well. It was great to see you at the weekend, thanks for coming over to us in the west and joining us in "hanging off the edge of the cliff," as you put it! I promise the house will be in better order next time you come to see us, but I'm finding it so difficult to settle down after traveling for months.

Settling into a new home, in a new village, in a new county is an adventure for us. Everybody is so friendly here and our Irish is gradually coming back to us. We don't have neighbors as exciting as you seem to have in your new apartment, although if it makes you feel any better your father told me to tell you that the whole of Ireland has a complaint to make about its neighbors: being stuck between America and Britain.

You're my wonderful brave baby girl, Rosie, and your dad and I are so, so proud of you. I hope you know that. You are so strong, you never allow anything to knock you back and you're the best mother to Katie. She's a feisty young lady now, isn't she? She's definitely her mother's daughter. I'm sorry Dad and I left you at such an important time of your life, it just broke my heart having to leave you and Katie when you were going through all that stuff with what's-his-name. But you're a tough cookie and what doesn't kill you only makes you stronger.

Remember Rosie that you can take on the world and win time and time again. I hope you know that. I'm not around enough now to tell you that. Don't mind what Alex said about you never doing anything right. I can understand that you were upset about it but he only said it to hurt you in a moment of anger. None of us are perfect. Don't allow this argument with Alex to end your friendship. He's been there for you all your life and you for him. I've seen you both grow together over the years and you surely can't expect to grow in the same way all of the time, you have to take your own paths.

It would be such a shame for you to miss his wedding. I was talking to Sandra earlier on and she was telling me that they're planning a very big Christmas wedding. They want to be married before the baby is born, and Bethany doesn't want to be showing too much in her dress. Sandra would love for you and Rosie to be there, they've watched you grow up over the years too. I get the impression she's not a huge fan of Bethany's herself but she loves Alex and she wants to go to support him.

Sandra said that Dad and I are invited but unfortunately we can't go because we are spending Christmas with Stephanie and Pierre in Paris, as you know. Christmas in Paris will be beautiful no doubt and I'm excited to meet granddaughter number two! It's such a shame that you and Katie can't come too but I understand she wants to spend her first Christmas with her dad, and I know she wants to get to know her "other" grandparents too. I can't help feeling jealous that they'll be seeing my Katie on Christmas day, and I won't!

Kevin has met a girl, would you believe, and he's spending Christmas with her and her parents in Donegal. It must be serious. I think she's a waitress in the same hotel as him or something but I'm not too sure. You know Kevin; he's not too good at giving information out about his life.

Your dad says hello, he's tucked up in bed with a nasty flu. He only got it the day you left so you're lucky you missed out on that. He's been very tired since he returned from the trip. We're both in our sixties Rosie, how time went by so fast I'll never know. Anyway I better go because he keeps calling me. Honestly you would think he was on his deathbed by the way he's acting even though it's nothing more than a case of the sniffles.

I'm so proud of my two girls in Dublin,

Love you,

Mum

∾

Dr. Reginald & Miranda Williams
invite KATIE DUNNE *to join them in celebrating the*
marriage of their beloved daughter
Bethany Williams
To
Dr. Alex Stewart
At
The Memorial Church of Harvard University
& a reception at
The Boston Harbor Hotel
On the 28th of December
RSVP Miranda Williams (address overleaf)

∾

—∿—

CHAPTER 40

Welcome to the Relieved Divorced Dubliners chat room
There are currently six people chatting

Divorced_1:   Oh LonelyLady just stop crying for one
               minute of your life and think about your situ-
               ation. You should be angry not sad. Repeat
               after me, I am a strong woman.

LonelyLady: I am a strong woman.

Divorced_1:   I am in control of my life.

LonelyLady: I am in control of my life.

Divorced_1:   It is *not* my fault that Tommy left.

LonelyLady: It is *not* my fault that Tommy left.

Divorced_1:   And I don't care that he did because he is a
               bastard.

LonelyLady: I can't say that!

Divorced_1:   Look, let me put your life into perspective for
               you. He walked out on you after only 6
               months of marriage, took the furniture, the
               kitchenware even the damn bathroom mat,
               and left you a *note* for Christ sake, so repeat
               after me, I don't care that he left me because
               he is a bastard!

LonelyLady: I don't care that he left me because he is a
              BASTARD!

Divorced_1:   Screw him!

LonelyLady: Screw him!

Unsure One: Ladies I'm not sure that this is a very healthy
              way to help LonelyLady.

Divorced_1:   Oh shut up, you're never sure of anything.

LonelyLady: Oh shut up, you're never sure of anything!

Divorced_1:   LonelyLady I didn't mean for you to repeat
              that.

Wildflower: Ha ha ha ha.

Divorced_1:   Oh shut up.

UnsureOne: Gosh, I'm not sure anyone is ever allowed to
              have an opinion in here apart from you Di-
              vorced_1.

Divorced_1:   But you never *have* an opinion.

SingleSam: Look everyone, calm down. Don't be silly,
              UnsureOne; of course we all want to hear
              your opinion. How did you deal with
              Leonard having an affair and leaving
              you?

Divorced_1:   She cleverly moved into the spare room and
              stopped having a life.

SingleSam: Now, now Divorced_1 give her a chance.

UnsureOne: Thank you SingleSam, you're a gentleman.
              What I was going to say is that I don't believe
              in divorce. I follow the teachings of the
              Catholic church and the pope himself said
              that divorce is an "evil" that is "spreading
              like a plague" through society. I for one agree
              with him. The purpose of the family is to be
              together. And together we shall stay no mat-
              ter what happens.

Divorced_1:   Well the pope was never married to my ex-
              husband, that's all I have to say to that.

Wildflower: Ha ha ha ha ha.

UnsureOne: I'm not continuing with this conversation, I
              don't like your tone.
Wildflower: The Catholic church believes in annulments,
              UnsureOne, why don't you get one of those?
UnsureOne: No.
Wildflower: Why not? It's practically the same thing only
              the pope will give his, kind of, blessing to it.
UnsureOne: No.
Wildflower: But can't you at least explain why?
Divorced_1:   Because she doesn't want to end her marriage,
              full stop.
UnsureOne: No Divorced_1. I just don't think it would be
              right. For the children.
Divorced_1:   What's so right for the children about your
              husband taking the master bedroom with the
              TV and en-suite, forcing you to sleep in the
              spare room while you stay at home on the
              weekend and he goes out on dates? Your kids
              will get married thinking they're supposed to
              have separate rooms and multiple partners.
LonelyLady: You let him go out on *dates*?
UnsureOne: Oh they're not dates, don't pay any attention
              to Divorced_1, she's in one of her moods to-
              night. He goes out on business dinners. I can't
              very well stop him from doing that can I?
              And just because his boss is a woman I don't
              think I should worry. You wouldn't be at me
              about this if his boss was a man.
SingleSam: Yes, but UnsureOne, it was his boss that he
              was having the affair with . . .
Wildflower: Ha ha ha ha.
LonelyLady: I can understand UnsureOne's reasoning. At
              least she gets to live with the man she loves,
              sees him every day, talks to him, knows
              where he is and what he's doing instead of be-

	ing alone all day, every day. Who cares if he doesn't love her back?
UnsureOne:	I'm not sure about the part about Leonard not loving me but I know what you're getting at. You should really work things out with Tommy you know, 6 months isn't enough time to make a marriage work.
Divorced_1:	UnsureOne, Tommy *emptied* their bank account, *stole* her engagement ring, *swiped* the furniture, the TV, the CD player, all her CDs, clothes, *and* personal possessions and *disappeared*. Why on earth should she want him back other than to point him out in a lineup?
UnsureOne:	Because she loves him and marriage is forever.
Divorced_1:	But he is a *thief*. You ladies are nuts.
Wildflower:	Well you know they say love is blind.
Divorced_1:	*And* deaf *and* dumb in this chat room.

Buttercup has joined the room

Divorced_1:	Oh good here comes the voice of reason to sort you lot out.
Buttercup:	He's a bloody bastard you know that? He bloody well married her.
Divorced_1:	Oh well. Screw him.
SingleSam:	Did he contact you yet?
Buttercup:	No, haven't heard a thing from him since he told me not to contact him.
SingleSam:	I thought maybe he would have sent a last-minute invitation.
Buttercup:	Not a chance, the selfish little—
UnsureOne:	Well you were very rude to him Buttercup, accusing him of marrying that woman for all the wrong reasons.

LonelyLady: I wish my dad could give Tommy a job pro-
             motion. He'd definitely come back to me then.

Divorced_1: Yes what a wonderful loving foundation to
             base your marriage on, very healthy, Lonely-
             Lady. So why doesn't your dad jump in and
             save you from your misery by giving Tommy
             a promotion?

LonelyLady: My dad is dead.

Divorced_1: Oh. Sorry.

Buttercup: Imagine inviting a 13-year-old girl to Boston
             all by herself. The man has gone insane.
             That's it; he is officially no longer my best
             friend.

LonelyLady: Can I be?

Divorced_1: You sad, sad woman.

LonelyLady: What *now*?

Wildflower: But would you have gone to the wedding had
             he invited you Buttercup?

Buttercup: Not if he paid me.

UnsureOne: Well then, I'm not sure that I understand the
             problem.

Divorced_1: You never do.

Buttercup: At least then I would have had the choice
             whether to go or not. This way *he* made the
             decision for me and I don't get to make my
             statement.

LonelyLady: He probably just didn't bother printing up an
             invite because he knew you weren't going to
             attend. Invites are very expensive, you know. I
             remember Tommy and me going through the
             wedding list together. We were so happy then.

Divorced_1: Probably because he knew he wasn't going to
             stick around long enough to meet half of the
             guests.

LonelyLady: That's unfair.

Buttercup: Well these people are not short of money, be-

	lieve me, and why else would he invite Katie and not me, if not but to rub it in my face? Smear it right in there like an exfoliating face pack that *scrapes* away at your skin—
UnsureOne:	Katie is his goddaughter. He couldn't *not* invite her.
Buttercup:	And I'm his best friend. Anyway he could have at least included a plane ticket and an offer of accommodation for the poor girl. She's only 13. But I'm almost sure their wedded bliss will be short-lived. He'll be joining us on this chat room shortly and I'll be able to say those four magical words, "I told you so." I don't want to have to say it though. He's my friend and I want him to be happy. But that woman is evil, I can sense it.
Divorced_1:	No, divorce is evil, isn't that right UnsureOne?
Wildflower:	Ha ha ha ha.
UnsureOne:	That's not funny.
Divorced_1:	All she's done is laugh all night. I think Wildflower has been sampling the wildflower if you know what I mean.

UnsureOne has left the room

Wildflower:	You're too hard on her, Divorced_1.
Divorced_1:	Oh don't be silly, she loves it. She comes back night after night doesn't she? I think we're the only bit of adult conversation she has all day.
Buttercup:	So did everyone enjoy their Christmas?
Wildflower:	I haven't stopped partying all week. It's been great. I've never sat on so many Santas' laps in my life. Ha ha. Anyway I have to go; I have to get ready for a fancy dress tonight. I'm going as a playboy bunny. Bye!

Wildflower has left the room

Buttercup:	What about everybody else?
Divorced_1:	I think I put on about two stone.
LonelyLady:	It was, you know, a quiet one.
SingleSam:	Television was good this year though.
Divorced_1:	Yeah.
Buttercup:	Yeah, I like the Christmas specials.
Divorced_1:	Good for occupying the kids too.
Buttercup:	Yeah.
SingleSam:	Good documentaries too.
Buttercup:	Mmmm.
Divorced_1:	Watched that one on polar bears last night.
Buttercup:	I saw that one too . . .
SingleSam:	I hadn't realized that all polar bears are left-handed.
Buttercup:	Yes, that was interesting . . . and the snails . . .
Divorced_1:	They're left-handed too?
SingleSam:	No but they can sleep for three years apparently.
Buttercup:	Lucky buggers . . .
Divorced_1:	Yes TV is good at Christmas alright . . .
SingleSam:	It's kind of nice to be alone at Christmas, to have a bit of peace and quiet.
LonelyLady:	*Total* peace and quiet.
Buttercup:	Yes it's *very* quiet . . .
SingleSam:	You know, myself and my ex, we used to have big parties every Christmas, busy all the time, out every night or entertaining whenever we were home. We hardly had any time to ourselves. But this is quite different. No one around. No parties, no guests this year . . .
Buttercup:	Same with me.
Divorced_1:	Oh who are we kidding? It's awful; this is the worst Christmas I've ever had.
Buttercup:	Me too.

SingleSam: Me too.
LonelyLady: Me too.

Click on this icon to print the conversation

FROM: Julie Casey
TO: Rosie
SUBJECT: Fax for you

Don't want to disturb you while you're so "busy" working (how is Ruby?), but a fax just arrived in my office a few minutes ago. It wasn't addressed to you but on reading it I discovered that it could *only* be for you as which of my other employees would give out *my* fax number for *their own* personal use?

There's some sort of childish scribbled note on the top of the article and having a bit of a flashback I presumed it was Alex coming back from the past to haunt me and ridicule me but luckily it's not. I think I can just about make out a "Form Josh" signed at the bottom. Come into my office and collect it. Oh and while you're at it, divert all your calls to my office; bring two cups of coffee and a packet of cigarettes in with you.

"SOCIAL LIVES" BY ELOISE PARKINSON

For those of us who were lucky enough to attend the wedding of the year (or surely, *at least,* the wedding of the week) we have lived to tell the tale of extravagance, sophistication, and splendor that was displayed for the lucky three hundred guests of Bethany Williams and Dr. Alex Stewart.

No expense was spared at the wedding ceremony that took place at the Memorial Church of Harvard University, where vibrant displays of red roses and red candles lined the aisle, like lights illuminating a runway for the exquisite couple to take off to their future life of happiness together.

Bethany, 34, was looking flawlessly stunning, as always, in an elegant white one-piece dress designed especially for her by the famous friend-of-the-stars (and mine) Jeremy Durkin. The solid-boned bodice was embellished in ten thousand pearls (and disguised that five-month pregnancy everybody is whispering about). The ballerina-style full skirt, made up of layers and layers of soft tulle, swished as she floated up the aisle on the arm of her proud prominent father, Dr. Reginald Williams.

Miranda Williams looked every bit the perfect mother of the bride in her scarlet red Armani trouser suit accompanied by her fabulous Philip Tracey hat that almost stole the spotlight from her daughter. Catwalk models (and *very* new friends of Bethany's) Sara Smythe and Hayley Broadbank acted as Bethany's two bridesmaids and wore sexy red silk spaghetti-strapped dresses that clung to their barely-there curves, half a dozen roses resting between their French manicured fingers. The bride's bouquet was made up of half a dozen red roses and half a dozen white roses (and was caught by none other than *moi*). Her usually flowing long blond hair was tied back tightly in a French bun that sat low on her head and helped the mother-to-be look every inch the perfect bride.

At the top of the aisle a confident-looking Prince Charming looked down on his princess proudly, dressed in a classic black three-button cutaway coat with white wing collar and red tie, accompanied by a single red rose in his lapel. Everything was certainly "rosie" on this day.

The extravagant reception was held at the Boston Harbor Hotel, where the finest speech by far was made by the best man, 8-year-old Josh Stewart, son of the groom from a previous marriage to college sweetheart Sally Gruber.

The day lived up to the expectation (and standards) of "Social Lives" and it was clear for all who witnessed the

newlyweds dancing for the first time as husband and wife
that this marriage was forever. May they live a long, happy,
rich, and fashionable married life together. As for me, your
favorite wedding columnist, I'm off with my bouquet, to
find myself a beau.

TO ALEX
HAPPY 34TH BIRTHDAY YOU GRAND DAD!
YOUR LOVING GODDAUGHTER,
KATIE

DEAR ROSIE,
HAPPY BIRTHDAY, DAUGHTER!
LOVE MUM AND DAD XXX

HAPPY BIRTHDAY SIS,
GETTING ANCIENT NOW AT THE RIPE OLD AGE OF 33!
ENJOY THE NIGHT (STAY AWAY FROM HARD-BOILED
EGGS!)
KEV

ROSIE,
HAPPY BIRTHDAY, FRIEND.
ANOTHER YEAR, HERE WE GO AGAIN.
RUBY

FROM: Stephanie
TO: Rosie
SUBJECT: Your visit

Can't wait for you to come over and meet Sophia next
month, she's excited to meet you too and Jean-Louis is as
hyper as always.

Happy 33rd sis, no doubt you and Ruby will be out until
the early hours. Enjoy!

FROM: Josh
TO: Katie
SUBJECT: Coming over

Dad is bringing me over to Ireland next month to
stay with Uncle Phil and Aunt Margaret and their three
hundred kids. Bethany is coming too and I'm gonna meet
her family too. Hopefully we can meet up with you and
your mom. It's so stupid that they don't talk anymore.
And it'll get real boring just being with the adults all the
time.

Can't wait to come over though. Hope I can meet up with
you and Toby.

FROM: Katie
TO: Josh
SUBJECT: Re: Coming over

We're not going to be here when you come over! That's
really crap! We're going over to France to meet my new little
cousin, Sophia. She's only a few months old. It would have
been great to set Mum and Alex up.

Maybe next time.

DEAR ALEX AND BETHANY,
CONGRATULATIONS ON THE BIRTH OF YOUR BABY
BOY.
WE WISH YOU EVERY HAPPINESS FOR THE FUTURE
AND ARE DELIGHTED THAT JOSH HAS THE BROTHER
HE WISHED FOR!
ROSIE AND KATIE

HAPPY 14TH, MY LITTLE ANGEL,
HAVE A GOOD NIGHT AT THE DISCO TONIGHT AND
REMEMBER NO DRINKING, NO SEX, AND NO DRUGS. BE

GOOD AND REMEMBER TO PLAY HARD TO GET! (JOKE)
LOTS OF LOVE,
MUM

You have an instant message from: ROSIE

Rosie: Who is this boy I heard you were kissing and slow dancing with on Friday night, Katie Dunne?

Katie: Can't talk Mum, Mr. Simpson is teaching something extremely important for the end of year exams and it's vital that I listen.

Rosie: Liar.

Katie: I'm not lying. I'm sure it is important whatever it is.

Rosie: Come on spill the beans, who was the boy?

Toby: Hi Rosie.

Rosie: Oh Toby, good timing. I was just quizzing my daughter on the mystery man at the disco on Friday night.

Toby: Oh ha ha. News travels fast.

Katie: Don't tell her, Toby.

Rosie: So it's true?

Toby: Yep.

Katie: Yeah and Toby was snogging the face off Monica all night as well.

Rosie: Oh no Toby, not moany Monica.

Katie: Ha ha.

Toby: Why do you two always call her that? She's not a moaner when she's with me.

Rosie: That's because we don't kiss her in front of everyone at school discos.

Katie: Ha ha.

Rosie: So come on darling daughter, bond with me and share details of this budding romance.

Katie: His name is John McKenna, he's fifteen, he's in the year ahead of me, and he's really nice.

Rosie: Ooooh an older man.

Katie: I know Mum, I've got taste.

Rosie: What do you think of him Toby?

Toby: He's OK; he's on the school football team. He's good.

Rosie: You'll have to keep an eye on him for me, won't you?

Toby: Absolutely!

Katie: Mum! Now he'll never shut up!

Rosie: Did you have sex with him?

Katie: Mum! I'm 14!

Rosie: I see 14-year-old girls on the TV who are pregnant these days.

Katie: Well not me!

Rosie: Good. Did you take any drugs?

Katie: Mum! Stop! Where the hell would I get drugs from??!

Rosie: I don't know, well you see 14-year-old pregnant girls on TV who are on drugs these days.

Katie: Well not me!

Rosie: Good. Did you drink alcohol?

Katie: Mum! Toby's mum drove us to the school and collected us, when would we have had time to drink?

Rosie: I don't know. You see drunken pregnant 14-year-olds who are on drugs on the TV these days.

Katie: Well that's definitely not me!

Toby: What TV programs are you watching?

Rosie: Mainly the news.

Katie: Well don't worry; you've lectured me enough to know that it's stupid to do all of those things. OK?

Rosie: OK but remember kisses are nice but that's as far as it should go. Ok?

Katie: Mum! That's all I want!!

Rosie: Good, now you two get back to your work. I expect you to get A's in this subject!

Katie: Well we won't if you keep bothering us!

Ruby: So what are you going to do for the next two months
         now that the kids are off school? You're so lucky get-
         ting such long holidays. Randy Andy told me I'd
         used up all my holidays already which is ridiculous
         because all those days were supposed to be sick days.
         He said there's no way someone could have been sick
         for 65 days of the working year and still be alive.

Rosie: Oh no, so you can't take any holidays?

Ruby: I can now, I told him that if he'll give me two weeks
         off that I'd mention Randy Andy's Paperclip Com-
         pany when Oprah invites me on her TV show after
         me and Gary win the World Salsa Championship.
         What are you going to do?

Rosie: I'm not too sure. Julie mentioned something about
         being able to do adult courses at the school. She
         says I should take a course in hotel management like
         I always wanted to do. Like it's that simple.

Ruby: Why can't it be that simple? Look Rosie, you don't
         know until you try. Ever since I met you you've been
         going on about working in a hotel. You're obsessed
         with them; your home is like a tribute to hotel mer-
         chandise. You can barely open the bathroom door
         for all the stolen mats in the way. I can't claim to
         understand your fascination with them but I know
         that working in one is an absolute dream for you.

         Most people dream of becoming millionaires or of
         traveling to space. Most people's dreams are unat-
         tainable. Yours isn't. It's a very normal, everyday
         person's kind of job.

Rosie: Julie said that if I don't take the course she'll fire
         me. And she said that when I finish the course she's
         firing me anyway.

Ruby: You need to listen to her; she's been a good teacher
         to you over the years.

Rosie: But Ruby, it takes three years to get a degree, and

it's expensive, and I'll have to work by day and
study by night. It'll be tough.

Ruby: Oh but, but, but Rosie Dunne. What's the problem,
have you got anything better planned for the next
three years of your life?

Dear Rosie,

Apologies for the delay in getting back to you, the past
few months have been very busy for Alex and me indeed.
Adjusting to married life and a newborn baby all in a matter
of months is hard work.

We were delighted to receive your little card and we hope
you and Katie are keeping well over in Ireland.

Best wishes,
Bethany (and Alex, Theo, and Josh too)

You have an instant message from: ROSIE

Rosie: You're right Ruby, it doesn't look like I'll be getting up to all that much for the next three years of
my life. Why not educate myself? I've nothing better to do.

Hi Mum,

Winter *again*. You would think once in a lifetime would be enough, nobody even *likes* it. It's scary how the months fly by so fast. They turn into years without me even noticing. Katie is like my calendar, watching her grow and change. She is growing up so fast, learning to have opinions of her own, learning that I don't have the answers to everything. And the moment a child begins to understand that, you know you're in trouble.

I'm still on my journey, Mum, still caught in that in-between stage of life where I've just come from somewhere, have left it well and truly behind and I'm now working my way toward something new.

I suppose what I'm trying to say is that my mind isn't settled yet. Still. I mean, you and Dad have done nothing but travel for the past year, you haven't been in one country for more than a few weeks at a time but you are both more settled than me, and I haven't left for the past year. You both know where you want to be. I suppose that's because you have each other and anywhere Dad is feels like home to you.

I've learned that home isn't a place, it's a feeling. I can make the flat look as pretty as I can, put as many flower

boxes on the window sills as I want, put a welcome mat
outside the front door, hang a Home Sweet Home sign over
the fireplace, and take to wearing aprons and baking
cookies, but the truth is that I know I don't want to stay
here forever.

It's like I'm waiting at the train station, busking to make
a few quid, just enough to catch the next train out of here.
And of course the most important thing to me is Katie and
everywhere I am with her should feel like home, but it
doesn't because it's up to me to make the home for her. I
know that Katie is going to leave in a few years and she
won't need me like she does now.

I have to set my own life up for when Katie goes. I *need*
to set my own life up for when Katie goes because I don't
see any Prince Charmings coming along to rescue me. Fairy
tales are such evil little stories for young children. Every
time I'm in a mess I expect a long-haired posh-speaking
man to come trotting into my life (on a horse of course,
literally trotting himself . . .) Then you realize you don't
want a long-haired posh-speaking man trotting into your
life because he's the one who put you in the bloody mess in
the first place.

I'm like Katie's coach right now, gearing her up for the
big fight. She's hardly thinking of life after me, sure she has
her dreams of traveling the world and DJ-ing for a living
without me but the *without me* part hasn't hit her yet. And
so it shouldn't, she's only fourteen. Anyway she is not up to
making her own decisions yet, and I've put my foot down on
the quitting school idea.

Although lately I haven't had to force her out of bed in
the mornings because of John, this new boyfriend of hers.
The pair of them are inseparable; they go to discos every
Friday night in the GAA club near where he lives. He's a
real GAA man and plays hurling for the Dublin minors. In
fact we're going to see Dublin v. Meath in Croke park on
Sunday. It's tricky for me because I obviously don't have a

car nor can drive so I sometimes put Ruby on driving duties. She calls it Driving Ms. Lazy. John's mother is a very nice lady though and she's kind enough to collect Katie and drop her home some weeks. I haven't seen or heard much of Toby but I met his mother at the school when she was dropping off her youngest and she told me he was acting more or less the same as Katie with his new love, Monica.

I never dated when I was fourteen. The youth of today are really changing . . . (I sounded SO OLD there!) OK, OK mum I can hear you fuming from here, I did become pregnant at the age of eighteen without having a job or education or man and almost gave you a nervous breakdown, but in some countries of the world that's old, so you should thank your lucky stars that I didn't get started even sooner.

Kevin called up for the weekend; he brought his girlfriend with him. She's very sweet but I don't know what she sees in Kevin. Did you know that they've been going out for a year now? Honestly that brother of mine is so secretive; you practically have to beat the information out of him. You never know, there could be more wedding bells in the air for the Dunne family! Tell Dad to get that dirty old tuxedo out of the attic and to brush the cobwebs and mothballs off in preparation. He'll be happy to know he won't have to walk down the aisle this time. (Honestly he had *me* nervous at my wedding!)

As for my North Strand Palace, we might as well have no windows here at all for all the wind they let in. It's so cold and windy tonight, the rain is pelting off the windows. That lamppost from outside shines directly into this flat, if only it could be moved a bit to the right then it could annoy Rupert instead. Although it does save me money on the electricity. I'm half-expecting Gene Kelly to be standing outside dancing around with his umbrella. Why is it movies can make everything look fun?

Every morning I rise when it is pitch black outside (and

you know it's not natural to be up if the sun couldn't even be bothered to get up), the flat is freezing, I hop from the shower to my bedroom shivering like hell, I make my way outside to the world where I have to walk ten minutes to my bus stop in the wind and rain. My ears ache and my hair is in strings around my head, I may as well not wash and blow-dry it at all. My mascara is running down my face, my umbrella has blown inside out, and I look like a disheveled Mary Poppins. Then the bus is late. Or too full to stop. And I end up late for work, looking like a drowned rat with clothes completely soaked through after having at least a few fights with a few bus drivers already, while everyone else has their makeup, clothes, and hair all perfect because they all got out of bed an hour later than me, hopped into their cars, drove to work, arrived at the school fifteen minutes before classes started, and have a cup of coffee as a nice start to their day.

Singing in the rain, my bum.

Notice I'm writing to you today and not e-mailing and that's due to the guy in the Internet café downstairs catching me one too many times staring at him. I think he's on to me so I decided to stay home tonight. The other reason for me writing is that I'm pretending to Katie that I'm studying. We both have Christmas exams coming up and I told her she needed to take them more seriously. Well I walked myself straight into that one. So here we both are, crammed at the kitchen table with our books, folders, papers, and pens pretending to look intellectual.

I have so much study to catch up on that I haven't been able to cook dinner all week. So it's been downstairs' delights for the past few days. Luckily Sanjay is giving us forty percent off our takeaway meals and he's even created a new dish called Rosie Chicken Curry. He sent it up free last night with our order. We tasted it and sent it back down. Just joking. It's basically chicken and curry. All he did was add the Rosie. I'm flattered all the same at the sight of my name on an Indian menu and it's interesting late at night to hear my name being yelled by drunken men in deep slurred voices. I keep thinking that my Romeo is standing on the pavement below my window calling me and throwing stones up to awaken me from my slumber. Then I remember that it's Saturday night, one o'clock in the morning, the pub has just closed, drunken men are shouting their special order over the counter, and the stones against my window are the rain. But a girl can always dream.

Speaking of dreams I had one last night that I was a chicken and that I was being chased around a huge hotel kitchen by chefs, waiters, and the guests and they were trying to kill me. Take from that what you may.

Every time I pass by Sanjay's wife she rolls her eyes and tuts. He's still asking me out on dates, he even asks me when she's standing right beside him. So I say very loudly that what he is asking me is wrong considering his marital status, that he needs to have more respect for his wife, and that even if he wasn't married I would say no. I say it so loudly so that she can hear but yet she stills tuts and Sanjay smiles at me and throws a few poppadoms in the bag for me for free. The man is insane.

Rupert (my other neighbor) asked me if I want to go to the National Concert Hall at the weekend. Apparently the National Symphony Orchestra is playing Brahms Piano Concerto Number 2 in B flat major, op. 83, which is his absolute favorite. It's not a date or anything. I think Rupert is completely asexual and that he just likes company. That suits me because that's how I define myself right now anyway. Plus the "I Love Mother" tattoo on his arm would be a real turn-off. That quote by James Joyce really upsets me too, because Rupert is so tall that when I look straight ahead I'm faced with his chest and I constantly read this "Mistakes are the portals of discovery." It's like a sign or something, like Rupert was put in the flat beside me to make me understand. Only I wish the message made more sense than that. Mistakes are more like the potholes of discovery. It's a bloody long bumpy road to discovery and you're more likely to die in a car crash than a plane accident. I wish it said "Chocolate is good" instead.

Speaking of mistakes, I still haven't spoken to Alex and it's been over a year. All we've been doing is sending stupid cards back and forth to each other. It's like we're having a staring competition and neither of us wants to be the first one to blink. It's silly really, because I miss him like crazy. There are so many things that happen to me, silly little everyday things that I go to tell him, like the postman this morning was delivering the post across the road and that stupid little Jack Russell dog called Jack Russell was attacking him again. So I looked out the window and I saw the postman shaking the dog off his leg as he does every morning but this time he kicked the dog in the stomach by mistake and the dog fell over and didn't move for ages. Then the owner came outside and I watched as the postman pretended that Jack Russell was like that when he got there. The owner believed him and there was pandemonium as they tried to help the dog. Eventually Jack Russell got up and when he took one look at the postman he whimpered and ran away into the house. It was so funny. The postman just shrugged and walked off. He was whistling by the time he got to my door. Things like that would have really made Alex laugh, especially as I had told him all about the stupid dog keeping me awake all night barking and always stealing my post from the poor postman.

Despite my loneliness for him I know this phase isn't going to last forever. He'll come around sooner or later. I just hope I won't be six feet under by the time he does. Katie is trying to sneak a peak off my page . . .

MASLOW'S THEORY OF HIERARCHY

Ha ha, that'll put her off the scent. OK I better go now and actually do some work. See you both soon. Tell Dad I said hello and that I love him.

Oh by the way Ruby has set me up on a blind date on Saturday night. I nearly killed her but I can't cancel it. Cross your fingers for me that he's not some sort of serial killer.

> Lots of love,
> Rosie

You have an instant message from: ROSIE

Rosie: Hi Julie. I've signed you up to be one of my instant message buddies. Whenever I see that you're online I can send you messages.

Julie: Not unless I block your name from my list.

Rosie: You wouldn't dare.

Julie: Why would you set up an instant messaging service with me when I am in the next room?

Rosie: It's what I do. It means I can multitask. I can speak to people on the phone and also do business with you online. What is it that you do, Ms. Casey? All I see you doing is terrorizing innocent children and having meetings with pissed off parents.

Julie: That's about all I do Rosie, you're right. Believe me you were one of the worst kids to teach and one of the worst parents to meet with. I hated calling you in.

Rosie: I hated coming in.

Julie: And now you've added me to your messaging list. How times change. By the way I'm having a little get-together for my birthday next week and I was wondering if you would like to come.

Rosie: Who else is going?

Julie: Oh just some other kids that I used to scare the hell out of 20 years ago. We love to gather and reminisce about the days gone by.

Rosie: Seriously.

Julie: No, just a few friends, a few members of my family for a few drinks and a few nibbles for a few min-

<table>
<tr><td></td><td>utes to mark the occasion and then you can all leave me alone.</td></tr>
<tr><td>Rosie:</td><td>What age will you be? I only ask so I can buy you a birthday card with a number on it. Maybe get a badge for you too.</td></tr>
<tr><td>Julie:</td><td>You do and you're fired. I'm going to be 53.</td></tr>
<tr><td>Rosie:</td><td>You're only 20 years older than me. I used to think you were ancient.</td></tr>
<tr><td>Julie:</td><td>Funny isn't it? Imagine I was only your age by the time you left this school. The kids must feel that you're ancient now too.</td></tr>
<tr><td>Rosie:</td><td>I feel ancient.</td></tr>
<tr><td>Julie:</td><td>Ancient people don't go on romantic blind dates. Come on, spill the beans, what was he like?</td></tr>
<tr><td>Rosie:</td><td>His name is Adam and he is a very, very attractive man. All through the night he was polite, a terrific conversationalist, and very funny. He paid for the meal, the taxi, drinks, absolutely everything and wouldn't let me open my purse (not that there was any money in it to spend). He was tall, dark, and handsome, dressed impeccably, and I could tell a lot of attention to detail was paid. Plucked eyebrows, straight teeth, and not a nose hair in sight.</td></tr>
<tr><td>Julie:</td><td>What does he do for a living?</td></tr>
<tr><td>Rosie:</td><td>He's an engineer.</td></tr>
<tr><td>Julie:</td><td>So he was polite, handsome, and had a great job. He sounds too good to be true. Is there the possibility of meeting again?</td></tr>
<tr><td>Rosie:</td><td>Well after the meal we went back to his penthouse apartment. He lives along Sir John Rogerson's quay, the place was fabulous. I stayed over, he asked me out again, and I said no.</td></tr>
<tr><td>Julie:</td><td>Are you crazy?</td></tr>
<tr><td>Rosie:</td><td>Probably. He was such a good man but there was nothing there.</td></tr>
<tr><td>Julie:</td><td>But it was only your first date. You can never really</td></tr>
</table>

tell these things by a first date. What did you want, fireworks?

Rosie: No actually, quite the opposite. I want silence, a perfect moment of quietness.

Julie: Silence?

Rosie: Oh it's a long story. But last night only proves that you can put me with a guy that's perfect in every way and too good to be true and I'm still not ready. Everyone around me needs to stop rushing me.

Julie: OK, OK, I promise I'll stop trying to set you up with men until you give me your permission. How's the studying going?

Rosie: It's tough working, studying, and being a mother all at the same time. I end up staying up till all hours of the night pondering life, the universe, and all that's in it.

Julie: Don't worry, we've all had those days and believe me by the time you get to my age you stop caring. Is there anything I can do to help?

Rosie: Yes actually a pay rise would be a terrific help.

Julie: No chance. How's the saving going?

Rosie: It would be going fine if I didn't have to feed, clothe, educate my child as well as pour rent money into the shoebox I'm living in.

Julie: That always seems to get in the way of things, that whole looking after your child part. Have you spoken to Alex yet?

Rosie: No.

Julie: Oh Rosie, you are both being ridiculous. It's been over a year now. I spent my life trying to separate you two from each other but now the fun is over. Tell him Ms. Big Nose Smelly Breath Casey has given you both permission to sit beside each other again.

Rosie: That'll never work; he never listened to you anyway. And it's not like we're not in contact at all, Katie keeps in touch with him all the time and I send cards for every occasion and he does the same back. Every few months I get a postcard from a different exotic country with boring weather reports from him, and when he's not holidaying he's working all hours. So we're not completely ignoring each other. It's a very civilized kind of argument we're having.

Julie: Yes, apart from the fact that you don't even talk. Your best friend has a 6-month-old baby that you haven't even bothered to meet. All I'm saying is that if you let this carry on much longer, the years will multiply and before you know it it'll just be too late.

CHAPTER 42

—⁓—

DEAR ROSIE AND KATIE DUNNE,
SEASON'S GREETINGS FROM ST. JUDE'S HOSPITAL.
MY WIFE, TWO SONS, AND I HOPE THAT THE YEAR
AHEAD BRINGS YOU AND YOUR LOVED ONES GOOD
HEALTH AND HAPPINESS.
MERRY CHRISTMAS AND A HAPPY NEW YEAR FROM
THE STEWARTS.
ALEX STEWART, M.D.

TO ALEX STEWART MD RIP BLA BLA BLA,
MAY THE COMING YEAR BE FILLED WITH WARM
WISHES FOR YOU AND YOUR FAMILY.
BEST WISHES,
ROSIE DUNNE R.E.S.P.E.C.T.

You have an instant message from: ALEX

Alex: What do you know about respect?
Rosie: Oooh, talking to me now are you?
Alex: It's been long enough. One of us should be adult

enough to make contact, remember I'm not the one
who started this in the first place.

Rosie: Yes you did.

Alex: Rosie, no I didn't.

Rosie: Yes you did!

Alex: Oh *please!* Last year I told you Bethany was pregnant at which point you went ape shit and ranted
about how being male is some sort of disease. And
for your information I proposed to her one night
before we went to an award ceremony. Bethany said
yes, and naturally being excited, she told her parents at the table (as any normal person would do).
Her father was presented his award and during his
speech he announced that his daughter has just gotten engaged (as a normal proud father would on
just learning that his daughter was to be married).

The press was there; they went back to their desks
and reported on the evening in time to make the
next day's papers. I went out and celebrated my engagement with my fiancée and her family. I got
home to bed and woke up the next day to phone
call after phone call from my family wanting to no
why the hell hadn't I told them I was getting married. My inbox was full of e-mails from confused
friends and I was just about to deal with them when
I got an instant message from you accusing me of
doing all sorts of things.

So I sent you and Katie a wedding invite anyway
thinking that even though you disapproved of my
choice of wife and concocted pathetic stories about
why I was marrying her, you might still have behaved like the friend you claim to be by attending
my wedding and being supportive.

Clearly you couldn't do that and stopped all forms

of communication for months so I didn't think it
was necessary for me to continue making an effort
when you obviously couldn't be bothered.

But in the meantime I have received your array of
Christmas cards, happy new year cards, St. Patrick's
Day cards, postcards, and gifts for Theo and likewise and I hope you have received mine. So I apologize for the last card you received, your name was
on my mailing list, but this particular card was intended for my patients and not you. Anyway, I
didn't think you would appreciate the family photo
in front of the Christmas tree. It's not something I
imagine that's being displayed on your mantel.

Rosie: I didn't receive any wedding invite!

Alex: What?

Rosie: I got no invitation to your wedding. There was one
         for Katie alright but none for me. And Katie
         couldn't very well go because she was only 13 and
         where would she stay? And I couldn't bring her over
         because frankly I couldn't afford to—

Alex: Stop! Now let me think about this for a moment.
         You received *no* wedding invite?

Rosie: No. Just one for Katie.

Alex: What about your parents?

Rosie: Yeah they received one but they couldn't go because
         they were visiting Steph in Paris and—

Alex: OK! Yours wasn't sent there by mistake?

Rosie: No.

Alex: But my parents, didn't they tell you?

Rosie: They said they would love me to go but they don't
         control the invites, Alex. You never asked me to go.

Alex: But you were on the list, I even *saw* your invite on
         the kitchen table.

Rosie: Oh.

Alex: So what happened?

Rosie: Don't ask me! I didn't even know there was an invite!

Alex: There was one!

Rosie: OK! Who posted them?

Alex: Bethany and the wedding planner.

Rosie: Hmm . . . OK so somewhere between Bethany
        walking toward the post box and the invite actually
        going in the slit, something happened to my invite.

Alex: Oh don't start Rosie, it wasn't Bethany. She's got
        much better things to be doing with her time than
        hatching plans to get rid of you.

Rosie: Like doing lunch with the ladies?

Alex: Stop.

Rosie: Well I'm in shock.

Alex: So you thought all this time that I didn't want you
        at my wedding?

Rosie: Yes.

Alex: Oh. But why didn't you say something? An entire
        year and you didn't say something? If you didn't
        invite me to your wedding I would at least *say*
        something.

Rosie: Excuse me, why didn't you ask me why I wasn't
        there? If I invited you to my wedding and I noticed
        that you hadn't turned up, I think I would at least
        say something.

Alex: I was angry.

Rosie: Me too.

Alex: I'm still angry about the things you said.

Rosie: Answer me this, Alex. Did you or did you not tell
        me only months previously that Bethany was not
        "the one" for you and that you didn't love her?

Alex: Yes but—

Rosie: And were you or were you not going to break up
        with her just before she announced her pregnancy?

Alex: Yes but—

Rosie: And were you or were you not worried about your
        job when you refused to marry Bethany?

Alex: Yes but—

Rosie: And were you or were you not—

Alex: Listen to me. Or read me. Reginald Williams is not
         my *boss*. It doesn't work like that in hospitals. He
         couldn't just fire me out of the blue.

Rosie: Yes but I bet he could make life really difficult for
         you at the hospital.

Alex: He could.

Rosie: And would he have?

Alex: Yes.

Rosie: So I really don't think that I was that far from the
         truth, Alex Stewart.

Alex: That perhaps may be about 1% of the truth but
         coupled with the fact that I wanted to be a part of
         Theo and Bethany's life.

Rosie: So if you *did* invite me to your wedding and I was
         partly correct on what I said, why did we spend the
         entire year sending tacky cards to each other?

Alex: What I want to no is where the hell your wedding
         invite went to. The wedding planner had everything
         arranged. Unless it was . . .

Rosie: Who?

Alex: Not *who* but *what* . . .

Rosie: *What*, then?

Alex: Jack Russell the Jack Russell.

Rosie: Oh yeah . . .

Alex: Next time I see him I'm going to wring his neck.

Rosie: Oh you can't do that.

Alex: I can do whatever the hell I want to that post-
         nicking little—

Rosie: He's dead. The postman kicked him in the stomach
         a few mornings in a row completely by mistake (I'm
         a witness) and on the final morning he did it, Jack
         just stopped moving.

Alex: A bit of justice in the world after all. I'm not sorry
         to hear that.

Rosie: I'm sorry though Alex.
Alex: Me too. Friends again?
Rosie: I never stopped being your friend.
Alex: Me neither. Well unfortunately I have to go because
        my baby is pouring his breakfast on his head and
        massaging it into his scalp with a look of pure con-
        centration on his face. I fear it may be nappy-
        changing time again.
Rosie: Oh no! I don't envy you that job!

FOR OUR BEAUTIFUL DAUGHTER,
WE LOVE YOU WITH ALL OUR HEARTS, HERE'S TO A
NEW YEAR,
HAPPY BIRTHDAY, ROSIE!
GOOD LUCK WITH YOUR EXAMS IN JUNE, WE HAVE
OUR FINGERS CROSSED FOR YOU.
LOTS OF LOVE,
MUM AND DAD

FOR MY SISTER,
YOU'RE FINALLY CATCHING ME, ROSIE, WHICH I'M
GLAD OF BECAUSE I DON'T WANT TO BE THE ONLY
ONE NEARING FORTY!
BEST OF LUCK WITH YOUR EXAMS, YOU HAVE TWO
MONTHS TO LEARN IT ALL, YOU CAN GET IT DONE.
I'M SURE YOU'LL FLY THROUGH THEM!
HAPPY BIRTHDAY,
LOVE,
STEPHANIE, PIERRE, JEAN-LOUIS, SOPHIA

HAPPY BIRTHDAY, MUM,
HOPE YOU LIKE YOUR PRESENT. IF IT DOESN'T FIT
YOU, I'LL HAVE IT!
LOVE,
KATIE

TO A SPECIAL FRIEND,
HAPPY 36TH BIRTHDAY, ROSIE, I'M WORKING ON A
NEW EXPERIMENT TO SLOW DOWN TIME, FANCY
JOINING IN WITH ME?
ENJOY YOUR DAY AND I HOPE TO SEE YOU SOON!
ALEX

TO ROSIE,
HAPPY BIRTHDAY AGAIN. AFTER THIS CELEBRATION
THERE WILL BE NO MORE DISTRACTIONS, YOU HAVE
TO PASS THESE EXAMS WITH STRAIGHT A'S. YOU CAN
DO IT AND YOU'RE MY ONLY HOPE OF GETTING OUT
OF HERE. I'M STILL DREAMING OF THAT JOB AS AN
ENTERTAINER AT THAT FINE HOTEL OF YOURS.
LOVE, RUBY

You have an instant message from: ROSIE

Rosie: 16. My little angel is 16. What the hell am I sup-
         posed to do now? Where's the rule book?
Ruby: Why? It's not like yesterday she was 2 years old you
         know. You have to have known this was coming.
         You did have a total of let's see, 16 years prepara-
         tion, this shouldn't come as a shock to you.
Rosie: Ruby you unsentimental witch, do you not feel any-
         thing? Are you numb to all emotions? How did you
         feel when your Gary turned 16?
Ruby: I just don't look at things like you do. I don't think
         much of ages, or birthdays, they're just another day
         to me. They don't symbolize anything but a bunch of
         definitions and generalizations people have created to
         make conversation, debates, and media discussions.

         Katie is not going to go off the rails because sud-
         denly she wakes up one morning and she's 16. Peo-

ple do whatever the hell they want to do at any age they fancy. Last month you were 36. That means you're 4 years from 40. Do you think that the day you reach 40 you will be any different than you were at 39 or 41 for that matter? People create little ideas about ages so they can write silly self-help books, stick stupid comments in birthday cards, create names for Internet chat rooms, and look for excuses for crises that are happening in their life.

For example the man's so called "midlife crisis" is just a bunch of hype. Age is not the problem; it's the male brain that's the problem. Men have been cheating since they were apes (insert your own joke there), since cavemen times (and again there) all the way up to now, the age of what is supposed to be the civilized man. That's the way they were made. Age is not the issue.

Your baby will remain your baby past the point when she has her own little baby. Don't worry about that.

Rosie: I don't want my baby to have a baby until she's grown up, married, and rich. I mean, when I think of the things I did on my 16th birthday . . . actually I can't remember what I did.

Ruby: Why not?

Rosie: Because I was being incredibly juvenile and stupid.

Ruby: What did you do?

Rosie: Me and Alex forged our mums' signatures and wrote notes to school saying we would both be absent for the day.

Ruby: Coincidentally.

Rosie: Exactly. We went to some old man's pub in town where ID wasn't a necessity and we drank all day. Unfortunately it was ruined by the fact that I fell and hit my head, had to be raced to hospital in an ambulance where I received 7 stitches and my stomach was pumped. The parents were none too pleased.

Ruby: I bet they weren't. How did you fall? Were you doing some of your funky moves on the dance floor again?

Rosie: Actually no. I was only sitting on my stool.

Ruby: Ha ha *only you* could fall on the floor while you were sitting down. Very dangerous, that sitting down nonsense.

Rosie: I know that's weird isn't it. I wonder how it happened!

Ruby: Well you should ask Alex, he was there too after all.

Rosie: Good idea! He's online now so I'll ask.

Ruby: It's not that bloody important but any old excuse to talk to him I suppose. I'll hold on here and try to make myself look busy while you ask.

You have an instant message from: ROSIE

Rosie: Hi Alex.

Alex: Hi there, do you ever do any work? Every time I log on you're on too!

Rosie: I'm just chatting to Ruby. It's cheaper this way. We don't have to answer questions at work about the telephone bill. An Internet bill is more accepted and typing makes us look like we're busy. Anyway I just wanted to ask you a quick question.

Alex: Fire ahead.

Rosie: Remember on my 16th birthday, I fell and hit my head bla bla bla.

Alex: Ha ha how could I forget? Are you thinking of this because Katie's birthday is coming up? Because if she's anything like you, you should be afraid, be very, very afraid. What should I get for her anyway, a sick bucket?

Rosie: Age is only a number, not a state of mind or a reason for any type of particular behavior.

Alex: O . . . K then. What's your question?

Rosie: How on earth did I fall and hit my head on the floor while I was sitting down?

Alex: Oh my lord. The question. *The* Question. The *Question.*

Rosie: What's wrong with my question??

Alex: Rosie Dunne I have been waiting 20 years for you to ask me that question and I thought you never would.

Rosie: What??

Alex: Why you never asked is beyond me but you woke up the next day and claimed to have no knowledge of what had happened. I didn't want to bring it up; you had brought enough up the night before! Ha ha.

Rosie: You didn't want to bring what up?! Alex *tell me!* How did I fall off my stool??

Alex: I don't think you're ready to no.

Rosie: Oh shut up. I'm Rosie Dunne after all; I was born to be ready for anything.

Alex: OK then, if you're so sure of yourself . . .

Rosie: I am! Now tell me!

Alex: We were kissing.

Rosie: We were *what??*

Alex: Yep. You were leaning across on your high stool, kissing me; the stool was very wobbly and lodged unsafely between the cracks of a very old uneven tiled pub floor. And you fell.

Rosie: WHAT??

Alex: Oh the sweet nothings you whispered into my ear that night, Rosie Dunne. And I was gutted the next day when you woke up and forgot. After me holding your hand while you puked all night.

Rosie: *Alex!*

Alex: What?

Rosie: *Why didn't you tell me?!*

Alex: Because we weren't allowed to see each other and I didn't want to tell you in a note. And then you said you wanted to forget everything that had happened that night so I thought that maybe you vaguely remembered and you just regretted it.

Rosie: You should have told me.

Alex: Why, what would you have said?

Rosie: Em . . . that's really putting me on the spot Alex.

Alex: Yeah sorry.

Rosie: I can't believe it. Because I fell, we got caught and I had to stay home for a week while your punishment was to start work in your dad's office, where you met Bethany. The girl you said you were going to marry . . .

Alex: That's right I said that!

Rosie: Yeah you did . . .

Alex: Well I actually said that just to test you but as you didn't seem to care too much I went out with her anyway. That's funny. I had forgotten I had said that! Bethany would love to hear that! Thanks for reminding me.

Rosie: No no, thank *you* for reminding *me* . . .

You have an instant message from: RUBY

Ruby: Come on Ms. Bumps, I need to look like I'm busy here. You find out what happened yet?

Rosie: Yes I found out I'm the biggest idiot in the *whole entire world*.

Ruby: I waited around for *that*. I could have told you that, *ages* ago.

DEAR KATIE,
FOR MY DAUGHTER,

HAPPY SWEET SIXTEENTH!
LOVE, MUM XXX

FOR OUR GRANDDAUGHTER,
HAPPY SWEET SIXTEENTH BIRTHDAY!
TO KATIE, LOTS OF LOVE,
GRANDMA & GRANDDAD

FOR MY GIRLFRIEND,
HAPPY SWEET 16!
LOTS OF LOVE,
JOHN

TO KATIE,
HAPPY BIRTHDAY YOU PAIN IN THE ASS, ANOTHER
FEW MONTHS AND THOSE BRACES WILL BE OFF. THEN
I WON'T BE ABLE TO TELL WHAT YOU'VE EATEN FOR
DINNER.
TOBY

FOR MY DAUGHTER,
CONGRATULATIONS KATIE, HAPPY SWEET SIXTEEN!
I HOPE JOHN DOESN'T TRY TO KISS YOU!
LOVE, DAD

Dear Mum and Dad,

I'm never speaking to Rupert again. *Sweet* sixteen my *arse*.

Katie demanded that I give her the money that I would
have spent on her present, so that she could go into town
and pick her own clothes, which suited me fine because then
I didn't have to bother spending sleepless nights trying to
think of the "perfect" gift that she would inevitably hate and
hide under her bed. Anyway she walked into the flat, hand
in hand with the big friendly giant (John), beaming from ear
to ear so I immediately knew something suspicious was

going on. She lifted her top, lowered her trousers an inch, and there it was.

The tattoo from hell.

An awful-dirty-disgusting-very ugly-I've-just-realized-I'm-beginning-to-sound-like-you-mother kind of tattoo. It sat there on her hip bone sticking its tongue out at me.

Mum, it's ugly. Mind you it was bleeding and beginning to grow a scab by the time I saw it. Apparently Rupert said his clients only needed to be sixteen to get a tattoo which I strongly disagree with so I came downstairs to check the Internet. It turns out he's right but if I could just find some sort of loophole that would allow me to kick his ass.

Cute Internet café guy asked me if I was OK and he looked really concerned, which I thought was possibly the beginning of something new for the both of us. But then I realized I was thumping the keyboard with my fists so he was probably only concerned about his computer. I don't know about you but I have no time for selfish men like that in my life so I've decided there's no chance of a steamy love affair occurring between us after hours on the computer desks. Purely my decision though.

What makes it even worse is that I was trying to study for my *final* exams and the drilling coming from the tattoo parlor downstairs was really distracting me. What I didn't realize was that I was listening to the mutilation of my own daughter's body.

It was kind of difficult giving Rupert a piece of my mind because I couldn't express my hatred of tattoos without offending him seeing as he is an actual walking tattoo. It would be like slagging one of his family members.

The tattoo is the least of my worries. She also got her tongue pierced. Rupert threw that part in for free. She sounds like she's got hot potatoes in her mouth when she speaks. So no wonder I got such a shock when she walked in with a scary look on her face and said, "Aah, uck at I aa-oo," and then proceeded to lift up her top. John got one as well but he got a tattoo of a Hurley stick and a hurling ball on his hip bone. You don't even want to know what that picture resembles. Rupert drilled the ball too close and on the wrong end of the stick if you know what I mean.

I suppose it could be worse, they could have gotten tattooed with each other's names. And there are worse tattoos Katie could get than a tiny little strawberry the size of my thumbnail.

Perhaps I'm overreacting?

How on earth must you and Dad have felt when I told you I was *pregnant*?

Now that I think of it perhaps I should give Katie some sort of *award*?

Anyway I should go back upstairs and face the (very loud, banging) music, plus I need to continue with my studies. I can't believe I've reached my final year. Three years flew by and while it was virtually impossible studying by night, working by day and trying to be a mother at both those times I'm glad I didn't pack it in the hundred times a day that I said I would. Imagine, I'll have a graduation ceremony! You and Dad will finally be able to sit in the crowd while I collect my degree in my unflattering robe and hat. It's only fifteen years later than originally planned, but I suppose it's better late than never.

However I won't get to the graduation ceremony if I don't pass my exams so, *no more distractions*, I am going to study!

> Love,
> Rosie

FROM: Rosie
TO: Alex
SUBJECT: Dad

Something awful has happened. People at work said you were in surgery but please as soon as you get my messages and this e-mail can you ring me?

Mum called me just a minute ago in tears; Dad has had a massive heart attack and has been rushed to hospital. She's in huge shock but she told me not to travel over to her because my first exam is starting tomorrow. I don't know what to do. I don't know how serious it is, the doctors won't tell us anything yet. Can you maybe ring the hospital and see what's going on, you understand all that stuff. I don't know what to do. Please get this e-mail on time, I don't know who else to call.

I don't want to leave Mum on her own, although Kevin is going over to her now. I don't want Dad to be alone either. Oh this is so confusing.

Oh god Alex, please help. I don't want to lose my dad.

FROM: Alex
TO: Rosie
SUBJECT: Re: Dad

I tried calling you but you must be on the phone. Just stay calm. I rang the hospital and had a word with Dr. Flannery in the hospital, he's the doctor looking after your dad and he explained Dennis's condition to me.

What I suggest you do is pack a bag for a few days and get on the earliest bus you can to Galway. Do you understand what I mean?

Forget about your exam, this is more important. Keep calm, Rosie, and just be there for your mum and dad. Tell Stephanie to come home too if she can. Keep in touch with me during the night.

—⁓—

CHAPTER 43

Alex, he's gone. I can't believe he's gone.

Oh Rosie, I'm so sorry for you.
I'll book a flight today and I'll be in Ireland at the weekend.

Dear Alex,
    Coffin sizes can be no wider than 76cm; can be made of
chipboard with approved veneers and plastics for cremation
purposes. Did you know that? Ferrous screws are acceptable
in small numbers and wood braces will give extra strength
but must *only* be placed in the inside of the coffin.
    The coffin must have the full name of the deceased on the
lid. Wouldn't want to get anyone mixed up I suppose. The
thing that I really wished I hadn't learned was that the coffin
should be lined with a substance known as "Cremfilm," or
use absorbent cloth or cotton padding because apparently
fluid can leak from a body.
    I didn't know any of this.
    There were forms. Lots and lots of forms. Form A, B, C,
F, and all the medical forms. No one mentioned anything
about D and E. I didn't know you needed so much proof to

show you were dead, I thought the fact you've stopped living and breathing was a huge giveaway. Apparently not.

I suppose it's like going away to live in another country. Dad just had to get his papers ready, get dressed in his Sunday best, arrange his mode of transport, and off he went to his final destination, wherever that may be. Oh, how much Mum would have loved to have gone on this particular trip with him, but she knows she can't.

She just kept repeating to everyone at the funeral, "He just didn't wake up, I called him and called him, but he wouldn't wake up." She hasn't stopped shaking since it's happened and she looks like she's aged twenty years. Although she looks older, she seems younger. Like a lost little child who looks around her and doesn't know where to go, like suddenly she's in a whole new place and she doesn't know the way.

I suppose she is. I suppose we all are.

I've never been here before. I'm thirty-six years old and I've never lost anyone close to me. I've been to ten funerals in my life and they were of distant relatives, friends of friends and family of friends whom my life is none the worse off without.

But Dad going? God, that's a big one.

He was only sixty-six years old. Not old at all. And he was healthy. What causes a healthy sixty-six-year-old man to fall asleep and never wake up? I can only comfort myself with thoughts that he saw something so beautiful that he just had to go. That's the kind of thing Dad would do.

There's something completely unnerving about seeing your parents upset. I suppose it's because they're supposed to be the strong ones, but that's not just it. Ever since people are kids they use their parents as some sort of measurement for how bad a situation is. When you fall on the ground really hard and you can't figure out whether it hurts or not you look to your parents. If they look worried and rush toward you, you cry. If they laugh and smack the ground saying "Bold ground," then you pick yourself up and get on with it.

When you find out you're pregnant and feel numb of all emotions you look at their expressions. When both your mum and dad hug you and tell you it's going to be OK and that they'll support you, you know it's not the end of the world. But depending on the parents, it could have been pretty damn close.

Parents are the barometers of emotions for children and it has a domino effect. I had never seen my mum cry s o much in all of my life which scared me and made me cry which scared Katie and made her cry. We all cried together.

As for Dad, he was supposed to live forever. The one who could open all the jar lids nobody else could, who fixed whatever was broken, was supposed to do that forever. The man who let me sit on his shoulders, climb on his back, chase me around while making monster noises, throw me in the air and catch me, spin me around so much until I felt dizzy and fell over laughing.

And in the end without being able to say thank you and a proper good-bye, my final memories of him turn into coffin sizes and medical forms.

I'm still over in Galway with Mum. In the wild, wild West. But it's a beautiful summer and it doesn't feel quite right. The atmosphere doesn't suit the mood, there's the sound of children's laughter floating up from the beach down below, there are birds singing and dancing around the sky, swooping low and catching their fresh meals from the sea. It doesn't feel right to love the world and see such brightness when something so awful has happened.

It's like hearing gurgling babies echoing in the church at the funeral. There's nothing more uplifting than to hear the sound of an innocent child being so happy in a place that people are sad. It reminds you that life goes on and on and on, just not for the one you're saying good-bye to. People come and people go and we know this happens, yet we get such a shock when it does. To use that old cliché, the only certainty in life is death. It's a certainty, it's the one condition of living that we're given but we often let it tear us apart.

I don't know what to do or say to Mum to make her feel better; I don't suppose there really is anything that would accomplish that but watching her crying to herself all day tears me apart. I can hear her pain in her tears. Maybe she'll just run out of tears.

Alex you're a heart doctor. You know the heart literally inside and out, what is there you can do when someone's heart has broken? Have you any cures for that?

Thanks for coming over to the funeral, it was so good to see you. It was just a shame that it was under these circumstances. It was good of your parents to come too, Mum really did appreciate it. Thanks for getting rid of what's-his-name too; I really wasn't in the mood to have any discussions with him at the church. It was good of him to come but if Dad had seen him he would have leaped out of that coffin and thrown what's-his-name in his place instead.

Stephanie and Kevin headed home a few days ago but I'm going to stay on for a little while longer. I just can't leave Mum alone. The neighbors are being so good to her I know she will be in good hands when I do finally leave. I've missed all my exams and by the sounds of things I'll have to repeat the entire final year if I do want to complete the course. I don't think I could be bothered doing it all over again.

Anyway I'll have to go home in a few days as no doubt the bills have been piling up in my post box since the day I left. I really need to get back before they cut everything off and evict me.

Thanks for being there for me once again Alex, but it's so typical of us for a tragedy to finally get us together.

     Love,
     Rosie

FROM: Rosie
TO: Alex
SUBJECT: Dad

I just returned home from Connemara to be greeted by an overflowing mailbox. Among a pile of bills was the following letter. It was posted the day before Dad died.

Dear Rosie,

Your mum and I are still laughing from your last letter about Katie's tattoo. I do love it when you write to us! I hope you're over the trauma of your daughter becoming a fully fledged teen. I remember the day that happened with you, I think it hit you before Stephanie! You were always eager to try new things and go new places, my fearless Rosie. I thought that when you finished school you were going to set off around the world and we would never see you again. I'm glad that didn't happen. You were always a delight to have around the house. You *and* Katie. I'm only sorry we had to leave you when you needed us both. Your mum and I questioned our actions time and time again. I hope we did the right thing.

I know you always felt that you were in the way or that you were letting us down, but that's far from the truth, it just meant that I got to see my little girl grow. Grow from being a baby to an adult and grow as a mother. You and Katie are a great team and she is a fine example of the good parenting she received. A bit of ink on her skin doesn't tarnish the goodness or dim the brightness that shines from her. A tribute to her mother.

Life deals each of us a different set of cards and out of all of us there's no doubt that you received the toughest hand of all. But you shone through the tough times. You are a strong girl and you grew even stronger when that idiot of a man (what's-his-name, your mother told me to say) let you down.

You picked yourself up, dusted yourself off, and started all
over again, set up home with Katie, found yourself a new
job, provided for your daughter, and did your dad proud
once more.

And now you're only days away from your exams. After
all you went through you'll now have a degree. I'll be proud
watching you accept that scroll Rosie; I'll be the proudest
dad in the world.

> Love,
> Dad

FROM: Rosie
TO: Alex
SUBJECT: Degree

There's no way I'm giving this college course up now. In
the wise words of Johnny Logan, what's another year? I'm
going to do these exams and I'm going to get this degree in
Hotel Management. Dad wouldn't want himself to be the
reason for me missing out.

It's the good-bye I needed, Alex. What a wonderful,
wonderful gift to be given.

FROM: Julie
TO: Rosie
SUBJECT: Staying with me?

So you're staying with me another year then?

I'll allow you, but after that, once you have your degree
I'm serious when I say I'm firing you. I'm 56 years old; I
don't have much longer at this job to be waiting for you to
fulfill your dreams.

This year the courses will be a breeze, first because
you've done it before and second and more important

because you have the good wishes and pride of your
father behind you. That's the best motivation a person
could get.

Do you mind me asking what is it about these hotels that
you love so much?

FROM: Rosie
TO: Julie
SUBJECT: Why I love hotels!

I just get this feeling when I walk into really nice hotels.
For me they represent everything in life that's luxurious and
full of splendor. I love that people pamper you and look after
you. Everything is so clean and pristine, so completely
perfect. So unlike home, well my home anyway.

I love that people go to enjoy themselves; it's not so much
a place of work as being a host in paradise.

I get excited by the sparkling bathrooms, the big fluffy
robes, the slippers, and the décor. Where else would you find
chocolate on your pillow? It's like the tooth fairy and Santa
Claus all at once. There's 24-hour room service and bouncy
padded carpets, turned-down beds and minibars, bowls of
fruit and free shampoo. I feel like I'm Charlie in the
chocolate factory. Everything you want is at your disposal,
all you have to do is pick up the phone and press the magic
number and the people on the other end of the phone are
only too delighted to help.

To stay in one is the ultimate treat; to work in one would
be an everyday pleasure. When I finish this course I'm
automatically placed in a hotel as a temporary manager in
training so I just know that there's a job for me at the end of
the rainbow.

You have an instant message from: RUBY

Ruby: Hello stranger.

Rosie: Oh hi Ruby, sorry it's been so long; I've had a lot
         on lately.

Ruby: No apologies needed. How's your mum?

Rosie: Not great. That tear reservoir still hasn't dried up.
         She's coming to stay with me for a little while.

Ruby: In the flat?

Rosie: Yes.

Ruby: How's that going to work? You don't have any
         spare rooms.

Rosie: Oh gosh it has been ages since I spoke to you. After
         many days of deliberations with Brian the Whine I
         eventually gave in and have decided to allow Katie
         to stay with him in Ibiza for the summer. I must be
         crazy because no matter how much Brian the Whine
         assures me that he's a responsible father who will
         keep an eye on his daughter, I can't stop thinking of
         the fact that he ran off when he found out I was
         pregnant and only returned when she was 13. I'm
         not too keen on his definition of responsible. Plus
         he will be working nights so I don't know how he'll
         know what she's up to.

Ruby: The good thing about Brian being her father is that
         he's the owner of a seedy night club on the part of
         an island where he's used to seeing what exactly 16-
         year-olds get up to. He will not want his daughter
         joining in with that kind of fun. Trust me. Anyway
         she'll be on her own, how much partying can a girl
         do on her own?

Rosie: You really want the answer to that question? Any-
         way her boyfriend John is going to join her for a
         few weeks and Toby and his girlfriend are going
         over for a holiday too. But I can't put up too much
         of a fight because Brian the Whine is good enough
         to spend most of the year here for Katie and he
         needs to be over there during the summer. There

has to be a bit of give and take, and Katie has never actually seen her own father's home. Also Brian said he would make sure she gets a bit of experience DJ-ing while she's there which would be brilliant for her.

Ruby: Have you convinced yourself enough yet?

Rosie: God does it really sound like that?

Ruby: Yep.

Rosie: Well, without wanting to sound like a complete moan (because we all know I'm not one to moan) this summer is going to be really lonely for me. I could be really selfish and not let her go just for my sake and Mum is only staying with me a short while before she's off again. A few people Mum and Dad met while they were on their cruise last year got in touch with Mum. They're planning a trip to South Africa and they're going to stay for a month. That was the next place Dad wanted to go to. He always used to watch *National Geographic* and swear he would one day go on a safari. Well he's going now because Mum is taking his ashes and scattering them with the tigers and elephants. She's really happy with the idea so I'm not going to get in her way. Kevin is a bit upset about it, he wants to have a place for Dad so that we can all visit, but Mum insists this is what Dad would want. She's the woman who knew him best; I don't know why Kev is causing such a fuss. He barely visited Dad when he was alive, I can't imagine him visiting his cremation site every day. Come to think of it, maybe that's what his problem is.

Anyway she doesn't want to stay in Connemara a moment longer on her own so she's coming to stay with me for two weeks before she heads off. But after that, everyone is gone. Mum, Dad, Katie, Steph,

Kev, and Alex. I'm all alone and because it's the
summer and the school is closed all I have to do is
to study.

Ruby: You think that maybe this is a sign to meet more
people?

Rosie: I know, I know. I'm alone by my own choosing.
When I was 18 everyone my age wanted to talk
about boys not babies, at 22 they wanted to talk
about college not teething, at 30 they wanted to talk
about marriage not divorce, and now when I'm 36
and finally willing to talk about men and college, all
people want to do is talk about babies. I've tried all
these coffee morning things, I've tried chatting to
other mothers as we waited at the school gates for
our children. It didn't work. Nobody understands
me like you do Ruby.

Ruby: And even I have trouble with that. You're unique
Rosie Dunne, you're definitely unique. But I'm here
for you and unless me and Gary miraculously become Ireland's salsa champions and are whisked off
to Madrid for the European championship, I ain't
going nowhere.

Rosie: Thanks.

Ruby: No problem. So when are you going to start dating
again? It's been a few years since you've been in
action!

Rosie: Excuse me, did I not go out on a date with Adam,
whom you set me up with? Anyway apart from that
enjoyable night with Adam, it's not like dating was
ever that brilliant for me to miss.

Ruby: Really?

Rosie: Oh please, sex with what's-his-name was so me-
chanical. He used to move in time to the bloody
bedside alarm clock that ticked so loudly it would
keep me awake (at night of course, not during
sex).

Sex with Brian the Whine was a mere drunken fumble in the dark so I can't even remember that. I've only ever been with 3 men and two of them aren't the greatest advertisements for men either. I don't think I'll ever meet my Don Juan. I don't really care either. What you don't know, you don't miss.

Ruby: But doesn't what you don't know make you even the teeny tiniest bit curious?

Rosie: No. I have a shit job with shit pay, a shit flat with shit rent. I have no time for shit sex with a shit man.

Ruby: Rosie!

Rosie: What? I'm serious.

Ruby: I just cannot believe my ears. I'm flabbergasted by this news. OK I'm taking you out clubbing at the weekend.

Rosie: Clubbing? Do you really think bringing me to a place where I am 10 years older than everyone is really going to make me feel better? You think young hot-blooded males are interested in 36-year-old, out of shape, single mothers these days? I don't think so. I think they're interested in women with breasts resting *above* their belly buttons.

Ruby: Oh don't exaggerate. You're 36 not 96! And I met my Teddy in a nightclub and he may not be Brad Pitt but what he lacks in looks he makes up for in the bedroom department.

Rosie: Really? You mean to tell me that sex is *good* with Teddy?

Ruby: Well I'm not with the man for conversation am I?

Rosie: Of course not, I'm not that stupid. I knew there was *something* keeping you two together, but sex was the last thing on my mind.

Ruby: Well all that's going to change now, so come on let's go out and have a good time.

Rosie: Honestly Ruby, thanks but no thanks. I really have no interest in meeting anyone. And if I did what

would I do, bring him home to meet my grieving
mother sleeping in the room next door?

Ruby: I suppose you have a point, but I'm not letting you
get away with this for much longer. Sooner or later
you're going to have to start enjoying yourself
again. You recognize that word, Rosie? Enjoy. To
have fun.

Rosie: Never heard of it.

Ruby: Fine then, we'll go to the pub again this weekend
but after that I'm putting you back on the market.

Rosie: OK but trust me when I say I'm only going for full
asking price. And if no one's interested in buying
I'm not taking on any renters.

Ruby: What about squatters?

Rosie: Ha ha ha. All trespassers will be prosecuted.

Ruby: I can just picture you standing there with a shotgun
in hand ordering men off your land.

Rosie: Now you're getting the picture.

—⁓—

CHAPTER 44

Dear Mum,

Sorry I didn't write sooner but I've been so busy ever since I landed that I haven't had the chance to pick up a pen. It's really hot here at the moment so I'm trying to work on my tan before John comes over. I want him seeing me as a complete beach babe!

Dad collected me from the airport which was a weird experience. Weird to see him dressed up, or I should say dressed *down* in shorts and flip-flops. I didn't know he had legs. You would have laughed if you'd seen him, he was wearing this navy blue Hawaiian-style shirt with yellow flowers splattered all over it, although he insisted it was black (by the way I believe you now about his debs suit being navy, he is completely color-blind).

He has an electric blue convertible which is pretty cool (he thinks it's black) as I've never been in a convertible before. The island is so beautiful. He lives in a really nice complex just outside the busy part of town and there are about ten white painted villas that share a swimming pool. There's a really cute guy that lives straight across from Dad who just swims and sunbathes all day. He's so brown and muscley and such a babe so I spend the entire day by the

pool drooling. Dad is freaking out and keeps telling him to
put his shirt on. He's trying to be funny but no one really
laughs. Speaking of cute guys I can't wait for John to come
over, I miss him like crazy. Two weeks is far too long to be
without him and I still have another week to go, it's not
natural.

Toby and Monica are coming over next week which
should be good fun as long as Monica keeps her gob shut.
They're both staying in a hotel in town and there's loads of
cool clubs around them. But before you go ape shit let me
tell you that the day I arrived, Dad brought me up and down
the street of bars and clubs and introduced me to all the
bouncers and managers and told them I was his daughter. I
thought he was doing it so that they'd recognize me and let
me in but when I went up to one of the bars last week not
one of them let me in. Not *one*. I thought they were doing it
because they hated Dad and they were trying to piss him off
or something, but yesterday a bouncer from the club down
the road came up to Dad's club with his fifteen-year-old son
who was staying with him for the summer too and
introduced him to Dad and all the head doormen. Then I
heard Dad tell the guys at the door to remember the boy's
face and not to let him in. That's obviously the way it works
around here.

I've just been going to Dad's club most nights. I was
allowed to stand in the DJ box all night just watching the DJ
work. It's crazy over here. Dad's club is really cool. It's
packed every night and you can barely move on the dance
floor. No one seems to care though; it seems the more
packed and stuffy a place is, the more popular it is.

The resident DJ is DJ Sugar (He. Is. Gorgeous!) and he
was showing me what to do all night and he even let me take
over for a few minutes. The entire point was for the crowd
not to notice I had taken over because I wanted to sound as
good and professional as Sugar but I looked up and
everyone was staring at me because Dad had a massive

camera in his hand and was trying to get people to pose for
the camera in front of the DJ box. It was so embarrassing.

I met Dad's girlfriend.

She's twenty-eight, her name's Lisa, and she's a dancer in
the club. She dances on a podium that's about ten feet off
the ground over everyone's heads, in the center of the club.
She dances inside a ring of fire in a tiger-print piece of
material that she wraps around her body (I wouldn't even
call it a dress). She's from Bristol in England and she moved
over here to become a dancer when she was my age. She said
she worked in a club down the road (which I'm presuming
is the strip club) and she met Dad and he offered her a job (I
don't want to know *how* or *where* they met).

She's talking about bringing a snake into her act next
because she bought a new snakeskin costume and she thinks
it'll look cool. I told her to dance with Dad. (I think you
possessed my body for a minute.) Anyway, Dad thinks she's
crazy and refuses to get her a snake and they've been
arguing about it all week. I didn't have the heart to tell her
that everyone is so drunk in the club I don't think they'd
notice if Lisa was dancing with an elephant, never mind a
snake. She says she wants to do it so she can put it in her
CV. Dad asked her if she was planning on applying for a job
with the circus. They're funny to listen to. It's not *arguing*
arguing, it's like a comedy act. I've never heard two people
disagree on so many things but still get along so well. I
think they both enjoy it.

I've just realized that you and I have never been on a sun
holiday together. In fact apart from visiting Steph and Alex
have you ever been *away* away? You and me can go away
next year when I've finally finished school and I'm enjoying
my freedom. You'll have finished your degree by then too so
the two of us can celebrate!

I hope your studying is going well, at least you don't have
me there distracting you from your work. If Rupert blares

his music too loud just bang down on the floor and he'll turn it down. That's what I do.

> I'll write again soon. I miss you!
> > Love,
> > Katie

Dear Rosie,

I'm writing to you from Cape Town in South Africa which is so stunning you would hate me for being here. The rest of the group are taking good care of me so don't you worry about that. And because they all knew Dennis from the cruise it's nice to be able to talk to them about him and remember the funny times we had. There's another lady here who has also lost her husband and this is her first holiday alone so we both tend to get teary-eyed together at times. I'm glad she's here because we both understand each other and what we're going through.

I miss Dennis very much. He would have loved this holiday. In a way he is here with me. I don't care how nuts Kevin thinks I am, I've scattered your father's ashes. Some into the air, some into the water, and some into the ground. He's all around me now. I know this is what he would have wanted. He told me not to let him rot away six feet under or remain a pile of ashes on the mantelpiece. This way he's floating through the air all around the world. Seeing more of it than me now. I saw it as sending him off on his final adventure.

Some days are very difficult and I just want to phone you up and have a good cry, but being here is a nice distraction. Not only that, it's a nice place to grieve if you have to. Kevin doesn't understand me at all, he thinks I should be wearing black and visiting a graveside every day like a miserable old soul. But I won't do it. Honestly I don't know where he gets his way of thinking at all. We have three weeks left and already the gang are talking about traveling some more

after! They have a lot of contacts in the travel world so we
could get some really terrific deals. I may as well keep
spending my savings because it's no good wherever I'm
going next.

I hope Katie is getting on well in Ibiza and that Brian is
taking good care of her. He seems to have turned into a
decent, hardworking man so I wouldn't worry, my dear
Rosie. Could you please pass on the enclosed letter for
Katie, I wasn't sure of her address.

I'm sure you're delighted to have a bit of peace and
quiet while you're studying. I hope Ruby is leaving you well
alone too and not dragging you out for too many nights on
the town!!

Good luck with the studying, love.
> I love you and miss you,
> Mum

FROM: Ruby
TO: Rosie
SUBJECT: Bye!

Hi Rosie, just a quick e-mail to let you know the great
news! Teddy and I got a cheap last-minute holiday to
Croatia today. €199 each for a fortnight including
accommodation and flights. How cheap is that?! The reason
for the cheapness is because the flight is leaving tonight! So
I'm throwing all my clothes into my case at the same time as
typing this (multitalented, I know). Do you think it's too late
for me to get the perfect beach bod? Maybe I won't eat the
food on the plane and we'll see what difference that'll make.
Maybe I'll fit into that thong after all, ha ha.

Just wanted to wish you farewell my friend, I'm sure
you'll be delighted I'm gone as you'll finally have a bit of
peace to study now. I hope you've fun when Alex and co.

come over on their hols but remember he's a married man
now so don't do anything I wouldn't do!!

> Take care,
> Ruby

Rosie,
Greetings from Hawaii!
As you can see there was a change of plan! My
crazy wife decided that Hawaii would be a far nicer resort than Ireland, why on earth I have no idea!!

The weather is fantastic, the hotel a dream (I've
taken the liberty of stealing a few things for you from
my room which should be enclosed in the package. A
shower cap and bath gel all the way from Hawaii! I
hope the cap fits).

Restaurants are great too.

You're probably delighted we're not coming over as
now you finally get a bit of peace and quiet to study. I
hope Kevin leaves you alone and stops annoying you
about your mum. I think she's right.

> Lots of love,
> Alex, Josh, Theo (and dare I say Bethany)

Rosie,
Hello from Cyprus.
Weather nice. Hotel nice. Food nice. Beach nice.
Hope you're enjoying your summer of silence and study.
(If Steph and the rest of the troop don't invade your home.
By the way we need to talk about Mum scattering Dad's
ashes.)

> Kevin

Hello from Disney World!
Hi sis, having a brill time. Feel like I'm ten years old!
Met Mickey Mouse yesterday and we all had to get a photo

with him (as you can see I look slightly star struck. Pierre was a little worried about me). The kids are in heaven, there's so many things for them to look at I think they're going to make themselves dizzy! There's so much to do here that we decided to stay an extra few days so unfortunately we won't be able to stop off in Dublin on the way home like we'd planned.

Hope the studying is going well and that you're enjoying your peace and quiet. Don't let Rupert from next door drag you to the National Concert Hall anymore, just tell him you need to study.

> Lots of love,
> Steph, Pierre, Jean-Louis, and Sophia

Hi Rosie,

I called around earlier but you weren't here so I thought I'd leave you this note. I'm going away for a few weeks with the choir I sing in, we're going to sing for the people of Kazakhstan. We're touring the country and I'm really looking forward to it.

I'm closing the shop while I'm gone so you'll be pleased to know that there won't be any noise coming from either the shop or the flat while I'm gone. You should be able to study now that we're all away. I've left my key with you in case there are any emergencies.

Good luck with the studying, enjoy your peace and quiet, and I'll see you when I get back. Maybe by the time I'm back you'll have asked that Internet guy from downstairs out on a date. I think he likes you—he keeps asking after you.

> Rupert (from next door)

Rosie Dunne,

You have an outstanding bill of €6.20 owed from the last time you were here to use the Internet. Please pay it immediately or we will take legal action.

> Ross (from the Internet café downstairs)

You have entered the Relieved Divorced Dubliner's Internet
Chat room
There are currently no people chatting
Buttercup has entered the room

Buttercup: Ah not these guys too, they're not supposed to
             have lives . . . where the hell *is* everyone?

CHAPTER 45

—∞—

You have an instant message from: TOBY

Toby: I bet you had a salad sandwich for lunch again.

Katie: How do you no?

Toby: It's KNOW not NO. I can see the lettuce hanging out of your braces again. I'm surprised you haven't taken to eating mashed foods by now or at least something you could suck through a straw. Solids are a bit of a no-no.

Katie: This time next week you won't be able to slag me anymore. For the end of an era has come. The braces are coming off. After three and a half years behind bars, my teeth, my now *straight* teeth may I add, will be free.

Toby: Well it's about time. I can't wait to see how they come off.

Katie: Not gonna happen.

Toby: Why not?!

Katie: You didn't think that I'd take three and a half years of listening to your annoying metal mouth jokes lying down did you? This is my revenge. Next week

I'm bringing my mum with me and she can take a photo for you.

Toby: Ah Katie, don't be ridiculous! You can't do this! I've been to every single one of your appointments and you leave me out for the final one, the biggest one of all? I *need* to see them come off.

Katie: I think they'll teach you that stuff at college Toby, I don't think you need to worry at all. You don't actually *need* to no everything *before* you even study it at college. The general idea is to learn it there.

Toby: Well I haven't been accepted yet have I? I could screw up in my exams and not get enough points for the course.

Katie: You'll get in Toby.

Toby: The points are really high Katie.

Katie: You'll get in.

Toby: Trinity College is really popular though, what if I do get the points but then so do hundreds of other people? Then they'll raise the points even higher.

Katie: You'll get in.

Toby: We'll see. Have you figured out what course you're going to do yet? You better decide soon because we need to fill out our CAO forms soon.

Katie: The stress of it all. How the hell are we expected at the age of 16 (and 17 in your case) to decide what we want to do for the rest of our lives? The decision is next to impossible. Right now all I want to do is get *out* of school, not start planning to get into another one. You're lucky you've always known what you want to do.

Toby: Only thanks to you and your manky teeth. Anyway, you've known what you wanted to do for longer than I have. Be a DJ.

Katie: I can't study that in college though, can I?

Toby: Who says you have to go to college?

Katie: Everyone. The career guidance teacher. My mum. My
         dad. All the teachers. God. Rupert. Sanjay even said I
         should go and that he will take care of Mum for me.

Toby: Well I wouldn't listen to Sanjay because he's got
         (scary) ulterior motives. I wouldn't listen to the ca-
         reer guidance teacher either because his job is to
         take you for half an hour every week and discuss
         college courses to his heart's content. Do you think
         he really cares what you do? Who cares what Rupert
         thinks, your dad is only agreeing with your mum,
         and your mum is only saying you should go because
         she thinks you want to. And don't mind God, as
         your mum always says, he's only having a laugh.

Katie: But Mum has worked so hard to finally get around
         to studying what she wants and it's been such a
         struggle for her to get to the final year. Now I have
         the opportunity to go to college, because let's face it
         if I study really hard from now until June we both
         no I could do well. I've nothing in my way, nothing
         to hold me back, and I think Mum thinks I'm jump-
         ing for joy at the idea.

         She wanted this opportunity so much at my age and
         I kind of got in the way and now it's my turn and
         I've nothing in the way. For her this is a big deal, for
         her I'm a really lucky person. Meanwhile I just can't
         think of anything I would be bothered studying for
         another four years of my life. It sounds like a prison
         sentence. Dad said that I could go over to him for
         the summer again and work in the club behind the
         bar for a few nights a week. Sugar will train me on
         the other nights. He says if I really want to do it I
         might as well start taking it seriously.

Toby: He's right.

Katie: Well you don't sound like you're going to miss me
         too much!

Toby: Of course I won't. If you don't go, then I'm the one
          who has to listen to you moan for the rest of my
          life. Apart from that, you should look at your mum
          as being the perfect example, she missed out on her
          chance when she was your age and now she's only
          months away from finally reaching it. You on the
          other hand have your dream on a plate right in front
          of you.

          Of all the mothers in the world yours is the least
          likely to be pushy about college. She's only encour-
          aging you because she thinks that's what you want.
Katie: You're right. I never thought of it like that.
Toby: I'm always right.
Katie: It's our final year Toby. Who new we would ever get
          here? After all those days of detention, I will finally
          never have to wear another tie again. For you dear
          Toby, your tie-wearing days are just beginning.
Toby: No more double computer class on a Monday morn-
          ing and I can assure you that if I get into college I
          will not be wearing ties.
Katie: Brown cords and long hair then, and you can listen
          to Bob Dylan all day while you're flaked out on the
          grass, man. I'm actually beginning to think that dou-
          ble computer class on a Monday morning could ac-
          tually be easy compared to moving away from Mum
          and Grandma. Oh my god, what about John?
Toby: John has legs, he'll be able to walk on to a plane, sit
          down, fly to Ibiza or wherever you may be, get off
          the plane, and see you. I noticed you didn't mention
          me there. Will life be that easy without me?
Katie: Yes of course it will. No but honestly, aren't there
          any dentistry colleges in Ibiza?
Toby: Not where you're going, unless you include extract-
          ing people's teeth using your fist.
Katie: Well then I guess it's Ibiza for just me and Dad then.

To Katie and Rosie,

Good luck to the both of you in your exams, I'm praying for my girls.

Love Mum/Grandma

To Rosie and Katie,

Good luck!

Love Steph, Pierre, JeAN-LOuiS, and Sophia

To Rosie and Katie,

My best friend and goddaughter, best of luck in your exams. You will both excel as you always do. Let me no how the first one goes.

Love,
Alex

To Rosie,

After these exams can you start going out again? You're becoming an awful bore and an intelligent bore at that which is even worse. The quality of conversation with Teddy and Gary is declining week by week and last week I was forced to listen to hours and hours of "discussion" about whether the Aston Martin DB7 is as good or as fast as a Ferrari 575. Oh yes my family likes to get down to the nitty-gritty and discuss the important things in life.

I know I encouraged you to go for this degree but if you fail these exams this year and have to repeat I'm giving you the official warning that I have the firm intention of making a new friend. One that won't be so ambitious. You do know that ambition was Macbeth's downfall don't you? (It was either that or the crazy wife.)

So absolutely no pressure there. Good luck,
Ruby

To Mum,
     Here we go, in a fortnight we'll both be free.
          Best of luck,
          Katie

To Katie,
     Good luck honey, thanks for being my study partner. No
matter how you do I'm proud of you.
          Love,
          Mum

Exam results: Rosie Dunne.
Student number: 4553901-L
Course: BA in Hotel Business Management
Recognized by Irish Hotel & Catering Institute (MIMCI) &
Catering Managers Association of Ireland (MCMA)

Subject	Grade
Accounting	B
Computer Applications and Data Summary	B
Economics	B
Hospitality Ethical and Legal Studies	B
Financial Control and Marketing	B
Human Resource Management	A
Enterprise Development	A
Languages (Irish)	A
Tourism and Hospitality Industry Studies	A

     Graduates qualify for membership for a period of profes-
sional internship in the hospitality industry.

YES! YES! YES! YES! YEEEEEESSSSSS! ALEX I DID IT! I
FINALLY DID IT!!

Rosie I'm so happy for you! Congratulations!

FROM: Rosie
TO: Ruby
SUBJECT: Let's celebrate!

Now we can definitely go out! By the way, Katie is coming out with us too so get your dancing shoes on (of course in your case I don't mean that literally. No one wants to see salsa shoes in a nightclub). She did brilliantly in her exams and got accepted to a few college business courses but she's going to stick to her original idea of trying out DJ-ing.

Toby got enough points for dentistry in Trinity College which is wonderful news so overall everyone is happy, happy, happy!

You know when I was 18 I missed out on going to Boston and I thought my world had ended. While all my friends were partying and studying I was cleaning dirty nappies. I thought my dream was lost. Never in a million years did I think that I would be able to share this special moment with my teenage daughter.

Everything does happen for a reason. I'll just be so sad to see my baby go away. The day I've been preparing for has finally arrived, Katie is spreading her wings and moving on and I must do the same. I think I might be close to gathering enough money to buy that train ticket out of here.

Rosie Dunne is leaving the station and moving on. *Finally*.

Rosie Dunne,	Principal Julie Casey,
Apt. 3,	St. Patrick's Primary School
Northstrand	
Dublin 1,	
Ireland	

Dear Rosie,

Congratulations on your recent exam results, you have proved yourself to be a true achiever and should feel proud.

Keeping my promise, I am delighted to inform you on behalf of all of us here at St. Patrick's Primary School that your services are no longer required. Your contract with us will not be up for renewal in August.

We are sorry to see you go but you have to. My retirement was one year later than planned but it was worth hanging around to see you succeed. Rosie Dunne, you have been the longest project of my life, my eldest and longest-serving student, and although we may have had a rocky start and an even rockier middle, I am so glad to see you succeed at the end.

Your hard work and dedication are an inspiration to us all and I wish you all the best for the future. I do hope you keep in touch and I would love to see you attend my retirement party for which you will receive an invitation shortly. I ask that you forward on an invitation to Alex Stewart too.

After years of separating the two of you it would be nice to see you both in the same room again after so many years. I do hope that he can make it.

      Congratulations again.
      Keep in touch,
      Julie (Big Nose Smelly Breath) Casey

Katie,

My baby girl is moving away! I'm so proud of you, love, you are so brave to be doing this. Make sure your dad doesn't forget to feed and clothe you.

I'll miss you so much, I loved having you here with me but I hope I'm welcome to visit you lots!

If you need me, just call and I'll come running.

      Lots of love,
      Mum

Dear Brian,

This is a huge responsibility, please take care of Katie and don't let her get up to anything stupid over there. You know what eighteen-year-old males are like, you yourself were one. Keep her away from them as best you can. She's over there to learn, not party and make babies.

Let me know *everything* that's going on with her. Even the stuff she's afraid to tell me. A mother needs to know. Please listen to her and be there for her all the time. If you even sense that something is wrong and she won't confide in you, just let me know and I'll subtly find out.

And last but not least, thank you so much for giving my baby, *our* baby her dream.

Best wishes,
Rosie

Dear Rosie Dunne,

Congratulations on completing your BA in Hotel Business Management.

We are pleased to inform you that your professional internship in the hospitality industry will be undertaken at the beginning of August. Each graduate's employment has been randomly selected and chosen by a computer without discrimination or prejudice and all jobs are on an equal par with one another. Once a placement has been made the graduate cannot change or demand another.

The contract of twelve months is for the position of assistant manager and is to be held at the Grand Tower Hotel in Dublin's city center.

You are to begin on Monday, 1st of August at nine a.m. For more information regarding your placement please contact Cronin Ui Cheallaigh, manager and owner of the Grand Tower Hotel. The phone number, details, and map of directions to the hotel are provided overleaf.

We wish you luck in your new venture and hope it brings
you success in the future.

> Yours sincerely,
> Keith Richards
> Hotel Business Management Course Director, St.
> Patrick's Primary School Night Courses

Alex: Very impressive Rosie, the Grand Tower Hotel?
Sounds very prestigious indeed.

Rosie: Oooh I know! That's what I thought! I'm not famil-
iar with the hotel though are you?

Alex: Oh you're asking the wrong person Rosie. Every
time I'm back in Dublin some new building, office
block, or apartment block has popped up where
there was nothing. I don't no where anything is anymore. You should go down and take a look yourself.

Rosie: No! I couldn't do that! What if they caught me
snooping around and then I arrived the next day
claiming to be the manager. They'll think I'm a freak.

Alex: A freak? No. Interested and eager? Yes.

Rosie: Nobody likes an eager beaver Alex. After we hung
up the other night, I was thinking and do you know
you're losing your accent?

Alex: Rosie I have been here 20 years. I've spent more
years here than in Ireland. My kids are American; I
have to keep up with the lingo! (Irish expression
added entirely for you.) Of course I'm going to lose
an accent.

Rosie: Well you're not so much losing an accent as gain-
ing an accent. Anyway 20 years . . . how did that
happen?

Alex: I no, time flies when you're having fun.

Rosie: If you call the last 20 years fun, then I don't want to
know how fast time goes by when you're really enjoying yourself.

Alex: It hasn't been so bad for you, has it Rosie?

Rosie: Define bad.

Alex: Oh come on . . .

Rosie: No it hasn't but I wouldn't complain if it became a whole lot better.

Alex: Well, none of us would . . . the job must be exciting for you.

Rosie: It really, really is. I feel like a kid on Christmas Eve! I haven't felt like that for a long, long time. I know the job is temporary and that I'm only in training but I've waited a long time for this opportunity.

Alex: You've waited too long for it. I of all people no how much you've wanted this. I used to hate it when you made me play Hotel.

Rosie: Ha ha, I remember that. I was always the person in charge and you had to be the customer!

Alex: I hated being the customer because you would never leave me alone. You kept fluffing my pillows and lifting my feet up on stools for the customer's "comfort."

Rosie: My god, I'd forgotten all about that! I used to try to be like the guy on *Fantasy Island* who looked after his guests so much he would use magic to give them their dreams.

Alex: I don't call forcing me to go to bed at two in the day, tucking me in so tight that I could hardly breathe a comfort/dream-providing service! I don't no what type of manager you were trying to be but if you behave like that with your real customers then a few of them will have restraining orders against you.

         These days people don't generally like being given daily schedules by their manager of what they *have* to do for their day in the hotel. (And if they don't obey the list, their manager will go home in a sulk and stay that way all day until the customer apologizes.) The phrase "The customer is always right" is one you'll need to remember Rosie.

Rosie: At least it wasn't as bad as playing Hospital.

Alex: Now that was a game and a half!

Rosie: It was a stupid game Alex. All it involved was you trying to trip me up in the school yard so I would cut myself and you would have to tend to me. Mum and Dad used to wonder where I was getting all the cuts and bruises from.

Alex: Yeah it was fun wasn't it?

Rosie: Well you have a distorted idea of what fun is. Like the last 20 years for example.

Alex: Obviously not *all* fun for either of us.

Rosie: No . . .

Alex: Hospitals and Hotels eh? Sounds like some kind of porn movie.

Rosie: You wish.

Alex: I *do* wish. I have a 4-year-old son who likes to get out of bed at 5 a.m. and sleep in between me and Beth. Any sex at all is like porn for me these days.

Rosie: Well a man smiled at me the other day and I crossed my legs. That's porn enough for me. I could join the nunnery and I don't think it would bother me in the slightest.

Alex: Oh I disagree!

Rosie: No really, *trust* me Alex. After the men I've been with, celibacy would be like a *gift*.

Alex: It wasn't the celibacy I was referring to; it was the vow of silence that would kill you.

Rosie: Funny. Well believe me Alex, there are certain kinds of silences that make you walk on air.

Alex: That, I no.

—⁓—

CHAPTER 46

Hi Mum,

Just a quick note to wish you luck (not that you need it) on your first day of work tomorrow. Your new suit sounds gorgeous so I'm sure you'll knock 'em all dead!

> Best of luck,
> Love,
> Katie

You have an instant message from: RUBY

Ruby: Well Ms. Assistant Manager, tell me all about it. How's work going?

Rosie: Very very sl o o o o o wly.

Ruby: Should I ask why?

Rosie: Are you ready for a rant? Because if you're not I'm giving you the opportunity now to get out of this conversation while you can.

Ruby: Believe it or not I came into this conversation prepared. Fire ahead.

Rosie: *OK* so I arrived on the road the hotel was situated on nice and early and proceeded to walk up and down the street for three quarters of an hour trying to find the very beautiful and *Grand* Tower Hotel. I asked shop owners and stall owners but none of them had any idea where this hotel was.

After ringing the course director almost in tears and in a complete panic over the fact that I was late for my first day of work, I also succeeded in accusing him of giving me the wrong address. He kept on repeating the same address over and over again which I told him couldn't be possible because the building in question was completely derelict.

Eventually he said he'd ring the hotel owner and double-check the directions with him so I sat down on the filthy front steps of the derelict building (dirtying the bum of my new suit) and tried not to cry about how late I was and what a bad impression this was making. Suddenly the door of the building behind me opened with a very loud farting noise at the hinges and this *thing* looked out at me. The thing spoke in a very strong Dublin accent, introduced himself as Cronin Ui Cheallaigh, the owner of the building, and insisted I call him Beanie.

At first I was confused by his nickname but as the day wore on it all became very clear. The hinges of the front door were not what made a farting sound; it was indeed the gaseous behind of Beanie.

He brought me inside to the ancient, damp building and showed me around the few rooms on the ground level. He then asked me if I had any questions and I of course wanted to know why I was in this particular building and when was I going to see the hotel. To which he replied proudly, " 'Dis is de bleedin' hotel. Nice, wha'?"

He then asked me if I had any ideas on how to improve the hotel after my first impression and I suggested displaying the actual name of the hotel on the actual building so as to make it easier for the guests. (Although not doing so was also a good marketing ploy.) I also suggested spreading the word of its existence among the surrounding businesses so they could help advertise the hotel (or at least be able to help give directions to completely lost tourists).

He studied my face very hard to see if I was being smart. Which by the way I absolutely wasn't. If my ideas seemed ridiculous to him then the fact that I had to even raise them was even more ridiculous. I'm currently waiting on a sign for the front of the hotel to arrive.

He then gave me a name tag which he insisted I wear. His reason for me having to wear this was so that if customers needed to complain, they would know whom to blame. A very positive-thinking man, as you can see. The problem with the name tag (other than having to wear it) was that he appeared to have misheard the spelling of my name over the phone.

I have been walking around the entire week as "Rosie Bumme." Something that Beanie seems to find incredibly humorous. Although after he had gotten over his laughing fit he was slightly disappointed. That alone is an example of his level of maturity and the seriousness with which he takes his job and general running of the so-called hotel.

How it has remained open up until now is beyond me. It is one of those beautiful houses that in Victorian, Georgian, Edwardian times (they're all the same to me) would have been extremely grand but that has been left to rot away. It's probably decaying underneath the floorboards with whatever else is causing the smell.

It was once redbricked but is now dirty brown. It has four levels and on the underground level, I have now learned, is a lap-dancing club also owned by Beanie. As you enter the ground level of the hotel, you are greeted by a tiny little desk made of dark mahogany wood (as is all the wood in the building), behind it is a messy collection of former guests' hats, umbrellas, and coats that are currently collecting dust.

The walls are wood-paneled from the floor to halfway up the wall which is a nice feature and the walls which were probably once a rich olive green color are now a more moldy green. Small lantern-like lights adorn the walls and throw out absolutely no light at all. The place is like a dungeon. The carpets look like they were laid in the '70s, they're dirty and smelly and have cigarette burns, black patches of stuck on chewing gum, and other stains the smell of which I don't wish to know.

This long corridor leads down to a large bar area which contains the same dirty smelly carpet, dark wood, paisley-covered stools and chairs, and when the sun shines through the tiny, paint-flaking window all you can see is the air thick with wisps of smoke probably still there from the old man who used to sit there with his pipe 200 years ago.

The dining area has twenty tables and a limited menu. It has the same carpet except it has the added feature of food stains. There are brown velvet curtains, and net blinds; the tables are covered in what was once white but now yellow lace tablecloth with rusty food-stained cutlery. The glasses are misty, the walls are white, which makes it the only room with light but no matter how much the heat is turned up it feels cold.

But the *smell*. It's like somebody died and was left to decay. It has since been absorbed into the furniture, the walls, and into my clothes.

There are 60 rooms, 20 on each floor. Beanie proudly announced that half of them are en-suite. You could imagine how happy I was to hear that, thinking immediately that I should ring up the TV and radio stations to advertise this wonderful feature. The fact that *some* bedrooms have bathrooms.

Two wonderful women, Betty and Joyce, each aged about 100 years old, clean the rooms three times a week which frankly I find rather disgusting. And given how slowly they move, I'd be surprised if they cleaned the room even that often.

I was also beginning to wonder what kind of customers a hotel like this would attract but it all became clear to me as I worked the late shift one night. As the lap-dancing club finished downstairs, the party continued upstairs. This gave me all the more reason to employ more chambermaids.

The place is far from being luxurious and I'm far from being the wonderful host welcoming the guests to paradise as I so desired to be. The only way someone would find a chocolate on their pillow is if the previous guest spit it out.

The only reason someone would wear the shower cap would be to protect their head from the yellow

water that runs through the pipes (though probably
safe, I'm sticking to my bottled water).

Last week a radio station rang up to ask if the hotel
could be part of a competition they're running. I
couldn't think of a good enough excuse to say no.
People had to write in and explain why they deserved a weekend of pampering in Dublin. They
would be treated to a night at the theater, an expensive meal, a day out shopping, and two nights bed
and breakfast at a central hotel, all expenses paid. It
was great for the hotel as we were advertised all
week on the radio and we got a good few guests as
a result.

The people who won had the most touching story
of all, I was nearly crying listening to their story
on the radio. So I had the honeymoon suite (completely the same as all the other rooms but I told
Beanie to put a sign on the door to make the win-
ners feel special. He ended up stenciling it on himself and spent an hour with a black marker in his
hand with his tongue hanging out in concentration) filled with beautiful flowers and left a compli-
mentary bottle of champagne for them. I really
tried my best with the room, squeezing enough
money out of the budget for new bed linen, etc.,
but there was only so much the meager profits
could get me.

Anyway when they found out they won, they were
so excited they kept ringing the hotel every day before they got here asking questions and making sure
everything was still OK. They walked in the door,
took one look at the place, and left within fifteen
minutes.

Ruby, the people had lost their *home*, the husband had lost his *job*, broken *both* his legs, lost their *car*, and had to leave their village. They had been given an all-expenses paid weekend and could stay in the hotel absolutely *free* and *still* they didn't want to stay. That's how *bad* this hotel is.

I think that train ticket I worked so hard to buy has left me stranded somewhere under a dark tunnel. The train is fine, it's the track that's broken and I have to wait while work is done before we can move. I'm hoping this won't be too long of a delay. I'll be back on track in no time, ha ha.

Rosie: Ruby?

Rosie: Ruby, are you there?

Rosie: Hello? Ruby, did you get all that?

Ruby: Zzzzzzzzzzzzzzzzzzzzz.

Rosie: Ruby!!

Ruby: Oh what?! Did I miss something? Sorry I must have nodded off about an *hour* ago when you *started* telling me about your job.

Rosie: I'm sorry Ruby but I warned you.

Ruby: Don't worry I managed to wander off and make myself a cup of coffee and came back when you were talking about olive green walls and decomposing bodies.

Rosie: Sorry it's been one of those months.

Ruby: Not all jobs turn out to be what you think they're going to be. Anyway would you rather be a secretary at the Randy Andy Paperclip & Co. or Assistant Manager of The Grand Tower Hotel?

Rosie: Oooh definitely assistant manager of The Grand Tower Hotel.

Ruby: Well there you go Rosie Bumme, life could be worse then couldn't it?

Rosie: I guess so. But I do have one other slight problem.

Ruby: Can you tell me what it is in less than 1,000 words?

Rosie: I'll try! Alex is coming over for Julie Casey's retirement party in a few months and he's bringing Bethany and they've booked themselves into the hotel for the weekend. You see I kind of told him that it was really nice . . . and they specifically requested a room with a view. At this stage I'm hard pushed to find a room with a *window* (OK not *really*) but under the circumstances, we at The Grand Tower Hotel consider a special request to be a room with a *bathroom.*

        I mean, view-wise, which do you think they'd prefer, a view of a butcher's or a view of a scrap yard?

Ruby: Oh dear . . .

You have an instant message from: ALEX

Alex: Hi Rosie, you're up late.

Rosie: So are you.

Alex: I'm 5 hours behind, remember.

Rosie: Katie's debs ball is on tonight. She's there right now in fact.

Alex: Oh I see. Can't you sleep?

Rosie: Are you mad? Of course I can't sleep.

        I helped shop for the dress, helped her get ready with her makeup and hair, took photographs of her being so excited on her special night. The night when she will see friends she probably won't see again for years or never again despite promises of keeping in touch. It was me and Mum twenty years ago.

        I know she's not me, she's her own person with her own mind but I couldn't help but see myself walking out that door. Arm in arm with a man in a tuxedo, excited about the night, excited about the future. Excited, excited, excited. I was so bloody young. Of course I didn't think I was at the time. I had a million plans. I knew what I was going to do. I had the next few years of my life all figured out.

But what I didn't know was that within a few hours all those plans would change. Ms. Know-it-all didn't quite know it all so much then.

	I just hope Katie comes home tonight when she should.
Alex:	She's wise Rosie and if you've raised her the way I think you have, then you have nothing to worry about.
Rosie:	I can't fool myself, she's been with her boyfriend for nearly 4 years now so I don't exactly think they've been holding hands all this time. But for tonight at least, on the night that changed my life, I wish her home early.
Alex:	Well then I'll just have to distract you until she comes home then, won't I?
Rosie:	If you wouldn't mind.
Alex:	So how is our hotel room set for next month? I certainly hope the manager can arrange the very best for us!
Rosie:	Well I'm actually only the *assistant* manager, remember, and the hotel isn't exactly . . .
Alex:	Isn't exactly what?
Rosie:	Well it's not as snazzy as the ones you're used to when you travel.
Alex:	Well this one will be extra special because my best friend will be running it.
Rosie:	I wouldn't want to take much credit for the general running of the hotel . . .
Alex:	Oh don't be silly, you never give yourself enough credit for what you do.

Rosie: Oh no *really* Alex, I wouldn't want to accept any
         responsibility for this hotel *at all*. You know, I'm
         only there a few months, I haven't had a chance to
         put my stamp on it at all. I only follow orders . . .

Alex: Nonsense. I can't wait to see it. How funny would
         it be if someone was poisoned in the restaurant
         and I had to be the in-house doctor that saved the
         day? Remember that was our plan when we were
         kids?

Rosie: I remember alright, and it may not be too far off a
         possibility. Wouldn't you and Bethany like to eat
         out that night? There are so many beautiful restau-
         rants you haven't been to in Dublin.

Alex: We might. I tried looking the hotel up on the Inter-
         net but nothing came up.

Rosie: Eh, yeah, the site is being updated right now. I'll let
         you know when you can see it.

Alex: Great. It'll be weird seeing Ms. Big Nose Smelly
         Breath Casey again. It's about time she retired. The
         children of the world need a break from her.

Rosie: Her name is Julie, remember that, and do *not* call her
         by the other name. And she has been very good to
         me over the past few years so please be good to her.

Alex: I will, I will. Don't worry I have been out of the
         house before, I do no how to deal with people.

Rosie: Of course you have Mr. Socialite Surgeon extraordi-
         naire.

Alex: Whatever image of me that you have in your head
         right now please get rid of it.

Rosie: What? The naked one? You can't tell me to get rid
         of that.

Alex: Ha ha. Well whatever image that is increase the size
         by ten.

Rosie: Jesus, ten inches, Alex?

Alex: Oh shut up! So how's your mum these days? Any
         word back from the hospital about those tests?

Rosie: No not yet. She's away with Stephanie right now
        taking a break from it all and when she comes back
        the results should be ready. They really don't seem
        to know what's wrong with her. I'm really worried.
        I looked at her the other day and it was as though I
        hadn't seen her properly for years. Without even
        noticing it, my young mum has gotten old.

Alex: She's only 65, she's still young.

Rosie: I know that but I had an image of her in my mind
        and that image was of her years ago. Somehow
        since I was young I've continued to see her like that.
        But the other day when I looked at her in the hospi-
        tal bed, she looked old. It was a bit of a shock.
        Anyway I just hope they find out what it is and fix
        it, she's really not feeling well at all.

Alex: As soon as you find out, let me know.

Rosie: I will. It's tough having to travel to Galway on my
        days off. As much as I love Mum, it's a bit of a trek
        for me. Between working incredibly unsociable
        hours, traveling to Mum, helping her, I haven't had
        any real days off for the past few weeks and I am
        tireder than tired.

Alex: Where is Kevin in all this? Can't he help out for
        once in his life?

Rosie: Ha! Good question. Well in all fairness to Kev, he's
        just bought a house and is in the process of moving
        in with his girlfriend. If he had more time I'm *al-
        most* sure he would help out.

Alex: No! Kevin? Mr. Commitment, bad. Freedom, good?

Rosie: The very man himself.

Alex: Wow, that's a shock. You should have a talk to him
        about all this, try to get him to help out a bit more.
        You can't be expected to do everything.

Rosie: Well I'm not exactly doing *everything*. Steph is
        looking after Mum for the week and Steph's got

two young kids so it's not exactly easy for her either. (*Looking after* Mum doesn't sound right does
it?) And I don't mind because I want to be there for
Mum, she's all alone and I know how that feels.

Alex: You asking for help from Kevin doesn't mean you
don't love and want to help Alice. Kev should be
told. And he shouldn't *have* to be told.

Rosie: Well I'll wait until he's settled into his new house
and when that's done and if he *still* hasn't pulled the
finger out then I'm not holding back. He didn't visit
Dad half as much as he should have and I know he's
paying for that now. I've never entirely understood
Kevin, he likes to keep himself to himself. He came
and went from the house and never filled anyone in
on what he was doing. Then when Dad died he suddenly thought he could take control of all the plans.
Now with Mum being sick he's backed off again.
Steph and I have tried to talk to him about it on numerous occasions but there's just no getting through
to him. He's selfish, simple as that. Hold on, a
coach pulled up outside, wait while I run to the
window and check.

Alex: Is Katie in it?

Rosie: No.

Alex: Oh. She'll be—

Rosie: Oh *thank god*, there she is. I better switch off the
computer and dive into bed. I don't want her thinking I was waiting up. Oh thank you god for bringing my baby home. Night Alex.

Alex: Night Rosie.

—&&—

CHAPTER 47

Mother dearest,

Good news! Tony Spencer, an English bloke who owns Club Insomnia down the road, was here in Dad's club last night when I was doing my set, and he was so impressed he asked if I'd like to work for him. How cool is that?! He also organizes a few summer dance festivals so I'll be off around Europe during the summer playing at those. I'm really excited!

Club Insomnia is a really popular club and it goes on till about six or seven in the morning. I'll only be on the decks from about 10 p.m. till midnight just to get started. He pays really well though and as soon as I get my first decent check, I'll send some home to you. I've met a really cool crowd of people over here who are also just out of school a few years and are doing bar work. Me and three other girls, Jennifer, Lucy, and Sara, are talking about renting an apartment together.

I don't no when John is coming over. Ever since he started college in September he's been out all night every night with a bunch of people I've never heard of. He keeps bumping against his phone and accidentally ringing me when he's out and all I can ever hear are loads of drunken people screaming in the background. It's just been really weird with the two of us. Only more so every time we meet up after weeks apart. It's not the same at all and I don't like it. I thought I'd be with him forever but the rate we're going I can barely imagine being with him until the end of the summer. He's annoying me that much.

Meanwhile, I haven't heard from Toby in a long, long time. It's entirely my fault because he rang me loads of times at the beginning when I moved over here and it was my turn to start making an effort but time just ran away. I keep on saying I'll call him tomorrow but it's been months. The last time I spoke to him he was having a great time at college, making friends with lots of teeth, no doubt. I'll call him tomorrow.

I hope everything at work is OK. I can't believe you got your contract extended, I thought you hated the place. Let me no what's going on there, I'm confused.

Alex wrote to me a while back and told me what happened when he and Bethany stayed in the hotel when they were over for Ms. Big Nose Smelly Breath Casey's retirement party. How funny! Didn't you no it was going to be the Northside Pole Dance Club's Christmas party? I don't think Alex seemed too disturbed by the sight of red and white fluffy-bikini-clad Mary Claus's dancing around the bar. I can't believe Bethany refused to stay the night. That woman really doesn't have a sense of humor. Those two just so aren't right for each other, I don't no what he sees in her. I've only met her a few times but she's so uptight and he's so laid-back I really don't see them lasting together for much longer. I can't believe Alex had to tend to one of the guests in the restaurant, was the man poisoned? What kind of food is your restaurant serving?! Just as well there was a doctor in the house.

Anyway I better go and figure out what tracks I'm doing tonight. Dad's giving me a two-hour set just to prepare me for Insomnia. Lisa keeps trying to persuade me to play

eighties music so she can do her flash-dance routine. If it's
not snakes she wants it's something worse like shoulder pads
and perms.

When Grandma gets better, you and she should come
over to me for a few weeks. There are loads of nice relaxing
areas to go to with lovely beaches and scenery; it's not all
pubs and clubs. Think about it, maybe a break would be
good for Grandma.

> Miss you.
> Love,
> Katie

You have an instant message from: RUBY

Ruby: I've been dumped.

Rosie: *What?* By Teddy?

Ruby: No! Don't be silly that man doesn't know how to
put the bins out never mind dump me. No, the cul-
prit is in fact my adoring son. He has informed me
that my services are no longer required and he's
traded me in for a younger model.

Rosie: Oh no, Ruby I'm so sorry. Who's the other woman?

Ruby: Actually I pretend to be mad but I'm not really.
Well, that's a lie, at first I was *really* angry and ate
an entire chocolate cake myself, Gary's favorite
cake that I had bought for him coincidentally.
Halfway through it I was just angry and then while
I was spooning the last mouthful into my mouth I
began to think rationally (that's what it does to me
you see). So I devised a plan whereby I was going to
invite this "other woman" into my home for dinner
so that I could poison her just like in the movie.

I needed to find out who she was, what made her so
much more qualified than me, and why on earth

Gary left me for her. As it turns out she's only in her late 20s, is from Spain, teaches Spanish at the school (that's where Gary met her, where he works as a custodial engineer), she's thin, pretty, and a very beautiful person.

Rosie: She's everything you would usually hate, right?

Ruby: *Usually* yes. But this time it's different because she and my Gary have found love.

Rosie: Ooooh!

Ruby: I know! Isn't it great? So I had no problem stepping aside and hanging up my dancing shoes. To tell the truth I was thinking of parting with Gary soon anyway. I'm not far off 50 now, I need to dance with someone more my own age who won't have the energy to be flinging me across the other side of the room. I'm not up to it anymore. I'm just happy Gary has finally found someone. Maybe Maria will make him move out of my house and in with her.

Rosie: Would you be upset by that?

Ruby: As upset as I would be if I found a million euro under my bed. The boy needs to realize he is a grown man now and move out. I can't cook him his dinners and clean his clothes forever. Anyway enough about me, how's your mum?

Rosie: Not great.

Ruby: That's a shame.

Rosie: It is. It just seems that bit by bit everything is failing on her. Her arthritis has gotten so bad now that she's almost crippled. It wasn't so much of a problem when she and Dad were traveling because then they had the hot weather. Now though I don't think hanging off a cliff in cold Connemara is really the best place for her. But she won't move from there. I'm worried for her. She's in and out of hospital with infections and problems with parts of her body

	that I didn't even know existed. It's as if when Dad died, her body just gave up.
Ruby:	She's a toughie though Rosie, she'll pull through.
Rosie:	Let's hope.
Ruby:	How are things at Fawlty Towers?
Rosie:	Ha! Well I won't have to put up with the place for much longer because I'm leaving at the end of the month.
Ruby:	You say that every month and you never do. You might as well just wait until your contract is up next year and then leave. Anyway unless you actually *look* for another job you're not going anywhere.
Rosie:	Between working all hours and traveling back and forth to Mum, I just don't have *time*. I mean when's the last time I even saw you?
Ruby:	Yesterday.
Rosie:	Well apart from when you drove by me at the bus stop beeping and waving. Thanks for speeding up, driving through the puddle on the side of the road and saturating me, by the way.
Ruby:	We were going in different directions and you looked like you could do with a shower.
Rosie:	Whatever. Anyway it's been at least a month since I've been out properly. It's ridiculous. I have no life. I really want to go visit Katie, and Alex has invited me over to him loads of times but I can't do any of those things.
Ruby:	When your mother gets better everything will be a lot easier.
Rosie:	She's not *going* to get better Ruby. She doesn't want to get better. She's just waiting now. She's practically wheelchair-bound at this stage and she's only 68.
Ruby:	Get lazy Kevin to help.
Rosie:	What would Kevin do? He wouldn't know where to start and I know Mum feels more comfortable

with me helping her. Anyway we'll just have to
keep on going.

TO JOSH,
YOU'RE A TEENAGER!
HAPPY 13TH BIRTHDAY,
LOTS OF LOVE,
ROSIE

To Rosie,
   Thanks so much for my present and card. It's really cool.
Wherever Katie is tell her I said hi. She sends me postcards
all the time from different countries and she sounds real
happy. She's got the coolest job! I never hear about her old
friend Toby anymore. I guess they lost touch or something.
Anyway thanks again for the present. I'll be able to buy a
new computer game with it.

           See you soon,
           Form Josh

       To Mum,
       Hello! I'm in Amsterdam, met a gorgeous guy who
   picks strawberries for a living. Doesn't speak English
   but we get along just fine.
       Everything here is great, got loads of gigs, and the
   cafés are nice too!
       Love,
           Katie

TO ROSIE,
HAPPY 38TH!
HOW SCARY IS IT THAT WE'RE SO CLOSE TO 40?! HAVE
A DRINK FOR ME.
LOVE,
ALEX

Rosie if you think thirty-eight is bad, just imagine how I must feel. Fifty next year. Aaaah! We'll have a *huge* party.

Just you and me invited.

Happy birthday again.

      Ruby

Hi Mum,

I'm in Andorra. Met this gorgeous guy who's my ski instructor who's trying to teach me how not to break my neck. He doesn't speak a word of English but we get along just fine. Everything is great here, you and I should go skiing some time, you'd love it! The winter festival is going really well, got a few small gigs to do. I'll be home for Christmas so we can catch up on all the gossip! Can't wait to see you!

      Love,

      Katie

Hi Mum,

Do you want to stay with me for Christmas? Katie is coming home and it can be the three of us. I think it would be really nice, you can have Katie's room and I'll set up a sofa bed for her. I'm so excited about the idea. Beanie has given me Christmas day off so please say yes!

      Rosie

Rosie,

I'd love to come over honey. Thanks for the invite. Can't wait to see little Katie. Not so little anymore I suppose!

      Love,

      Mum

FROM: Katie

TO: Mum

SUBJECT: Coming home

Thanks so much for Christmas dinner it was absolutely yummy as always. It was good for us 3 to be together again. Just the girls!

Grandma has changed a lot since the last time I saw her and you look tired. I was thinking of coming home for a few weeks and helping out. Maybe I could get a job around Dublin for a short while? I want to help out (plus there's the added bonus of meeting up with that guy I met while I was there!).

Let me no.

FROM: Rosie
TO: Katie
SUBJECT: Re: Coming home

Do *not* come home! That is an order! Everything is just fine here. You need to live your life too so you can continue on with your travels, work hard, and enjoy yourself! Don't worry about your grandma and me, we're absolutely fine!

I'm really enjoying the job and I don't mind the long hours. It's also nice to be able to go away every week to breathe the fresh air of Connemara. Although I do have one favor to ask, Ruby and I would love to go over to you for a week sometime in February if you could fit us into your schedule. Ruby said she wants to go to a foam party and win a wet T-shirt competition before she's fifty!

Let me know when a good week is for you.

FROM: Rosie
TO: Steph
SUBJECT: Mum

I've a favor to ask. Do you think you might be able to take Mum for another week in February? I'm sorry I know

you're really busy too but Beanie has finally given me a
week off and I really wanted to get over to Katie to check
out how she's living these days. I want to meet her friends
and see where she's working; you know, annoying things
that mothers do.

If you can't then I understand. Perhaps I could twist
Kevin's arm into caring about someone else for a change.

Give my love to the family.

FROM: Steph
TO: Rosie
SUBJECT: Re: Mum

Of course I'll take Mum. In fact I'll go one better and
take the family over to Connemara for the week. Pierre
dragged me to his mother and father's for Christmas dinner
so I think I'm entitled to have my turn!

You deserve a break Rosie. I'm so sorry you're stuck over
there doing everything. Sometimes I feel like going over
there and giving Kev a good kick. I'm going to have a good
talk with him when I go over and perhaps he may even want
to see his niece and nephew for a change.

Have fun with Katie. I can't believe how grown up she is
now. When she stayed with us a few months back I felt like
I was talking to you.

Enjoy the week with Ruby, I need to spend some quality
time with Mum anyway.

FROM: Alex
TO: Katie
SUBJECT: Surprise 40th

I don't no where you are in the world right now but I
hope you're still checking your e-mails! Seeing as your mum
is going to be 40 next month and you are going to be 21, I

thought it would be a good idea to have a double birthday party. But I was hoping that we could fly you home and surprise your mum with a party?

You can invite all your friends and we can organize all of Rosie's friends too. Perhaps we can bring Ruby in on this too for help? Let me no if you think it's a good idea. Noing Rosie the way I do, I think she would love it.

Rosie: I'm 40 in a few days Ruby. *40.* The big 4-0.

Ruby: So?

Rosie: So it's *old.*

Ruby: Then what does that make me, ancient?

Rosie: Oh sorry you know what I mean.

Ruby: No not really.

Rosie: Well we're not exactly 20 years old are we?

Ruby: No thank god for that because if that was the case I would have to go through a shit marriage and a divorce all over again. We would have to go out and look for jobs, be all uncertain about our lives, care about dating and how we look and what car we're driving, what music we're playing in it, what we wear, whether we'll get into certain clubs or not bla bla bla bla. What's so good about being 20? I call them the materialistic years. The years we get distracted by all the bullshit. Then we cop on when we hit our 30s and spend those years trying to make up for the 20s. But your 40s? Those years are for enjoying it.

Rosie: Hmmm good point. What are the 50s for?

Ruby: Fixing what you fucked up on in your 40s.

Rosie: Great. Looking forward to it.

Ruby: Oh don't worry Rosie. You don't need to make a song and dance about the fact the world has spun around the sun one more time. We should just take it as a given by now. So what do you want to do for your 40th?

Rosie: Nothing?

Ruby: Good plan. Why don't we go down to my local on
        Friday night for one too many?

Rosie: Sounds perfect.

Ruby: Oh hold on though. It's Teddy's brother's birthday
        that night too and we're all gathering in the Berke-
        ley Court Hotel.

Rosie: Oh very snazzy! I love that hotel!

Ruby: I know, I think he's on the fiddle again. Honestly
        you would think he'd know the gardai are watching
        him after he's just got out of prison. Some people
        never learn.

Rosie: Oh well, would you rather change it to Saturday
        night then?

Ruby: No! Will you collect me from the hotel and we can
        head to the pub together?

Rosie: Why don't I just wait for you at the pub?

Ruby: Because. If you come and meet me then they'll
        know that I actually do have plans and that I'm not
        lying and trying to get away from them. Besides if
        you're not there to drag me away they'll never let
        me leave.

Rosie: I don't want to get stuck talking to Teddy's brother
        though. The last time I met him he tried to put his
        hand up my skirt.

Ruby: He had only been out of prison a few days though
        Rosie, you can understand how he was feeling.

Rosie: Whatever. When I turn up, we're gone. Out of there.

Ruby: Absolutely, like a flash.

Rosie: So what time should I pick you up?

Ruby: 8p.m.

Rosie: 8p.m. are you joking?! What time does it start?

Ruby: 7:30p.m.

Rosie: Ruby! You'll have to stay a lot longer than that! I'm
        not arriving to take you away after only a half an

hour; everyone will think I'm so rude! I'll come at 9:30p.m. At least that way you'll have two hours.

Ruby: No! You *have* to come at 8p.m.!

Rosie: Why?

Ruby: Well, for one thing the party is in the *penthouse suite* of the Berkeley Court Hotel.

Rosie: Oh my god why didn't you just say so? I'll be there at 7:30p.m.

Ruby: No! You can't!

Rosie: What is wrong with you, why can't I?

Ruby: Because you're not invited and they'll think you've a cheek just turning up like that. If you come at 8p.m. you can quickly see the place and then leave.

Rosie: But I want to stay at the penthouse. Have you any idea how much that would mean to me?

Ruby: Yes I do . . . but I'm sorry you can't stay. Anyway once you meet the rest of Teddy's family you'll want to leave straight away.

Rosie: OK fine but I hope you know that you're breaking my heart and I don't care what you say, anything in the bathrooms that isn't stuck to the floor is going in my handbag. Actually I think I'll bring my camera!

Ruby: Rosie, it's a birthday party. I'm sure lots of people will have cameras.

Rosie: Yes I know but I'll take some photos for Katie too. She'd love to see what it looks like. I was hoping she would be able to come over but she can't. Bless her she works so hard. It's her 21st birthday a few weeks after me and I was hoping we could celebrate it together but unfortunately it's not to be. Mum is going over to stay with Stephanie again so she'll miss it as well. I was a bit upset about that but she's been so ill lately I didn't want to cause a fuss. I was just glad she said she wanted to go somewhere, even if it was on my birthday.

So it will just be you and me once again, but at least this year I'll get to sneak a peak at the penthouse suite! I'll steal a few ideas for my own hotel. What a treat!

Ruby: Looking forward to seeing the look on your face when that happens, Rosie. See you at 8p.m., room 440.

PENTHOUSE SUITE
440

SURPRISE ROSIE!
HAPPY BIRTHDAY ROSIE & KATIE!!

Happy 40th Rosie,

I had a wonderful weekend at your party, we really did surprise you, didn't we?! It broke my heart pretending to you that I was staying with Stephanie but it was worth it to see the look on your face (and the tears in your eyes). Alex arranged the entire thing. He's a lovely, lovely man Rosie. Shame about the wife though, I always thought you and he would get together when you were children. Silly isn't it?!

Anyway thank you, thank you, *thank you* for being a wonderful daughter and for all of your help over the past few years. Your father would be proud of you, I'll be sure to tell him all about you when I see him!

You are a beautiful young woman Rosie Dunne, your father and I did well!

                    Lots of love, Mum

—m—

HAPPY 70TH MUM!
YOU MADE IT TO THE BIG 7-0 AND YOU LOOK AS
BEAUTIFUL AS EVER! WE'LL HAVE YOU OUT OF
HOSPITAL AS QUICK AS WE CAN; IN THE MEANTIME
HERE ARE SOME GRAPES TO MAKE YOU FEEL *REALLY*
SICK!
LOVE YOU ALWAYS AND FOREVER MUM.
LOVE,
ROSIE

Hi Kev. Steph here. Can't get you on the phone. You might
want to come to Connemara now. It's time.

Hi love, get in touch with ur dad ASAP. He's booked u a
flight home 2morrow. I know it's short notice but Grandma
has been asking 4 u. Kev will collect u from airport t bring
u here. C u 2morrow.
Love mum.

Dunne (nee O'Sullivan)
(Connemara, Co. Galway and
formerly Dundrum, Dublin 10)
-Alice beloved wife of Dennis and
loving mother of Stephanie, Rosie,
and Kevin; will be missed by her
grandchildren Katie, Jean-Louis, and
Sophia, son-in-law Pierre, brother
Patrick, and sister-in-law Sandra.
Removal at 4:45p.m. today from
Stafford's Funeral Home to
Oughterard Church, Connemara.
May she rest in peace.
"Ar dheis lamh De go raibh a
anam uasal."

THIS IS THE LAST WILL dated the 10th day of September, 2000, of ALICE DUNNE

HEREBY REVOKING all former Wills and Testamentary Dispositions made by Alice Dunne.

If my husband survives me by thirty days I GIVE, DEVISE, AND BEQUEATH the whole of my estate to him and appoint him my executor. If my husband does not survive me by thirty days the following provisions shall apply:

1. I APPOINT Rosie Dunne (hereinafter called "my Trustee") to be executrix and trustee and appoint her trustee for the purposes of the Settled Land Acts, Conveyancing Acts and Section 57 of the Succession Act.

2. I GIVE, DEVISE, AND BEQUEATH to my Trustee the whole of my estate upon trust to sell the same (with power to postpone such sale in whole or in part for such time as they shall think fit) and to hold the same or the proceeds of sale thereof on the following trusts . . .

You have an instant message from: STEPH

Steph: How's my baby sister holding up?

Rosie: Oh hi Steph. I'm not sure. There's an eerie silence in
         my world these days. I find myself switching on the
         TV and the radio just to fill the background. Katie
         had to head back to work; people have stopped
         ringing and calling around to offer their sympathies.
         Everything is calming down now and I'm left with
         this silence.

         I'm not quite sure what to do with myself on my
         days off now. I'm so used to hopping on the bus and
         traveling over to Mum in the west. Life is strange
         now. Before even when she lay in bed looking frail
         and weak she still managed to make me feel safe.
         Mothers do that don't they? Their very presence can
         help. And even if I ended up mothering her in the fi-
         nal days, she still was taking care of me. I miss her.

Steph: I do too and at the oddest times too. It's only when
         you get back to the normal routine of life that you
         really feel it. I keep on having to remind myself that
         when the phone rings it's not her. Or when I get a
         free moment in the day I pick up the phone to call
         her and then I remember that she's not there to call.
         It's such an odd feeling.

Rosie: Yeah it is. Kevin is still in a huff with me.

Steph: Ignore Kevin; he's in a huff with the entire world.

Rosie: Maybe he's right though Steph. Mum has put me in
         such an awkward position by leaving me the house.
         Perhaps I should sell it and split the profits three
         ways. It's fairer.

Steph: Rosie Dunne you will not sell that house for me and
         Kev. She left it for you for a reason. Kev and I are
         both financially secure, we both have houses, we re-
         ally don't need the Connemara house. It would be

different if we were both broke but Mum knows
that me and Kev are OK so that's why it was left to
you. You work harder than the two of us put together and you still can't get out of that flat. Mum
discussed it with me before and I agreed with her.
This is the best way. Don't listen to Kev.

Rosie: I don't know Steph; I'm not hugely comfortable
with it . . .

Steph: Rosie trust me, if I needed the money so badly I
would tell you and we could work something out.
But I don't. Neither does Kevin. It's not like we
were forgotten about in the will. We're both fine,
honestly. The house in Connemara belongs to you.
You do with it whatever you wish.

Rosie: Thanks Steph.

Steph: No problem. So what are you going to do over there
on your own Rosie? I hate you being all alone. Do
you want to come over here for a while?

Rosie: No thanks Steph I really have to work. I'm going to
throw myself into this job and make it the best
damn hotel in the world.

The Grand Tower Hotel
Tower Road,
Dublin 1

Dear Mr. Cronin Ui
Cheallaigh,

Following our visit to The Grand Tower Hotel we at the
Department of Public Works are sending you an emergency
order due to an imminent and substantial hazard to the life,
health, and safety of occupants.

After their visit last week, the Department of Building
Inspection listed more than 100 code violations, including
missing smoke detectors, water damage, and inadequate
lighting.

The bathrooms are noted as being unsanitary and during our visit rodents were spotted in the kitchens.

According to our records you have received many warnings over the years to improve the maintenance of the building and you were advised to make the necessary improvements in order to keep the building acting as a hotel. These warnings were ignored and we have no choice but to shut you down.

The business on the ground level may remain open.

Please be in touch with our offices as soon as you receive this letter. Details of the Health and Safety Act are overleaf.

> Yours sincerely,
> Adam Delaney
> Office of Public Works

FROM: Katie
TO: Mum
SUBJECT: Your job

I'm so sorry to hear about you losing your job, I no you hated it but still it's never nice to have to leave when it's not your own decision. I couldn't reach you on the phone, you've either been on the phone all day or they've cut you off. Either way I thought I'd e-mail you instead. I completely forgot to tell you that when we returned to Dublin after the funeral that what's-his-name called around to the flat to see you.

I didn't want to call you because you were upset enough as it was so I took a message. He dropped in some post that had been delivered to his house for you and said that he hoped that they would be some sort of help to you now that your mum and dad are gone. He said he understood how you felt as his mum died last year and he didn't want to be the cause of your loneliness.

He seemed sincere but who can ever tell with him. It was

odd seeing him after so many years. He's really aged.
Anyway I hope whatever is in the envelopes isn't too
important but let me no what they are all the same. I left the
two envelopes in the bottom drawer of the living room
cabinet.

∽

Dr. Reginald & Miranda Williams
invite ROSIE DUNNE *to join them in celebrating the*
marriage of their beloved daughter
Bethany Williams
To
Dr. Alex Stewart
At
The Memorial Church of Harvard University
& a reception at
The Boston Harbor Hotel
On the 28th of December
RSVP Miranda Williams

∽

Rosie,

I'm returning to Boston tomorrow but before I go I
wanted to write this letter to you. All the thoughts and
feelings that have been bubbling up inside me are finally
overflowing into this pen and I'm leaving this letter for you
so that you don't feel that I'm putting you under any great
pressure. I understand that you will need to take your time
trying to decide on what I am about to say.

I no what's going on, Rosie; you're my best friend and I
can see the sadness in your eyes. I no that Greg isn't away
working for the weekend. You never could lie to me; you
were always terrible at it. Don't pretend that everything is

perfect because I *see* what's going on. I see that Greg is a selfish man who has absolutely no idea just how lucky he is and it makes me sick.

He is the luckiest man in the world to have you, Rosie, but he doesn't deserve you and *you* deserve far better. You deserve someone who loves you with every single beat of his heart, someone who thinks about you constantly, someone who spends every minute of every day just wondering what you're doing, where you are, who you're with, and if you're OK. You need someone who can help you reach your dreams and who can protect you from your fears. You need someone who will treat you with respect, love every part of you, *especially* your flaws. You should be with someone who can make you happy, really happy, *dancing on air happy*. Someone who should have taken the chance to be with you years ago instead of becoming scared and being too afraid to try.

I'm not scared anymore Rosie. I am not afraid to try.

I no what that feeling was at your wedding—it was jealousy. My heart broke when I saw the woman I love turning away from me to walk down the aisle with another man, another man she planned to spend the rest of her life with. It was like a prison sentence for me. Years ahead without me being able to tell you how I feel or hold you how I wanted to.

Twice we stood beside each other at the altar, Rosie. *Twice*. And twice we got it wrong. I needed you to be there for my wedding day but I was too stupid to see that I needed you to be the *reason* for my wedding day. But we got it all wrong.

I should never have let your lips leave mine all those years ago in Boston. I should never have pulled away. I should never have panicked. I should never have wasted all those years without you. Give me a chance to make them up to you. I love you, Rosie, and I want to be with you and Katie and Josh. Always.

Please think about it. Don't waste your time on Greg, this is *our* opportunity. Let's stop being afraid and take the chance. I promise I'll make you happy.

All my love,
Alex

—◆◆◆—

CHAPTER 49

FROM: Ruby
TO: Rosie
SUBJECT: Are you OK?

I haven't heard from you in almost two weeks. Is everything OK? I called around to see you at the flat but Rupert told me you had gone to Galway. You just packed up and left without saying good-bye, something must be up. How long are you planning on staying there and why didn't you tell anyone?

Your mother's phone has obviously been disconnected so I didn't know how else to reach you. I understand that you probably just need some time to yourself, losing parents is really difficult. As much as I complain about how mine were, it was still tough dealing with their loss. I know I joke around a lot but I'm seriously here for you Rosie if you need someone to talk to, a shoulder to cry on, or even someone to scream at.

I would say I'm sorry that you lost your job at the hotel but I'm not sorry at all. You were better than that hotel; you had bigger dreams that extended far beyond those crumbling walls. Now the world is your oyster.

Please just respond to let me know you're OK or I'm coming down there myself to check up on you and that's not a threat, it's a promise.

**Welcome to the Relieved Divorced Dubliners Chat room
There are currently 2 people chatting**

LonelyLady: The guy from my reading group asked me out yesterday. To go out on a date, like. This weekend. Just me and him. But I just don't know . . .

Wildflower: You don't know what?

LonelyLady: Well I don't know if I should start dating again. I mean I don't know if I'm ready, being so soon after Tommy and all . . .

Wildflower: So soon? *So soon?* In case you haven't noticed it's been 10 *years* since Tommy left you.

LonelyLady: Oh. It doesn't *feel* like 10 years.

Wildflower: Well if you ever stopped whinging and moaning about how lonely you were, you would be able to think rationally about your life. Which guy in your reading group are you dating?

LonelyLady: The *only* guy in the reading group.

Wildflower: I bet the ladies will drop out like flies now. But the all important question for you is, does he have a criminal record?

LonelyLady: No I checked.

Wildflower: God, I was only joking! But at least you know your TV won't go walkabout when you go to the toilet.

LonelyLady: A luxury which most women don't appreciate.

SureOne has entered the room

Wildflower:	Well he sounds perfect for you then. I see no reason why you shouldn't go out with him. Good luck with the date.
SureOne:	LonelyLady are you going out on a *date*?
LonelyLady:	You say it like it's a disease.
Wildflower:	Well it could turn into one I suppose.
SureOne:	No I'm just shocked! But in a good way! Congratulations!
LonelyLady:	Thank you! Hey, you changed your name!
SureOne:	I know, I was granted my annulment. See I told you the church had sense. They agree that Leonard is a complete prick.
Wildflower:	SureOne! Well it's a change to hear that come from you! I'm not quite sure the church thinks exactly *that* but it's a start . . .

Buttercup has entered the room

LonelyLady:	Well congratulations anyway SureOne.
Buttercup:	Why, what are you celebrating SureOne? (Nice name change by the way.)
Wildflower:	She got her annulment.
Buttercup:	Oh congrats!
SureOne:	Thanks girls!
Buttercup:	So I take it I haven't missed anything?
SureOne:	No. We haven't heard from you in a while Buttercup, where have you been lately?
Buttercup:	I've been staying in the house in Connemara for the past few weeks. I've had a lot of thinking to do.
Wildflower:	Is everything OK?
Buttercup:	No not really.
SureOne:	Do you want to tell us about it? Maybe we can help.

Buttercup: Well my mother died, I lost my job, and I'm
              afraid to say the words of the "something
              else" in case it validates it and causes me to
              have a nervous breakdown. Because if it be-
              comes true, then it would officially declare
              the past 10 years of my life to be utterly use-
              less and a waste of time.

LonelyLady: Well we're all experts on that subject. You
              know by now that what goes on in this room,
              stays in this room, maybe we can shed some
              light on it for you.

Buttercup: Thanks. OK then, here goes . . . I came
              across a letter that was written just after my
              30th birthday. A letter that was meant for me
              but that never made it into my hands. It was
              from Alex.

LonelyLady: Oooh, what did he say in the letter?

Buttercup: Here's the tough part. He said he loved me.

Wildflower: Whooooah!

SureOne: Oh. My. God.

LonelyLady: No! So where did you find the letter?

Buttercup: What's-his-name returned it to me. He
              "didn't want to be the cause of my loneliness
              anymore," he said.

LonelyLady: He had kept it all these years?

Buttercup: Why he would keep it all these years I have
              no idea. I haven't quite figured that out yet.
              Although I never truly figured him out at all
              while I was married to him. I can't really
              think anything now, I'm in so much shock.

Wildflower: So have you spoken to Alex?

Buttercup: How can I speak to him, Wildflower? Know-
              ing what I know, how can I even *think* of him?

Wildflower: Very easily I would imagine. He's just told
              you that he loves you!

Buttercup: No LonelyLady, he told me over 10 years ago
                that he loved me. *Before* he got married, *be-*
                fore he had Theo. I just couldn't bring myself
                to talk to him. He's been writing and phoning
                but the thought of that missed opportunity
                makes me so sick to the stomach that I can't
                respond to his messages.

LonelyLady: But you have to tell him, you know!

Buttercup: I was going to. I was half fearful, half excited.
                I was going to ring him on the phone and say
                it to him casually at first to test the waters
                and see how he felt and then go a bit further.
                But that morning his annual Christmas card
                arrived in the post box. With the photo of his
                wife and two sons on the cover of the card,
                all wearing colorful knitted Christmas
                jumpers, Theo with his two front teeth gone,
                Josh with his beaming smile just like his dad.
                Bethany hand in hand with Alex. And I
                couldn't tell him. What would he care now
                anyway?

                He's married. He's happy. He's over me and
                even if he's not, I wouldn't expect him to jump
                out of that perfect Christmas photo for me.

SureOne: Take it from me Buttercup, you're right to
                leave the family alone.

Wildflower: But she *loves* him! And he loves her! And
                everyone airbrushes their photos these days!

SureOne: What age are you now Buttercup, 42?

Buttercup: Yes.

SureOne: Right. He wrote that letter 12 years ago, be-
                fore he got married. It's not right to bring it
                up now. She could break too many little
                hearts by telling him.

LonelyLady: SureOne would know, seeing as it happened
              to her.

Wildflower: Oh don't listen to those two Buttercup, you
              hop on a plane and go to Alex and tell the
              man that you love him.

Buttercup: But what if he doesn't feel that way about
              me anymore? I've never ever picked up
              on any vibes from him over the past 10
              years.

SureOne: Because he's *married*. He's a good man But-
              tercup. He follows the rules.

Wildflower: Oh rules were made to be broken!

SureOne: Not when people get hurt Wildflower.

Buttercup: She's right Wildflower.

Wildflower: Oh don't let people walk all over you Butter-
              cup. It's your life. If you want something,
              you need to get out there and grab it by the
              horns because no one is going to give you
              what you want on a plate. Good girls always
              come second.

SureOne: Good girls have a conscience and that way
              they can live with themselves. And anyway
              we haven't even thought about the fact that
              Alex's feelings may have diminished for But-
              tercup over time.

Wildflower: Oh why don't we just slit her wrists *for* her
              SureOne?

Buttercup: She's right Wildflower. I need to cover all an-
              gles before I jump into this headfirst. God I
              feel sick. OK so what happens when I tell
              Alex that I received his letter and his feelings
              have changed? What do I do then? Things be-
              tween us could or would never get back to
              normal ever again and I would lose my very
              best friend and I don't think I could cope
              with that.

Wildflower: Yes but then what if when you tell him how you feel, he grabs you passionately, relieved you finally know his true feelings, and the two of you live happily ever after.

SureOne: Yeah sure, in between one messy divorce, child custody court fights, a heartbroken ex-wife . . .

Wildflower: And a partridge in a pear tree.

SureOne: If you can live with yourself by doing that, then by all means go ahead, but I for one couldn't.

Wildflower: But she can't pretend nothing happened.

SureOne: Your friendship will remain strong with Alex and the happiness in his life will also remain intact, just as it did when Alex heard no reply from you all those years ago. He kept on as normal, as though nothing had ever happened.

Buttercup: Why did he keep on as normal? I remember him asking about a letter and I told him I didn't get it. Why didn't he just tell me then?

Wildflower: He could have chickened out.

SureOne: Or he saw that you were in love with your husband.

Buttercup: This is all very confusing. LonelyLady, you've been very quiet. What do you think?

LonelyLady: Well I of all people know what it's like to feel all alone and there were times that I thought I would do just about anything to find love, *but* SureOne has put it into perspective. Knowing the hurt she has gone through, I wouldn't look for my own happiness at the expense of others. I would carry on as normal, as though nothing had happened.

Wildflower: You 3 are unbelievable. Learn to live a little. Do unto others as others have done to you. You have all been screwed with by people.

Buttercup:	Yes we have and as much as I don't like Bethany she has never done anything to hurt me.
Wildflower:	Apart from marrying Alex.
Buttercup:	I don't *own* Alex.
Wildflower:	But you could.
Buttercup:	People can never *own* people but whether I can be with him or not right now, the answer is no. Not now. Maybe in another time.

FatherMichael has entered the room

Wildflower:	Ah don't tell me you're through a divorce yourself Father?
SureOne:	Don't be silly Wildflower, have a bit of respect! He's here for the ceremony.
Wildflower:	I know that. I was just trying to lighten the atmosphere.
FatherMichael:	So have the loving couple arrived yet?
SureOne:	No but it's customary for the bride to be late.
FatherMichael:	Well is the groom here?

SingleSam has entered the room

Wildflower:	Here he is now. Hello there SingleSam. I think this is the first time ever that both the bride and groom will have to change their names.
SingleSam:	Hello all.
Buttercup:	Where's the bride?
LonelyLady:	Probably fixing her makeup.
Wildflower:	Oh don't be silly. No one can even see her.

LonelyLady:	SingleSam can see her.
SureOne:	She's not doing her makeup; she's *supposed* to keep the groom waiting.
SingleSam:	No she's right here on the laptop beside me. She's just having problems with her password logging in.
SureOne:	Doomed from the start.

Divorced_1 has entered the room

Wildflower:	Wahoo! Here comes the bride, all dressed in . . .
SingleSam:	Black.
Wildflower:	How charming.
Buttercup:	She's right to wear black.
Divorced_1:	What's wrong with misery guts today?
LonelyLady:	She found a letter from Alex that was written 12 years ago proclaiming his love for her and she doesn't know what to do.
Divorced_1:	Here's a word of advice. *Get over it*, he's married. Now let's focus the attention on me for a change.

SoOverHim has entered the room

FatherMichael:	OK let's begin. We are gathered here online today to witness the marriage of SingleSam (soon to be "Sam") and Divorced_1 (soon to be "Married_1").
SoOverHim:	WHAT?? WHAT THE HELL IS GOING ON HERE? THIS IS A *MARRIAGE CEREMONY* IN A *DIVORCED PEOPLE CHAT ROOM*??

Wildflower:	Uh-oh, looks like we got ourselves a gate crasher here. Excuse me can we see your wedding invite please?
Divorced_1:	Ha ha.
SoOverHim:	YOU THINK THIS IS *FUNNY?* YOU PEOPLE MAKE ME SICK, COMING IN HERE AND TRYING TO UPSET OTHERS WHO ARE GENUINELY TROUBLED.
Buttercup:	Oh we are genuinely troubled alright. And could you please STOP SHOUTING.
LonelyLady:	You see SoOverHim, this is where Single-Sam and Divorced_1 met for the first time.
SoOverHim:	OH I HAVE SEEN IT ALL NOW!
Buttercup:	Sshh!
SoOverHim:	Sorry. Mind if I stick around?
Divorced_1:	Sure grab a pew; just don't trip over my train.
Wildflower:	Ha ha.
FatherMichael:	OK we should get on with this; I don't want to be late for my 2 o'clock. First I have to ask, is there anyone in here who thinks there is any reason why these two should not be married?
LonelyLady:	Yes.
SureOne:	I could give more than one reason.
Buttercup:	*Hell* yes.
SoOverHim:	DON'T DO IT!
FatherMichael:	Well I'm afraid this has put me in a very tricky predicament.
Divorced_1:	Father we are in a divorced chat room, of course they all object to marriage. Can we get on with it?
FatherMichael:	Certainly. Do you Sam take Penelope to be your lawful wedded wife?
SingleSam:	I do.

FatherMichael: Do you Penelope take Sam to be your law-
                 ful wedded husband?
Divorced_1:   I do (yeah, yeah my name is Penelope).
FatherMichael: You have already e-mailed your vows to
                 me so by the online power vested in me, I
                 now pronounce you husband and wife. You
                 may kiss the bride. Now if the witnesses
                 could click on the icon to the right of the
                 screen they will find a form to type their
                 names, addresses, and phone numbers.
                 Once that's filled in just e-mail it off to me.
                 I'll be off now. Congratulations again.

FatherMichael has left the room

Wildflower: Congrats Sam and Penelope!
Divorced_1:   Thanks girls for being here.
SoOverHim: Freaks.

SoOverHim has left the room

Wildflower: Funny, we've been chatting about our most
                 intimate life details for years now and we
                 never even knew each other's real names. I'm
                 just looking down the witness form right
                 now, LonelyLady I see your name is Lynne,
                 SureOne, I see yours is Sinead . . . the name
                 Rosie Dunne . . . it suits you Buttercup.
Buttercup: Why thank you Wildflower.
Wildflower: Right, you love birds I'm off. Enjoy your hon-
                 eymoon and I expect to never see you in here
                 again. LonelyLady good luck with that date.
                 SureOne enjoy the start of the rest of your life,
                 and Rosie Dunne, what *are* you going to do?

Ruby: *What do you mean* you're moving to Co. Galway?
Rosie: I mean exactly that. I'm leaving that horrible flat in
        Dublin once and for all and I'm moving to Con-
        nemara for good.
Ruby: But *why?*
Rosie: Ruby there's nothing there for me in Dublin. Apart
        from you of course. I have had a string of unsatis-
        factory jobs, have no family there, had my heart
        broken twice there, have no money, and no man. I
        don't see a reason why I should stay.
Ruby: Well forgive me for being the bearer of bad news
        but you have no job in Galway, no family, and no
        man. Unless you're going to take to herding sheep.
Rosie: Oh yes the common city person's misconception of
        the country. There are shops and restaurants here
        too you know. Anyway I may not have all those
        things but I have a *house.*
Ruby: Have you gone nuts Rosie?
Rosie: Probably! But think about it. I have a great big
        modern-built 4-bedroom house right on the coast in
        Connemara.
Ruby: Exactly! What are you going to do all on your own
        with no job, in a 4-bedroom house, hanging off the
        cliff in Connemara?
Rosie: You could be close to guessing!
Ruby: Well I was thinking very much of you committing
        suicide so I hope I'm not.
Rosie: No silly! I'm opening up a Bed and Breakfast! And I
        know I've always said I hate B&Bs but I'm planning
        on turning the house more into my own mini hotel.
        And I am going to be manager/owner extraordinaire!
Ruby: Wow.
Rosie: What do you think?
Ruby: I think that . . . wow. I can't think of anything sar-
        castic to say actually. I think that's a great idea. Are
        you sure you want to do this?

Rosie: Ruby I've never been surer in my life! I've done my re-
         search, with my inheritance from Mum and Dad I can
         afford the insurance. I've asked all the B&Bs around
         and the place is *crawling* with tourists. It's a bit tough
         in November and December but they generally make
         enough in the rest of the months to get through that.

         The area is beautiful, the coastline is dramatic and
         rugged, the boglands have a foggy mysteriousness
         to them, the sea just crashes and whips against the
         cliffs letting everyone who lives here know who's
         boss. It's just nature and all the elements at their
         best, who wouldn't want to come here? Who
         wouldn't want to live here?

Ruby: Well *I* wouldn't but I appreciate what you're saying.
         I think it's a great idea Rosie. Congratulations you
         little genius. I hope that whatever it was that sent you
         packing isn't going to chase you away any farther.

*Rosie Dunne will be your hostess in Buttercup House.
The building is a modern four-bedroom home approved by
Bord Failte, the Irish Tourist Board. All of the rooms are en-
suite with private baths and toilets. Double, twin, and family rooms are all available. The rooms are centrally heated
and there is a telephone in each room.*

*Buttercup House is the ideal location to explore Con-
nemara, enjoy hill-walking, mile-long sandy beaches, an-
gling, fishing in Lough Corrib, Ireland's largest natural
inland water mass, a favorite with fishermen for salmon and
brown trout. Scuba-diving, sailing, and surfing are accessible
along the coastline.*

*Connemara National Park is a 2,000-hectare state-owned
conservation center with mountains, bogs, grasslands, and
spectacular wildlife. Traces of ancient settlements can be
seen, including 4,000-year-old megalithic tombs. There are
golf courses aplenty, with rocky hills and ocean inlets pro-*

*viding the ultimate challenge for the keen golfer. Walking,
horse riding, and cycling are wonderful ways to explore the
terrain, and mountaineering is also popular with rock-
climbing enthusiasts.*

*The television lounge is comfortably furnished with log
fire, board games, and plenty of books for our guests to relax
with after their active days. Breakfast is served in the dining
room and the conservatory offers panoramic views of the
mountains and Atlantic Ocean.*

Rates are €35 per person per night.

Contact Rosie Dunne to make your reservation now!

FROM: Katie
TO: Mum
SUBJECT: Wow!

Wow, Mum that looks fantastic! The photographs look so
beautiful, you've really done so much to the place. You are
finally Rosie Dunne, General Manager and Owner of
Buttercup House! I'll come over next week and help with all
that's left to do and we can go shopping for more things to
fill this big house! Grandma and Granddad would be so
proud of you using the house like this. They always said it
was such a waste of space only having the two of them there.

Well done! See you next week.

Dear Rosie,

I just wanted to no if everything between us is OK?
You've been sounding a little, well, odd on the phone lately.
Have I done something to upset you in any way? I can't
think of anything that I may have said to piss you off but do
let me no. It seems I have to do nothing these days in order
to succeed in upsetting the women in my life. Bethany starts
a fight with me if I even look at her these days. If I have
unintentionally done the same to you Rosie, please let me no.

Bethany is going crazy about organizing Theo's tenth birthday party next week. She has invited more of her own friends than Theo's and Josh keeps stealing my car and driving it around all night with his new girlfriend. She's a sweet girl but I don't no what she sees in my son, that's for sure. He's a madman. I can't seem to get him to settle down and study (I sounded like my own dad just then). He's supposed to be starting college next September but considering the fact he hasn't applied for anywhere and can't figure out what he wants to do other than drive my car, I'm presuming that he'll be taking a year out before he heads off to educate himself further.

Luckily Theo thinks Josh is nuts. He's actually afraid of him. So we're hoping that Theo can be the son that we can talk about and admit to having. That of course is a joke.

Things at the hospital are going well. I'm still doing the same old thing but my life has been made massively easier due to the retirement of Reginald Williams. I can breathe now without having to explain it. Working with your father-in-law is as advisable as living with his daughter. Joking once again, *of course*. Well, kind of, but we won't go into that.

I have to go now but I wanted to make sure things were OK between us. The brochure for the B&B looks fantastic! I wish you well with it Rosie, you deserve the best!

> Love,
> Alex

FROM: Rosie
TO: Alex
SUBJECT: Sorry

I apologize for sounding off with you on the phone. I was a little distracted by a few things that popped up from the past in my life that I was previously unaware of. They were holding me back for a little while but they've let go of me now and I'm back on course.

I'm ready to move on and spend the next 10 years of my life tending to my quest for greatness and happiness. You are more than welcome to stay with me *whenever* you are ready to.

FROM: Alex
TO: Rosie
SUBJECT: Thank you

Thank you very much for that generous offer Rosie. I'll be sure to take you up on that whenever my wife isn't looking.

FROM: Rosie
TO: Alex
SUBJECT: Flirt

Now, now, are you flirting with me Alex Stewart?

FROM: Alex
TO: Rosie
SUBJECT: Re: Flirt

Why, Rosie Dunne, I do believe I am. Get in touch with me in 10 years time when your quest for greatness has reached its pinnacle.

PART 5

CHAPTER 50

—◆—

You have an instant message from: KATIE

Katie: Happy birthday, Mum! How does it feel to be 50?!

Rosie: Hot.

Katie: Are you having another flush?

Rosie: Yes. How does it feel to be almost 31? Any sign of my only daughter settling down, getting a decent job, and giving me grandchildren?

Katie: Hmm . . . I'm not sure, although there was a little baby boy playing on the beach making sand castles this morning and for the first time ever I thought it was cute. It's possible that I'm coming around to the rest of the world's way of thinking.

Rosie: Well that sounds hopeful. I thought dreams of you getting a respectable job would have to die, but you've given me hope. Perhaps I can start telling people I actually have a daughter now.

Katie: Funny. How's the B&B going?

Rosie: Busy, thank god. I was just in the middle of updating the website when you messaged me. Buttercup House now has *seven* en-suite bedrooms.

Katie: I no, the place looks terrific.

Rosie: It's KNOW not NO.

Katie: Sorry us DJs don't need to be able to spell. OH MY
        GOD I almost forgot to tell you! I can't believe this
        isn't the first thing I said to you! You'll *never* guess
        who I met in the club last night!

Rosie: Well if I'll never guess I don't think I want to play
        this game.

Katie: Toby Quinn!!

Rosie: Never heard of him. Is he an old boyfriend?

Katie: *Mum!* Toby Quinn! *Toby!*

Rosie: I don't see how repeating his name is going to help.

Katie: My best friend from school! *Toby!*

Rosie: Oh my lord! Toby! How is the little pet?

Katie: He's fine! He's working as a dentist in Dublin just
        like he wanted and he's over here in Ibiza for a holi-
        day for two weeks. It was so weird seeing him after
        10 years but he hasn't changed a bit!

Rosie: Oh that's fabulous. Tell him I was asking for him,
        will you?

Katie: I will. He had lots of lovely things to say about you.
        Actually I'll be seeing him again tonight, we're go-
        ing out for dinner.

Rosie: Is it a date?

Katie: No! I couldn't date Toby. It's Toby! We're just go-
        ing to catch up.

Rosie: Whatever you say Katie dear.

Katie: Honestly Mum! I couldn't date Toby, he used to be
        my best friend, it would be too odd.

Rosie: I don't see anything wrong with dating your best
        friend.

Katie: Mum it would be like *you* dating *Alex!*

Rosie: Well I would think that would be perfectly normal
        too.

Katie: Mum!

Rosie: What? I don't see the big deal. Anyway have you
        been speaking to Alex lately?

Katie: Yeah just yesterday. He's on the couch again so to
          speak. Bethany is tormenting him again. Honestly I
          think they're both stupid to wait until Theo heads
          off to college.

Rosie: Well they were both stupid for getting married in
          the first place. You know what Theo is like though
          Katie, he's such a softie. His parents breaking up
          would break his little heart. But he's going to have
          to deal with it from Paris at Art College so I'm not
          quite sure why they feel that will be better for him.

Katie: Well the sooner the better, they're a match made in
          hell, I've said it all along. Josh says he can't wait for
          Alex and her to split up. He can't stand her.

Rosie: Well they lasted longer than anyone thought they
          would. Tell Josh I said hi.

Katie: Will do. I better go and tell Alex about Toby, he'll
          never believe it! Don't work too hard on your birth-
          day, Mum!

You have an instant message from: KATIE

Katie: Hi Alex.

Alex: Hello my wonderful god daughter, how are you and
          what do you want?

Katie: I'm fine and I don't want anything!

Alex: You women always want something.

Katie: That's not true and you no it!

Alex: How's my son? I hope he's working hard over there.

Katie: Still alive at least.

Alex: Good. Tell him to phone me a bit more often, as
          good as it is hearing from you and all, it would be
          nice to hear about his life from him.

Katie: I understand; I'll pass it on. Anyway the reason why
          I'm messaging you is because you'll never guess who
          I met in the club last night!

Alex: If I'll never guess then I don't want to play this game.

Katie: That's exactly what Mum said! Anyway I met Toby Quinn!!!

Alex: Is he an ex-boyfriend or someone famous? Give me a clue.

Katie: Alex! Honestly you and Mum are getting forgetful in your old age. Toby is my best friend from school!

Alex: Oh that Toby! Wow there's a blast from the past, how is he?

Katie: He's fine. He's working as a dentist in Dublin and he's just over in Ibiza for a few weeks holiday. He was asking about you.

Alex: Great well if you see him again give him my regards. He was a good guy.

Katie: Yeah I will. I'll actually be seeing him again tonight; we're going out for dinner.

Alex: Is it a date?

Katie: Honestly what is it with you and Mum? He used to be my best friend. I couldn't go out with him.

Alex: Oh don't be stupid, there's nothing wrong with dating a best friend.

Katie: That's what Mum said too!

Alex: She did?

Katie: Yeah so I tried to put it into perspective for her by explaining that would be like *her* dating *you*.

Alex: And what did she say to that?

Katie: I don't think she was particularly put off by the idea. So you see Alex, whenever you get your lazy behind out of that house of yours, you no that there's one woman at least who'll have you. Ha ha.

Alex: I see . . .

Katie: Jesus Alex, lighten up. OK I gotta go and get ready for dinner.

You have an instant message from: ROSIE

Rosie: Hello old woman, what are you up to?

Ruby: Sitting in my rocking chair knitting. What else? No, Gary, Maria, and the kids just left and I'm knackered. I can't run after them like I used to.

Rosie: Do you really want to anyway?

Ruby: No and stiff muscles are a great excuse for not having to play hide-and-seek 24/7. What are you up to?

Rosie: I'm just taking a break from clearing away all the dust from the builders. Honestly have they ever heard of the words vacuum cleaner?

Ruby: No and neither have I. Is it a new invention? How is the new wing looking?

Rosie: Oh it's great Ruby, I'll have so much more privacy now. I can stick to my side of the house and the guests can have theirs. I've decorated a room just the way you like it so it can be yours when you stay. Let me know when you can come over. I'm heading off out with Sean tonight.

Ruby: Again? Well this is really becoming a regular occurrence indeed.

Rosie: He's a lovely man and I really enjoy his company. Even though the house is always full of strangers, I can still feel alone so it's nice to be able to meet up with him once in a while.

Ruby: I know what you mean. He seems a real gentleman alright.

Rosie: He is.

Ruby: I read in the newspaper that Alex's marriage had ended. It was in some silly gossip page.

Rosie: Ruby his marriage barely even started never mind ended. Unfortunately for him.

Ruby: How do you feel about it?

Rosie: Sad for him. Happy for him.

Ruby: Now you can tell me the truth. How do you *really* feel?

FROM: Katie
TO: Mum
SUBJECT: Oh Mum

Oh Mum.

Oh my god Mum.

The most bizarre thing has happened.

I've never felt so . . . *odd* in my whole entire life.

Forgive me for speaking like a 12-year-old but that's exactly how I feel right now. Last night was the weirdest night of my life. I met up with Toby and we went to dinner at Raul's restaurant in the old part of town. In order to get there we had to walk up a really steep cobbled stone hill, passing by women dressed in black from head to toe who were just sitting on wooden chairs outside their houses, enjoying the warmth and silence.

The place only had a few tables and as we were the only tourists there I almost felt bad for intruding but they were so friendly and there was such a good atmosphere. It's not a part of the island that my job allows me to see very often unfortunately.

The manager of Toby's hotel suggested the restaurant and it was such a good choice because it sat high on a mountaintop overlooking the island on one side and the sea on the other. The air was warm, the stars were twinkling, a man played on the violin in the corner. It was like something out of a movie only it was so much better because it felt real and it was happening to me.

We chatted and chatted and chatted for hours until well after we had finished eating and eventually we were asked to leave at 2a.m. I don't think I've ever laughed so much in my life. We continued talking as we strolled along the beach and the air felt so magical! We talked about old times and caught up on new times.

Mum I don't no if it was the wine, or the heat, the food, or just my hormones but there were some forces in motion last night. Toby touched my arm and I felt all . . . *zingy* from head to toe. I'm almost 31 years old and I've never felt that before. And then there was this silence. This really weird silence. We stared at each other as though we were seeing each other for the very first time. It was like the world stopped turning just for us. An odd magical silence. The very same one that you told me you had with someone all those years ago.

Then he *kissed* me. *Toby* kissed me. And it was the best kiss I have ever had in all my 30 years. And as our lips pulled apart my eyelids opened slowly to see him staring at me, looking as though he was going to say something. And in true Toby form he said, "I bet there was pepperoni in your dinner."

How embarrassing.

Immediately my hands flew to my teeth remembering how he used to always comment on the food stuck in my braces all the time and tease me about it. But he grabbed my hands and pulled them gently away from my mouth and said, "No, this time I could taste it."

Is that heart-wrenching stuff or what? My legs nearly buckled from underneath me. It felt so odd that it was Toby that I was kissing but in another way it felt completely natural and I think that's what the odd thing was about it if you no what I mean.

We spent all day together again today and my stomach is doing somersaults at the thought of seeing him again to-night. I now no what all my friends were talking about when they tried to describe this feeling. It's so good it's indescribable. Dad kept teasing me for walking around with a silly grin on my face all day.

Toby asked me to move back to Dublin, Mum! Not to live with him of course but just so that we could be closer. And do you no what? I think I'm going to. Why the hell not? I'll throw caution to the wind and leap into the darkness and all those clichés and we'll see where I land.

Because if I don't follow this feeling right now who nos
where I will be twenty years on from now.

How crazy does all this seem? What a 24 hours it's been!

FROM: Rosie
TO: Katie
SUBJECT: Yes!

Oh it's not crazy at all Katie! It's really not crazy at all!
Enjoy it, love. Enjoy every second of it.

FROM: Katie
TO: Alex
SUBJECT: In love!

So Mum was right Alex! You *can* fall in love with your
best friend! Who new?! I've packed everything up and I'm
heading home to Dublin with my heart filled with love and
hope and my head filled with dreams! Mum told me about
the silence she experienced years ago. She kept telling me
when I felt that silence with someone, it meant they were
"the one." I was beginning to think she made it up but she
didn't! This magical silence exists!

You have an instant message from: ALEX

Alex: Phil she felt the silence too.
Phil: Who, what, where, when?
Alex: Rosie. She felt that silence too all those years ago.
Phil: Oh the dreaded silence thing is back to haunt us, is
          it? I haven't heard you talk about that for years.
Alex: I knew I wasn't imagining it Phil!
Phil: Well then, what are you doing talking to me? Get

off the Internet you fool and pick up the phone. Or the pen.

Alex has logged off

My dear Rosie,

Unbeknownst to you I took this chance before many, many years ago. You never received that letter and I'm glad because my feelings since then have changed dramatically. They have intensified with every passing day.

I'll get straight to the point because if I don't say what I have to say now, I fear it will never be said. And I *need* to say it.

Today I love you more than ever; tomorrow I will love you even more. I *need* you more than ever; I *want* you more than ever. I'm a man of fifty years of age coming to you, feeling like a teenager in love, asking you to give me a chance and love me back.

Rosie Dunne I love you with all my heart, I have always loved you even when I was seven years old and lied about falling asleep on Santa watch, when I was ten years old and didn't invite you to my birthday party, when I was eighteen and had to move away, even on my wedding days, on your wedding day, on christenings, birthdays, and when we fought. I loved you through it all. Make me the happiest man on this earth by being with me.

Please reply to me.

All my love,
Alex

EPILOGUE

─⁓─

Rosie read the letter for what seemed like the millionth time in her life, folded it into four neat squares, and slid it back into the envelope. Her eyes panned across her collection of letters, greeting cards, e-mail printouts, chat room printouts, faxes, and scribbled notes from her school days. There were hundreds of them spread across the floor, each telling its own tale of triumph or sadness, each letter representing a phase in her life.

She had kept them all.

She sat on the sheepskin rug in front of her fire in her bedroom in Connemara and continued to take in the array of words spread out before her. Her life in ink. She had spent the entire night reading back over them and her back ached from stooping and her eyes stung. Stung from the tiredness and tears.

People she had loved had so vividly come alive in her head during those hours as she read their fears, emotions, and thoughts that had once been so real, but that were now gone from her life. Friends that had come and gone, workmates, schoolmates, lovers, and family members. She had relived her life all over again that night in a matter of hours.

Without her even noticing, the sun had risen, the seagulls

were dancing around the sky calling with excitement as their meals were thrown around by the angry sea. The waves crashed against the rocks threatening to come further. Gray clouds hung like smoke rings outside her window.

The bell from the front desk downstairs rang loudly. Rosie tutted and glanced at her watch. 6:15.

A guest had arrived.

She rose to her feet slowly, wincing at the pain of being crouched in the same position for hours. She held on to her bedpost and pulled herself up onto her feet. She slowly straightened her back.

The bell rang again.

Her knees cracked.

"Ouch, coming!" she called out, trying to hide the irritation in her voice.

She had been so stupid to stay up all night reading those letters, today was a busy day and she couldn't afford to be tired. She had five guests leaving and four more arriving not long after them. Their bedrooms needed to be cleaned, their sheets washed and replaced for the next arrivals, and she hadn't even started making breakfast yet.

She carefully tiptoed between the mess of letters scattered around the rug, trying not to step on the important papers she had saved all her life.

The bell rang again.

She rolled her eyes and cursed under her breath. She was not in the mood for impatient guests today. Not when she hadn't had a second's sleep.

"Just a *minute*," she called cheerfully, holding on to the banister and rushing down the stairs. She felt her toe hit against the luggage that had stupidly been placed by the end stair. She felt herself falling forward and then a hand grab her firmly by the arm to steady her.

"I'm *so* sorry," the man apologized and Rosie's head shot up. She took in the man that stood before her, nearly six feet in height with dark hair that had grayed along the sides. His skin was tired and wrinkled around the eyes and mouth. His eyes looked tired, as would anybody's who had just spent four hours in a car to Connemara after a five-hour flight. But those eyes sparkled and they glistened as the moisture inside them began to well up.

Rosie's eyes replied and filled up also. The grip on her arm tightened.

It was him. Finally it was him. The man who had written the final letter she had read that morning, begging her for an answer.

Of course after she had received it, it hadn't taken her long to reply at all. And as the magical silence once again embraced them, after almost fifty years, all they could do was look at each other. And smile.

ACKNOWLEDGMENTS

—◆—

Here I go again everyone!

There are so many special people who have been instrumental in making this happen for me.

A huge thank you to my editor Peternelle van Arsdale, Will Schwalbe, to Bob Miller, Ellen Archer, Beth Dickey, and the fantastic team at Hyperion for their constant support and belief in me.

Thank you:

Marianne Gunn O'Connor, super-agent and friend.

Mom, Dad, Georgina, Nicky, and Keano for your love, support, advice, laughter, friendship (and licks on the face!). We all make a great team!

David, for taking every step of this incredible journey with me. I share it all with you.

After the year that I've had, everyone near and dear to me deserves an even bigger thank you than ever. I'm lucky to be surrounded by such a huge support group, so special thanks to:

Fairy godmother Sarah, Olive, Enda, Rita and all the Kellys, all the Ahern family, Susana, Paula pea, Sarah-Jayne, Adrienne, Roel, Ryano & Sniff, Neil & Breda and the Keoghans, Jimmy & Rose, Lucy, Elaine & Joe, Gail, Eadaoin,

Margaret, Gerald & Clodagh, Daithi & Brenda, Shane & Gillian, the Byrne family, Gallaghers Paul & Helen, Drew Reed, Vicki Satlow. My grandparents Olive, Raphael, Julia, and Con, who must be pressing magical buttons way, way up there.

Thank you God, I owe you (more than) one.

To everyone who has welcomed my books into their hearts. You've all put a smile on my face and a lump in my throat so I thank you with all my heart.

And finally, thank you Rosie Dunne, for nagging me all night, every night until your story was told.

If you enjoyed *Love, Rosie,* be sure to check out Cecelia Ahern's most recent novel, *If You Could See Me Now,* available in mass market paperback from Hyperion.

An excerpt follows.

Elizabeth's heart hammered loudly against her chest. She banged the front door behind her and paced the hallway in uneven strides. With the phone pressed hard between her ear and shoulder, she balanced herself against the hall table and pulled off her broken-heeled shoe. Another bit of chaos to thank her sister for.

She stopped pacing long enough to stare at her reflection in the mirror. Her brown eyes widened with horror. Rarely did she allow herself to look so bedraggled. So out of control. Strands of her chocolate-brown hair were fleeing from the tight French plait and mascara nestled in the lines under her eyes. Her lipstick had faded, leaving only her plum-colored lip-liner as a frame, and her foundation clung to the dry patches of her olive skin. Gone was her usually pristine look. This caused her heart to beat faster, the panic to accelerate.

Breathe, Elizabeth, just breathe, she told herself. She ran a trembling hand over her tousled hair, forcing down the strays. She wiped the mascara away with a wet finger, pursed her lips together, smoothed down her suit jacket, and cleared her throat. It was merely a momentary lapse of concentration on her part, that was all. Not to happen again. She transferred the phone to her left ear and noticed the impression of her Claddagh earring against her neck; such was the pressure of her shoulder's grip on the phone against her skin.

Finally someone answered and Elizabeth turned her back on the mirror to stand to attention. Back to business.

"Hello, *Baile na gCroíthe Garda Station*."

Elizabeth winced as she recognized the voice on the phone. "Hi, Marie, Elizabeth here again. Saoirse's gone off with the car," she paused, "again."

There was a gentle sigh on the other end of the phone. "How long ago, Elizabeth?"

Elizabeth sat down on the bottom stair and settled down for the usual line of questioning. She closed her eyes, only meaning to rest them briefly, but at the relief of blocking everything she kept them closed. "Just five minutes ago."

"Right. Did she say where she was going?"

"The moon," she replied matter-of-factly.

"Excuse me?" Marie asked.

"You heard me. She said she was going to the moon," Elizabeth said firmly. "Apparently people will understand her there."

"The moon," Marie repeated.

"Yes," Elizabeth replied, feeling irritated. "You could perhaps start looking for her on the motorway. I would imagine that if you were heading to the moon that would be the quickest way to get there, wouldn't you? Although I'm not entirely sure which exit she would take. Either way, I'd check the motor—"

"Relax, Elizabeth; you know I have to ask."

"I know." Elizabeth tried to calm herself again. She was missing an important meeting right now. Her nephew Luke's fill-in babysitter had fled. Elizabeth could hardly blame the girl. Her nephew's mother, Elizabeth's younger sister Saoirse, was unmanageable and the frantic young babysitter had called Elizabeth in a panic. Elizabeth had to drop everything and come home. Luke's nanny, Edith, had left for the three months of traveling she had threatened Elizabeth with for the past six years. She was, however, surprised that Edith, apart from the current trip to Australia, was still turning up to work every day. Six years she had been helping Elizabeth to raise Luke, six years of drama, and still after all her years of loyalty, Elizabeth expected a phone call or her letter of resignation practically every day. Being Luke's nanny came with a lot of baggage. Then again, so did being Luke's adoptive parent.

"Elizabeth, are you still there?"

"Yes." Her eyes shot open. She was losing concentration. "Sorry, what did you say?"

"I asked you what car she took."

Elizabeth rolled her eyes and made a face at the phone. "The same one, Marie. The same bloody car as last week, and the week before and the week before that," she snapped.

Marie remained firm. "Which is the—?"

"BMW," she interrupted. "The same damn 330 black BMW Cabriolet. Four wheels, two doors, one steering wheel, two wing mirrors, lights, and—"

"A partridge in a pear tree," Marie interrupted. "What condition was she in?"

"Very shiny. I'd just washed her," Elizabeth replied cheekily.

"Great, and what condition was Saoirse in?"

"The usual one."

"Intoxicated."

"That's the one." Elizabeth stood up and walked down the hall to the kitchen. Her sun trap. Her one heel against the marble floor echoed in the empty high-ceilinged room. Everything was in its place. The room was hot from the sun's glare through the glass of the conservatory. Elizabeth's tired eyes squinted in the brightness. The spotless kitchen gleamed, the black granite countertops sparkled, the chrome fittings mirrored the bright day. A stainless-steel and walnut heaven. She headed straight to the espresso machine. Her savior. Needing an injection of life into her exhausted body, she opened the kitchen cabinet and took out a small beige coffee cup. Before closing the press, she turned a cup 'round so that the handle was on the right side like all the others. She slid open the long steel cutlery drawer, noticed a knife in the fork compartment, put it back in its rightful place, retrieved a spoon, and slid it shut.

From the corner of her eye she saw the hand towel messily strewn over the handle of the cooker. She threw the crumpled cloth into the utility room, retrieved a fresh towel from the neat pile in the press, folded it exactly in half, and draped it over the cooker handle. Everything had its place.

She placed the steaming espresso cup on a marble coaster to protect the glass kitchen table. She smoothed out her trousers, removed a piece of fluff from her jacket, sat down in the conservatory, and looked out at her long swath of garden and the rolling green hills beyond which seemed to stretch on forever. Forty shades of green, gold, and brown.

She breathed in the rich aroma of her steaming espresso and immediately felt revived. She pictured her sister racing over the hills with the top down on Elizabeth's convertible, arms in the air, eyes closed, flame-red hair blowing in the wind, believing she was free. *Saoirse* meant *freedom* in Irish. The name had been chosen by their mother in her last desperate attempt to make the duties of motherhood she despised so much seem less like a punishment. She felt by naming her this, her second daughter could some way bring her freedom from the shackles of marriage, motherhood, responsibility, reality.

Elizabeth and Saoirse's mother, Gráinne, had met their father when Gráinne was just sixteen. She was traveling through the town with a group of poets, musicians, and dreamers and got talking to Brendan Egan, a farmer in the local pub. He was twelve years her senior and was enthralled by her wild, mysterious ways and carefree nature. She was flattered. And so they married. At eighteen Gráinne had their first child, Elizabeth. As it turned out, her mother couldn't be tamed and found it increasingly frustrating being held in the sleepy town nestled in the hills she had only ever intended to pass through. A crying baby and sleepless nights drove her further and further away in her head. Dreams of her own personal freedom became confused with her reality and she started to go missing for days at a time. She went exploring, discovering places and other people.

For as long as Elizabeth could remember, she looked after herself and her silent, brooding father and didn't ask when her mother would be home. She knew in her heart that her mother would eventually return, cheeks flushed, eyes bright, and speaking breathlessly of the world and all it had to offer. She would waft into their lives like a fresh summer breeze bringing excitement and hope. The feel of their bungalow farmhouse always changed when she returned; the four walls absorbed her enthusiasm. Elizabeth would sit at the end of her mother's bed, listening to stories, giddy with delight. This ambience would last for only a few days until her mother quickly tired of sharing stories rather than making new ones.

Often she brought back mementos such as shells, stones, leaves. Elizabeth could recall a vase of long fresh grasses that sat in the center of the dining room table as though they were the most exotic plants ever created. When asked about the field they were pulled from, her mother just winked and tipped her nose, promising Elizabeth that she would understand some day. Her father would sit silently in his chair by the fireplace, reading his paper but never turning the page as he got lost in his wife's world of words.

When Elizabeth was twelve years old her mother became pregnant again and, despite the newborn baby being named Saoirse, this child didn't offer the freedom her mother craved, and so she set off on another expedition. And didn't return. Her father, Brendan, had no interest in the new baby and waited in silence by the fire for his wife to return. Reading his paper but never turning the page. For years. Forever. Soon Elizabeth's heart grew weary of awaiting her mother's return and Saoirse became Elizabeth's responsibility.

Saoirse had inherited her father's Celtic looks of strawberry-blond hair and fair skin, while Elizabeth was the image of her mother. Olive skin, chocolate hair, almost black eyes; in their blood from the Spanish influence thousands of years before. As she grew from adolescence, Elizabeth resembled her mother more and more, and she knew her father found it difficult. She grew to hate herself for it, and along with making the effort of trying to have conversations with her father she tried even harder to prove, to her father and to herself, that she was nothing like her mother, that she was capable of loyalty.

When Elizabeth finished school at eighteen she was faced with the choice of moving to Cork to attend university, a decision that took all her courage to make. Her father regarded her acceptance of the course as abandonment; he saw any friendship she created with anyone as abandonment. He craved attention, always demanding to be the only person in his daughters' lives, as though that would prevent them from moving away from him. Well, he almost succeeded and certainly was part of the reason for Elizabeth's lack of a social life or circle of friends. She had been conditioned to walk away when polite conversation was started, knowing she would pay for any unnecessary time spent away from the farm with sullen words and disapproving glares. In any case, looking after Saoirse as well as going to school was a full-time job. Nevertheless, Brendan accused her of being like her mother, of thinking she was above him and superior to Baile na gCroíthe.

She had begun to understand how her mother must have felt living in such a suffocating home where she felt bored and trapped by marriage and motherhood. Like her mother, she found the small town claustrophobic. It was a place where every action of every person was monitored, frowned upon, commented on, kept, and stored for gossip. A place that managed to attract the tourists but repel the women of the Egan family. Elizabeth felt the dull farmhouse was dipped in darkness, with no sense of time. It was as though even the grandfather clock in the hall was waiting for her mother to return.

"And, Luke, where is he?" Marie asked over the phone, bringing Elizabeth swiftly back to the present.

Elizabeth replied bitterly, "Do you really think Saoirse would take him with her?"

Silence.

Elizabeth sighed. "He's here."

Saoirse was more than just a name to call Elizabeth's sister. To her sister it was an identity, a way of life. Everything the name represented was passed into her blood. She was fiery, independent, wild, and free. Saoirse followed the pattern of the mother she could not remember, to such a degree that Elizabeth found herself watching Saoirse to keep her from disappearing like their mother. But Elizabeth kept losing sight of her. Saoirse became pregnant at sixteen and no one knew who the father was, not even Saoirse. Once she had the baby she didn't care much for naming him but, when pressed, she gave her baby boy a name that was like a wish. Lucky. So Elizabeth named him Luke. And at the age of twenty-eight, Elizabeth found herself once again responsible for a child who wasn't her own.

There was never as much as a flicker of recognition in Saoirse's eyes when she looked at Luke. It startled Elizabeth to see that there was no bond, no connection at all. Granted, Elizabeth had made a pact with herself *never* to have children. She had raised herself and raised her sister; she had no desire to raise anybody else. It was time to look after herself. After having slaved away at school and college she had been successful in starting up her own interior design business. She had reached her goals by being in control, maintaining order, not losing sight of herself, always being realistic, believing in fact and not dreams, and above all, applying herself and working hard. Her mother's and sister's example had taught her that she wouldn't get anywhere by following wistful dreams.

Despite that pact with herself, there was no one else in the family capable of providing Luke with a good life, so Elizabeth found herself thirty-four years old and living alone with a six-year-old in a house she had made her haven, the place she could retreat to and feel safe. Alone because love was one of those feelings that you could never have control of. And she needed to be in control. She had loved before, had been loved, had tasted what it was to dream, and had felt what it was to dance on air. She had also learned what it was to cruelly land back on the earth with a thud. Having to take care of her sister's child had sent her love away and there had been no one since. She had learned not to lose control of her feelings again.

The front door banged shut and she heard the patter of little feet running down the hall.

"Luke!" she called, putting her hand over the receiver.

"Yeah?" he asked innocently, blue eyes and blond hair appearing from around the doorway.

"*Yes*, not yeah," she corrected him sternly. Her voice was full of the authority she had become a pro at over the years.

"*Yes*," he repeated.

"What are you doing?"

Luke stepped out of the doorway into the hall and Elizabeth's eyes immediately went to his grass-stained knees.

"Me and Ivan are just going to play on the computer," he explained.

"Ivan and I," she corrected him and continued listening to Marie at the other end of the phone arranging to send a Garda car out. Luke looked at his aunt and returned to the playroom.

"Hold on a minute," Elizabeth shouted down the phone, finally registering what Luke had just told her. She jumped up from her chair, bumping the table leg and spilling her espresso onto the glass. She swore. The black wrought-iron legs of the chair screeched against the marble. Holding the phone to her chest, she raced down the long hall to the playroom. She tucked her head around the corner and saw Luke sitting on the floor, eyes glued to the TV screen. Here and his bedroom were the only rooms in the house she allowed his toys. Taking care of a child had not succeeded in changing her as many thought it would; he hadn't softened her views in any way. She had visited many of Luke's friends' houses, picking him up or dropping him off, so full of toys lying around they tripped up everyone who dared walk in their path. She reluctantly had cups of coffee with the mothers while sitting on teddies, surrounded by bottles, formula, and nappies. But not in her home. Edith had been told the rules at the beginning of their working relationship and she had followed them. As Luke grew up and understood Elizabeth's ways, he obediently respected her wishes and contained his playing to the one room she had dedicated to his needs.

"Luke, who's Ivan?" Elizabeth asked, eyes darting around the room. "You know you can't be bringing strangers home," she said, worried.

"He's my new friend," Luke replied, zombie-like, not moving his eyes from the beefed-up wrestler body-slamming his opponent on the screen.

"You know I insist on meeting your friends first before you bring them home. Where is he?" she questioned, pushing open the door and stepping into Luke's space. She hoped to god that this friend would be better than the last little terror, who had decided to draw a picture of his happy family in Magic Marker on her wall, which had since been painted over.

"Over there." Luke nodded his head in the direction of the window, still not budging his eyes.

Elizabeth walked toward the window and looked out at the front garden. She crossed her arms. "Is he hiding?"

Luke pressed pause on his computer keypad and finally moved his eyes away from the two wrestlers on the screen. His face crinkled in confusion. "He's right there!" He pointed toward the beanbag at Elizabeth's feet.

Elizabeth's eyes widened as she stared at the beanbag. "Where?"

"Right there," he repeated.

Elizabeth blinked back at him. She raised her arms questioningly.

"Beside you, on the beanbag." Luke's voice became louder with his anxiety. He stared at the yellow corduroy beanbag with intensity, as though willing his friend to appear.

Elizabeth followed his gaze.

"See him?" He dropped the control pad and got quickly to his feet.

This was followed by a tense silence and Elizabeth could feel Luke's hatred for her emanating from his body. She could tell what he was thinking: Why couldn't she just see him, why couldn't she just play along just this once, why couldn't she ever pretend? She swallowed the lump in her throat and looked around the room to see if she really was missing his friend in some way. Nothing.

She leaned down to be on an even level with Luke and her knees cracked loudly in the silent room. "There's no one else but you and me in this room," she whispered softly. Somehow saying it quietly made it easier. Easier for herself or Luke, she didn't know.

Luke's cheeks flushed and his chest heaved faster. He stood in the center of the room, surrounded by computer keypad wires, with his little hands down by his sides, looking helpless. Elizabeth's heart hammered in her chest. *Please do*

not be like your mother, please do not be like your mother.
She knew only too well how the world of fantasy could steal
you away.

Finally Luke exploded and stared into space. "Ivan, say
something to her!"

There was a silence as Luke looked into space and then
giggled hysterically. He looked back at Elizabeth and his
smile quickly faded when he noticed her lack of response.
"Do you not see him?" he squealed nervously, then more angrily repeated, "Why don't you see him?"

"OK, OK!" Elizabeth tried not to panic. She stood up
back to her own level. A level where she had control. She
couldn't see him and her brain refused to let her pretend. She
wanted to get out of the room quickly. She lifted her leg to
step over the beanbag and stopped herself, instead choosing
to walk around it. Once at the door, she glanced around one
last time to see if she could spot the mystery Ivan. No sign.

Luke shrugged back into space, sat down, and continued
playing his wrestling game.

"I'm putting some pizza on now, Luke."

Silence. What else should she say? It was at moments like
this she realized that reading all the parenting manuals in the
world never helped. Good parenting came from the heart,
was instinctive, and not for the first time she worried she was
letting Luke down.

"It will be ready in twenty minutes," she finished awk-
wardly.

"What?" Luke pressed pause and faced the window.

"I said it will be ready in twen—"

"No, not you," Luke said, once again being sucked into
the world of video games. "Ivan would like some too. He
said pizza is his favorite."

"Oh." Elizabeth swallowed helplessly.

"With olives," Luke continued.

"But Luke, you hate olives."

"Yeah, but Ivan loves them. He says they're his favorite."

"Oh . . ."

"Thanks," Luke said to his aunt, looked to the beanbag, gave the thumbs-up, smiled, then looked away again.

Elizabeth slowly backed out of the playroom. She realized she was still holding the phone to her chest. "Marie, are you still there?" She chewed on her nail and stared at the closed playroom door, wondering what to do.

"I thought you'd gone off to the moon as well," Marie chuckled.

Marie mistook Elizabeth's silence for anger and apologized quickly. "Anyway, you were right, Saoirse *was* headed to the moon but luckily she decided to stop off on the way to refuel. Refueling herself, more like. Your car was found blocking the main street with the engine still running and the driver's door wide open. You're lucky Paddy found it when he did before someone took off with it."

"Let me guess, the car was outside the pub." Elizabeth already knew the answer.

"Correct." She paused. "Do you want to press charges?"

Elizabeth sighed, "No. Thanks, Marie."

"Not a problem. We'll have someone bring the car around to you."

"What about Saoirse?" Elizabeth paced the hall. "Where is she?"

"We'll just keep her here for a while, Elizabeth."

"I'll come get her," Elizabeth said quickly.

"No," Marie said firmly. "Let me get back to you about that. She needs to calm down before she goes anywhere yet."

Inside the playroom, she heard Luke laughing and talking away to himself.

"Actually, Marie," Elizabeth added with a weak smile, "while we're on the phone, tell whoever's bringing the car to bring a shrink with them. It seems Luke is imagining friends now."

• • •

Inside the playroom, Ivan rolled his eyes and wiggled his body down further into the beanbag. He had heard her on the phone. Ever since he had started this job, parents had been calling him that and it was really beginning to bother him. There was nothing imaginary about him whatsoever.

They just couldn't see him.

CECELIA AHERN, author of the international bestsellers *If You Could See Me Now* and *PS, I Love You,* is the daughter of Ireland's prime minister. Foreign rights to her novels have been sold to more than forty countries, and film rights have been bought by Walt Disney Pictures and Warner Bros. She lives in Dublin.